"You know, Caroline," Nathaniel began, his eyes focusing disarmingly on hers as he reached out and took her hand in his, "if two of the wealthiest business people in Boston can't succeed in something as elementary as making love, I don't hold out much hope for our generation."

She exhaled a long, tense breath. "No. I suppose not."

"Don't you think we've tortured each other long enough with all this?" he continued.

She nodded. *"Oui.* But I must warn you that I'm not sure I'll be much good at it."

"So, I'll teach you," he said softly, smiling at her. "I'm honored, in fact, to be your teacher."

"I'm glad that it's you, as well," she murmured, before he silenced her with a kiss . . .

CAJUN CARESS
ASHLAND PRICE

ZEBRA BOOKS
KENSINGTON PUBLISHING CORP.

ZEBRA BOOKS

are published by

Kensington Publishing Corp.
475 Park Avenue South
New York, NY 10016

First printing: August, 1990

Printed in the United States of America

To the readers of *Autumn Angel*,
the first book in this saga.

To Marcy, Kristie, and 94 East
for all your moral support through the years.

And, finally, to Ann S., Linnea, Diane,
and the rest of my long-lost clan.
May every adoption search end
as happily as mine did.

Chapter 1

Caroline Brenton stood just outside the front door of Monsieur Blanchard's farmhouse, listening to the two-step stomping rhythm and the sprightly fiddling of that evening's *fais dodo* music. It was a warm night, and the sound of the crickets chirping almost rivaled the loudness of the music within. Caroline loved dancing to the Acadian tunes of her mother's people, but she half hoped that she wouldn't be asked to dance anymore that night. She hated seeing the hopeful twinkle in her partners' eyes, hated having to refuse their requests to continue seeing her in the days that followed. She would have thought that word of her reluctance with Cajun men would have spread about the ribbon farms in the region by now. She had assumed that everyone knew by this time she didn't intend to marry a Cajun, that her parents wanted her to marry a businessman of some sort instead, a man with

7

the drive and worldliness necessary to help Caroline manage the Brenton family shipping business one day. But, with each *fais dodo* she attended, it became more and more clear to Caroline that there were still many young hopefuls among the Cajun bachelors, and she was realizing now that she was only being cruel to them by continuing to be present at such gatherings.

She wasn't a girl anymore, she silently reminded herself. She couldn't expect to go on taking part in such social functions as the *fais dodo,* without some kind of romantic entanglements occurring. She loved living here with her maternal grandfather and her brothers, loved the simple life among the Cajuns, yet she was finally realizing that she couldn't continue to spend her summers here. Her life and the family's business, to which she was the heir apparent, were both miles away in New Orleans. What was more, she had, at last, reached the age where she would be considered a spinster if she didn't settle upon a suitable mate soon and begin the next generation of the Brenton family line.

She looked down in those seconds to see that the skirt of her long linen dress was swaying to the gentle spring of the music within the farmhouse. She was, she thought wistfully, Acadian at heart. She spoke the language better than she ever had her father's English, and she displayed the Cajuns' openhearted, easygoing ways. Yet she knew, deep inside, that she really didn't belong here anymore, that she wouldn't be allowed the luxury of living out her days here as her younger siblings, Étienne and William, would. They had no desire to assume the duties of managing the family business. So, when the time came for their father to retire, those duties would come to rest upon Caroline's shoulders, she being the first-born of this generation of Brentons, and it occurred to her from time to time that this was probably for the best.

Despite Caroline's love for this community, part of her knew that she had never really blended in with her mother's people, that she was Acadian on the inside but not outside. Hers, after all, was the only head of blondish curls beneath an Acadian bonnet at the festivities this night. The rest of the women had long black hair, like their French and Indian ancestors. Unlike her brothers, Caroline, who was also half English, looked it. In fact, she greatly resembled one of her paternal aunts in distant Boston, a woman her father had always teasingly called "Pudding" and one Caroline had only had occasion to meet a few times in her twenty-one years of life.

But, in spite of her looks, she'd never been made to feel like an outsider by the Cajuns, and she knew she only had herself to blame for feeling that she didn't always fit in. The truth was, of all the societies she'd heard or read about, this one was probably the most accepting of outside blood. Indeed, it was her maternal ancestors' very acceptance of, and interbreeding with, the Indians of Maritime Canada that had enabled them to survive the perilous ocean-front winters of that land.

One could become a full-fledged Cajun in a few different ways: "by the blood, by the ring, and by the back door," as their saying went. And, though these were not people who placed a great deal of importance on material wealth, Caroline's future holdings as the heiress to a thriving shipping business with branches in both New Orleans and Boston was certainly no hindrance to her being pursued by Cajun men.

Although Caroline and her family had never flaunted their wealth during their stays on the Acadian Coast, it wasn't easy to hide in a community as rustic and unmoneyed as this one, and, even before Caroline had been born, talk had begun among the occupants of the ribbon farms as to which lucky Cajun family would sire a spouse for the Brentons' first-born child. In the end, however, the answer to this would have to be none of them. This was because Cajun men, on the whole, did not seem well suited to dealing with the world of Colonial commerce, and that talent would be crucial for any man who aspired to be Caroline's consort.

Caroline's mother had, therefore, begun urging Caroline to seek the courtship of some local French-speaking plantation owner, a man who knew how to manage large holdings and who also shared her French background. Her father, on the other hand, favored her marrying one of the Creole businessmen who sought her affections in New Orleans. The Creoles, after all, were among the most powerful of populations in Louisiana. Their Spanish lineage helped to wield great influence in this now Spanish-owned territory.

Because she wished to please *both* of her parents with her choice of a spouse, this question of who to marry had naturally become quite a quandary for Caroline in the past couple of years. She agreed with her parents, that it would be best for her to marry a man with some business savvy, someone who would be well equipped to help her when the time finally came for her to take ownership of her family's holdings. She also knew that in the end she was best off marrying someone who was at least as wealthy as she; for she

10

could then be a bit more certain he was marrying her for more than just a life interest in her estate. So far, however, Caroline just hadn't met anyone she could honestly say she loved, and, being a romantic at heart, she believed that loving the man she married was the most important criterion.

She gave forth a pensive sigh, as she continued to lean against one of the wooden columns of Monsieur Blanchard's front porch. Just as with the heavy, corseted clothing she had to wear when she spent the rest of the year among the fashion-conscious citizens of New Orleans, life had become burdensome and complicated since she'd reached adulthood. Consequently, her spirit continued to relish the relaxed way of life among these Cajun farmers, much as her body now relished the light, unencumbering feel of her simple Acadian dress.

She was clinging to her past, a voice within her admonished, clinging to the happy childhood days she had spent here at her grandfather's home, just as surely as her mother's people had clung to all the old ways of that distant northern land the British had forced them to leave some twenty years earlier. And Caroline knew for certain that such cleaving was not a luxury a young businesswoman of the future would be allowed to enjoy much longer.

Her thoughts were suddenly interrupted, and she gave forth a slight yelp as someone came up behind her and pinched her bottom. She turned about to see who it was, her eyes blazing with indignation. But, she reminded herself in that same instant, by choosing to step outside for a while, she had put herself at risk for this sort of thing. It was common knowledge among the Cajuns that at *fais dodos* the drink and the drinkers were not allowed inside, where they might discomfit the young ladies. So Caroline had quite simply let herself in for such outrageous treatment when she decided to come out for a breath of night air.

She froze with surprise as she raised a hand to slap her attacker. It wasn't a drunken neighbor at all but her brother Étienne who had pinched her. He stood before her now, dark and handsome, a teasing smile spreading across his tan face.

"What ya doin' out here, *chère?* Best get yaself inside, 'fore the folks start to talk about ya," he drawled in the lazy, sloppy dialect the Cajuns had come to call their own.

He was eighteen now, three years Caroline's junior but clearly a man. His muscular form more than filled the amply cut, linen shirt and suspendered pants he wore. Caroline had watched him grow by leaps and bounds, long after she'd reached her full height of just five feet four, and as he'd finally begun to tower over her, she had reluctantly started addressing him as the adult he'd obviously become.

"I should, shouldn't I?" she conceded with an awkward laugh. "The mosquitoes are having quite a feast on me, really."

"They aren't the only ones be feastin' on ya, *ma soeur,* if ya don't get yaself back inside soon," Étienne warned again, a smirk tugging at one corner of his lips.

Caroline narrowed her eyes suspiciously, as she looked up into his face. "You're not usually so concerned about me. What are you trying to hide, Éti? Why are you so anxious for me to go back in?"

He gave a careless shrug. "No reason, *chère.* No

12

reason t'all. Just thought it might be time ya go back in . . . See ya later, at *Grand-père's,"* he called back to her, as he turned away and shuffled down the porch's front steps.

Caroline, certain now that her brother was up to something, lingered for a moment or two longer on the porch, watching his figure grow dimmer. Then, seconds later, when he was several yards from the farmhouse, she saw someone walk up to him. It was Madeleine, the young Cajun girl he had been courting of late, and Caroline saw the two of them join hands and hurry off into the cloaking darkness of the neighboring woods.

Such unchaperoned rendezvous were greatly frowned upon by these people, because they often led to unseemly entanglements among the Cajun youth. Nevertheless, as she turned to go back into the dance, Caroline knew that she wouldn't be reporting this tryst to her Grandfather DuBay. Nor would she mention it to her parents when she returned to their New Orleans home at summer's end. Étienne was a man now, after all, old enough to be assigned most of the backbreaking work on their grandfather's farm. And Madeleine had reached the ripe age of seventeen; so, she was certainly old enough to know the risks and consequences inherent in such liaisons.

Far from wanting to bear witness against them, Caroline found herself almost smiling at the fact that the young couple had made such a successful getaway. These maneuvers could be very difficult under the watchful eyes of all the village elders who inevitably lined the dance floor at such functions. What Caroline felt now was not annoyance but envy. With all her heart, she wished that her life could be as uncomplicated and spontaneous as Étienne's. She would gladly have given up her role as heir apparent of the Brenton clan for such a tryst with a handsome Cajun gentleman that night. The music, the warm evening breeze, the starry sky would all have helped to make a wonderful setting for being ravished to ecstasy on a nearby forest floor. She knew, however, that her virginity was simply not expendable. It was, in fact, yet another asset, one more enticement to be used in eventually acquiring what her parents would, hopefully, deem to be just the right husband for her. Accordingly, she had guarded her virtue quite painstakingly for what seemed like ages to her.

Just as Caroline felt herself beginning to sink into a bout of self-pity, a young man appeared before her, and she was quite relieved to realize that, unlike so many of the others, he was a male whose attentions she would not have to discourage. It was William, her eleven-year-old brother, smiling up at her, his arms extended to lead her into the crowd of two-steppers on the dance floor.

He, too, was dark-haired and dark-eyed, like their mother, and, though he was young yet, Caroline could see that he was destined to grow into a handsome, strapping man like Étienne. William had been named after their Puritan grandfather, but clearly that appellation was where the English part of him ended.

"Viens danser, Caroline," he coaxed in a voice that still possessed a boyishly high pitch. "My friends say you're the prettiest girl here, so you'd honor me if you'd agree to dance."

Caroline found herself stunned for a moment by the

14

praise. William was usually such a brat, she was invariably taken aback whenever he displayed a fleeting moment of civility. But, after looking about and seeing that a small circle of his friends were indeed watching them quite closely, she realized that this invitation was precisely what William had said it was, an opportunity to show off a bit in front of his peers. It would be his way of emphasizing the fact that the fair-haired heiress to the Brenton estates really was his older sister, someone who found herself hard pressed to refuse his flattering request.

Caroline smiled down at him and reached out to take his hands in hers. As they began to move about the dance floor seconds later, she again felt a wave of envy run through her at seeing how well William fit into this society; how clearly, in both his nature and appearance, he belonged here. Caroline's dark eyes, on the other hand, were the *only* part of her that even hinted at her maternal lineage—her eyes and her talents as a healer. Her mother had been known as a *sage femme* in Acadia, a healer and herbalist, and now, in this new southern territory, Caroline was called a *traiteur,* a treater of those who were sick or injured.

Even though Caroline had become quite good at this craft over the course of her twenty-one years, it was a gift she never displayed, except during her stays on the Acadian Coast. She knew enough about the city dwellers of New Orleans and Boston to realize that revealing such talents to them would probably only lead to her being called a sorceress. So, once again, the Cajun half of Caroline remained unapparent, suppressed, free to emerge only at times like these, when she was among her mother's people.

To Caroline's surprise, her thoughts and her dance with her little brother were both suddenly interrupted by a heavy tapping on her shoulder. She stopped abruptly, thinking it was yet another hopeful bachelor come to cut in on her dance with William. She saw instead that it was a local footboy, a lad who often brought supplies and mail to the Acadian Coast from New Orleans. What was more, the troubled look he wore told her that he had something far more weighty in mind than simply asking her to dance.

"What is it?" she blurted out, realizing now that he'd been running, for he seemed almost too winded to speak.

"Come out where you can . . . can hear me, Mademoiselle Brenton," he stammered, fighting to catch his breath. "Come outside with me for a moment."

Caroline gestured for little William to stay behind. Then she followed the footboy out onto the porch, swallowing uneasily. In a community where most messages were conveyed relay-style, from one front porch to the next, it went without saying that such special delivery meant very bad news.

"What is it?" she asked again, taking a deep breath now in an effort to brace herself for what he had to say.

"It's your father, *mademoiselle* . . . Monsieur Richard Brenton. I have just come from New Orleans, and your mother paid me to return here to you and tell you that he is very ill," he concluded, his tone ominous. "She says you must come right away. You must head back to your home in New Orleans tonight."

"Oh, mon Dieu!" Caroline exclaimed, clapping a hand to her mouth. "But what is it? What's wrong with him?"

16

The footboy shook his head. "I do not know, *mademoiselle*. Your mother sent for me just as I was leaving with a consignment of food and supplies, and there wasn't time for her to tell me more. I only know that you must go to your parents now."

"Bien, bien," Caroline replied anxiously, reaching into one of her dress pockets in search of some coins to offer him for his trouble.

He shook his head. *"Non. Non . . .* as I've said, your *maman* already paid me. Just you go now, *mademoiselle*. It's a long ways in the dark."

Caroline, feeling almost too stunned to move, forced herself to turn in those moments and go back in to the dance. She hurried over to the set of benches along the far left wall of Monsieur Blanchard's front room, where she'd seen her mother's cousin, Élise, sitting with Luc, her husband, minutes earlier. Now in their mid-forties, they were among the most respected of the village elders, and, because a few of their younger children were present at the dance tonight, they'd felt obliged to attend as chaperones.

As Caroline stood before them, her words flowed out in a frantic gush. "It's Papa. He's taken ill. Maman sent word that I must return to New Orleans at once. *Oh, mon Dieu,"* she concluded tearfully, wringing her hands now, "what if he should die, before I can reach him?"

The couple sprang to their feet, Élise with a consoling hug for her cousin's daughter and Luc with the assurance that he would accompany Caroline to the city with all due haste. Then the pair began walking Caroline toward the door, so she could go back to her grandfather's farm and pack her things.

"Be sure to tell Grand-père and Étienne and William. They must be told," Caroline muttered, still in a dazed state, as they moved her along through the crowd.

"We will," Élise promised. "We'll take care of everything here. Just get yourself off to the city now, and tell your *maman* our prayers are with her."

Chapter 2

Caroline was still numb with shock when she arrived, after two A.M., at her parents' New Orleans town house. Her mind was too clouded with worry for her to notice, as she usually did, the stark contrast between the bucolic Acadian village she'd just left and the baroque-facaded neighborhood in which she lived in the city. Try as she might to fight it, her mind kept returning to the worst possible scenarios. Perhaps her father had died while she was en route and she'd never have the chance to speak to him again. Or maybe he was so far gone now that not even Caroline's extraordinary healing abilities, or those of her mother, could rescue him from death.

When Élise's husband, Luc, escorted Caroline up the steps to the front door of the house, they were greeted at the threshold by a maid whom Caroline had gotten to know very well through the years. This was, after all, the home where Caroline had spent most of her life. Because she'd never gone abroad for schooling as her father had always encouraged her to do, she had not only spent every autumn, winter, and spring since childhood here, but she'd been tutored here, in her later years, by a professor from Paris. Then, at the young age of seventeen, she'd begun to serve as one of her father's business apprentices, and, at the end of each trying day she had spent at the nearby shipping office, this elegant town house had provided her with an oasis of peace and quiet.

She therefore believed that she knew every inch of this place. Yet it all seemed so foreign to her now: the elaborately carved staircase which led to the second floor, the foyer's cut-glass chandelier—its candles still lit at this hour—illuminating the huge entrance hall before which the maid stood. The servant's expression in those seconds was also foreign to Caroline, utterly unreadable. The scene seemed to freeze for her, as she studied the elderly maid's face. Was it a mourner's sympathy she saw in the woman's eyes? Or was it simply relief that Mademoiselle Caroline had made it home so quickly and safely?

"How is he?" Caroline heard herself croak, as the maid stepped aside to let them enter the stately dwelling.

"Better, *mademoiselle,*" the sevant answered with a smile.

At this, Caroline reached up and reflexively crossed herself. It was an expression of gratitude to God. In lieu of her father providing any Puritanical instruction, her mother had simply chosen to raise Caroline and her brothers in the Catholic faith of the Acadians.

"The physician has left. But he did prescribe several weeks' bed rest, I'm afraid," the maid continued, stepping forward and leading them, with lit candle in hand, across the foyer and up the darkened staircase.

Caroline, once again dressed for the city, in an absurdly wide French farthingale-style gown of the day, picked up her billowing skirts and began climbing the steps, with Luc bringing up the rear. "What is it? What's . . . what's wrong with him?" she stammered, her heart continuing to race despite her efforts to tell herself that things were not as serious as they'd seemed.

As the servant reached the top of the stairs, she turned back to address them. "Catarrh of the lungs, I believe the doctor said." With that, she began leading the way down the upstairs corridor to Monsieur Brenton's bedchamber.

Though the door of his suite was open and it was now clear that the patriarch was not on his deathbed, Caroline could hear Luc's footsteps cease behind her, several feet from the bedchamber door, and she turned back to him with a questioning expression.

"You go on in, *chére,*" he said softly. "I think I'll wait out here for a while."

Caroline, unsure why he was hesitant to go any farther, simply found herself offering him a befuddled smile. She'd come to realize through the years that her mother's relatives were rather strange in this way. They seemed quite ill at ease on those rare occasions when some family matter brought them to New Orleans, and Caroline was never sure whether they were uncomfortable because they knew they were not dressed for such settings or because some of them had never really forgiven her father for taking part in the British expulsion of the Acadians from their northern homeland some two decades earlier. This had been the military campaign on which her father had met her

21

mother, and, though the expulsion had led to the two of them falling in love, Caroline knew it had not ended nearly as blessedly for most of the other Acadians involved. Consequently, she'd simply never found the nerve to question her maternal relatives about their feelings toward her father, and she knew that this was definitely not the time to open such a discussion. Instead, she blew Luc a grateful kiss to thank him for having escorted her so far and then turned back to head into her father's suite. As she did so, she saw her mother peer around the side of a wing chair positioned near the bed.

"Oh, Caroline," her mother greeted her with marked relief, rising from the chair and crossing to the doorway. "I'm so glad my message reached you. I had Nona keeping an eye out for you," she explained, reaching out and embracing Caroline.

"Oui. I know, Maman," Caroline replied, smiling slightly over her mother's shoulder at the maid, who stood just inside the bedchamber door now. "She let us in. How's Father?" she asked, lowering her voice to almost a whisper, as her mother ended their hug. "The footboy you sent said things were very grave."

Caroline's eyes searched her mother's face for an instant answer as she made this inquiry. Even at forty-three, Angeline Brenton still looked remarkably young. The only lines evident in her complexion were those about the corners of her mouth, the flattering creases caused by years of donning warm smiles and speaking their native French with all its mouth-contorting accents. Her long black hair had, for quite some time, been highlighted by streaks of gray, but her lovely dark eyes still twinkled with the youthful joie de vivre that Caroline remembered seeing in them from her earliest days. In spite of her obvious attempts to appear cheerful now, however, Angeline did look as if she were in desperate need of a few hours' sleep. Even though it was the middle of the night, she was still fully dressed in a red afternoon gown, and her hair was still swept up and held in place by the Spanish combs considered fashionable by some of the Creoles in the city.

"I know," Angeline replied, keeping her voice low as well now. "You see, even though the doctor concluded that it was nothing more than catarrh, I know it was his heart, and I was terribly afraid that, if I didn't send for you immediately, he . . . he might die before you could reach us," she explained tearfully. "Then, thank the Lord, his chest pains suddenly subsided."

"Oh, do stop whispering as though you were at my wake, you two!" Richard Brenton snarled from where he lay on his canopied bed. "I assure you that, whatever my ailment was, I'm still very much alive. Now, do come over here, daughter, and give your father a kiss. It seems months since you left for that mosquito-ridden coast, and your mother and I have missed you terribly," he concluded, easing himself up into a sitting position and leaning back heavily upon the bed's headboard.

Caroline instantly crossed to her father and reached out to take his hand as she sat down on the edge of his bed. As always happened when she met his gaze, she marveled at what a good-looking man he still was at the old age of fifty-four. The sharp Brenton cheekbones and the regal line of his nose—the very same features that had won Caroline so many compliments through the years—seemed never to be overshadowed by the wrinkles and lines in his face. He remained forever handsome, yet his eyes were different now. Even in the dim candlelight about his bed, Caroline could see the pain in them. What was more, she couldn't help noting how cold his hand was as she continued to hold it in hers.

"It's your heart, isn't it?" she queried in a serious tone. "Catarrh would never leave you feeling so cold to the touch."

He shrugged and tried to continue smiling. "Ah, well, you know these expensive physicians. They can't bear to have their diagnoses match those of a mere *sage femme* like your mother."

"Oui. It is his heart," Angeline affirmed, coming up beside where her daughter sat. "I tried to tell the doctor this, but he wouldn't listen," she explained, her nostrils flaring with indignation.

"Well, whatever it is," Richard Brenton continued, "we're all in agreement that I shall be bedridden for quite some time to come. And that's why I had your mother send for you, Caroline—"

"Oh, Richard . . . not tonight," his wife interrupted in a beseeching tone.

"Yes. Tonight, my dear," he said firmly. "It's late, and I'll be brief because I know we could all use some sleep. But she has to be asked now. Things have never been more peaceful between the rebels and the redcoats as in these last few months, and I'm convinced that this is the safest time for her to go to Boston."

"Boston?" Caroline echoed in confusion.

"Yes," her father replied, looking directly into her eyes. "It's that trip I was planning to make this

24

month. Clearly, I can't go now, not under the circumstances. So, I thought it best to ask you, daughter, to go in my stead."

Caroline found herself feeling a little taken aback by this request. She'd only traveled to Boston a few times to date, and she'd always done so with her father at her side, so, the idea of making the trip unchaperoned struck her as very strange indeed. "Well, of course . . . of course I'll go for you, Father," she stammered. "But what, for heaven's sake, is the rush? You're acting as if this trip is suddenly quite urgent."

"It is. The rebels really shouldn't be kept waiting any longer. They're expecting the guns and ammunition no later than the fifteenth of July."

Caroline furrowed her brow in perplexity. *"Pardonnez-moi.* I'm afraid I'm not following you."

"Your father has been supplying the rebels in Boston with guns and other smuggled goods for quite some time now," Angeline explained, keeping her voice so low it was clear to Caroline that she didn't want anyone but the three of them to hear.

Caroline could feel an odd little smile forming on her lips. "You *have?*" she asked, meeting her father's eyes once more.

"But, of course, I have," he said with a rakish laugh. "I've waited a lifetime to see the Colonies overthrow the king's rule. Why wouldn't I back them now?"

Caroline continued to smile at him in wonderment. "So all those trips to Boston in the last four years . . . you were using them as an excuse to smuggle weapons to the rebels?"

"In part. We also have a branch of the family business to manage in Boston, remember," he added coolly. "You don't think I'd trust Pudding and that dolt she calls a husband to keep your Aunt Margaret at bay all the time, do you?"

"Well, no," Caroline conceded. "It's just that at your age, Father, I figured—"

"Figured that my military days were behind me?" he interrupted, a resentful edge to his voice.

"Something of the sort."

"Not at all," he retorted. "Freedom from tyranny comes at a high price for *all* of us, no matter our gender or age, as you know, Caroline. That's why I'm certain you'll agree to take my place this time around."

"Richard," Angeline repeated sharply.

"Your mother doesn't think you should go," he explained. "She thinks I should ask one of my other apprentices to go in my place and rendezvous with my rebel contacts."

"Mais oui," Caroline's mother interjected with a nod.

"But what she doesn't realize, dear daughter, is that, whether another of my apprentices agrees with this family's views on the War of Independence or not, he will doubtless agree to my request, simply because he's in my employ and doesn't wish to anger me. With you, on the other hand, I'm confident that your views align with my own, and this is a journey you will undertake out of dedication to the cause of liberty."

"Well . . . yes, Father," Caroline hesitantly replied, still feeling rather dumbfounded by this unusual request.

"What is more," her father continued, "it's common knowledge these days that a family is best advised to be quiet about its political loyalties. Granted, this is not as true here in Louisiana as it is in the Colonies, but secrecy is nevertheless the wisest course. And I simply don't want any more people involved in this than are absolutely necessary, my dear. I'm sure you understand."

Caroline nodded.

"Consequently, I feel it's best to send you in my stead. I doubt the British will suspect a young lady like yourself of such things. I'm sure they'll simply assume we've sent you up to Boston to seek out a suitable husband or some such thing."

At this Caroline felt her cheeks flush with embarrassment, and she let her gaze drop down to the bed linens. "Oh, Father . . . am I really such a spinster as that?"

Richard reached out and patted one of her hands consolingly. "Heavens, no! That's not what I meant at all. You know that your mother and I want you to take all the time you feel you need in choosing just the right husband for yourself. Good God, I was over thirty by the time I was wed."

Caroline furrowed her brow in annoyance and stared up at him once more. "That was different, Father. You're a man."

"Well, in any case," he continued, "all I meant was, the redcoats aren't likely to suspect a young lady like yourself of such things. Not in the way they'd suspect a man."

"But there may be a search at Boston Harbor. How am I to get through that?"

"They may search through the ship's cargo, yes," her father agreed. "But it is highly doubtful that they would go so far as to search through a young lady's personal trunks."

"'Highly doubtful,'" Mrs. Brenton mocked, shaking her hands at the ceiling. "This is our Caroline we're talking about here, Richard! *Mon Dieu!* How can you even *think* of subjecting her to such dangers?"

At this, Richard Brenton's eyes traveled over to meet his wife's, and he sat staring at her quizzically. "And who else can I trust with this, Angeline? You tell me. Who?"

"Étienne?" she offered weakly.

"Étienne?" he fired back, gaping with amazement. "You must be joking. As we've already established, the boy has no business acumen whatsoever, and, given his untamable nature, he'd stick out a mile in Boston! At least Caroline knows something of the city and its people. At least *she* knows how to present herself."

At this, Angeline sank down once more onto the wing chair beside the bed and, with a mulish air, crossed her arms over her chest. "It's too dangerous," she maintained, "sending her up there without a chaperone."

"If you're so worried about her going alone, why don't you go with her?"

Angeline Brenton's eyes suddenly widened, as though she were astounded that he'd even suggest such a thing. "You would agree to that? To the possibility of losing both of us?"

Her husband gave forth a dry, confident laugh. "I won't 'lose' either of you. I've been taking guns to the rebels for years now, and I've always returned to New Orleans unscathed . . . and in far less peaceful times than these, I might add."

Angeline Brenton issued a cluck of disgust and leaned back in her chair. "My place at a time such as this is with you, Richard. I don't care whether that fancy physician believes me or not! I know we came very close to losing you this evening, and what's more, I know you know it, too!"

Caroline, who had been watching her mother issue this reply, turned back to her father now to see what effect her mother's incisive glare was having upon him. She wanted to determine, if possible, whether or not he agreed with his wife's assessment of his condition. To Caroline's dismay, in those seconds his expression did become rather acquiescent.

"Very well, *ma chèrie,*" he said with a soft smile after a moment. "If you wish to stay at my bedside for all the boring weeks to come, suit yourself. I'm in no condition to try to prevent it."

That was all he said about the matter, but Caroline could see that his adoring eyes were saying the rest, thanking her mother for continuing to prize his life and their marriage above all else.

"Besides," he continued hearteningly after a moment, "Caroline can hardly be deemed to be 'unchaperoned' with an entire schooner's crew about her night and day en route to the Colonies."

"A crew of nothing but *men,*" Angeline Brenton retorted pointedly. "Quite unseemly, Richard. What will people think?"

"Who cares what people think? Have I ever, in all the years you've known me, cared a damn what people 'think'?"

At this Angeline Brenton appeared to be fighting a laugh. "No . . . I guess not," she conceded.

"Caroline is a businesswoman now, my dear," Richard declared, "and people in business, especially those in the shipping business, must travel to distant ports now and then. What is more, that crew wouldn't dare lay a finger on her, knowing she's my daughter. On the contrary, I'm sure that most of them would rather suffer in her stead than have to come back here and report to me that she's come to any harm."

"Yes . . . well, I suppose you're right," Angeline Brenton said reluctantly after a moment.

Richard Brenton met his daughter's eyes once more. "Ah, *oui,* you'll be safe enough en route. It's once you've arrived in Boston that you must keep your guard up, *ma petite."*

Caroline smiled at him, thinking that he was teasing, attempting to make light of her mother's obviously excessive concern about her safety. "What, Father?" she asked with a smirk. "What should I be wary of in Boston, pray tell?"

Caroline was surprised to see that he looked quite serious as he replied.

"Two things," he answered without an instant of hesitation. "The first of which, of course, is your Aunt Margaret and her endless conniving."

Caroline knew he wasn't joking about this. She had only met her father's fraternal twin, Margaret, on a few occasions, but one look had confirmed that this paternal aunt was every bit as wicked as the Brenton family had always warned Caroline she was. Having been born a few minutes before Caroline's father, Margaret had always believed that it was she, and not Richard, who should have been named the heir apparent to the Brenton family business and holdings. When it had become evident that the position would fall to her twin brother, she began to retaliate, even going so far as to sell Caroline's mother into slavery when Angeline had first arrived in Boston from Acadia in 1755. After that incident, Caroline's paternal grandparents expelled Margaret and her husband from the family estate and the entire Brenton clan realized that Margaret would go to just about any lengths to have her way in the family's affairs. Consequently, they had all come to distrust her.

Their cautiousness with her wasn't always enough, however. Margaret was most assuredly a master of stealth, always mounting her attacks in the most insidious ways possible. What was more, she was capable of being quite charming at times, in spite of her rather forbidding appearance. She, therefore, often won the support of other local proprietors, those in a position to influence the inner workings of the Brenton shipping business. As a result, her schemes were sometimes carried out before anyone in the family could put a stop to them.

Unfortunately, the situation had only gotten worse since Caroline's paternal grandparents had died and Richard Brenton had appointed his younger sister Amelia and her husband to oversee the Bostonian branch of the family business. Amelia was good-hearted but sometimes rather simple and gullible, so Richard Brenton found himself having to sail up to Boston a couple of times a year simply to make certain that Margaret hadn't gotten her talons too far into the business once more.

Margaret's latest shenanigans concerned her continued drive to get the Brenton shipping business involved with slave trade. It was indisputably a very lucrative trade, and Margaret, though still receiving her fair share of the company's profits, was, of course, anxious to up the ante. Richard, however, had always been opposed to slavery, especially after having seen so many of his wife's people rounded up and expelled from Acadia to work as serfs in the Colonies. He had therefore decreed that the Brenton Shipping Company would definitely not become involved with such dealings.

For her part, Caroline had only to reflect upon the atrocities committed against the black slaves who worked on some of the plantations near her grandfather's farm to know where she stood on the issue. She'd once asked a plantation owner why there was a shallow ditch dug near his slaves' quarters. When he'd explained, with a casual smile, that the ditch was used to accommodate the huge bellies of pregnant Negresses, so the unborn came to no harm while their mothers were being whipped, Caroline had felt herself growing far too nauseous and weak to continue the tour of the grounds. From that day on, she knew that a person had only to encounter one such atrocity in order to realize how wrong such practices were and how sinful it was to take part in supplying slaves to buyers in the New World. She also reflected now—with a very dry swallow—upon the fact that, as the child of an Acadian mother, slavery could have been her fate as well, had it not been for the intervention of her father.

Fortunately, Caroline's nightmarish reflections on all of this were suddenly interrupted by her father's continued admonitions. "Just steer clear of Margaret," he advised. "Don't speak to her, except perhaps to make polite conversation, and, for heaven's sake, don't let her know too much about your comings and goings."

Caroline stared at him incredulously. "Oh, Father, you don't honestly believe she'd turn me in to the redcoats, do you?"

"Let us never forget, my dear, that the Bible teaches us the first murder occurred between *brothers,*" he replied in a forebodingly low voice.

He was right, of course, Caroline acknowledged with another dry swallow. No friend, neighbor, or acquaintance ever possessed the familiarity or the occasion to harm one quite as incisively as a member of one's family could. It was a bitter truth, but one she knew she shouldn't ignore.

"The second of these pitfalls is the young men of Boston," her father continued, a slight flush coming to his cheeks.

His obvious uneasiness with the subject only served to make Caroline a bit blushful as well in the seconds that followed, and she directed her gaze downward as she replied.

"I know, Papa. I shall be careful." After a moment, however, she lifted her head rather proudly and looked her father in the eye once more. "But, when it comes to that realm, I must tell you that I have always considered myself to be in complete control."

To her surprise, her father looked quite unconvinced of this, in spite of her obvious certitude.

"You've never been in Boston long enough to be wooed by the likes of such men, I assure you," he began again. "They are not the polite farm boys of the bayou, nor even the cultured gentlemen of New Orleans—I was one of them once, you know," he reminded her, again looking a bit embarrassed.

"And a perfect gentleman with Maman," Caroline

shot back imperiously.

"Not always," he confessed, lowering his voice, and Caroline couldn't help noticing in those seconds, out of the corner of her eye, how her mother snapped open the folding fan, which hung from her right wrist, and began nervously breezing herself with it.

"The main point, Caroline," Richard Brenton began again to pursue his thoughts, "is that there will be bachelors in Boston who possess more guile than you ever thought possible in a man. And it will be cloaked in such disarming charm, they'll have done their dirty deeds with a lass before she even knows what's happened."

Caroline couldn't help laughing a bit at this. Then she reached out and pressed a silencing finger to his lips. "Oh, enough, Papa! You said it yourself; I am, first and foremost, a businesswoman now. You've taught me much in the past four years, and you can rest assured that I'm shrewd enough not to be duped by some pompous buck in a powdered wig! That, I promise you, will be the least of my worries in Boston."

Her father's expression as he spoke again told Caroline that she was actually starting to convince him of this claim. "Very well, then. I shan't lecture you any further on the subject. It is *you* and not me who shall be at the helm on this trip, after all. So I must trust that you'll do well . . . Just remember to be at Bentley's farm, at noon on the fifteenth of July to make your contact with the rebels. Bentley's is just on the west edge of Boston. Anyone you ask is sure to know the way . . . and don't write this time and place down anywhere, *ma petite.* You must commit both to memory, lest we risk having the enemy intercept this information. Boston is said to be swarming with British spies these days . . . And do try to keep your dear Aunt Amelia and that bungling husband of hers out of all of this," he added. "I'm certain they share our sentiments about this war, but I see no profit in getting them involved in our dealings. It would only serve to frighten Amelia—"

"Enough. *Enough,* Papa," Caroline interrupted with a weary laugh. "I think you've told me all I'll need to know for tonight. It's time you lie down and try to get some sleep. Don't you think?"

He pressed his lips together in a slight pout and finally nodded. "Yes. I suppose it is."

As he eased back down into a reclining position seconds later, Caroline bent forward and kissed his forehead. "*Bonne* . . . good night." She corrected herself, remembering that he usually insisted she speak English when at home. He wanted her command of the language to stay sharp enough for her to use it in their dealings with the Bostonian branch.

"Good night," he replied with a soft laugh, obviously pleased at her adherence to this request. "And thank you, Caroline, for agreeing to take my place in all of this."

"It's nothing, Father. No trouble at all." With that, she rose, kissed her mother good night as well, and left the suite.

She'd said it was "no trouble at all," and the words still echoed in her mind. Yet she knew in her heart that she didn't feel in the least bit certain this assignment would go smoothly for her. In fact, a voice within warned her that there was some very insidious trouble ahead, and she always listened to that voice because it seemed to be related to the gift of clairvoyance she'd inherited from her mother.

Yet what other answer could she have possibly given her father tonight but yes? This was the question she couldn't help asking herself as she said good night to Luc and then made her way down the long upstairs corridor to her own bedchamber. Her loyalties, like her family's, clearly had to rest with the rebels now. Even her mother's distant, ancestral homeland of France had chosen to intervene in the war on the side of the Colonists. What was more, every Louisianan knew that, though their tightly knit settlements to the north kept them well protected from redcoat attack, they were sure to be invaded sooner or later. There were just too many British forts along the Mississippi for this region to remain uninvolved much longer.

Knowing all of this, Caroline could hardly have refused her father's request. Still, rather than feeling confident that traveling to Boston to aid the rebels was the right thing to do, she felt only misgivings, and she resolved to do her level best in the next few days not to let them show.

Chapter 3

Boston—Ten days later

Nathaniel Hamlin's dark eyes never left the girl's as
he stood beside the bed, calmly, methodically disrob-
ing. So far he'd removed his buckle-topped shoes, his
flared coat, and his waistcoat, and he was, at present,
untying his lacy cravat. For an instant, he let his gaze
travel down the length of his partner's now-naked
body, taking in her soft curves in the peachy glow of his
candlelit bedchamber. But then he forced his eyes to
meet hers again, to continue to convey the silent,
intense message that he was not a man to be toyed with,
that she had taken matters this far and he didn't intend
to be dissuaded from making love to her.

Fortunately, she didn't so much as flinch at his
mesmeric stare. In fact, her only response in those
seconds was to roll toward him a bit on the canopied
bed. Then she came to rest on her right side and
propped herself up on her elbow, letting her face fall
into the palm of her upturned right hand. She

concluded these moves by flashing him a sportive smile. "Are you always this slow about it?" she asked with a laugh.

He returned her smile, but he knew that his was a much more incisive expression. "No sense in tossing my clothes into a wrinkled heap, is there, my dear? Not when I know how important anticipation is to you ladies," he explained, undoing the cuff buttons on his ruffled shirt sleeves with a practiced agility while still keeping his eyes fixed upon hers. "Wouldn't want you as dry as the desert when the time comes, now would we, Meredith?"

He could see her cheeks color a bit at this retort, and he took pleasure in it. He always enjoyed getting the upper hand. Then, still facing her, he sank down upon the bed and began untying the drawstring closing at his neck. He pulled the shirt up over his head and reached out to set it upon the carefully folded pile of clothing on the adjacent night table.

"You've got wonderful eyes," he said softly, as he removed his breeches and stockings. "Surely I can't be the first man who has told you that."

"No, you're not," she admitted with a somewhat bashful laugh.

"I'm not the first man in any regard, am I?" he acknowledged, seeing how her eyes reflexively raced to survey his privates now that he was unbreeched.

She smirked, seeming quite pleased with what she saw. "That's hardly what one would call a gentlemanly question, is it, Mr. Hamlin?" she asked, in a coy tone that set Nathaniel's teeth on edge.

He disliked women who were too sophisticated, disliked losing control in any realm, but especially in the bedchamber. "You needn't answer it, my dear. Your response at seeing me aroused is answer enough."

She bit her lip, as though fighting a laugh when he stretched out beside her, mirroring her casual, side-propped pose. "Oh? . . . And what do most of your ladies do when they see how well-endowed you are? Whimper with fear?"

He smirked as well, still looking her squarely in the eye. "Some of them. Yes."

"And is that what you want me to do?"

He threw back his head and issued a dry laugh. "Well, it wouldn't break my heart if you whimpered a bit and played at being the tremulous virgin. I don't suppose any man minds that," he replied, reaching out to stroke the sausage curl that hung down over her cleavage. She had glistening, blondish hair that looked almost the color of gold in the candlelight, and Nathaniel had to admit to himself that he'd taken quite a liking to blondes in the last few years. Though he was considered by all to be a man of great restraint, he couldn't deny that he'd come to find some of Boston's fair-haired females positively irresistible at times.

"Very well, *Master* Hamlin," she agreed, rolling onto her back once more and drawing her legs together so tightly that it seemed to Nathaniel a lever might be required to pry them apart. In that same instant, she clapped her open palms over her breasts.

"Oh, bravo," he praised, a sarcastic edge to his voice. "You know, in that pose you very much resemble a nutcracker my brother purchased while in the tropics. Charming, indeed!"

"Well, how should I act, then?" she asked impatiently. "I do wish we could get on with this. I haven't all night, you know."

"Ah, but lest we forget, it was you who sought me out this evening, not the reverse. I believe you said you did so upon the recommendation of a friend."

"Well . . . yes," she conceded.

Nathaniel drew closer to her in those seconds, his air suddenly more amorous, and he began to ease her arms downward, away from her ample breasts. "Then you must have been told I'm much like a leisurely, relishable feast, Meredith—not some sandwich you devour when otherwise engaged . . . And you really need not pretend to be a timorous maiden with me," he continued, running both of his large, warming palms down the sides of her body now, as he lifted himself up over her and straddled her thighs with a masterful smile. "Why, I predict that, in a moment or two, there will be no need to pretend at all, my dear. In fact, I *defy* you to be the silent sophisticate, once I enter you." With that he lay more fully over her and lowered his lips to her neck, which he began to kiss with a whisper-lightness that made her draw her shoulders upward as chills ran through her.

"What was that I heard?" he whispered in her ear, his breath pouring forth now in a hot caressing stream. "Was that a spontaneous moan from the self-possessed Meredith?"

She seemed capable now of doing nothing more than softly moaning again in response, and Nathaniel could feel her legs easing apart beneath him.

His thumb and forefinger deftly led the way an instant later, and he felt, with relief and satisfaction, that she was quite wet and ready for him. Perhaps all the claret he'd drunk at the party was clouding his judgment, he thought. Maybe more prudence and restraint were in order. But, whatever it was that was welling up so defiantly inside him, he knew there'd be none of the usual courteous groping tonight, none of that polite "easing into" business he practiced with most of his bed partners. He would thrust deeply into her without a second of hesitation, simply for the satisfaction of hearing her groan with shock and pleasure. And that was precisely what he proceeded to do, opening her first with his fingers and then driving the entire length of himself into her like a wave crashing upon a seashore.

He was gratified to hear her emit a stirringly deep sound in response an instant later, a sound that definitely reflected a combination of surprise and titillation. "What was that?" he whispered again teasingly, doing his best to ignore his own feelings of arousal in those seconds as he forced himself to stay completely still within her. "Was that a groan, my dear?"

Her eyes were squeezed shut now, as he continued to prop himself up over her and stare down into her face, but the expression she wore in those seconds told him that she was overwhelmed. It was as if every nerve in her body had been pleasurably affected by his penetration. "Noth-nothing," she stammered in an enraptured tone. "Just keep moving! For God's sake, don't stop!"

Again he smirked, this time with pride. He'd gotten what he wanted from her, after all; complete surrender, and now he knew it was time to allow himself to be swept up in the heavenly feel of the act as well. Just as he proceeded to do so, however, just as he withdrew from her and began surging back into her once more, there came a thunderous knocking at his bedchamber door.

He and his partner froze in that instant, breathlessly clinging to one another as they tried to place the sound.

"Nathan . . . Nathan," a male voice called from the other side of the suite's main door.

"Go away, John," Nathaniel ordered, recognizing the voice as being that of his only brother. "I'm . . . I'm *indisposed* at the moment. I told you I didn't wish to be disturbed!"

The voice in the corridor sounded rather apologetic now. "Yes. Yes, I know. But it's Mr. Smythe. He says he must have a word with you."

Nathaniel reflexively clenched his teeth and snarled at this news. Then he looked down to see that his partner's eyes were open once more and bore almost a beseeching expression. She looked even more unhappy at the idea of them having to uncouple than he was.

"Can't it wait until morning?" he called out wearily.

"No. I'm afraid not. I asked him that myself, and I'm afraid he said it couldn't," John answered.

"Oh, bloody hell." Nathaniel snarled again. "That disgusting man!"

"Who is he?" Meredith inquired softly in a cheerless tone.

"Just . . . just a messenger," Nathaniel stammered, knowing better than to tell her too much. He'd succeeded in keeping his loyalty to the British Crown a secret from all but his immediate family for the past five years, and he had no intention of divulging such information now, especially to a woman he'd known for only an hour or two.

"A messenger?" she echoed. "At this hour? . . . It must be something terribly important."

Nathaniel could feel his lips turning up into a roguish smile. "Not so important that we couldn't steal a few minutes more, if you wish."

"Oh, yes. I do wish," she replied, smiling as well and giving her hips a seductive swivel.

At this, Nathaniel's eyes fell shut, and he emitted an involuntary moan.

"John?" he called out again, his voice loud enough to be heard but his tone so dreamy he felt certain his brother could tell from it precisely how far he and the young lady had gotten. "Go downstairs and show Mr. Smythe to my study. Then tell him he'll have to wait a few minutes."

"Very well," his brother replied rather hesitantly. To Nathaniel's relief, he heard John's footsteps fading away down the upstairs corridor seconds later.

"Now . . . where were we?" Nathaniel asked in a winning whisper, as he smiled down at his bed partner once more.

"We were here," she answered, an enticing twinkle in her eye. She again rotated her hips and caused her innermost parts to close around him with irresistible pressure.

Nathaniel moaned once more. "Oh, yes," he murmured, and, without another instant of hesitation, he began moving in and out of her with great force and rapidity. The young lady, in response, bent upward and muffled her outcries against his chest and shoulder as his body continued to glide over her in a torrent of motion.

When at last their lovemaking ended, in a sublime, climactic rush that seemed to envelop them both, Nathaniel eased himself upward and softly kissed his partner's forehead. He hoped this gesture would somehow assuage any disappointment that came with his having to slip out of her now. "Very nice, my dear. Very nice, indeed," he praised in a low, provocative voice. "I do hope you'll consider staying for the short time it will take me to rid myself of this caller, because I'd very much like to return to you and do it all again . . . Of course, on a second time around, I could give far more attention to the matter of pleasing you."

The young lady gave forth a slight gasp, as he slid down and punctuated this last statement by easing her legs even farther apart and pressing a wet, lingering kiss to the creamy interior of one of her thighs, at a point that was titilatingly close to that part of her he had, only minutes before, penetrated.

Her gasp was immediately followed by a demure laugh. "Very well," she agreed, "since you put it *that* way. . . . There's no denying that you're vain, Nathaniel Hamlin," she added with a laugh. "But, having *known* you now, I'm tempted to say that vanity might actually be justified."

Nathaniel offered her an appreciative smile and kissed her again. Then he slowly moved away, drew the bedsheet up over her with a markedly chivalrous air, and rose to get his dressing gown from the nearby wardrobe.

"What is it, Mr. Smythe?" Nathaniel inquired irritably minutes later, as he entered his study to find the British sergeant, not in uniform, surveying his rather impressive collection of books.

At this, Smythe wheeled around from the bookcase with a startled expression. "Oh, Master Hamlin. I didn't expect to find you in your dressing gown. Did I wake you? I'm terribly sorry." The apology was made with his usual disingenuous air of cordiality.

Nathaniel, choosing not to dignify the inquiry with an immediate response, simply closed the study door behind him and crossed to sit at his huge mahogany writing table. Smythe's brown-nosing ways didn't sway him in the least. He'd had enough conversations with the man to know him for what he was; one of those uneducated, underpaid sergeants; a fellow who couldn't even afford to pay for a respectable rank in His Majesty's Army, let alone buy himself out of service altogether, as Nathaniel had. He, therefore, found Smythe's attempts at playing the part of a gentleman repulsive.

Given all of this, Nathaniel couldn't help clucking at the messenger as he sank into his spacious desk chair. He hadn't had time to take off his bagwig and let his long dark hair hang loose, so he knew it had to be quite evident to Smythe that he hadn't retired for the night. Smythe had simply made the inquiry in an effort to pry into Nathaniel's personal life, as had come to be his habit in the past several months.

"I wasn't asleep," Nathaniel answered coldly. "But I *was* indisposed, so I sincerely hope Commander Rushton has some very good cause for sending you here at this hour."

Smythe donned an odd, knowing sort of smile as he helped himself to one of the wing chairs positioned before Nathaniel's writing table. "Oh, yes. In fact, your next quarry is due to arrive in Boston tomorrow morning, so there was no time to waste in informing you of her."

"Her?" Nathaniel echoed, clearly surprised. His previous spying assignments for the Crown had always involved informing upon males, turning in this or that moneyed Bostonian for collaborating with a secret Whig committee, that sort of thing. It had simply never occurred to him that the commander would ask him to help entrap one of the fair sex, and the thought of doing so made him a bit uneasy.

"Yes, sir," the messenger replied. "It's a Mademoiselle Caroline Brenton of New Orleans. She's the Brenton Shipping Company heiress, an outfit with which I'm certain you're familiar."

"Yes," Nathaniel answered, with, he was sorry to note, a defensive edge to his voice. "Our company does business with Brentons' sometimes. That's only natural, given that they're in shipping and we're in shipbuilding. What of it?" he concluded, suddenly concerned that Smythe meant to imply his company's dealings with the Brentons somehow linked him with any of their subversive activities.

"Oh, nothing, sir. Nothing at all," Smythe assured him. "In fact, the commander couldn't help feeling that's precisely what makes you the best man for this task . . . tell me, sir, have you ever met Caroline Brenton?"

Nathaniel shook his head. "No. I believe I've heard her name once or twice, but we've never had occasion to meet. As you said, she lives in New Orleans, doesn't she?"

Smythe nodded. "Aye, she does. But we're told she's been to Boston a few times, and she should arrive here again tomorrow morning, according to intelligence we've received from the South. It is believed she'll be carrying a shipment of weapons and ammunition for the rebel forces here in Boston. Even without word from our sources, we could probably safely assume this suspicion to be true, because we've known for quite some time now that her father, Richard Brenton, has made a habit of smuggling weapons to the rebels whenever he is here on business."

"Well, if you already know the Brentons are guilty of smuggling, why haven't you arrested one of them? Why don't you simply apprehend Miss Brenton upon her arrival?"

The messenger's chinless face seemed to flatten into his long, thin neck as he drew his head back and critically crinkled up his nose at Nathaniel. "Oh, no. It's not as simple as that, sir. No. Not at all," he retorted with a patronizing chuckle which Nathaniel found quite irksome.

"Well then, kindly explain to me your rationale," Nathaniel growled. "It's well past the time I usually retire, Smythe, and I've really no patience for making trifling conversation with you tonight."

"Well, it's very simple, you see, sir. The commander would like to be able to arrest not only Miss Brenton but her rebel contacts as well. Catch all of them 'at it,' as it were, and make a public example of them. Put the fear of God and King back into them. At the very least, it's sure to turn your fellow Bostonians back into obedient subjects for no less than a month or two, thereby lightening our load a bit . . . or so the

47

commander reasons. In any case, that is where you come in, sir. We need to have you befriend the young lady straightaway and try to determine when and where she's to meet her contacts. We will require a date, place, and time."

Nathaniel leaned back in his desk chair with an exasperated sigh. "In that case, why don't you simply have her followed, Mr. Smythe? You're good at that sort of thing, aren't you? You hardly need *me* for a task as simple as that."

"Well, I asked the commander that question myself, sir, and he said that, given the nature of her mission, she's sure to be expecting to be followed, and she'll probably only end by giving us the slip. We'll keep an eye on her comings and goings, of course. But I'm afraid it will be up to you, sir, to try to extract the precise information about her rendezvous with the rebels . . . that is," he continued, clearing his throat with an admonishing air, "if your loyalties still lie with the Crown."

"Of course they do," Nathaniel snapped. "I assure you, my dear man, that you would never be let into this house if they didn't!"

"Very well, then," Smythe replied, looking rather taken aback but surprisingly unwounded by Nathaniel's outburst. "May I assume then that you'll agree to this assignment?"

Nathaniel leaned forward at his desk and looked Smythe squarely in the eye. "And what exactly makes the commander think that *I'm* going to be able to get such information out of a woman I've never even met?"

To Nathaniel's surprise, the messenger responded with an awkward, almost sheepish, smile. "Well . . .

she's looking for a husband, you see, sir. She's twenty-one and still unmarried, and we believe one of the reasons her father is sending her to Boston in his stead is the hopes that she might find a suitable spouse while she's here."

Nathaniel's mouth dropped opened in amazement. "Am I to understand, sir, that the commander wants *me* to pretend to be seeking her hand?" The furious rise to his voice clearly reflected how outrageous he felt it was for anyone, including the English Crown, to ask such a favor of him. And, to add insult to injury, the fact that Smythe had come to him with this assignment only served to indicate how closely he'd been watched by the English forces in the past few years. They obviously knew him to be a ladies' man, despite the discretion he took such pride in practicing in his personal life.

"Well . . . something of the sort, sir," the messenger replied, looking quite ill at ease now at hearing this preposterous expectation echoed back to him in Nathaniel's question. "But you must understand that it would hardly be as binding as that. The commander simply wants you to woo Miss Brenton a bit, if possible. Nothing serious, of course. Just try to win her confidence, so that she might tell you a bit about her dealings with the rebels. . . . It shouldn't be so terribly difficult to induce her to speak of them, after all, sir," he added with a shrug. "Most of the Whigs seem fairly vocal about their allegiances these days. It tends to be you Loyalists who stay quiet about what you feel."

"And for good reason," Nathaniel retorted, scowling at him. "Why, if the rebels knew I was in cahoots with the commander, they would have this entire estate burned to the ground and before you redcoats could arrive here with a single bucket of water!"

"Granted, sir," the messenger said amenably. "That's why I'm always so careful not to come here in uniform. You've been of great service to His Majesty in the past few years, so you really can rest assured that none of us would do anything to betray your loyalties."

Nathaniel was silent for several seconds as he pulled his chair more tightly up to his writing table and pressed his index fingers to his lips, giving the assignment further thought. "Caroline Brenton from New Orleans," he said pensively. "Isn't her father the one who married an Indian woman from Acadia?"

Smythe nodded. "Yes . . . well, I'm told she was really much more French than Indian, sir, if that makes matters any easier for you."

"I suppose it might," Nathaniel replied tentatively, still immersed in thought. He just couldn't help wondering in those seconds what kind of uncivilized creature he would be stuck with having to finesse if he agreed to this assignment. Pretending to be enamored of a woman at the behest of a British commander would be trying enough, but such a task would be almost impossible if said woman proved to be too unattractive for Nathaniel to find even somewhat palatable.

"Does that mean, sir, that you intend to agree to this request?" Smythe asked again anxiously.

Nathaniel was still too buried in thought to give an immediate answer. In spite of his misgivings about the assignment, he again acknowledged that his loyalties to England were very deep-rooted. His family stood to lose a great deal indeed if the Colonists succeeded in this ridiculous, starry-eyed plan to sever ties with their mother country. For his own part, Nathaniel and his siblings had inherited a large parcel of land just outside London, property that earned them considerable amounts year after year in the form of rent from tenant farmers. If the Colonies broke with England, such holdings could very well be invalidated. What was more, experience had taught Nathaniel that the Americans needed Britain's financial and commercial support, to say nothing of her military protection against other European powers that might wish to invade and conquer the Colonies. It went without saying that the motley collection of farmers and craftsmen that had come to be known as the Continental Army would ultimately prove no match for well-trained, well-equipped forces from abroad. In fact, Nathaniel was quite at a loss to understand why the redcoats hadn't already defeated the rebels.

Whenever he questioned the commander on this, however, he was informed that His Majesty and the ministry continued to view the Colonists' rebellion not as a war but merely as an uprising that required little more than policing. The British authorities had therefore refused to send any more soldiers to the Colonies than were absolutely necessary to reclaim the land from the rebellious faction of the Colonists. They seemed oblivious to the fact that such reclamation was futile, unless there were enough redcoats here to occupy those cities they had succeeded in winning back in battle. Because of this policy, men like Commander Rushton were destined to keep fighting the same battles over and over again. As a result, redcoat morale had never seemed lower to Nathaniel than it was now.

Furthermore, matters were sure to get worse if the English ministry didn't conclude their arguments over how to deal with the ever-widening conflict and begin to institute firmer, better-organized action against the rebels.

In light of all of this, Nathaniel could hardly refuse this assignment from the commander, and he knew it, just as Smythe did.

"It really shouldn't require too much of your time, Master Hamlin," the messenger declared. "And there is no telling how much this simple, little task might do to help reestablish the King's peace here in Boston," he added, an almost beseeching gleam in his eye.

"Yes, You're right . . . of course," Nathaniel said softly, trying to put out of his mind the nagging awareness that befriending and betraying a young lady could be a great deal more complicated and precarious than his previous assignments with men had been. The English forces would do all they could to shield him from any pitfalls, however, he stoically reminded himself, drawing in a long bolstering breath. What was more, he had to remember that this sort of covert work constituted a much less life-threatening way to serve the Crown than having to march into battle against the rebels, as men like Smythe did. "Tell the commander that I've agreed to this request," he declared at last, fixing his jaw resolutely and rising from his writing table.

"Splendid," Smythe replied with a broad smile, and, to Nathaniel's relief, he rose.

"And tell him that I shall go to work at once upon the task of arranging to meet Miss Brenton," Nathaniel continued, crossing to his study door now to make his exit and finally rid himself of the messenger. "I shall do my best to make her acquaintance within twenty-four hours of her arrival."

"Aye. We've every faith in you, sir. I will return here Saturday next at four o'clock to see how you are progressing with the young lady. Will that be convenient for you?"

Nathaniel nodded. "I trust you know your way out," he said simply.

"Aye."

Then, without offering so much as a good night in response, Nathaniel turned away from him. He crossed the huge entrance hall that led to the staircase and began to climb back up to the company of a woman of his own choosing.

It wasn't that Nathaniel believed he would fail at this assignment for the commander. He had certainly seduced enough young women in his time to succeed in getting just about any information out of this "Mademoiselle" Brenton. It was just that he already knew, given his quarry this time around, the undertaking was sure to be the stickiest, most difficult of those he tackled for the king.

Chapter 4

As her carriage drew up to the Brenton family estate on this sunny, June morning, Margaret Brenton Prentiss looked down and saw that her fingers had tightened in a knuckle-whitening grip about the drawstring of her purse. Now, as always when she visited the family manse, she was filled with rancor at recalling how her father had expelled her, along with her husband and children, from it some twenty years earlier. Her feelings of hostility were even more acute this morning, however, because she'd just learned, through Boston's inevitable grapevine, that her niece, Caroline, was due to arrive in Boston on this day. What was more, Margaret's younger sister, Amelia, was said to be planning a welcoming reception for the girl. It was to take place just two days hence, and Margaret hadn't so much as received word of it from her family, let alone an invitation to the function.

As incensed as Margaret was about this, however, she knew she couldn't afford to let her anger show. Amelia, while not overly bright, was certainly sensitive enough to be aware of people's moods, and it wouldn't take long for her to invent some way to flee from Margaret if she detected her sister's fury. So, needing to converse with Amelia and to somehow, obtain an invitation to the reception for Caroline, Margaret was determined to keep her feelings under wraps. This, of course, wouldn't be easy for her because she had never had much patience with people, especially those, like Amelia, who were simply too timid to really stand their own ground. But, Margaret told herself determinedly, she had to muster her patience this morning.

Upon the death of her parents, her twin brother, Richard, had, for some reason that still baffled her, appointed Amelia and her husband, Meldon Thorwell, to serve as the occupants of the Brenton family's Bostonian estate and to oversee the local branch of the family business. So, like it or not, Margaret must deal with Amelia on all matters having to do with the family and its shipping company. She, therefore, forced a smile onto her face and strove to achieve a pleasant tone as she told her coachman to pull over to the side of the carriage entrance and await her return.

Then, with his assistance, Margaret climbed out of the vehicle, rearranged her lacy towering headdress, and slowly, deliberately made her way up the walk to the estate's front door. She shouldn't rush, a voice within her warned. She should take her sweet time and appear as gracious and unhurried in her mission as a duchess.

To her dismay, however, she was greeted at the door minutes later, not by Amelia or her husband, as sometimes happened, but by a maid, a woman who had certainly come to recognize her throughout the years.

Margaret instantly realized that this was to her disadvantage. The servant was sure to go and warn her mistress as to who the caller was, and this would allow Amelia enough time to come up with a plausible excuse for not receiving her. Margaret also realized, however, that in such a case it would simply be up to her to employ her well-cultivated wiles to convince the maid that it was crucial she be allowed to speak to her sister. So, confident in her powers of persuasion, she did her best to appear unruffled as the maid showed her in and asked her to take a seat on one of the entrance hall's elaborately carved settles. Then the servant went off to "find" her mistress.

As Margaret waited, she couldn't help scanning the huge hall, as well as the rooms visible beyond it, and, as usual, an aching lump began to form in her throat. From the time her father had expelled her from this place, decades earlier, she had hated coming back here, hated being treated like a common caller in what had for over thirty years been her home. She couldn't bear seeing the impressive collection of gilded weaponry that adorned the foyer's walls, the dining room's breathtaking cut-glass chandelier, all of the expensive furnishings. She honestly believed that by birthright, they should have been hers. She was first-born, after all, and such was a first-born's due. Yet, cruel as life was, she'd ended up in a rustic, ill-furnished saltbox on the southern edge of town. She'd come into her old age, not in the lap of luxury as her younger sister had, but in a drafty clapboard dwelling which, despite her constant reprimands, her husband could not seem to keep in good repair.

Heaven knew she hadn't given up without a fight.

She and her husband had even tried to use the knowledge they'd gleaned from assisting her father in the family business to start a rival shipping company here in Boston. Lacking the capital to get the enterprise sufficiently under way, however, they'd failed, and they now spent their days farming the parcel of Brenton land on which their humble abode had been built. It was a modest existence, to be sure, and terribly trying for Margaret, who'd known the life of a pampered aristocrat until she was middle-aged. Nevertheless, she and her husband and their six children had managed to survive, having long since learned to make the most of what dividends Margaret's now-deceased parents had willed to them.

At present, however, with Caroline, who was being groomed to manage the Brenton family holdings, coming to Boston alone in such turbulent times, Margaret's hope of regaining power in the clan had been rekindled. Caroline was, after all, the spitting image of her rather brainless Aunt Amelia. It stood to reason, therefore, that Caroline might also have inherited Amelia's simplemindedness. Margaret couldn't be sure of this, of course. She'd only met her niece a couple of times, and one really couldn't fully assess the mental capacities of a young lady who was only in her teens. Now that Caroline was in her twenties, she was sure to manifest such capacities, and Margaret intended to keep a very careful eye on her. She would have to be able to determine where Caroline was vulnerable, if she were to have any hope of somehow doing away with her.

Perhaps, Margaret thought hopefully, Caroline would prove to be stupid enough to simply be charmed and manipulated. On the other hand, maybe it would take something more heavy-handed to get her out of the way. In any case, it was common knowledge in the family that Richard Brenton's two sons were not at all disposed to take over the reins of the Brenton interests, should Caroline somehow fail to do so. Amelia had no children, and Margaret's only other sibling, Louisa, had died of dysentery as a young spinster, so the only alternative would be for one of Margaret's offspring to become heir apparent, and this would be, to Margaret's way of thinking, poetic justice indeed. It was certainly her due, after having been denied the title herself, and she found that the very thought of reclaiming such a position of power within the Brenton clan was making her heart throb with excitement.

Then, to Margaret's surprise, her thoughts were interrupted, not by the return of the maid but by the sudden appearance of Amelia. Her sister was descending the carved staircase, clad in a dressing gown. While relieved to see that Amelia had sumoned the courage to face her, Margaret couldn't help feeling that she should at least have made some effort to conceal her dread.

"Good morning, Amelia," Margaret said brightly, rising from the settle and doing her best not to let her voice waver in response to her sister's blatantly unwelcoming expression.

"Good morning," Amelia croaked, as though it was her first utterance of the day and she'd only just been roused at this relatively late hour of nine o'clock A.M.

Is it possible, Margaret wondered, that Amelia could really be in the habit of sleeping until such a decadent time? It didn't seem likely. Yet, given her disheveled appearance, and since she'd never had any screaming children about to put her in the habit of waking for early feedings and such, Margaret decided it was entirely possible. "Oh, did I wake you?" she asked in the most apologetic tone she could muster.

Amelia stopped, on the third step up from the foyer, and began at once to try to impose some semblance of order on her mop of blondish curls. "No . . . of . . . of course not," she stammered, her eyes widening as though she were having some trouble getting them to focus. "What do you want, Margaret?" she asked coldly after several seconds.

Margaret realized in that instant that most people would have been taken aback by such a rude inquiry. Nevertheless, she was not. She had, sorrily, grown accustomed to being treated by her family with suspicious chilliness throughout the years. "Well . . . well, nothing," she replied, taking a few steps toward Amelia now and donning the most disarming smile possible. "Can't I simply pay my baby sister a call from time to time without being treated as though I intend to steal the silver?"

At this, Amelia scowled, one honey-colored brow angling higher than the other as both drew closer together in the tender furrow that formed between her eyes. It was really rather a silly little scowl, one that seemed to Margaret more befitting a child than a grown woman. But, in spite of her efforts to view Amelia critically in those seconds, Margaret had to admit to herself, however grudgingly, that even in the most unflattering circumstances, Amelia was capable of looking quite angelic. She and Louisa had inherited the kind of fair-haired, luminous beauty bards praised in their sonnets, while Margaret, the only other female child, had ended up with the harsh brunette hair and chalky complexion of her paternal aunts, and this had never seemed fair to her. What was more, Margaret was positively confounded by the fact that, though she and Amelia were only five years apart in age, Amelia always looked a full decade younger.

"We're . . . we're terribly busy at present," Amelia continued, interrupting Margaret's thoughts now. "We're expecting a houseguest, so please state your business because I've . . . I've really no time to stand about chatting with you today."

Again Margaret did her very best to look unaffected by her sister's attempts at brusqueness. "Well, you see, it is *because* of your houseguest that I've come. I've just heard that little Caroline is arriving today from New Orleans and that you and Meldon plan to host a reception for her Friday night."

"So?" Amelia retorted defensively.

"So I thought it was Richard who was scheduled to sail up here this month." As she spoke these words, Margaret's eyes were locked upon her sister's face, ready to pounce upon any little telling twitch or expression. She truly didn't know why her twin brother had suddenly chosen to send his daughter up to Boston in his place, but she had her suspicions. She knew Richard well. He was both a perfectionist and a workhorse, so she had already come to the conclusion that he was not coming because he was either very ill or dead, and, if he had died, Margaret was sure that her family had some legal obligation to tell her so. She, therefore, could only conclude that he was ill. "He's sick, isn't he?" she blurted out, a knowing gleam in her eye that she felt certain her sister couldn't ignore.

Amelia, in response, instantly shifted her gaze downward, to the stairs. "No," she quickly responded, and Margaret knew she was lying. "Well . . . that is . . . he really didn't say. We only just received the dispatch from him yesterday, saying that Caroline was coming instead. I guess he just feels it's time she began learning to handle the business details up here on her own."

"And you've decided to give her a little welcoming reception, introduce her to Bostonian society as an adult at last?"

Amelia responded to this question only with a gulp and a nod.

"Well, I think that's a marvelous idea," Margaret declared, going closer to her sister and ceremoniously opening her drawstring bag. "And, since she's my niece, too, I only thought it right that I should contribute to the costs of the affair." With that, she delved into her purse and withdrew a generous mound of coins.

As Margaret had hoped, Amelia looked flabbergasted by this offering. Then her astounded expression began to give way to an uneasy blush. "Oh . . . heavens no, Margaret," she said, gesturing for her sister to put the money back into her purse. "That isn't necessary. Meldon and I have ample funds for this sort of thing. You keep your money. I'm sure you need it for your children."

"Oh, nonsense," Margaret retorted in a voice that dripped with graciousness. "It's the least we can do for our little Caroline. As I've said, we all think this reception is a wonderful idea. Really wonderfully clever of you!" With that, Margaret rushed right over to her sister and began pouring the coins into one of the pockets of her dressing gown.

"Meldon!" Amelia called up the stairs, and her look of panic told Margaret that she knew she'd not only lost control of the situation but that she felt herself virtually drowning in her older sister's insistent gush.

In that instant it was all there for Margaret's perusal, the blush on Amelia's cheeks revealed that she was chagrined at having been caught in the act of planning a family reception behind her sister's back, the guilty glimmer in her eye indicated that this rare act of generosity was absolutely the last thing she'd have expected from Margaret, and the telltale crack in her voice, as she again called out for Meldon, completely betrayed the fact that she didn't have the slightest idea of how to get Margaret to go away and forget about the blasted reception.

"Margaret, really," Amelia exclaimed at last, pulling away from her sister's grasp and digging into her gown's pocket in an effort to remove the many coins that had been deposited there. "This is not necessary. All of the arrangements have already been made and paid for. I do wish you'd just keep your money."

Margaret took a step or two backward and looked into her sister's eyes with a deeply questioning expression. "You do?"

"Yes, yes. I do," Amelia answered, nodding emphatically and stepping forward to redeposit the coins in her sister's still-open purse, her fingers trembling.

Margaret let all but a few of the coins slip back into her bag. Then she abruptly drew it shut. "Very well," she answered resignedly, letting the purse dangle at her side once more. "Very well, then we'll simply have to do our part in another way, I guess. We'll simply have to agree—the children and I, I mean—to attend the reception as part of the serving staff. Do our part in labor," she concluded, coming up alongside Amelia now and turning to wrap an arm about her shoulders with a feigned air of sisterly warmth.

Amelia instantly tried to shrug free of the embrace. "No! No, Margaret! As I've told you, we've already hired the necessary staff. It's all been arranged."

At this, Margaret drew away from her slightly and donned a thoughtful look. "Oh, I guess you're right. It really wouldn't do to have members of the Brenton family acting as servants, now, would it?"

A grateful smile appeared on Amelia's face, as though she were immeasurably thankful for whatever it was that had so miraculously gotten her off the hook. "No, it wouldn't," she agreed. "It wouldn't do at all."

"You're right," Margaret said again, reciprocating her sister's relieved expression. Then she drew even farther away from her, taking a step or two toward the door before turning back to face her once more. "I guess we'll simply have to come as your guests then. We'll be here at the stroke of seven Friday night."

Before the stunned Amelia could even choke out a word of protest, Margaret strode to the door, her posture as straight and proud as a peacock's, and took her leave. She was already climbing back into her carriage, and pretending to be out of earshot, by the time she heard her sister calling after her from the estate's entryway.

Having just helped her back up into the vehicle, Margaret's coachman paused to look up at her with a puzzled expression. He obviously wondered why she was failing to respond to her sister's shouts.

"Just go," she snarled at him. "Drive us out of here, my dear man, and look lively about it!"

Fortunately, the coachman managed to do so with ample haste, and Margaret glanced back, over her shoulder, to see that Amelia hadn't even made her way down the front walk before the carriage turned onto the main road.

With a satisfied smile, Margaret leaned back in the spacious seat of the livery carriage as the vehicle continued to speed along. She knew she hadn't recovered all of her coins from her sister. She estimated that half a dozen or more remained in the pocket of Amelia's gown. Considering, however, that the ploy had helped her to invite herself to Caroline's reception, she considered the money very well spent. She probably wasn't going to have many chances to get a stranglehold on Caroline while her niece was visiting Boston, so she'd have to make every opportunity count.

The wind along Boston's coast blew Caroline Brenton's golden, ringleted hair backward, over her shoulders, as she stood on the deck of one of her father's schooners. Though it was already late June, she'd begun to find the weather chilly as they traveled northward, and on this morning, as had come to be her habit while on deck, she wore a russet-colored capuchin of shimmering crepe over her billowing dress.

She'd had many worries as she and the crew had made this journey. The first of these, of course, was the nagging fear that her father might die before she could return to New Orleans. Then there were her professional misgivings—her apprehension about having to interact with the staff at the Bostonian branch of her family's business, about having to give orders to male employees, some of whom were twice her age. Her father's right-hand man in Louisiana had, of course, acquainted her with the particulars of the business transactions she was to handle in Boston. Nevertheless, she couldn't help feeling anxious about it all now. This was relatively uncharted territory for her, and, of the three homes she'd known since infancy, the Brenton Bostonian estate was the one at which she'd spent the least amount of time.

All of these concerns seemed to fall by the wayside for her, however, as the schooner she was aboard finally neared Boston Harbor and she saw the fleet of British ships that seemed to be standing guard at its mouth.

"They're enormous, aren't they?" she said to the senior crewman who stood just a few feet aft of her, surveying the British ships through a spyglass.

He must have seen how she was squinting to make out the details of the closest of the warships, because he reached over and handed her the glass a few seconds later. "Aye, *mademoiselle,* that they are. Have a better look, if you wish."

Caroline accepted the spyglass from him with a gracious smile. "Thank you."

He was one of the seamen the company had sent down to New Orleans from Boston, and he was a fairly new arrival in the Colonies, so his Old-World accent sometimes made it difficult for Caroline to understand his English. She did her best, however. He, like all of the men on board, had been nothing but courteous to her during the week or so at sea. Yet, probably for fear of being accused of making overtures to Caroline, the crew had seemed reluctant to converse with her, and after so many days of segregation, she was finding herself starved for social interaction.

Her feelings of loneliness and isolation were overshadowed now, however, by her terror at the prospect of being greeted at the harbor by a fleet of British ships. As she studied the nearest vessel through the glass, she saw that it was more than twice the size of the pale yellow and gray schooner she was presently aboard. It appeared to be fully manned, and its twenty gunports clearly sported ready cannons. Caroline realized that she had never, in her two decades of life, seen anything so awesome.

"Do they ever fire upon Boston?" she asked the crewman in a tremulous voice.

"Not in the last several months, *mademoiselle*. I guess they haven't had much cause to," he answered evenly. "They are out there mainly to lend support to the English garrisons on land, is all."

"So, there is fighting in the city now?" Having not been to Boston since the war began four years earlier, she truly didn't know the answer to this.

"Skirmishes, I guess you'd call them. This or that pack of marauding redcoats bullying those they think are Whigs. They really are a nasty lot, the grenadiers. Forever gambling away their wages and whoring about," he added. Then an uneasy flush came over him, as though he regretted having made mention of such a thing to so genteel a maiden. "Well, you seize my meaning, I'm sure. I'll just let it suffice to say that a young lady, such as yourself, would do well to steer small and avoid the British troops while you're here."

"Oh, I intend to," Caroline assured him. "But it does look as though we're about to sail straight into a nest of them, doesn't it? Will they insist upon searching our ship?" She lowered the glass now and handed it back to him, only to see that his initial response to this question was simply a careless shrug.

"Probably. But we've nothing to hide, so I shouldn't worry myself over it, *mademoiselle*."

Caroline could feel her lips quivering a bit as she smiled at him once more. "Right," she said with a dry swallow, and then, finding that she was too weak-kneed to go on staring out at the warships while the schooner continued to near the harbor, she went below deck, to her quarters.

She couldn't help feeling intermittently angry with herself as, frozen with fear, she sat on her bunk in the minutes that followed. Where was all of that anti-monarchical, Enlightenment rabble-rousing of hers now that she was so near the enemy? Had she forgotten that her Acadian ancestors had taught the rebels the guerrilla warfare that had won them so many battles? Even the Bostonians' "tea party," one of the initial acts of rebellion in all of this, had been of Acadian invention. The very soldiers sent by England to expel her mother's people from New Brunswick and Nova Scotia twenty-four years earlier were among the men who opposed the king now, and they, like the Acadians, dressed themselves in Indian buckskins and war paint in order to carry out their acts of defiance anonymously. So, where was Caroline's pride in her heritage? Where was her confidence in her father's judgment? Where was her righteous courage now, as she sat nervously fingering the large bow at the neckline of her capuchin and listening to her heart pounding with dread?

She began eying her two traveling trunks, those fateful containers that, if searched by the redcoats, would doubtless get her shot as a smuggler, and she started to think that maybe her mother had been right. Perhaps it *had* been unwise for her father to send such a sheltered, pampered young lady on a mission this risky. At this, she rushed over to the two trunks and plopped herself down on them, so that her splayed legs traversed the lengths of both as the schooner continued to pitch and rock with the morning tide. Between the luxuries her father's money provided and all the love and nurturing she'd always received from the maternal side of her family, she'd never really known a moment of hardship or terror. She was sorry to note that she'd become that most superfluous of beings, a perennial nestling.

Then a voice within her began to scold. What good would it do to be sitting here and berating herself once the enemy soldiers boarded the schooner and began their search? Her trepidation was sure to show if she didn't get a grip on herself soon. What did the Enlightenment philosophers espouse, after all, if not logic, the "natural" order of things? It stood to reason that, if a young lady had something to hide in her trunks, she would do precisely what Caroline was doing now, sprawl upon them, her face flushed and her palms sweaty. Therefore, she had to summon the courage to get back up on deck and face the intruders squarely. The very fact that she'd agreed to make this trip in her father's place showed that she wasn't really a coward. She was a Brenton and the heir apparent to the family's holdings to boot, and it was clearly time to gather all of her nerve and climb back up to present a brave front to the foe.

Having decided this, Caroline took a deep breath, stood up, and smoothed down her skirts. Then she squared her shoulders, straightened the hang of her capuchin, and left her cabin with as bold a stride as she could muster.

Half an hour later, Caroline was leaning heavily up against the port rail as a dozen redcoats swarmed all about her in their hurried search of the now-docked schooner. She'd never even seen an enemy soldier before this morning, so finding herself virtually surrounded by them was taking her breath away.

She was surprised to note that they didn't seem like Englishmen at all. Rather, they were aliens to her, like the fearsomely masked and armored Japanese warriors she'd once seen depicted in a book. What was more, though she spoke English with some facility, the redcoats' Old-World accents were so thick, she was able to make out very few of the words they were hastily bellowing to one another as they bustled about the vessel.

The only thing that confirmed they were indeed human beings capable of focusing upon more than just this hunt for smuggled goods, was the occasional look she'd receive from some of them. Their eyes would lock upon her figure, scan the length of her so suggestively that chills ran through her, and then they'd shift away from her as once more the soldiers hurried about their business. That she was a woman, and the only one aboard this vessel, had not escaped their notice. Their intermittent looks certainly confirmed that, yet there probably was no harm in simply looking, Caroline told herself. God knew she was doing her share of it as well.

She had, thus far, managed to take in every detail of their imposing uniforms. Their coats were bright red, of course, faced with black, and their breeches and vests were white. Each had white ruffled shirt cuffs protruding from his coat, and every man was armed, with a bayonet at the end of his musket and a scabbarded sword as well. All in all, their get-ups were so impressive, they made the schooner crew, in their simple bell-bottomed trousers, pea jackets, and flat-brimmed hats, look like a complement of mice.

They were said to be a highly disciplined lot, these redcoats, quicker and tougher in battle than any Continental Army soldier could ever hope to be. It was rumored that it was not uncommon for them to be sentenced to two hundred lashes or more for even the slightest violation of army regulations, yet it was clear to Caroline now that there was also that inexplicable, reckless, marauding side to them, which the senior crewman had mentioned. She could see it in the voracious gleams in their eyes, and she knew the crewman had been absolutely right to advise her to avoid them at all costs. In fact, she was now convinced that she'd simply faint dead away if any of them so much as made an effort to speak to her.

She was wrong about that, however. She realized this minutes later when she felt someone tapping her right shoulder rather emphatically and turned to see a high-ranking redcoat officer with gold epaulettes on his broad shoulders.

"Are you Caroline Brenton?" he asked sternly.

Caroline could feel a lump forming in her throat as she looked up to meet his gaze, but, to her amazement, she was still standing. *"Oui* . . . um, yes." She corrected herself with a nervous smile. In those seconds she had to fight an almost overwhelming impulse to dash to the closest schooner crewman and hide behind him.

The Englishman nodded, then paused as though mulling her answer over.

"Of the Brenton Shipping Company?" he pursued.

Caroline swallowed loudly and did her best to continue to look the man in the eye as she answered again. "Yes," she replied, feeling certain now that this line of questioning usually preceded one's arrest.

To her amazement, however, the officer's only response was a strange, almost knowing smile. "Good enough, then," he declared seconds later, tipping his tasseled grenadier's cap to her. Then, to her further surprise, he simply turned and walked away.

The next voice she heard, as the officer began rounding up his men, apparently to disembark now, was that of the senior crewman to whom she'd spoken earlier.

"What was all that about?" he asked under his breath.

Caroline shrugged, still gaping. "I'm not sure. He simply asked me my name."

The crewman scowled. "That's odd. I should have thought he'd received a full list of those aboard from the captain. Perhaps he simply wanted to confirm the information."

"Perhaps," Caroline answered, still feeling quite

71

shaken by the encounter.

"They didn't search our quarters," the crewman continued.

Caroline turned to face him more fully. "Pardon me?"

"I say, they didn't search below deck for some reason. Seems they're simply playing at it this morning."

"Oh? Why would they do that?"

"No one higher ranking about," he answered with a shrug. "Or maybe they've finally come to realize that the only ships they truly have to fear are those of the privateersmen, and most of those crews have more sense than to lie at anchor in a British-occupied harbor, such as this."

"Yes. I suppose you're right," Caroline replied, keeping her voice low as well now. "But that officer wore the strangest expression as he spoke to me. It was as though he knew me, somehow."

The crewman seemed to ponder this observation for several seconds. Then he gave forth a dry laugh. "No. He only wishes he did, miss. I'm sure that was all."

Caroline felt her face flush a bit at the compliment, but she was still too shaken up to formulate a modest response. "Yes. Well . . . thank you, and thank you, too—all of you—for looking after me on this voyage," she stammered.

"Oh, it was nothing, *mademoiselle*. Our pleasure," the man answered, blushing a little himself now.

Maybe he is right, Caroline thought, as she began to make her way below minutes later to gather up her things in order to disembark. Perhaps, there really was nothing to the officer's coy look, only more of the lecherous intent she'd seen in his men. Nevertheless, she couldn't seem to shake off her feeling that the officer had known perfectly well that she was in the process of smuggling goods to the rebels. But if he had, why hadn't he acted upon it? Why hadn't his men even bothered to complete their search by checking below deck?

None of it made any sense to her, so she decided to try to put the incident out of her mind. It had been a long lonely trip, after all, and her craving for the anemities of land and the comfort of familiar faces was probably causing her to blow things out of proportion. It had simply been the terror of the moment, she reasoned, that had caused her to read so much into the redcoat's expression.

Chapter 5

To Caroline, it seemed to take an eternity for her trunks to be loaded onto a coach bound for the Brenton estate. Though the redcoats had long since left the schooner, they continued to mill around the piers, like cocks of the walk in their red and white turned-back coattails. They would presumably be there all day, conducting searches of other incoming vessels, and Caroline knew that she would not really relax until she was away from them, until she was safely packed up and headed for the family manse.

She took in the passing scenery with great interest half an hour later, as the coach she had boarded finally began to roll along. Boston had grown a bit in the four years since she'd been there, but the biggest change, of course, was the pervasiveness of the redcoats. They seemed to be everywhere she looked: coming out of the taverns in packs, sitting on the village greens, laughing and surreptitiously swilling pints, even loitering near the doorways of blacksmiths' and milliners' shops, chatting with the proprietors and calling after any passing females in the swaggering manner of a plundering enemy.

But then, of course, they were the enemy, Caroline reminded herself. In the years since she had last been here, the Colonies had declared themselves independent of the king's rule, and what had been the protecting forces had become the foe. There no longer appeared to be a "friendly" army, yet Caroline knew one existed. It simply wasn't visible, except to those in the know, because it came in the form of just about every "civilian" Colonist her coach passed along the carriageway. It was made up of illegally armed farmers and shopkeepers and, doubtless, even the rebel strumpets who knew that many of the redcoats' military secrets were best discovered between the sheets. The revolutionary forces were out there, and they were strong, skilled, and determined; yet Caroline found herself strangely unable to take much comfort in that knowledge this morning.

Ever since her father's schooner had sailed into Boston Harbor earlier, she had felt very much as if she were suffocating little by little, and she wasn't really sure why. In the truest sense she could, of course, breathe. The air was no different here, no less breathable certainly than it had been in Louisiana. Yet, this inexplicable feeling remained with her, and finally she knew it had to do with her perception that she was on foreign soil.

She tried to assure herself that the Colonists were fine. They appeared to be carrying on with their lives as before, going about their respective businesses and doing their best to continue to be good neighbors and compatriots to one another. Still, the redcoats seemed to Caroline like the segments of a constricting snake, wrapping themselves about every street and edifice and threatening to crush the whole of Boston at any time.

Nevertheless, the Colonists were clearly still able to communicate, Caroline told herself. Her Aunt Amelia's letters to her father still came regularly and showed no signs of having been opened or censored. Yet for Caroline, the Colonists' situation was distressingly reminiscent of the subjugation of the black slaves in Louisiana, those poor souls who had even had their native tom-toms taken from them by their owners for fear that the drums would be used to sound the signal for revolt from one plantation to the next. Communication was always the first freedom to be hampered at such times, and Caroline was finally realizing that slaves were all the Colonists were to His Majesty—subjects to be taxed and governed without representation, no better than serfs. Finally acknowledging this, finally seeing one of the colonies so infested with enemy troops, Caroline felt her eyes begin to fill with tears. She didn't like what had happened to Boston in her absence. She was learning firsthand that war was a very sad business indeed.

But she had to get a grip on her emotions, she told herself. The Brenton estate was only a quarter of a mile away at this point, and she couldn't greet her aunt and uncle with unexplainable tears in her eyes. Her father had asked her not to discuss her rebel loyalties with his sister and brother-in-law, and she knew it was best to honor that request. She was just travel weary, she rationalized, as she reached into the pocket of her capuchin and withdrew a handkerchief with which to blot her eyes. She was still a bit shaken by the redcoats' search, and she had spent one too many restless nights, tossing about on her berth as the schooner navigated the turbulent currents along the coast of the Colonies. After a decent night's rest and a few good meals at the estate, she would surely be herself again.

To her surprise, however, it wasn't continued sadness Caroline felt when the coach finally arrived at the Brenton estate and she made her way up the walk to the front door, but an odd sort of shyness. She hadn't seen her aunt and uncle since she was seventeen, and she'd always had her parents with her when she'd come to visit them before. To make matters worse, she realized that she would be stuck with the wrenching task of having to inform her aunt and uncle of her father's condition if the dispatch her parents had sent on the day before she'd left for Boston had not reached Amelia yet. It was with a great deal of apprehension that Caroline rapped on the door with the knocker and then stood waiting for a response as the coachman came up behind her with one of her trunks in tow.

Her uneasiness was unwarranted, however, and she realized it the instant she saw Amelia's sunny face peeking out at her through one of the door's long side windows. This was a face she'd known since childhood. It stirred only the happiest of memories in her. What was more, it was already clear to her that Amelia had received her parents' dispatch because she didn't look the least bit surprised at seeing Caroline standing on the front stoop alone.

Caroline didn't have a chance to utter so much as a hello before the door swung open and "Pudding" stepped out to greet her with a hearty hug and a squeal of delight. She returned her aunt's hug, her eyes nearly tearing up once more at the sweet familiar scent of the Parisian perfume Amelia always wore.

In those same seconds, Caroline's eyes focused upon her Uncle Meldon, who now stood just inside the doorway. He was casually coatless and holding a smoking meerschaum pipe in his upraised hand.

"Good to see you, Caroline. How was your trip?" he said by way of greeting. "I do hope the redcoats were enough of a welcoming committee for you down at the harbor," he added with a teasing chuckle.

Caroline was a bit taken aback by his blatant reference to the British troops. Clearly, the Colonists weren't as close-mouthed about their political feelings as she and her father had thought they would be.

"*Oh, mon Dieu!* More than enough!" she said with a groan. "They're a frightening lot, aren't they."

He nodded and rolled his eyes, again with a laugh. "Indeed they are. Indeed, my dear. In fact, your aunt keeps threatening to invite them all onto the gazebo some afternoon for a pitcher of poisoned lemonade!"

Amelia waved him off with a scowl. "Oh, I do no such thing," she snarled, looking thoroughly unamused with him at this point. "Now, do step aside, Meldon, so the poor girl can come in and make herself comfortable."

Meldon obediently moved out of the doorway, and Amelia ushered her niece into the estate with an unmistakably maternal air. She and Meldon had never had children of their own, and Amelia, therefore, had made it quite clear throughout the years that Caroline was very dear to her. "You should have been born to me, you know," she'd often say with a wistful smile. "You look so much like me."

As Caroline stepped into the huge entrance hall an instant later, she was amazed to note how familiar it seemed, the flood of pleasant childhood memories it brought to mind. She hadn't been to Boston often in the past, but, when she and her parents had come, their stays were usually several weeks long, due to all the travel time required to get there from Louisiana. She also realized in those seconds that, because of the length of those stays, this home was as much a part of her as her grandfather's beloved ribbon farm on the Acadian Coast, and, surprisingly, she found herself feeling almost equally as welcome. But that heart-warming feeling was dampened a bit by the guilt she felt at having expected to find this Bostonian estate, as well as its occupants, strange and unfamiliar.

"Oh, thank you," she suddenly gushed, hugging her aunt to her once more. "And you, too, Uncle Meldon."

"For *what?*" Amelia asked, confused and flushed.

"For being here to greet me this morning. For not just allowing me to arrive at an empty estate."

Her aunt continued to look befuddled by this.

"Well, where else would we be?" her uncle asked, raising an eyebrow at Caroline and issuing a puzzled laugh. "We *live* here, and we'd hardly dare to leave the place for very long, not with the redcoats out pillaging at every turn."

"Nonetheless, thank you," Caroline said, again in a burst. "Nine days on a ship can seem like forever when one has no familiar faces about." To her chagrin, her voice cracked tearfully, and she knew that her relatives were now aware of all the emotion welling up inside her. She, therefore, made no effort to hide her handkerchief as she reached up to again blot her eyes.

"Oh, silly," Amelia said softly, reaching out to pat her on the back. "You're just overtired, that's all. You come on upstairs now and have yourself a nice nap and a bath, while the cook finishes preparing the noon meal."

With that, Caroline found herself being ushered up the stairs, and she turned back awkwardly and offered her uncle a hurried, parting smile.

"Have you more than the one trunk?" Amelia asked, once they reached the upstairs corridor and began heading in the direction of the suite in which Caroline usually stayed.

"Yes, two," she answered, again trying to get a grip on her emotions. "And a portmanteau as well, and three hatboxes."

"Well, don't you worry," Amelia continued, with a steadiness to her voice that Caroline found quite comforting. "I'll see to it they're all brought in."

"Thank you," Caroline said again, as they entered her accustomed suite a moment later. She set her drawstring purse down upon a table and then she sauntered farther into the sitting room that, in turn, led into the bedchamber. "Ah, it's all just the same," she noted appreciatively, breathing in the sweet scent of the freshly cut lilacs that her aunt had clustered about the room in cut-glass vases.

She scanned the suite's various pieces of Chippendale furniture. "I've always loved these rooms. They're so bright and cheerful."

"Yes," Amelia replied. Then a melancholy look eclipsed her smile. "I don't suppose you would remember this, because you were so young the first time you came here, but this used to be your grandparents' suite. I've tried to keep it just the way your grandmother did . . . filled with flowers and all the blinds raised to let in the sun."

Caroline sank down onto one of the room's camel-back chairs, in the hope that the constant rocking motion she still felt from her days at sea would soon leave her. "I don't remember Grandmother very well," she said sadly. "What was she like?"

Amelia cocked her head thoughtfully, as though trying to fully recall. "Well . . . she was most like your late Aunt Louisa, I guess, except that she had a slightly darker coloring, more like your Aunt Margaret's. Well, you can see for yourself again, in the portrait of her in the dining room. I won't have to pick you up this time to see it, will I, Caroline?" her aunt concluded with a funny mix of laughter and tearfulness.

Caroline laughed as well. "No. I guess not, Auntie. I'm big enough to look her squarely in the eyes these days, am I not?"

"Indeed. Big enough now to oversee the whole of the Brenton business, if need be. . . . How is your father?" Amelia inquired, great concern in her eyes as she sat down in the camel-back chair that was positioned just a few feet from the one Caroline occupied. "The dispatch really didn't say much."

Caroline tried to muster an unwavering smile as she answered. "I think he'll recover. He's certainly following the doctor's orders and staying in bed, but I must admit that all the peace and quiet seem to be driving him quite mad," she laughed softly.

"And was it really nothing more than catarrh?"

Caroline shrugged and let a thoughtful sigh escape her. "Maman and I don't think so, if you want the truth. We both tend to think the problem was with his heart. He wasn't the least bit feverish on the night he took ill, you see. Quite the contrary, he was cold to the touch."

Amelia nodded with a sad sort of knowingness. "Yes. His heart. That was what killed your grandfather. But it wasn't drawn out in any way. It happened very suddenly. So, perhaps, with rest and enough of your mother's sagacious care," she added hearteningly, "your father will be on his feet again soon. I'm sure he wouldn't have risked sending you so far away from home if he really thought his end was near."

Caroline didn't agree with this conclusion, but she resisted the temptation to tell Amelia so. She was afraid that contradicting her aunt now would only lead to having to allude to her father's primary concern in sending her to Boston, the pressing need of the rebels for supplies. Nothing, not even critical illness, would have kept him from seeing to that. So, finding herself unable to think of a relevant response at this point, Caroline bit her lower lip and began to gaze out of the adjacent window at the estate's lush back acreage.

"Well," Amelia spoke up, more brightly, after several seconds of silence had passed between them. "I'm sure you're exhausted after your long trip, so perhaps it's best that I leave you on your own for a while. I can catch up on all the news of your family over dinner. What do you say?"

"All right," Caroline agreed, respectfully rising from her chair as she turned back and saw her aunt doing so.

"But there is one thing I fear I must tell you before I go," Amelia continued, lowering her voice considerably. "Otherwise I'll risk having your Uncle Meldon overhear me at dinner, and I know he'd become terribly angry as a result."

Caroline couldn't help feeling rather concerned at seeing how ill at ease her aunt appeared to be now. "What is it?"

"Well, it has to do with your Aunt Margaret. Your uncle and I plan to give a welcoming party for you this coming Friday night, and I'm afraid your aunt found out about it and managed to invite herself to it. I'm frightfully sorry, my dear," Amelia concluded, her face now completely flushed with embarrassment.

For some reason, though she tried to fight it, Caroline responded to this with a resounding laugh. "That's it?" she asked. "That's the dreadful secret you must keep from Uncle Meldon?"

Unfortunately, this response only served to make Amelia look all the more embarrassed. "Yes . . . well, you see, I promised your father—many years ago— that I'd do everything in my power to keep Margaret away from you during your stays here."

"But that was years ago, Auntie," Caroline reminded her with a confident smile. "I'm old enough now to contend with her on my own, if need be."

Amelia appeared a bit surprised by Caroline's self-assurance on this score. "Very . . . very well, then," she stammered. "I guess you'll have to on Friday night. I honestly couldn't seem to say no to her. I mean . . . I tried," she continued, rolling her eyes helplessly, "but she was gone before I could say another word!"

At this, Caroline crossed to her and gave one of her shoulders a consoling pat. "I quite understand. I'm sure you did your best. And I won't let on to Uncle Meldon that you had anything to do with Aunt Margaret's presence at the party . . . I just think it's wonderful of you to organize such an affair in my honor!"

Amelia looked assuaged by her praise. "Well, it's nothing really. Just a few of our friends . . . and several of Boston's most eligible young men." She added this last part with a waggishly designing wink that seemed so patronizing Caroline would have been tempted to strike her, had she been anyone but her father's beloved "Pudding."

"How very nice," Caroline said coolly. "I look forward to it. Really, I do. And I promise you I'll try not to let Aunt Margaret anywhere near me."

Amelia donned an awkward smile at this assurance and began to make her way to the door. "Yes. Well . . . enough said about it, I guess. I'll leave you to rest. And be sure to call down for some hot water, should you wish to bathe."

"I will, Auntie. . . . And, Auntie," Caroline called out as Amelia left the suite.

Her aunt stopped just outside, in the corridor, and turned back to her with a questioning expression.

"Would you be so kind as to see to it that both of my trunks are brought up here straightaway? I've need of some of the articles in them for my bath, so the sooner the better, please." Caroline was relieved to note that she'd managed to keep her voice admirably even as she'd made this request. Surely, Amelia couldn't have guessed that her real reason for wanting her luggage so promptly was fear that the coachman, if allowed enough time, might chance to discover what was hidden in it.

Just as she'd hoped, Amelia only nodded and smiled in response. Then she strode off, down the corridor.

Caroline, in turn, walked over to the suite's door and quietly shut it. Then she went back into the sitting room to collect her thoughts. She couldn't help chuckling again at the mortified expression Amelia had worn as she'd admitted to being unsuccessful in diverting Margaret. Caroline had thought, from the looks of things, that Amelia had been about to confess to committing a murder or something equally appalling, so she'd been greatly relieved to learn it was nothing more than a simple blunder.

As Caroline sat in one of the camel-back chairs once more and bent down to remove her shoes, she realized that her father had been dead right about Amelia; she really wasn't much good at family politics. In fact, Caroline shuddered to think what the poor dear would do, if entrusted with something as awesome as smuggling weapons to the rebels.

Chapter 6

Meldon Thorwell, of the Brenton Shipping Company, looked quite surprised to see Nathaniel Hamlin sitting in his office at the warehouse that afternoon. Having heard Meldon approach the back office, Nathaniel had already turned about in the comb-back chair before the desk and was staring backward at the doorway as Meldon entered.

Despite his obvious surprise, however, Meldon didn't hesitate to give Nathaniel a proper greeting. He crossed to him immediately and offered him a warm smile and a handshake, before going to sit behind his desk. "Nathaniel, I haven't seen you in months, it seems. How are you?"

Hamlin reciprocated with a broad smile. "Quite well, thank you, Meldon. And yourself?"

"Fine . . . fine, indeed. What brings you over here?" Meldon inquired, his tone still cordial and nonchalant as he settled into his desk chair.

Nathaniel had prepared for this question all night, or so it seemed, yet he found himself without much of an answer now. "Oh, nothing . . . really. I mean, 'we'—the company—had a few bills to settle with your firm, and I thought, with the weather so clement, I'd walk over here and make the payment myself."

"Well, that was neighborly of you."

"Yes . . . well, we do our best, don't we?" Nathaniel replied, hating himself for not being better prepared for the small talk he'd known would come with this encounter. He'd already made some inquiries regarding Meldon's niece, Caroline, and he'd been told that she was coming to Boston primarily to take care of some matters at the shipping office, in her father's stead. Indeed, he had expected to find the *mademoiselle* scurrying about the place, garbed in some fancy French day dress and spouting orders to the staff. Instead he'd found that Meldon was the only management figure present, and before he could make a graceful getaway, some clerk had led him back to Meldon's desk to await Thorwell's return from whatever recess of the establishment he was frequenting.

Perhaps this was for the best, Nathaniel had told himself. Maybe there'd be something to gain by hanging about and chatting with the man. He might even learn a thing or two about Miss Brenton's plans for her stay in Boston. There was also, though Nathaniel cringed to think of it, the possibility that Meldon and his wife were somehow involved with this weapons-smuggling business, and Nathaniel realized that it wouldn't hurt to see what he could learn about those two as well. But something deep inside him told him that Meldon and Amelia simply weren't revolutionary sorts. They had always struck Nathaniel as being a little too lean-witted for anything quite so weighty. Nevertheless, here he was now, face-to-face with Meldon Thorwell, scouring his brain for something appropriate to say and coming up with precious little.

In spite of this loss for words, however, Nathaniel actually felt his mouth opening again to speak, and the question he heard himself asking confounded him. "Tell me, how are our ships holding up for you these days? No problems, I trust."

Meldon, dumbfounded, predictably enough, raised an eyebrow. "Well . . . none of them have sunk, if that is what you're asking," he replied with a clumsy laugh.

Nathaniel could feel his cheeks warming from embarrassment. "Good God, man, I should certainly hope not! I simply meant . . . well, what I meant to say was, if you need any assistance from us at any time, please don't hesitate to ask. Our businesses are so dependent upon one another, after all, aren't they, old chap?" he continued, trying to recover his composure and to smooth the conversation over by interjecting a fraternal theme. "I mean, the very nails that you good people ship in and sell to us could well be those used in the next vessel we build for you. One hand really washes the other here in the Colonies, doesn't it?"

Meldon nodded, but this was clearly only to be polite. He still didn't seem to have the faintest idea where this exchange was leading, and neither did his companion, for that matter.

Fortunately, Nathaniel finally recalled that Meldon had never really been a man for talking shop. The truth was he usually seemed too perplexed by the business world to comfortably converse about even the simplest aspects of it, and he far preferred talking about his personal life. It wasn't that all of this was evident when one first met the man. Meldon had, after all, always dressed the part of the proprietor, and he certainly knew how to charm his customers and associates. But Nathaniel remembered now that Meldon was much like the flavorless, yet luscious-looking English-made baked goods he'd sampled during his stays in London. Meldon looked and acted the part, but, when one bit in, one found that the expected qualities simply weren't there, that he was, in fact, quite devoid of all the things his exterior seemed to promise. He was, therefore, the perfect puppet for Richard Brenton. Though Brenton had purportedly appointed Meldon and his wife to run the Bostonian branch of the business, it was clear that they were little more than figureheads. Everyone knew most of the company's decisions were being made over a thousand miles away, in New Orleans. Recalling all of this, Nathaniel decided to take a different approach.

"I say, Meldon," he began, leaning back in his chair and coming up with as casual a smile as he could summon. "How are things at the club these days? Have you been there of late?"

Meldon looked markedly relieved at this change of subject. "Yes, of course. I go there regularly, Nathan. You know that."

"Indeed I do. It's just that I've been so busy with the company in the last several weeks, I haven't had even a spare hour to go there."

Meldon pointed a finger at him, assuming a playfully admonishing air. "So we've noticed, Mr. Hamlin. Don't think we haven't. The fellows so enjoy your dry wit, you know. You really should join us again soon."

Nathaniel nodded and gazed sheepishly down at his

shoes. "Yes. Yes, I suppose I should. I really miss the place when I let too much time go by between visits."

"Ah, well, we all know you've been frightfully busy, what with filling your father's shoes and getting your sisters so respectably married off. You've done quite a commendable job of it, I must say. And you've made some tremendous strides with your family's company. I'm sure your father would be very proud of you, were he still alive," Meldon concluded, his eyes glistening a bit now at recalling Nathaniel's father. The two men had been good friends. At these times, Nathaniel most hated the work he had to do for the Crown; in such situations the battle lines had to be secretly drawn and old friends unwittingly became the enemy.

"Yes . . . well, I hope so," Nathaniel said softly, honestly touched by the praise.

"But you ought to take more time for yourself, Nathan. That's always been one of your failings, in my opinion; you're just too hard on yourself. I fear your well-meaning father caned you boys too often when you were lads, and, consequently, neither of you seem to know how to stop working and simply enjoy life once in a while."

Nathaniel did his best to continue smiling and to keep his true feelings from showing. After all, it was dolts like Meldon Thorwell who were allowing the Colonies to fall into chaos while they were out "enjoying life"! And now the fool was giving the same misguided advice to him, of all people! Apparently, the witty side of Nathaniel, which he showed at their private club and in his social life, had everyone, including Meldon, more hoodwinked than he'd thought. They obviously didn't realize what a wise and cautious soul he was. He believed only in the tried and true. He trusted Mother England alone to keep the Colonies safe and prosperous. His faith was solely in the Crown, and he'd be damned if he'd make the mistake of going the merry, heedless way of most of his fellow Bostonians!

"You ought to take some time to find yourself a nice wife and start a family of your own," Nathaniel heard Meldon continuing to say. "Surely, your brother can assume more of the responsibility for the company, can't he?"

"Oh, yes," Nathaniel assured him, actually somewhat in agreement with Meldon on this particular point. Marriage and procreation were inevitable, of course, if he was to have heirs to whom he could pass on his name and holdings. It was just that he was quite familiar with both the pleasures and drawbacks of bachelorhood, and being rather reticent by nature, he was in no hurry to trade in the familiar for the unknown. "And, believe me," he went on, "John already has taken over some of my duties. So I alone am to blame, I fear, for my continued bachelorhood . . . but the day will come. I have every confidence that the right young lady will appear in due course."

At this Meldon's mouth suddenly dropped open, as though something very important had just popped into his head. Nathaniel, knowing this was a relatively rare occurrence, simply stared at him for a few seconds, awaiting his revelation.

"Perhaps she already has," Meldon declared with a knowing smile.

Nathaniel tried to look pleased at this news. "Oh?" It occurred to him that Meldon might have been referring to Caroline, and that he was about to make Nathaniel's task a great deal easier by offering to introduce him to her. He didn't want to get his hopes up just yet, however.

"Yes. My niece, Caroline."

A delighted chill ran through Nathaniel at that instant, but he was careful not to let it show.

"You two have never met, have you?"

Nathaniel shook his head.

"Well then, it's time you did, don't you think?" Meldon asked, his smile so broad it could have charmed a Canadian Indian out of his furs in the dead of winter.

"Yes . . . well . . . I suppose it is," Nathaniel stammered, striving to look amply hesitant about committing himself too soon.

"You won't be disappointed," Meldon assured him. "She's really quite lovely."

Nathaniel managed to fight the temptation to roll his eyes at this. He'd known enough doting parents and aunts and uncles in his time to realize that they deemed any of the family's progeny attractive, even if said children had boarish tusks protruding from their nostrils. "I'm certain you're right," he said with a polite smile.

"She's my brother-in-law's girl. Surely you remember Richard Brenton. He and your father did a lot of business together through the years."

"Oh, yes. I certainly do remember him. He lives in New Orleans now, doesn't he?"

"Yes, but he comes back to Boston a few times a year, and this time he chose to send little Caroline, who will be taking over the management of the Brenton interests, up here in his place." Meldon raised one eyebrow emphatically as he said this, as if to underscore the fact that his niece would one day be very wealthy.

"How nice," Nathaniel replied, refusing to appear overly enthusiastic. He was far too respectable a man to allow anyone to accuse him of being a dowry hunter, and he knew that his displeasure at this intimation must have shown.

"Yes. And how nice for whoever she chooses to marry!" Meldon added.

"But surely, to the young lady's credit, Meldon, she has more to offer than wealth, does she not?" Nathaniel inquired, determined now to steer this annoying exchange in a direction that might give him more inside information about the *mademoiselle*.

Meldon's smile faded a bit, as though it was finally beginning to dawn on him that emphasizing his niece's vast holdings was a bit gauche. "Well, yes. Of course."

"So . . . tell me about her, if you will. Her likes and dislikes. Pastimes. That sort of thing," Nathaniel prompted. He was careful not to ask for a physical description of Caroline. In truth, he realized, he was afraid to hear it, afraid it would only confirm what he'd been dreading—that she was not physically appealing. Such confirmation, he realized, would only cause him to delay the already distasteful task of befriending her and then informing on her.

"Well, she seemes to like music, and she likes to dance and go riding." Meldon shrugged. "I don't know. She spends almost all of her time with Amelia when she visits, you see. And they're always off frequenting the shops and calling on friends. You know . . . the kinds of things ladies do. Can't say much, though, about what she does in her native Louisiana—those bayou people are very unlike us—but for some reason she seemes to enjoy doing farm work down there of all things. Richard says she actually does almost a man's share on her grandfather's stead each summer."

"Ah . . . the 'sturdy' sort," Nathaniel grumbled to himself, the image of an obese spinster popping into his head. Unhappily, he realized in that instant he'd said it just loudly enough for Meldon to hear.

"Oh, she's not fat," Thorwell quickly declared. "No. Not in the least, my good man. On the contrary, she's quite petite. Very much like my little Amelia."

To his credit, Nathaniel did manage not to issue a skeptical hmm in response. Meldon, while being false in appearance, had never proven to be a liar. "Does she speak English?" Nathaniel prodded, trying to sound enthusiastic once more.

"Oh, yes. Of course. She has quite a capacity for languages, in fact. But she says she speaks French best. I mean, that being all they speak in New Orleans."

"And when will I be allowed to meet this lovely lass?"

"Why, tomorrow night, of course. Don't tell me you didn't receive an invitation. Amelia said she was planning to send one to you and John."

"Sorry, but I can't say I've received it yet, Meldon," Nathaniel replied calmly, though inwardly he was ready to gnash his teeth at the realization that this wrenching visit had probably not been necessary and he would have made the young lady's acquaintance soon enough in any case.

"Well, it will just be a little gathering. A light supper and a string concert out in the gazebo. Nothing too formal."

"Sounds as if it will be very enjoyable. What time should I be there?"

"Seven."

Nathaniel nodded and smiled at him again. "Very well, Meldon," he said, rising from his chair. "I shall come without fail, and we can resume this little chat at that time."

"I'll look forward to that," Meldon replied, rising to escort him out, and Nathaniel could almost see in his eyes what Meldon was thinking. He was proud of himself for having arranged for Nathaniel to meet his niece. He was thinking what a fine match Nathaniel would be for Caroline—and, of course, he couldn't have been more wrong.

Just as Nathaniel was finally about to extricate himself from this encounter, however, just as he was on the verge of saying good day to Meldon and taking his leave, Thorwell suddenly donned a woeful expression.

"Pity about Crosley Fergusson, wasn't it."

This comment sent a chill up Nathaniel's spine, and he found himself unable to respond for several seconds. Fergusson had been his previous quarry, the last man he had informed on to Commander Rushton, and though he knew perfectly well what Meldon was referring to, he pretended now that he didn't. "What happened?"

"Oh, surely you've heard, haven't you? He was hung, without trial. By the redcoats, they say, for smuggling guns to the rebels. Good God, Nathan, it has been a while since you've been to the club, hasn't it?" he added with an amazed laugh.

"I guess it has," Nathaniel agreed, relieved to see how unsuspecting Meldon seemed. Had he been in any way wise to Nathaniel's dealings, he would surely have been searching his eyes now, checking for any little change of expression that might confirm that Nathaniel was somehow responsible for their fellow club member's demise. Yet he was not doing so. And certainly, if he were suspicious, he wouldn't have been fool enough to invite Nathaniel over to meet his niece. Not even Meldon Thorwell was that daft.

Chapter 7

Nathaniel Hamlin was running late as he dressed to attend Caroline Brenton's welcoming reception the following evening. Consequently, he wasn't in the best of moods. He was rarely late for anything. He found tardiness inexcusable, especially in himself, and the fact that his brother, John, had, at the last minute, decided to come with him to the gathering wasn't making matters any easier.

Having thrown on a hodgepodge of somewhat wrinkled dress clothes, John now lay on Nathaniel's canopied bed, slowing his brother's efforts to get ready with his attempts to make small talk. Nathaniel was standing before his full-length looking glass, trying to get his ruffled cravat arranged to his satisfaction, and he glared into the mirror at such an angle that he was certain John could see his reflection. "Must you always go about looking like an unmade bed?" he snarled. "Why don't you ask the maid to fetch you up some ironed clothing?"

As Nathaniel could have predicted, his younger

brother responded with nothing more than a laugh. Then he rolled from his side onto his stomach and continued to stare into the glass at Nathaniel, his lips curled in an irksome smirk. Unlike Nathaniel, John took after their late mother, a pixieish redhead with Irish roots. While he was certainly handsome in his own way, he had a laugh like a hyena's, and his prankish vitality was enough to make Nathaniel want to take a buggy whip to him on some days. Indeed, at times, it seemed to Nathaniel that it had been rather cruel of his parents to die and leave him to take over the family business, especially with a brother as unmanageable as John at his side. It would have been far more tolerable had Nathaniel been allowed to appoint one of his levelheaded sisters to act as his assistant. But they were both married off now, wed, by Nathaniel's own arrangement, to two prosperous Bostonians, whom he was sure would do well by them, and Nathaniel was stuck with John as his right-hand man.

"These clothes are just fine, thank you," John finally retorted, continuing to chuckle. "It will be dusk in just an hour or two, and no one will be able to see a rumple here or there."

At this, Nathaniel again scowled into the mirror at his brother and issued a cluck of disgust.

"Good Lord, Nathan, I don't remember when I've seen you so on edge. She's just some little Cajun métis, after all. Don't tell me you're nervous about this."

"Well, yes. I guess I am. A trifle," Nathaniel admitted.

"All the more reason, then, to have me along. I'll help you keep matters in perspective . . . help you stay calm. I mean, you can hardly hope to woo anyone when you're so terribly growly, now, can you?"

"But can't you see? It's you who's causing my 'growliness,' as you put it. I do wish you'd simply oblige me and stay home tonight!"

Nathaniel could see in the mirror that his brother's smile was fading now. John further responded to this comeback by stubbornly jutting out his chin, which rested in the palms of his upraised hands. "Might I remind you that the Brentons' invitation was addressed to me, too?"

"But you know perfectly well that I work better alone. I mean, that would finish us, wouldn't it? Having us both implicated in a Tory spy ring. Don't you see? One of us has to remain alive to carry on the company and the Hamlin name. We owe Father that much, John."

His brother only shrugged at this appeal. "But I don't see why I always have to be the one who's stuck at home, tending the fire while you're out having your little intrigues!"

"Oh, for Christ's sake," Nathaniel snapped. "Do you want this assignment? Really? Do you truly want to find yourself having to woo some French and Indian girl from a Spanish-owned colony down south? My God, you flunked French altogether! You're even worse at it than I am. What on earth would you have to say to her?"

"Nothing, I suppose," John conceded. "I only wish that—just once—you'd let me take one of the commander's assignments. You always save the most exciting tasks for yourself, while I'm stuck year after year, acting as little more than the company's scrivener!"

"All right. Very well," Nathaniel agreed after a moment, crossing to his brother and giving his right shoulder a consoling squeeze. "The next one is yours. You have my word. Just do stop carrying on, will you? You're twenty-six years old, for God's sake. Sit up and act your age! I think I've been more than fair with you since father died."

Again his brother shrugged, but this time, to Nathaniel's relief, he did so with a good-natured smirk. "Yes, I guess you have. It's just that I'd hate to see anything happen to you, Nathan. I mean, I'm likely to find you floating facedown in the harbor one of these days, what with tongues flying as fast as they do in this town. When is the commander going to finally let you 'resign your commission' in all of this?"

Nathaniel was bent over now, with one of his feet up on the cedar chest situated at the end of the bed. He was busily putting the final bit of polish on his nicest pair of buckle-topped shoes. "Now is not the time to 'resign one's commission,' John. You know that. The redcoats have been virtually dormant for over a year, waiting for England to grant them further backing. This is, therefore, the worst of all times for any of us to 'resign.'"

"But can't you, at least, get this assignment over with more quickly this time? Last time around, I got saddled with every patron complaint, every disgruntled workman in the company for over three months, while you wiled away your days at the club, trying to wheedle information out of that poor fellow—what was his name again?" John asked with a snarl, obviously too irritated now to recall.

"Fergusson."

"Yes. Crosley Fergusson. Poor, dumb bloke."

"'Poor,' indeed. Meldon Thorwell informed me yesterday that a pack of redcoats actually hung him! And I must say it disturbed me. I understood that Fergusson's smuggling to the rebels would have to be stopped, but the commander never once informed me that he'd allow his men to resort to murdering him!"

"Yes, but what did you expect? It's not as though you, or any of the other Tories they employ, would agree to act as witnesses against the Whigs in public trials, now, is it?"

"I suppose not."

"Well, there you have it, then. You can hardly fancy that the redcoats would just set these fellows free, knowing they're gunrunners and such. This is a war, after all, and men die in wars. What does it matter if they die in battle or at the end of a rope?"

Nathaniel crossed back to the mirror to put on his last bit of finery, a Burgundy-colored silk bag into which he stuffed his black hair. Then he tied the tiny bag shut with a bow at the back of his neck. "Yes, but I still don't care for it much. A war should not preclude due process. It's bad enough men such as ourselves have to live in fear of having the Whigs torch our homes at the drop of a hat. Our side shouldn't be making matters worse by hanging people without trials."

John suddenly affected a waggishly knowing smile. "Do you know what I think? I think you're actually having some qualms about informing on this Miss Brenton. Don't tell me you're worried about what might become of her."

Nathaniel turned back to his brother with a glower.

"Good God, no! I don't even know her, for heaven's sake. What do I care what becomes of her?" Even as he said these words, however, he knew that on some level he probably would end up caring. He'd never before been asked to mix his espionage efforts with the realm of the boudoir, and the combination had had him on edge from the start. His love life was, after all, one of the few realms in which he allowed himself total abandon, and he truly did not want to spoil that carefree realm by permitting politics to be brought into it.

"Just wondering, is all," John explained.

"Well, do stop 'wondering' and get downstairs and make certain the coachman has brought the carriage around. It's already ten to seven, and the Brenton place is at least a five-minute ride from here."

At this, John dragged himself to his feet with the schoolboyish reluctance with which he met most of his brother's orders, and he headed for the door.

"And, John," Nathaniel called after him.

His brother turned back to him with a weary roll of his eyes.

"How do I look?"

"Fine. You'll sweep her off her feet."

Nathaniel turned back to the mirror to peruse his strapping form once more. Fortunately, he'd inherited the swarthiness of his father, and though entirely of British descent, he could well have passed for a dashing Spanish prince. "Do you really think so?" he asked again, doing his best to sound modestly uncertain.

"I really think so," John answered in a monotone.

"Oh, good. Because I want to be mercifully swift on this one. Hopefully, the dear girl will let the cat out of the bag before I'm forced to take her to bed," he concluded, giving his embroidered waistcoat a slight tug downward and straightening his cravat once more. Though his brother was gone an instant later, Nathaniel resisted the temptation to flash his reflection an admiring smile. It wasn't that he was not pleased with how he looked this evening, it was just that, given the news about Fergusson, smiling seemed a bit too callous.

Caroline was startled, and her quill left a sweeping blot of ink upon the page as she heard a deep voice address her from her sitting-room doorway. Though she'd been dressed for the reception for almost an hour, Amelia had asked her not to come down to the gathering until a respectable number of guests had arrived, so she sat, penning a letter to her parents and intermittently gazing out the back window at the site of the reception below. Now, as she looked up to see who had called her name, her heart began to pound with trepidation.

"Good evening, Caroline," the caller said. "Do you remember me?"

Caroline rose from the little slant-top desk, swallowing uneasily and trying to summon a smile. "But, of course, Aunt Margaret. Of course, I do."

"May I come in?"

Caroline nodded, taking in all of her aunt's features in an apprehensive scan. Margaret had aged quite a bit. Her hair was grayer now, and her face, even in this late-day light, showed signs of having wrinkled considerably since Caroline had seen her last. As usual,

Margaret was tastefully, but rather drably, dressed, and her hair was parted down the middle and pulled back with a severeness that doubtless culminated in an uninspired bun. The times, the fashions had changed, Caroline thought in that instant, but old Aunt Margaret never seemed to. Even her forced smile was as unsettling to behold as ever, and Caroline knew that conversing with her now would be the same as it had been. It would be as precarious as walking along the rim of a caldron of boiling water. People like Margaret only seemed more charming than most, because one instinctively knew how dangerously close by their nasty sides always hovered.

"Come in. Yes, of course," Caroline replied, doing her best to sound calm and collected.

Margaret immediately took her up on this invitation, sashaying over to her and clasping her with a tightness that nearly took Caroline's breath away.

"Well, well," Margaret declared, backing away from Caroline an instant later and surveying her from head to toe. "Aren't you a feast for the eyes this evening! That peach color really flatters you, my dear. My fellow Bostonians shall surely find themselves quite taken by you."

"Thank you," Caroline choked out, amazed at hearing her aunt gush so. She'd never seen much of this side of Margaret, probably because her parents had always been present when she was with her before and Margaret had seen no gain in acting this way. "You may sit down if you wish, but, in truth, I was just about to go downstairs and join the guests."

"Oh, I'm sure you were, and I promise not to keep you, Caroline. But, what with my being your only other aunt on the Brenton side of your family and all, it seemed that I should, at least, come up and see you alone for a moment."

Caroline responded with a clumsy laugh. "Yes. Well . . . it seems you have, doesn't it?"

Margaret wasn't going to sit down, thank heavens. Caroline could see that the woman's only aim at this point was to stay toe to toe with her, to keep her eyes locked upon Caroline's as much as possible and to extract whatever information she could from her, like a bee drawing up nectar from a flower.

"How is your father?" she asked. "I hope he's recovering nicely."

Caroline didn't know how to respond. She was sure that Amelia would not have been foolish enough to tell Margaret of her father's illness, yet Margaret sounded so certain of it. "Recovering?" she echoed.

"Yes. He's been sick, hasn't he?"

"Sick?" Caroline shook her head as though confused. "He seemed to be doing well when last I saw him." This wasn't really a lie, after all, she reasoned. Her father had appeared to have almost returned to health when she'd said good-bye to him and gone off to board the schooner, and, unfortunately, these sorts of marginal truths seemed necessary when one was conversing with a woman as treacherous as Margaret.

Caroline was gratified an instant later to see how befuddled her aunt looked at having gotten this response.

"Then . . . if he's well," Margaret stammered, "why didn't he come up here with you?"

"He had other matters to handle, I'm afraid. Besides, it is time I began learning my way about this branch of the business."

"Yes, I suppose it is," Margaret replied, nodding, but seeming unable to keep her eyes from revealing that she still didn't believe Caroline. Then, suddenly, her penetrating gaze shifted over Caroline's shoulder to the desk beside the window. "Whatever were you writing so feverishly as I came in, my dear? A letter home?"

Caroline saw no risk in answering this honestly. "Yes." With that, she turned and walked back to the desk to fold up the note. For a moment, she thought about how she might gracefully rid herself of it or stow it away, so Margaret couldn't come up later and read it. The only hiding place she could think of, however, was one of her trunks. They, at least, could be locked for safekeeping. But, given their contents, she knew the trunks were out of the question. She certainly couldn't afford to risk drawing Margaret's attention to them. So, anxious to get her aunt out of her suite and to take refuge in the crowd assembled below, Caroline slipped the letter into the bodice of her low-cut gown and turned back to face Margaret with a smile.

"Missing your home already?" Margaret asked pointedly.

Caroline gave forth a cool laugh as she crossed back to her aunt. "Oh, but you don't understand, Auntie, do you? Boston is my home. One of them, in any case." Noting in that instant that she had grown to be at least a full inch taller than Margaret, Caroline somehow found the nerve to politely but firmly turn her aunt about and walk with her out of the room.

Margaret seemed rather surprised by this boldness at first, her legs hesitant to match Caroline's quick stride. But she finally did lift her gown and make an adequate effort to keep up with her niece. "I gather we're headed downstairs now," she said.

"Yes," Caroline answered, flashing an imperious smile, and Margaret realized at this point that she really was going to have a fight on her hands with this one.

Chapter 8

Nathaniel was almost grateful for his brother's company as he stood on the back grounds of the Brenton mansion, sipping wine from a pewter goblet and doing his best to look at ease among the guests. Though he hadn't yet been introduced to Mademoiselle Brenton, he felt certain that he knew who she was. He'd spotted her almost the instant he'd arrived. She was the short lass in the rather risqué, scarlet gown *à la polonaise,* and she was wearing her raven-black hair in a towering cascade of curls which was absurdly elaborate.

"That's her," he said to John out of the corner of his mouth, his eyes moving up at such an angle that he felt certain his brother would see to whom he was referring.

John pondered this for several seconds as he mindlessly ran his right index finger about the rim of his wine goblet. "No . . . I don't think so," he said softly, shaking his head. "She's too salaciously dressed to be a Brenton."

"But she's also French and a Cajun, remember," Nathaniel countered, "and that's the sort of gown

French women wear."

"Well, then, if you're so certain it's her, why don't you go over and introduce yourself?" John gave his brother a teasing nudge.

Nathaniel brushed his hand away and scowled at him. "Certainly not! Meldon Thorwell was the one who invited me to this thing, and *he* can bloody well take responsibility for coming over here and introducing me to his niece." With that, Nathaniel stubbornly squared his shoulders and took a long swallow of his wine.

"Fine. Then I guess we're stuck standing here, watching her from afar."

"I guess we are . . . though I can tell you there are a hundred things I'd rather be doing this evening."

There was a surprised rise to John's voice as he spoke again. "What? You don't like her looks?"

"Not at all." Nathaniel was starting to feel as though he and his brother were a pair of voyeurs, as they stood a tasteful four or five feet from the edge of the crowd, surveying the scene. He knew that in some ways he would probably have been less conspicuous, had he forced himself to mingle, but part of him warned that it wasn't a wise thing to do. Considering the real reason for his having come, it seemed best that he keep a low profile and not deliberately bring his presence to anyone's attention. For all he knew, his association with Crosley Fergusson, just prior to Crosley's demise, was already suspicious to his fellow Bostonians, and he realized, therefore, that he couldn't afford to let himself be seen with Mademoiselle Brenton too often in the next few weeks. Fortunately, however, the melodic string music that started flowing from the gazebo, enveloping and somehow unifying the crowd, seemed to give him more license to simply continue to stand at the edge of the gathering and keep his distance from the *mademoiselle* and from everyone else.

Oh, dear God, he thought to himself, watching the disquietingly dark young lady intently as her ebony eyes flashed about the small circle of guests with whom she was chatting and laughing, she's a sorceress. Nothing less than a femme fatale! The sort of young lady who would obviously delight in tearing a gentleman's heart out!

Fool that he was, Nathaniel had already gone ahead and given Rushton his promise to try to court her! He'd made a big mistake by making such a pledge. Perhaps his biggest ever, and he found himself anxiously gulping down the rest of his wine and eying the crowd in search of another steward to refill his goblet.

"I'm in over my head," he said in a whisper to his brother.

John, his eyes still fixed on the exotic young woman, simply smirked. It was an expression that reflected both amusement and just the tiniest bit of delight at seeing his usually self-possessed brother becoming unnerved. "Yes, Nathaniel. I'd say that you are."

"I mean, maybe . . . if she were pretty, I could bring it off. But not with *her,"* he concluded, issuing a resigned sigh and shaking his head. "Dear Lord, I think I'd rather try bedding a serpent!"

"What's this about serpents?" The jovial voice came from behind Nathaniel.

He could have sworn that his feet left the ground as, with a start, he turned about to see who had spoken so loudly. To his further surprise, he found himself facing

Meldon Thorwell and an angel-faced young lady with a glorious mane of honey blond hair.

"Oh, Meldon, my good man . . . you scared me, I'm afraid," Nathaniel confessed with an awkward laugh.

"Sorry to sneak up on you, Nathan, but you and John were the first guests I saw as Caroline and I came out of the house just now, so I thought I'd introduce her to you."

Nathaniel felt his mouth drop open in that instant, and he did his best to close it and regain his composure. "Caroline?" he echoed in amazement.

"Yes. My niece. The one I told you about yesterday. Surely you recall," Meldon added, furrowing his brow.

"Well, yes. Yes, of course, I recall," Nathaniel replied with a laugh. "It is just that I was . . . I was hardly expecting anyone so . . . so ravishing."

The young lady appeared flattered by the praise, and Meldon went on to make a formal introduction. "My niece, Mademoiselle Caroline Brenton. Caroline, this is Nathaniel Hamlin and his brother, John."

The young lady offered a slight curtsy, and Nathaniel, still shaken by this turn of events, felt his fingers tremble a bit as he reached out and took her hand in his. He raised it to his lips, with as much courtliness as he could muster, and kissed the back of it, keeping his eyes fixed on hers all the while. *"Enchanté,"* he murmured, still feeling rather tongue-tied due to her luminous beauty.

"Merci," the *mademoiselle* answered softly, her cocoa brown eyes seeming to sum him up in one sweep. Then they moved on to survey John, as he reached out to kiss her hand as well.

Nathaniel would have paid just about any price to

know what she was thinking in those moments, what was behind those disarming, yet strangely calculating, eyes of hers. And then he realized that he hadn't even appraised her beautifully clad figure, as he did instantly with every other young lady he met. Instead, his eyes seemed affixed to Caroline's, inextricably linked to her lovely face and her full, softly colored lips. Then it dawned upon him that he wasn't allowing his eyes to travel down the length of her because he didn't dare to imagine her disrobed. He instinctively knew that such fancying was apt to make him feel even more smitten with her than he already was, and that wasn't something he could afford to let happen.

"Nathaniel and his brother own the Hamlin Shipyards, Caroline," Meldon explained to his niece an instant later.

Nathaniel noted that she did not turn back to look at her uncle as he spoke. Rather, her eyes traveled over to lock upon Nathaniel's once more.

"*Oui*. I know the name well, dear uncle," she said in a confident tone. "He's the man who recently refused a substantial offer from the English forces to build ships for His Majesty. Isn't that right, Mr. Hamlin?"

"That's right," Nathaniel replied, amazed that she had already heard this news when she'd only been in Boston a day or two. While Nathaniel and Commander Rushton had purposely started this rumor, and had done their best to see to it that it was spread about, Meldon Thorwell seemed a little too obtuse to have intercepted it and passed it on to his niece. "But how would you have known that, *mademoiselle,* what with being so far away in New Orleans?"

A soft smile tugged at the corner of her lips. "I make

it my business to know such things, *monsieur*. Our companies have far too many dealings for me not to."

"I think what Caroline's trying to say, Nathan," Meldon interjected, "if, indeed, it is permissible to say it . . . is that we all applaud your decision."

Nathaniel smiled. "Yes. It's permissible to say it. You have my word, Meldon, that I shan't repeat it to any Tory spies, if that is what concerns you," he added with a dry laugh.

This comment, predictably enough, brought a peal of laughter from Meldon, as well as an uneasy chuckle from John. Nathaniel noted that Miss Brenton's sedate expression didn't change in those seconds, however. "A little joke," he explained to her with a nervous cough.

"*Oui*. I'm aware of that."

"Oh, yes," Meldon chimed in again. "Our Caroline speaks English very well. No need to do any translating or explaining for her, my dear man."

"No. It doesn't appear so," Nathaniel agreed. "I just wanted to make certain that she knew I was simply speaking in jest."

Caroline donned a broad smile. "And so I did, Mr. Hamlin, and I must say it's been a pleasure meeting you and John. I do fear, however, that it's time I moved on to the rest of my uncle's guests. I'm sure you understand."

"Yes . . . well . . . yes," Nathaniel stammered. He was astounded that, before he could even gather his wits and really begin to converse with her, she was going to be on her way. To his further dismay, instead of thinking of something to say that might persuade her to stay, he reflexively reached out and took her hand in his once more. At this a voice within him instantly started scolding: What are you doing? You have already pronounced her "ravishing" and kissed her hand! It would certainly seem excessively forward of him to draw it up to your lips now and do it again.

In that case, what could he do with it? Offer her a clumsy handshake, perhaps, and tell her what a pleasure it was for the Hamlin Shipyard to do business with her company? No. That seemed even more awkward than kissing her hand a second time. Then, fortunately, his eyes focused upon hers once more, and he saw that she looked almost as surprised and embarrassed as he must have.

She laughed nervously, and Nathaniel spied the first glimmer of vulnerability in her. Seeing this, he realized that reaching out to her again was not, as he'd thought a moment earlier, the very worst blunder he could have made. It had, after all, drawn her out. It had cracked open that businesslike veneer of hers, and there was probably much to be learned from that.

Her eyes seemed to be searching his now, as though she were trying to determine whether he'd taken hold of her hand again intentionally or simply mindlessly—out of nervousness, perhaps. Then, apparently having attained her answer, she directed her gaze down at their joined hands once more and began to speak.

"Is that a ruby in your ring, Mr. Hamlin?"

Nathaniel seized the opportunity to take his hand from hers. He then drew it upward, fixing his attention on the stone as well. He was hoping, just as she obviously was that this new topic would dig them both out of the awkward situation in which they'd found themselves. "Why, yes. Yes, it is."

"That's good," she said, her voice seeming strangely

sympathetic. "Rubies are said to protect their wearers from danger, and I'm not sure why, but I sense that you're a man who could use such protection."

With that, she flashed Nathaniel and his brother a parting smile. Then she moved on to meet the rest of the guests. This, of course, left Meldon to linger behind for a couple of seconds and offer the two men an embarrassed, almost apologetic smile at his niece's Cajun reference to the magical properties of gems.

"So much for the 'love at first sight' approach," John muttered, once their host had left them as well. "She didn't seem the slightest bit interested in you."

Nathaniel gave his brother a biting sideward glance. "Which delights you no end, I'm sure." Nathaniel's outstanding success at seducing women had always been a sore point for his less popular brother, and Nathaniel was certain now that this was what was coloring John's interpretation of the encounter with Miss Brenton.

John, however, simply shrugged in response and raised his brows with an artless air. "Well, I don't care one way or the other, if you want the truth. I just think it's bound to make your work for the commander all the more difficult."

"But she looked at me. Her eyes were fixed upon mine almost the entire time she was standing here."

"Is it any wonder, the way you were ogling her? I'm sure she thought you had taken leave of your senses!"

"Well, I didn't expect her to be a blonde. Meldon never once said anything about her being a gorgeous blonde. If he had, I'm sure I would have come here better prepared to gain the advantage."

"Whatever you say," John replied, his smirk so

irritating that Nathaniel was tempted to wrestle him to the ground and thrash him.

"I need more wine," Nathaniel suddenly snarled, heading into the crowd now, in search of a wine steward.

"I'll come with you," he heard John declare, and it was clear that his brother was tagging after him as he continued to ease through the various clusters of guests.

"She didn't seem to care much for your Tory spy remark, did she?" John noted in a prudent undertone, as they moved along.

"This is hardly the time and place to be discussing that," Nathaniel hissed scoldingly.

"But she didn't, did she?"

"No, John. Clearly she did not."

"But then, I don't suppose I would either if I were smuggling weapons to the rebels."

Nathaniel brought his quest to an abrupt halt and turned back to glare at his brother. "If you don't cease your chatter on this subject at once, I swear to you I shall bind and gag you and carry you back out to the coachman to have you transported home!"

To Nathaniel's relief, this threat seemed to sober his brother a bit, and he again felt it was safe to continue on in search of another glass of wine.

"That talk about your ruby was rather unsettling, wasn't it?" John began again seconds later, in a more retiring tone.

Nathaniel gave forth a dry laugh as he paused once more to scan the scene for a steward. "It was nothing more than hocus-pocus, you fool. Simply her way of trying to keep the locals from getting too close to her."

116

"No. She *believed* what she was saying, Nathan," John countered. "I could see in her eyes that she honestly believed she was doing you a good turn by telling you about your ring's 'protective' properties."

"Well, fine then. What if she did believe it? I'm in the business of helping the commander, not saving maidens' souls from the perils of witchcraft. You don't know me as well as you might suppose if you think me frightened by such nonsense." With that, Nathaniel, having at last spotted a wine bearer on the far side of the gazebo, began walking once more.

John issued a frustrated cluck as he continued traipsing after him. "Well, she may have stared at you," he conceded, "but it wasn't because she found you comely."

"Oh, no? Then, pray, tell me why."

"It was because she disliked you. Any bloke with eyes could have seen that. She just flatly didn't like the looks of you. And were I in your place, I'd send for Mr. Smythe at once and tell him I was very sorry, but I was simply not going to make any headway with this one and they ought to engage some other fellow."

The very thought of being rejected by a girl of such dubious extraction was making Nathaniel's blood begin to boil, and he had all he could do to keep from reaching out and slapping John as he again came to a halt and turned back to address him through clenched teeth. "You must know by now, *little* brother, that when I want your advice, I shall ask for it! In the meantime, I'll thank you to stay out of my affairs! Now, I came here this evening expressly to win the favor of Meldon's niece, and that is precisely what I intend to do! There is a way into every woman's heart,

117

and you can bloody bet that, when it comes to Miss Brenton, I intend to find it!" Having said this, Nathaniel strode the rest of the way to the wine steward he'd spotted and, much to his relief succeeded in having his goblet refilled to its rim.

John was, of course, still on his heels, but, fortunately, as Nathaniel turned back to converse with him once more, he noticed that John wasn't the only one who had been following him. While it was apparent that Meldon and his wife had, for obvious reasons, been very careful not to invite too many of Boston's eligible maidens to this showcase for their niece, two or three of them had managed to gain admittance, and they'd finally caught sight of Nathaniel in the crowd. They were consequently upon him now, forming a small semicircle about Nathaniel and John, and tittering and nervously fanning themselves in the warmish evening air.

At first, this seemed nothing more than an annoyance to Nathaniel, yet another stumbling block to his efforts to remain inconspicuous. But, when he scanned the crowd once more and saw that the knoll upon which Miss Brenton was currently standing afforded her a perfect view of him and the trio of adoring young ladies, he seized the opportunity to make the most of the situation.

He proceeded to converse with the maidens in the minutes that followed, being careful to direct an occasional glance over their shoulders at the *mademoiselle,* to see if she was noticing. She didn't seem to be, so Nathaniel used some of his well-known wit on the ladies, in order to elicit some loud, attention-getting laughter from them. Unfortunately, this tactic failed as well. Not only did Miss Brenton seem oblivious to Nathaniel and his admirers, but it appeared that she was absolutely enthralled by the conversation she was having with Nathaniel's key competitor in the ship-building business, Earl McCrae.

Infuriated by this, Nathaniel excused himself from the young ladies and took John aside to confer.

"She's talking to that worm McCrae, and she has been for over five minutes now, I believe," Nathaniel explained in a heated whisper.

"Well, there's no law against it."

"But what could they possibly have to talk about for so long? The man's about as interesting as a rusty nail. Look at that. Just look," Nathaniel continued. "He's actually making her laugh! I've never heard Earl say anything that struck me as being even faintly amusing."

"Apparently Miss Brenton has."

"But I'm much funnier than he! Everyone has always said so."

"Yes . . . everyone at the club. But perhaps to a Cajun you are not, Nathan. I mean, I don't remember you saying anything amusing when Meldon introduced us to her. Just that Tory spy remark, and she obviously didn't find that funny."

"But the other ladies . . . I . . . I had them positively roaring a couple times just now."

"That's different."

"Why?"

"Because they adore you. They would doubtless roll over and do tricks for you like our beagles if they thought it would bring any of them closer to being courted by you. Miss Brenton, on the other hand . . . as I tried to explain to you earlier," he added gingerly, "doesn't seem terribly interested." With that, John began to turn away from his brother, obviously wanting to go back to the gathering of maidens Nathaniel had attracted and see what fallout he could glean from the situation—as had come to be his practice through the years.

Nathaniel reached out and captured his shoulder in a viselike grip. "Oh, no, you don't," he growled. "You stay here and offer me what advice you can, or, I promise you, I shall strive to make your life hell upon earth down at the shipyards in the weeks to come!"

At this threat, John turned back to face his brother, sighing resignedly. "Oh, very well, then. But I don't know what makes you think *I* will be of any help."

"You, dear brother, have to work at wooing young ladies, all the time. I, on the other hand, have become shamelessly lax about it over the years. I fear Boston's maidens have made it all far too easy for me of late."

This was, in its own way, a compliment to John. Nathaniel could tell, however, from the single brow his brother raised that it struck John as being a very backhanded one—both surprising and galling.

"Has it not occurred to you, Nathan, that the reason why McCrae seems to be having so much success with her is that he's one of the rebel contacts the commander is seeking?"

Nathaniel couldn't help smiling a bit at this possibility. "No. But I assure you that *nothing* would please me more!"

"Yes. It would be gratifying—wouldn't it?—having our chief competitor found hanging from a tree!"

Nathaniel's smile faded. "But what if he's *not* one of her contacts. What if it's just as it appears, two strangers talking, and he's over there making headway with her?"

"Well, there's only one way to find out, isn't there? You'll simply have to go over and interrupt them."

Nathaniel was clearly aghast at this suggestion. "What? Become an interloper? You must be mad! Why, she'd only scowl at me."

"No. You see, you don't walk over there pretending to want to speak to her, you pretend you want to speak to Earl. That way, she'll be obliged to stand there and compare the two of you as you match wits. Why, on looks alone, you'll make McCrae pale."

However immodest it seemed, Nathaniel couldn't help but agree with this last statement. Earl had never been a man one could call handsome. He was really rather plain-looking. In contrast to Nathaniel's strikingly dark coloring, his hair and brows were a thoroughly forgettable shade of ecru and his eyes were as cloudy brown as an aged dog's. Recalling all of this, Nathaniel began to smile again, and he reached out and gave his little brother a grateful slap on the back. "Why, that's capital, John. Thank you! But, what should I say to him? I mean, I haven't spoken to the man in over four years, not since one of the horses went lame in front of his office and I urgently needed some smithy tools. Won't it seem odd?"

"Who cares how it seems?" John asked scoldingly. "Just strut over there and pretend to be his dearest bloody friend, for God's sake! You're doing this for King and country, remember."

Nathaniel gave this some thought as he swallowed back the last of his wine. "So I am," he agreed after several seconds. "And certainly, as you say, it would be quite impossible for a cur such as McCrae to make me come off badly." With this, Nathaniel handed his empty goblet to his brother, gave his waistcoat a straightening, downward tug, and then strode off to join his competitor and the *mademoiselle,* his heart pounding with apprehension all the while. He might just as well have been marching into battle, he realized in those seconds, for his palms were moist and his throat dry.

"I say, Earl," he said loudly, as he finally reached the two of them. "I see you've met the guest of honor. Isn't she splendid?"

It didn't surprise Nathaniel in the least that McCrae met his interruption with the fiercest of scowls upon turning from the *mademoiselle* to see who was addressing him.

Miss Brenton, on the other hand, didn't look in the least bit annoyed. Rather, she appeared to be flattered and somewhat surprised.

"Nathaniel. What brings you over here?" McCrae coolly demanded, turning about more fully now and reaching out to give his competitor's hand a half-hearted shake. "Why, I haven't seen you since your father's funeral, six years ago," he noted in a biting tone.

Nathaniel issued an uneasy laugh and locked his eyes upon Earl's, silently cautioning him not to press his advantage too far. "No. I'm sure I've seen you since then, Earl. In fact, I keep meaning to stop by your office and pay you a call. There is some business I would like to discuss with you."

McCrae looked surprised by this, and rightfully so. "There is?"

122

"Why, yes, but let us not bore the young lady with such talk now. This gathering is meant to honor her, after all," Nathaniel continued, somehow summoning the courage to focus upon Caroline's heart-stirring eyes once more and unhappily seeing in them that same impenetrableness he'd found earlier. "Tell me, did you two meet before this evening?"

"No," McCrae answered, also gazing at Caroline and, to Nathaniel's dismay, exchanging a gentle smile with her. "Why do you ask?"

"Well, only because you seemed to be hitting it off so well. I simply thought you might have met before."

"No, Mr. Hamlin," Caroline answered incisively. "In fact Uncle Meldon *only just* introduced me to Mr. McCrae only a few moments ago."

"Oh," Nathaniel said, sensing just how unwelcome his interruption was to both parties. To make matters worse, Miss Brenton's expression became almost condolent, much like the one she'd worn when she'd commented on his ruby earlier, and Nathaniel had all he could do to keep from betraying his frustration and befuddlement. He'd never been pitied by anyone. He had, in fact, always been admired or envied by most of his fellow Bostonians, and he couldn't imagine what kept provoking this woman to flash him such patronizing looks. Of course, he had no intention of questioning her about it in front of McCrae, and, even if he had, that became a pointless consideration, for Caroline excused herself from the two men, claiming that they could surely converse much more freely without a lady present.

Nathaniel's heart sank as he stood alone with McCrae in the seconds that followed. He had no idea what else to say to the man. Fortunately, McCrae saved him the effort of coming up with something.

"What was that all about, Hamlin?" he growled. "Why, you haven't had a civil thing to say to me in over a decade. What could you possibly want now?"

McCrae's acidic tone was just enough to shake some of Nathaniel's ire loose as well. "What do you think I *want?* Anyone with half a brain would be able to deduce that much, McCrae!"

"Well, you can't have her," he snapped. "She's already agreed to accompany me to the Winthrops' ball Friday next, so go and find yourself another woman. Hell's bells, you practically have to peel the young ladies off yourself whenever I see you. What does it matter if you forgo bedding this one?"

Nathaniel could feel his nostrils flaring at McCrae's insinuation that he slept with every women who came his way, and he was on the verge of lashing out at the man once more when Meldon Thorwell suddenly walked up to them and announced that supper was about to be served.

McCrae, apparently seeing the rage in Nathaniel's eyes in those seconds, flashed him a parting glare and strode off the knoll, down to the rows of large trestle tables which had been set up for the meal. Nathaniel, in turn, felt his anger begin to subside as Meldon threw a friendly arm about his shoulders and explained in a low voice that he had made special arrangements for Nathaniel and his brother to sit next to his niece during the meal.

"Do go off and fetch John now, Nathan, will you?" he requested. "We shall await you at the head of the table, the one nearest the house."

Nathaniel offered his host a grateful smile and tried to compose himself after his unnerving confrontation with McCrae. "How thoughtful of you, Meldon. We would be delighted to dine next to your niece, but I fear she will not feel the same way," he confessed.

"Whatever do you mean?" Meldon asked, lowering his voice even more now and donning an expression of deep concern.

"Well, she doesn't seem to care for me much, I'm afraid, old chap," Nathaniel explained, though he was probably even more surprised now than Meldon to hear these words coming out of his mouth. He'd never before had reason to speak them, and he found them quite gut-wrenching. "That is to say, she seems to keep walking away whenever I'm near."

Meldon's brow was deeply furrowed at this point, as though this was absolutely the last thing he'd expected to hear. "Well, that's most odd, isn't it? A man as popular with the ladies as yourself, it just doesn't make sense, does it? Perhaps she's not feeling well this evening."

"She certainly seemed to be feeling fine when McCrae was speaking to her just now. She accepted his invitation to the Winthrops' ball, in fact."

"She did?"

Nathaniel nodded.

"Silly girl. Accepting the first invitation to come along! I thought she was more clever than that. I'll have Amelia speak to her," he replied, shaking his head and staring down at the ground. "Well, don't you worry yourself over it, Nathaniel," he advised, more hearteningly. "She'll take a fancy to you by and by, I'm sure. You know how fickle young ladies can be. Why, they don't know from one day to the next what mind they're of. Just you go find your brother and hurry down to the table now, and I'm sure you'll have our little Caroline chattering to you straightaway."

Nathaniel rather doubted this, but, wishing to cooperate with his host and hellbent on not having to admit defeat to Commander Rushton, he turned about and began heading back to where he'd left John in the crowd.

Chapter 9

Fortunately, Nathaniel didn't have to search too long for his brother. John was now heading in his direction, flanked by two of the young ladies who'd gathered about Nathaniel earlier.

"Nathan," he called out jubilantly. He was weaving a bit as he walked, and it was clear to Nathaniel that he'd tossed down a few more goblets of wine in his absence. "How did it go with McCrae?"

Nathaniel shushed him fiercely, as he finally reached him. "Disastrously," he answered in a furtive whisper. "It was the worst advice you could have given!"

John affected a slightly wounded expression as he came to a teetering halt before his brother. The two girls stopped as well and stood tittering at John, like a pair of adoring barmaids.

"Say good-bye to the young ladies now, John," Nathaniel instructed, not wishing to risk having his brother say anything more in their presence about his encounter with McCrae and Miss Brenton. "Meldon has arranged for us to sit next to his niece at supper, so you'll have to see them later."

Fortunately the women were gracious enough to excuse themselves and head on to the tables without further prompting, and this allowed Nathaniel a moment alone with John before they, too, had to join the rest of the guests.

"You're getting drunk," Nathaniel noted critically.

"Naah. Not really."

"Well, in any case, do you think you can refrain from belching, licking your fingers, or spilling food or drink on yourself until we're through this meal?"

John flashed him a silly grin. "Certainly."

"Fine," Nathaniel concluded, coming up beside him and firmly gripping his arm so he could walk him down to the tables and prevent him from stumbling in the fading sunlight.

"What happened with McCrae?" John inquired again, as they walked.

"He told me to push off, of course. I'd have done the same in his place, I suppose."

"He said that to you in front of Miss Brenton?" John asked with marked concern.

"No. Thank God. At least, he had the decency to wait until she'd walked away. But he'd already managed to invite her to the Winthrops' ball."

"Sounds as though you got over to them a little too late, then. Did she accept?"

"Yes. I'm afraid so. I can't imagine what she sees in him, though."

"Well, he probably knows enough to ask her lots of questions about herself, Nathan. You know, encouraging her to talk about what interests her."

Nathaniel's eyes narrowed as he and his brother

approached the designated table. "And I suppose what you're saying is that I, on the other hand, can only be expected to ramble on about myself all evening, like a shameless braggart!"

"Let us not get testy again. You're not at all charming when you're testy, big brother. It's not that you're a braggart; it's simply that, as you said, you've never had to work much at attracting the ladies. So just listen to me," he continued, with the sort of slurred bravado that only a drunken man could exhibit. "All you have to do is get her off by herself somehow, after supper. You've tried talking to her twice with others around, and you haven't succeeded. Now try getting her off alone and talk about what interests *her*."

"Such as?" Nathaniel prompted in a whisper, not wishing to risk being overheard as they came up to the table.

"Such as . . . rubies and . . . and politics," John suggested in an equally hushed voice. "She's obviously got some feelings about both of those topics." With that, John pulled free of his brother's guiding grasp and, with a mulish air, went over to sit on Miss Brenton's left side, at the head of the table.

Nathaniel then took his place, as Meldon directed, on Caroline's right. As he did so, he scowled at John, his eyes silently warning him to mind what he was doing and to strive to act more sober than he obviously was.

Then, realizing that Miss Brenton had caught him glowering at his little brother, Nathaniel turned and offered her an apologetic smile. "John had to rise very early this morning, I'm afraid," he explained under his breath. "A pressing project at the yards. And I think the wine is simply proving a little too potent for him."

"I quite understand," she replied in a tone that Nathaniel found surprisingly affable. "We probably kept everyone waiting far too long for supper," she added in a whisper, obviously not wishing to be heard by her aunt and uncle, who were seated just to Nathaniel's right.

"Your uncle asked John and me to sit on either side of you, *mademoiselle*. We could move, though, if you would prefer the company of someone else," Nathaniel added, still in a hushed voice. Fortunately her gaze was directed at him as he spoke. Had it not been, she would have seen John flash Nathaniel an approving grin and mouth an emphatic, "Precisely." John obviously felt that this was the first right thing Nathaniel had said to the young lady since they'd arrived.

He was evidently correct, because Caroline reached out in that instant and placed one of her soft hands over Nathaniel's in an obvious attempt at consolation. "Oh, heavens no, Mr. Hamlin. Your company will do just fine. Whatever made you think it wouldn't?"

It simply hadn't occurred to Nathaniel that acting humble would bring such a gush of feeling from the woman. The humble approach was not, after all, one he had often employed, so he wasn't much good at gauging its potential. "Well, I just thought that maybe you would rather have some other gentleman at your side now, say Mr. McCrae perhaps."

At this Caroline directed an amused smile at him, as though she were actually taking some pleasure in hearing the note of rivalry in his voice. "But I'll have all of next Friday evening to be with Mr. McCrae, you see, at the Winthrops' ball. So it only seems right that I have you and John next to me now."

"Well, me, in any case," Nathaniel retorted awkwardly, and he reaching out to rouse his brother who had slumped forward upon the table in a drunken slumber. "Most embarrassing, this," he added with a clumsy smile.

Caroline broke into soft laughter. "Oh, let him sleep if he wishes. I'm not offended. I quite understand, in fact. I've younger brothers, too, Mr. Hamlin."

This disclosure prompted Nathaniel to lean toward her with great interest. If John didn't show signs of life soon, he told himself, he'd have him removed by one of the servants and carried out to their coachman. In the meantime, he knew it was best to simply follow John's advice and take full advantage of this opportunity to talk to Caroline on his own. "You do?" he asked.

"Ah, oui," she answered with an even smile. "Two brothers. Étienne, who's eighteen, and William, who's eleven."

Nathaniel raised a surprised brow at her, and he couldn't help wondering how, with her sculptured features so beautifully framed by the red of the sunset, he was managing to keep his voice so calm. He could only conclude that she, too, had drunk some wine and that was what was making her more receptive to him. In any case, he somehow had more faith now that she intended to try to carry her end of their conversation. "Eleven? So young?" he queried.

"Oui. He is rather, isn't he? Quite a surprise to my parents," she added with a slight blush, which Nathaniel found so endearing his breath caught in his throat.

"I . . . I imagine," he choked out. What on earth is

happening to me? he wondered. He'd certainly discussed far more provocative subjects with young women before—far, *far* more provocative—and he'd never felt tongue-tied. Not like he was now.

"These things happen, though," she continued, lowering her voice even more, as a scullery maid arrived with the first of the brimming serving platters.

"Oh, indeed. Indeed they do," Nathaniel agreed, catching hold of the servant an instant later and requesting in a whisper that she see to it the estate's steward come out and collect John at his earliest convenience.

As Nathaniel turned back to the table an instant later, he saw that his supper goblet had, blessedly, been filled, and he reached out and helped himself to it, taking a long, badly needed swallow of the dinner wine. Unfortunately the *mademoiselle* chose that same instant to make her next utterance.

"I was already ten when little William was born, you see," she said with a strangely salty laugh. "And I remember that my *maman* had such a devil of a time trying to explain to me from where he had come!"

At this, Nathaniel's mouthful of wine was suddenly sucked back into some wrong passage in his throat, and he immediately began coughing into his serviette and intermittently gasping for breath.

"*Oh, mon Dieu!* Are you all right, Mr. Hamlin?" Caroline inquired, springing to her feet and coming around to slap him on the back. "I fear we shall have to haul *both* of you Hamlin men into the house, before the night is through."

"I'm . . . I'm fine," Nathaniel stammered seconds later. Finally managing to draw in some air, he reached up with his serviette to dab his tearing eyes. "Do sit down, *mademoiselle* . . . please. I'm fine," he insisted.

Fortunately, she obliged him, returning to her place at the table's head and staring over at him with great concern. "Did I say something that upset you, *monsieur?*"

"No . . . it's just that I don't believe I've ever heard a young lady say anything quite like that," he confessed, "and I'm afraid it took me by surprise. That's all."

"What took you by surprise? My speaking of William's birth?"

Nathaniel stared down at the table, fighting a smile. "Yes. I guess so."

"Oh, Mr. Hamlin. I am so sorry! I did not realize that you Bostonians consider it gauche to speak of having babies."

Nathaniel looked up and met her eyes again. "Well, it's not that we consider it gauche, Miss Brenton—"

"Please, call me Caroline."

"It's not that we consider it gauche, Caroline. It's just that it's not often discussed in mixed company," he explained, doing his best to sound brotherly now so that he wouldn't drive her away with any hint of amorousness. Perhaps the most he could hope for with this one was to simply befriend her, and, all things considered, maybe that was for the best.

She cocked her head and smiled. "What does this 'mixed' mean, then, Mr. Hamlin? Does it mean men and women together?"

"If I may call you Caroline, you must call me Nathaniel," he replied. "And yes, that is precisely what mixed means."

"Well, then, I do apologize again, Nathaniel. I didn't

133

intend to make you uncomfortable. You see, my mother is what we call a *sage femme* in Louisiana, a doctor of sorts, and she and I have delivered so many babies that it only seems a natural topic of conversation to me now. Why, the Cajuns have such large families they can scarcely think of names for all their children," she exclaimed with a laugh. Then she grew sober once more. "Oh, but I'm doing it again, am I not? Speaking of it in 'mixed' company, as you say. I am sorry."

To Nathaniel's great relief, the steward arrived at their table just then and, with the assistance of a footman, very discreetly hauled John away, promising that Nathaniel could find him in one of the manse's guest rooms whenever he decided to depart. With that sticky matter taken care of, Nathaniel turned back to the *mademoiselle*.

"There's no need to keep apologizing, Caroline," he said softly. "I understand that our upbringings were quite different. I realized it as soon as you commented on the ruby in my ring earlier."

"Oh, yes . . . that," she said, looking somewhat embarrassed. "I suppose I really shouldn't have told you what I did, not with the others present. It really was rather the sort of thing one ought to be told in private. It's just that there are so many guests here tonight, I wasn't certain I would have the opportunity to speak to you again, and I felt you should know."

"But that part about my being in danger," Nathaniel pressed, lowering his voice and nodding at a scullery maid who was offering him some of the sliced poultry she was serving. "How would you know that? Are you clairvoyant?"

"Ah, *oui*. A little. Most who inherit the gift of healing are, it seems."

"And just how am I in danger?" he inquired, still keeping his voice hushed, as a steady stream of servants came by with their offerings. As he'd told John earlier, he really didn't believe in such hocus-pocus, but it seemed to be the only topic he could think of at this point and it was surely of interest to her.

Caroline was now somewhat distracted by her efforts to consume a chicken drumstick. It was a task she undertook with more delicacy and grace than Nathaniel had ever seen a woman display while dining.

That done, she began again. "Well, such things are never very clear for me, Nathaniel. You see, it's little more than a lightning flash in my mind's eye. And it usually happens the instant I meet someone . . . just as it did when I met you."

"And what, exactly, did you see in that instant?"

Again she assumed that slightly pitying expression she had directed at him twice before. "It won't please you," she said gingerly.

Nathaniel did his best to produce a nonchalant laugh. "Oh, fire away, my dear. I think you'll find I'm not easily daunted." With that, he took another long swallow of his wine.

"Well . . . I . . ." she faltered.

He flashed her a sportive smile and gave her forearm a nudge. "You what?"

"I . . . I saw a grave."

He couldn't help gulping a bit at this. "A *grave?*"

"Yes, well, now you see? I told you you wouldn't like it," she said defensively.

He gave her hand a consoling pat to let her know he

didn't blame her for what she'd seen. "And . . . was I *in* this grave?" he asked, doing his best to keep his voice steady.

"*Oui,*" she answered softly, casting her eyes downward. "But you weren't lying in it," she continued hearteningly. "You were digging it."

Nathaniel furrowed his brow in confusion. "Digging it? Digging someone else's grave?"

"*Non.* Digging your own, I think . . . I, too, had thought, when I saw it, that it was someone else's, but I think now that it was yours," she concluded, again dropping her gaze to the plate of food before her.

"But that's ridiculous. I'm in the business of building ships, not digging graves! It makes no sense at all. What could it possibly mean?"

She looked up at him, a sympathetic glimmer in her eyes, and shook her head. "I don't know. Only you could know. The seer rarely understands as well as those she's seeing for."

Nathaniel had managed to keep his aggravation over all of this pretty well hidden, but a trace of it emerged as he posed his next question. "And what about McCrae? What did you see when you met *him?*"

She shrugged. "Nothing, I'm afraid."

"You mean to say this doesn't happen with everyone you meet?"

"No. Just with you so far this week."

"Well, why would it happen with me and no one else?"

Again she shrugged and offered him another sympathetic smile. "I truly don't know, *mon ami.* I wish I did."

They dined in silence for several seconds, and then Nathaniel couldn't resist the temptation to begin questioning her again.

"Tell me, Caroline, have you ever seen such an image before? I mean of a man digging a grave?"

She gave the question some thought. "Yes," she said finally. "Once . . . with a pirate I met in New Orleans. But he was a very different man than you are, I'm sure. He was a known murderer and a thief, so I imagine he dug quite a few graves in his day. He's dead now, however . . . fortunately."

Though she obviously found comfort in this last statement, Nathaniel did not.

"But how would a young lady as cultured and refined as yourself ever have come to meet a pirate?"

Caroline laughed. "Oh, one comes to know all kinds of men in a city like New Orleans. It's not nearly as homogeneous a place as Boston, you see."

"But didn't your father think it rather dangerous for you to converse with such a man?"

Again, she laughed. "I don't think he was present when I did so. I believe he had left the office early on that particular day. In any case, I don't think one need fear those who are arrant pirates so much as those who are pirates in honest men's clothing—do you follow me there, Nathaniel?" she asked, her eyes narrowing, her air earnest. "I fear my English does not reach as far as my thoughts at times."

"Oh, yes. I certainly do follow you, Caroline, and I couldn't agree more," he concluded, donning an equally serious expression. She was, he acknowledged, precisely what she was speaking of: a smuggler, a rebel, a pirate of sorts in the guise of a ravishing young maiden. Perhaps she was, in her own way, trying to warn him of this as well. This helped to explain the fact that, in spite of their ready dinner conversation, he knew he still wasn't truly cracking through that polite, professional veneer of hers. And that was what this was all about, he suddenly realized, this trying to divide her time equally between him and McCrae. It was all strictly commerce to her, the sort of social lubrication that made the wheels of business turn. Nathaniel had been employing such lubricative charm with Boston's upper crust and the more influential men at his private club for years. He simply hadn't recognized it for what it was with Caroline, because she was a woman, and women so rarely entered such arenas. Nor did most females play in them as well as she. Now, finally realizing how little physical attraction had to do with all of this, Nathaniel could put his blasted ego aside and play the game with equal shrewdness. It would have been easier, of course, had he been blindfolded and not had to look upon Caroline's loveliness all the while. Nevertheless, he swallowed hard, straightened his posture, and set about trying not to let her beauty interfere with his efforts to manipulate her.

"You know, Caroline," he began, "I must admit to feeling rather offended when I heard that you had already accepted Earl McCrae's invitation to the Winthrops'. I had planned, you see, to invite you."

Nathaniel was pleased to see that this statement seemed to catch her by surprise. "You intended to?"

"Oh, yes. And now, it seems, you've agreed to accompany McCrae, without so much as giving any of the rest of us the chance to invite you."

Her gaze again dropped to the plate before her, as though she needed to ponder this obvious faux pas on her part. *"Oui.* I suppose that wasn't very fair of me."

Nathaniel shook his head, the corner of his lips curling up into a good-natured smile.

She looked up at him again, wide-eyed, like a child. "But we have this evening together, don't we? I mean, we could dance later, after supper is through. That should be enough time for us to get better acquainted, shouldn't it?"

Again Nathaniel shook his head and offered her a gentle smile. "Enough for you, perhaps, but not for me. I'm sorry."

To Nathaniel's further satisfaction, she looked even more ruffled now than she had before. "Well . . . I . . . I could reserve another evening for you, I suppose, if you wish."

"Yes," Nathaniel replied, reaching out and placing his left hand over one of hers. "I wish it very much, Caroline. How long do you plan to be in Boston, by the way?"

"A month or two. It depends upon the demands of the company."

"Well, then, there should be plenty of time for us to get to know one another better."

"Yes. I'll . . . I'll see what I can arrange," she concluded, clearly very uncomfortable with this power play on his part. She was obviously the sort of woman who liked being in control of the situation, and now that she'd lost some of that control, a bit of the vulnerability Nathaniel had seen in her earlier was apparent once more.

"That is," he added with a provocative edge to his hushed voice, "unless you're afraid to be with me again."

She scowled. "Afraid?" she asked defensively. "Why

139

should I be afraid?"

Nathaniel laughed softly. "Why, because of the way you saw me in that 'lightning flash' vision of yours."

"Do you think I was only joking about that?" she asked with obvious surprise.

"Heavens, no. I think you were most serious. I think you truly believe you saw what you claim you saw. That's why I asked if you were afraid of being with me."

She was silent for several seconds. Then she smiled thoughtfully. "No. I don't think I am," she answered simply.

Nathaniel knew that no dance would give him quite as much opportunity with Miss Brenton as the last, so he made it a point to remain at the party long enough to claim it. And, since he had forgone all of the others with her, he knew she wouldn't be able to refuse him.

The guests were doing their minuets and reels on a makeshift dance floor made of rows of long planks. The sunset's reddish rays had long since disappeared, and the dance floor was lit by the warm glow of a huge square of translucent, colored lanterns, which were suspended overhead on rows of string tied to the limbs of nearby trees. Nathaniel was told that the lanterns had come from the Orient. Such was the lot of a shipper's family, he thought rather grudgingly. All that was novel and fashionable in the Colonies, every new invention from the Old World seemed to come to the shippers first, and Amelia Thorwell was just the sort of social butterfly who thrived most on such newfangledness.

While Nathaniel had had a few of his female admirers to dance with in the hours that followed supper, he was forced to spend most of his time looking on as the fair Caroline danced with one after another of her uncle's male guests. These were both the most pleasant and the most painful hours Nathaniel had spent in a long time, because, while watching Caroline's gracefulness and ease on the dance floor brought him great pleasure, part of him already resented seeing other men partnered with her. Though he had only known her for a short time, he already felt a bit possessive toward her, and he wasn't sure why. Perhaps, he told himself, it was simply because she alone could give him the particular information that he sought for the commander, and he was most eager to extract it from her and be on his way.

When, finally, Meldon Thorwell took his place in front of the musicians assembled in the gazebo and announced that the last dance of the evening was about to be played, Nathaniel strode onto the dance floor to take Caroline's hand. He could tell from her resigned expression that, no matter how she felt about him, she would not refuse him. He had simply waited too long, too patiently for her to do anything but cooperate. And when, in the midst of the whirling crowd of dancers, he began easing her into one of the shadowy corners of the dance floor, the one that was farthest from the house, she did not fight him either—though surely, to a young woman of her age and obvious worldliness, his purpose must have been clear.

Their bodies continued swaying in gentle unison to a ballad Nathaniel recognized as being French in origin. "What are the words to this, Caroline?" he whispered.

"I know I've heard them before, but I don't speak French well enough to make them out."

Though he couldn't see how she moved now, not as he had from his previous perspective as an onlooker, he could feel her body as it pressed up against his, and he knew she wasn't dancing with quite the same ease she'd shown with all the others. She was tenser, less pliable, more like the frightened virgins with whom he found himself most comfortable, and he liked this very much.

"It . . . it is called '*La chanson de Claudette*,' Mr. Hamlin . . . 'The Song of Claudette.'"

"It's Nathaniel, remember," he noted with a soft laugh.

"Ah, *oui* . . . Nathaniel."

"Had you forgotten my name, dancing with so many others since we dined?" He could feel how moist her hand had become since they'd begun dancing, and it was clear that she felt like a cornered ewe awaiting shearing. She obviously hoped that this lovely languorous tune would finally come to an end so she could break away. "Well, *I* didn't forget yours," he added in a winning whisper, very near her ear.

"No, Nathaniel. That much is clear."

"Is it?" he asked with a boyish hopefulness to his voice. "Yes. I truly hope it is. . . . So, tell me of the tune, Caroline. Who is this Claudette? And why did someone write such a poignant tune for her? So sad, so dulcet, so resigned to life."

"Well, yes . . . it is rather a sad tale . . . of a young girl who waits for her lover to return from the sea. And, when at last it is revealed that he never shall, that he and his mates were lost in a storm one night, far, far away, she still returns to wait for him at the shore each

142

evening at sunset. On some nights, she can almost see him once more, out on the ocean, standing near the starboard bow of the ship on which he departed."

"Very loyal, that one," Nathaniel said under his breath.

"Ah, but that is the English way of seeing it. The French would say instead that she was very much in love. Some souls, you see, are meant to be together, Nathaniel, whether or not that seems impossible at times. And I suppose when one feels that way about a lover, no other will ever do."

"You French are terribly romantic, *oui?*"

She gave forth a whisper of a laugh. *"Oui* . . . We're in the dark by the way," she added gingerly.

"What?" he asked in a dreamy tone. He couldn't seem to help himself now. He hadn't intended to become amorous with her. He'd simply planned to take her aside and ask when he could see her again. But he was getting swept up in the magic of the haunting ballad, coupled as it was with the ethereal scent of her perfume, and he reflexively bent down and let his cheek come to rest against hers as their bodies continued to move to the music.

"I said we are dancing in the dark. Shouldn't we get back to the others?"

"And let them see me kiss you?" Nathaniel asked in a voice that feigned both playfulness and shock. He knew he was taking a chance at this point, running the risk of getting her ruffled again and causing her to flee or, worse yet, having her slap him with the others so near. But kissing her was what he wanted to do most now—his will power with beautiful blondes being negligible—and he desperately wished to believe that it would be just the thing to finally break the ice between them. "That wouldn't do, now, would it? What would people say?"

At this she pulled away from him slightly, and he could see, in the dim glow from the lantern, the apprehensive gleam in her eye.

"What is it?" he murmured. "Have you never been kissed by a man?"

"*Oui.* Of course," she replied with an uneasy smile.

"Then never by a Bostonian?"

"No. That's not it either."

"Well, what then?" he asked, doing his best to remain patient with her.

"Never by a man I didn't . . . didn't feel something for," she explained. "I'm terribly sorry, Nathaniel." She eased out of his hold and stopped her soft swaying to the music. "You're a very handsome man. I've been told how popular you are with the ladies of Boston, and I'm sure it's true. I truly don't want this to affect the business our two companies do . . . I know this may be taken as a sign that I am shallow and fickle, neither of which are true, I assure you. But it's just . . . well, I've never really cared for brunets, and it hardly seems fair to lead you on. I'm sure you understand."

With a sheepish smile, she bent toward him once more and pressed a soft, consolatory kiss to his cheek. Then she headed back to the center of the dance floor and disappeared into the crowd, leaving Nathaniel gaping after her.

Chapter 10

Minutes later, Nathaniel regained his composure and went into the house to collect his brother. To his surprise, he was informed that John had already been taken home by their coachman, who had stated that he would return to the Brenton estate as quickly as possible for Nathaniel. Nathaniel, therefore, headed out to the carriage entrance to look for his driver, thanking God all the while that his path did not again cross Caroline's.

To his great relief, he spotted his coachman just as he emerged from the Brenton's front door. He hurried over to the man, anxious to find out how John was doing and even more anxious to put this whole humiliating evening behind him and get back to more familiar surroundings.

"How is John, Harold?" he inquired. "Why did you take him home?"

The coachman looked nonplused as he gazed down upon Nathaniel from the driver's box. "Because he asked to be taken home, sir . . . he and the young lady."

Nathaniel furrowed his brow. "What young lady?"

"Why, the one he had on his arm, sir, as he came out of the house about half an hour ago."

"You mean to say he was actually talking and walking without assistance?"

"Why, yes, sir. Why wouldn't he be?"

"Because he was out cold from too much wine at a quarter to eight," Nathaniel explained, climbing up to take a seat on the driver's box.

The coachman was clearly surprised by this. "You're sitting up here, sir?"

"Yes," Nathaniel answered windlessly. "I want to talk to you as we ride. Let's just be on our way, and quickly," he urged.

The coachman shrugged, and obediently began steering the horses past the other vehicles that lined the carriage entrance. "Master John seemed sober enough when I saw him, sir," he continued. "I guess he must have revived himself."

Nathaniel shook his head in puzzlement. "I guess so . . . who was the girl with him?" he asked, raising his voice as the carriage merged onto the main road and the evening breeze began to blow against them, muffling his words. "Did you know her?"

"No, sir. But I did chance to notice that she was quite a lovely redhead."

"Meara Miller," Nathaniel acknowledged with a resentful snarl. Meara had been the only lovely redhead he'd seen at the gathering that evening. He had noticed her sudden disappearance from the festivities roughly half an hour earlier, so it only stood to reason that she was the woman who'd left with John.

"What's that, sir?"

"I said 'Meara Miller.' Did you happen to notice whether or not John called her Meara?"

"Well, no, sir . . . But they weren't doing much talking, if you get my meaning," he added with a simper.

At this, Nathaniel leaned back on the driver's box and issued another snarl. Meara was one of his most prized admirers, and he couldn't help feeling a bit angry at John for stepping into his territory. "So, where did you say you took them, Harold?" he asked grudgingly.

"Back to your house, sir. Those were Master John's orders, after all. And, because he said that you wished to stay at the Brentons' for a while longer, I didn't think there was any harm in obliging him."

"Oh, no, no," Nathaniel said allayingly. "You didn't do anything wrong, my good man. Please don't think that I'm perturbed with you. It's John who's gotten me angry!"

"Pardon me, sir," the driver requested after a moment, in a chary tone. "I don't mean to offend. But it does seem to me that you can hardly expect the young ladies to wait for you forever. I mean, they're really not likely to stand about, waiting for the fruit to drop from the tree. They'll either climb up and pick it or gather what's on the ground, won't they? And it does appear that your good brother 'fell to the ground,' as it were, this evening, doesn't it?"

"Yes. Yes, it does appear so," Nathaniel absently agreed. He was so wrought up that he was biting the inside of one of his cheeks with blood-drawing pressure. Never in the many years since he and John had entered manhood, had John gone home to bed one of Boston's prettiest lasses while Nathaniel returned home alone. Never . . . until tonight. Never, until that infuriating Cajun girl sailed into Boston Harbor and turned Nathaniel's usually smooth-running life upside down! And the very thought of going home to the muffled sounds of lovemaking doubtlessly pouring from John's bedchamber was almost more than he could bear.

Though a bit shaken by her interaction with Nathaniel Hamlin that evening, Caroline was silently congratulating herself as she finally said good night to the last of her aunt and uncle's guests and then went upstairs to retire to her suite. All things considered, she believed she had handled Mr. Hamlin very well—certainly with far more tact than she felt he would have exercised, had he been in her place. Furthermore, she hadn't let her Aunt Margaret get the best of her either. Her Uncle Meldon had been the first to rescue her from Margaret, as they were heading out of the house hours before to join in the festivities. Then, fortunately, Caroline had been "rescued" by one after another of the guests, each unwittingly interrupting Margaret's attempts to corner her, and by the time the dancing began, Caroline knew that she was in the clear. She sensed that, if she made it from the dance floor back up to her suite at evening's end without Margaret intercepting her, she would be free of the woman—at least for the time being.

So now, as Caroline entered her sitting room and shut the door behind her, her sense of relief was mixed with triumph. She'd made it through her aunt and uncle's welcoming party, the first big hurdle in her Bostonian stay, and, as a result, everything else that she had to face seemed easier.

She immediately removed her shoes. They were new and therefore painfully tight-fitting. Then she took off her hose as well. After that, she reached back, unfastened a few of the midlevel buttons on her gown *à la polonaise,* and loosened the cinching of her stays. Feeling able to really breathe again, she bent down and gathered up her shoes and hose once more. Then she proceeded into her bedchamber, which one of the maids had been good enough to illuminate by lighting the sconce candles on either side of the bed.

She reflexively tossed her shoes and hose onto the travel trunk that stood near the door. Then she crossed to her canopied bed and flopped back upon it with a sigh. She wasn't sleepy, she realized, just a bit tipsy from the wine and exhausted from all the dancing and from having to make polite conversation with so many strangers all evening. She knew it would feel wonderful to finally disrobe and climb in between the freshly laundered bed linens, but her feet still ached too much for her to bring herself to rise and fetch one of her nightshifts from the wardrobe just yet. Consequently, she simply lay there for several minutes, enjoying the solitude and mulling over all she'd said at the welcoming party and all that had been said to her.

She thought of Earl McCrae, that fair-haired gentleman with the likable, easy manner, and she smiled. He would doubtless be pleasant company for her next Friday night at the Winthrops', and she was genuinely looking forward to seeing him. He seemed the sensitive, thoughtful sort, the kind of man who could really accommodate a woman, and she liked that very much.

Then, though she tried to fight it, her thoughts turned to Nathaniel Hamlin again, and she felt her smile sink into a frown. He was a troubling chap, that one. She'd heard about his well-known wit, how he could charm and amuse almost anyone, regardless of gender, and she wondered at this now. He had struck her as being far too smoldering and intense a man to make a woman feel like doing anything as frivolous as laughing in his presence. On the contrary, Caroline's first and only true response to him was to run back up to her suite and hide under the bed! He was simply too swarthy, his dark eyes too mesmeric for her to have felt anything but unnerved with him.

She realized now that she'd lied to him, and she hadn't really meant to do so. She just hadn't known what to say when he'd asked if she was afraid of him. She'd said she wasn't, not bothering to distinguish between what he was asking and whether or not her vision of him had frightened her. But, in truth, she had been afraid. She'd feared both him and the erotic energy he'd exuded as they'd danced. She couldn't quite put her finger on what she'd felt, but it had seemed like a kind of lurid dread mixed with arousal. And the very thought of it made the most unspeakable parts of her ache.

All she'd really known for sure, when she'd been with him, was that she wanted him to ravish her and have done with it or to set her free so she could go and hide from him. There just didn't seem to be any intermediate ground for her, not where he was concerned. His obvious intelligence, his worldliness, his gentility, none of these seemed to temper the odd animal magnetism he possessed. And she realized that he might just as well have been a pillaging Indian warrior, so uncomfortable she'd been in his presence.

Boston's ladies might think him a witty charmer, but he hadn't fooled Caroline for a moment! He was a predator of some sort. That much was clear to her. Each time his eyes had met hers, it was as though he were looking right through her. She felt like a doe he had spotted in a forest during a bow hunt, and on some strange, sexual level, which she didn't fully understand, he positively terrified her.

Finally, having finished reflecting on all of this, Caroline found the will to get up and cross to her wardrobe to fetch her nightclothes. She carried one of her nightshifts to the foot of the bed and laid it over the second travel trunk, which was situated there. Then she reached back and began trying to finish unbuttoning her dress. She hoped she could manage to get out of the garment on her own. After having to be with so many people all evening, she truly didn't want her solitude disrupted by the need for a maid. As she stood there, straining to get undressed, her eyes were focused downward, upon the trunk, and it was then she noticed that its key was resting in the lock. Yet, she was positive she'd stowed the key away a few days before. She distinctly remembered having hidden it inside one of the flower vases in the adjoining sitting room shortly after her arrival, and she was certain that she hadn't opened this particular trunk since. Acknowledging this, she froze, terrified by the implications of her discovery.

Margaret, she thought in that horrific moment. Her

151

Aunt Margaret must have sneaked into the suite sometime during the evening. Caroline dropped to her knees, swept her nightshift off the trunk, and hurriedly opened it to see if anything had been removed. A quick search revealed that nothing seemed to be missing. The box of jewelry she'd stored within was still filled to the brim with the pieces she'd brought along, and, beneath a concealing layer of undergarments, she found all of the guns and projectiles she had packed in New Orleans. It appeared that nothing had been removed, yet the layer of underclothes had clearly been disturbed. These items weren't in the same, neatly folded state in which Caroline had left them, and she was now certain that someone had rummaged through the trunk.

She sprang to her feet and hurried to the suite's main door. Trying to keep her voice calm, she called down the corridor for a maid, but it seemed her heart was pounding loudly enough for everyone in the house to hear.

Fortunately, she only had to wait a couple of minutes for a servant to report to her, and, rushing that young woman inside, Caroline shut the door of the suite behind her with the furtiveness of a spy.

"You called, *mademoiselle?*" the maid asked with an uneasy swallow.

"Yes," Caroline replied, hurriedly turning away from her. "Unbutton me, if you please."

Caroline's heart continued to race as the servant obliged her in the seconds that followed. "I wonder," she began again awkwardly, "I wonder . . . could you tell me if you know whether anyone came into my suite during the party tonight?"

The servant was silent for several seconds, as though

152

giving the question some thought. "Yes . . . umm," she stammered, "Yes, well, I do believe one of the footmen accidentally put that besotted gentleman in here for a while. But only very briefly, *mademoiselle*. The footman is new, and he didn't know this suite was assigned to you."

"The besotted gentleman?" Caroline echoed. "Do you mean John Hamlin?"

"The shipbuilder's brother. Yes, miss. That was the one."

"Well, how long was he in here?"

"Very briefly, *mademoiselle*." The maid sounded defensive, and was obviously concerned with protecting her fellow servant.

"In that case, who moved him out of here?"

"The steward, I believe, miss . . . but by that time, I guess, Mr. Hamlin was able to walk on his own in some measure. So, after a couple of hour's sleep in the other guest suite down the hall, I'm told he up and left by himself."

"You mean his brother didn't come up to fetch him?"

"No. He left quite some time before his brother did . . . I'm done, miss. You should be able to slip right out of it now," the maid added, having finished the unbuttoning. "Shall I unlace you, as well?"

"Thank you, yes . . . And how would you know when John Hamlin's brother left?"

"Well, that was Nathaniel Hamlin dancing the last dance of the evening with you, wasn't it, miss?" the maid asked sheepishly.

Now that her stays felt fully unlaced, Caroline clasped the front of her gown to her chest and turned back to face the servant with a smile, one brow raised in curiosity. "And how would you have known that?"

"Well, miss . . . we—the staff, I mean—well, I'm afraid we notice almost everything on evenings such as this. It is, after all, our duty to keep our eyes out for empty goblets and any guests in search of the water closets or their wraps and such . . . I'm only saying, miss, if that was Nathaniel Hamlin dancing the last dance with you, he must have left quite some time after his brother did."

"And you say John was fairly well up on his feet when he was taken out of my suite?"

The maid nodded. "Will that be all, *mademoiselle?* Can I help you into your nightclothes or get you something from the kitchen?"

"No, thank you. Just one more question, if you please."

"Yes?"

"Besides John Hamlin and the footman, you and the rest saw no one come into my suite?"

"No one, miss. I'm quite certain of that . . . Why?" she asked gingerly. "Is something missing?"

Caroline shook her head, determined now not to call too much attention to the situation. She knew that to do so might cause her aunt and uncle to be drawn into the matter, and she didn't think she would hold up well under their questioning. "No. Nothing," she answered honestly. As far as she knew, this was true. "It's just that things weren't exactly as I had left them, and I wondered who had been in here, you see. I'm afraid I do like my privacy."

"Of course, *mademoiselle.* That's only natural, isn't it? . . . Well, good night, then," the maid concluded, turning away and heading back to the door. "Or I

154

should say *bonne nuit*. Right?" she asked, looking back and flashing Caroline a good-natured smile.

"Yes. *Bonne nuit,*" Caroline answered, grateful for the staff's efforts to make her feel at home. "And thank you."

"You're quite welcome, *mademoiselle,*" the servant said in parting.

Once the maid had shut the suite's door behind her, Caroline went back into her bedchamber and slipped out of her gown, exchanging it for the feather-light comfort of a silken nightshift. The evenings weren't nearly as warm here as in Louisiana, and she was thankful for the quilt provided, as she climbed into her bed seconds later.

It doesn't make any sense, she thought, propping one of her pillows up against the headboard and leaning back upon it. Why would someone simply open a trunk filled with jewelry and such, and not take anything from it? What other reason but theft would have prompted a search for the trunk's key? Had it simply been curiosity? Just to examine what was hidden within? It really made no sense. What was more, whoever had done it had also made no effort to cover his or her tracks by relocking the trunk and returning the key to its hiding place. It was as though whoever had opened it *wanted* Caroline to know that it had been searched through.

Margaret, Caroline concluded again. Who else would have seen any advantage in rummaging through her belongings? And surely, Margaret had had some opportunities to do so that evening; she certainly hadn't been on Caroline's heels during the entire affair. There were all those hours of dancing left unaccounted

155

for. However, the maid had said the only ones seen in Caroline's room were John Hamlin and the footman, and the staff would most certainly have recognized Margaret if they'd seen her entering or leaving the suite. So, the only other possibility was John Hamlin, and perhaps his drunken state explained why the key hadn't been returned to its hiding place.

On the other hand, Caroline really had to wonder *why* a man like John would want to look through her trunks. It was widely known that the Hamlins were among the most well-to-do of Boston's citizens, so it wasn't likely that he was searching for money. He had, after all, passed up Caroline's jewels—most of which would have brought a very good price—so she felt she could rule out John Hamlin. Again, she was forced to conclude that Margaret, or perhaps one of her children, was behind this mysterious intrusion.

But how could she verify this? It really didn't seem wise to bring the trunks to Margaret's attention by questioning her about them. Even at her young age, Caroline knew that the direct approach was not the wisest when dealing with a woman as venomous as Margaret. What was more, if Margaret was behind it, Caroline was sure to discover it soon enough. It probably wouldn't take long for her aunt to set the local English authorities on her. There was, no doubt, probably nothing Margaret wanted more than to see the family's heir apparent jailed or executed for smuggling.

But Caroline now realized that she couldn't go on entertaining such dreadful thoughts. They were simply too frightening to contemplate, and she knew she wouldn't sleep a wink for the rest of her stay in Boston if she dwelled on them.

She would just take the weapons out of the trunk and hide them elsewhere. She'd bury them somewhere on the grounds, she concluded, climbing out of bed once more and rushing over to the trunk to begin unloading its contents. That way, if Margaret did send the redcoats over to search the place, Caroline could simply deny the accusation that she was a weapons smuggler. Then, just to be on the safe side and to put her mind at ease a little, she would go over to the Hamlins' tomorrow and fish around a bit with John and Nathaniel, see if they knew anything about her opened trunk. The encroachment might, after all, have been due to nothing more than the prankish behavior of a drunken man, and Caroline offered up a silent prayer that that really was all that was behind it.

Chapter 11

Nathaniel waited until he heard Meara Miller depart before going into John's bedchamber the following morning. This was a courtesy John had always extended to him throughout the years, and Nathaniel felt obligated to return the favor. He certainly didn't delay a moment longer than necessary, however. He was down the hall to John's room before he even heard the front door close behind Meara.

"Don't get up, little brother," he growled, as he entered John's suite.

John, still wearing his bagwig from the night before, lay naked on the bed, and he looked positively green, obviously hung over. "As long as my bedside basin is so close at hand, I have absolutely no wish to move, Nathan, believe me. And please do keep your voice down and take pity on my soul for the next few hours at least, will you? I know you're angry about Meara and all, but I truly do not have the strength to fight with you over her just now."

Nathaniel, suddenly compassionate, shook his head

and went over to sit on the side of the bed. He'd certainly had his share of such mornings, and he honestly pitied his brother. "No. I'm not angry about Meara," he explained, keeping his voice obligingly low. He'd had a whole night to simmer down and think things through, and he spoke the truth.

John furrowed his brow and his pained, squinting eyes narrowed all the more, now in obvious confusion. "You're not?"

"No. Not really. A bit offended, perhaps," Nathaniel confessed. "A bit disappointed in you two. But I suppose I can't expect the young ladies to wait for me indefinitely, after all."

John shook his head gingerly and emitted a groan as he reached up and ran his fingers along his forehead. "Dear God, even my face hurts," he exclaimed.

"Did you drink some more, when you and Meara came back here?"

John squeezed one eye shut, grimaced, and offered a weak nod.

Nathaniel fought a laugh. "Yes. Then I'd say it's normal. Now tell me, what went on last night?" he prodded knowingly. "That 'going out cold' business at the table was all for my benefit, wasn't it?"

John nodded again.

"So I was sure to have some time alone with her . . . was that it?"

"Yes. Did it help?"

"Sorrily, no. But don't worry. Nothing you could have done would have made much of a difference. She just doesn't find me attractive, I'm afraid."

"Ah, that's a shame," John replied, groaning again, and Nathaniel was relatively sure that the groan was reflective of sympathy this time as well as pain. "I . . . I did try to oblige you further, though," John added.

"In what way?"

"Well, you see, I knew if I pretended to be out cold, you'd probably have me hauled into the house for a while, and I figured that would afford me a golden opportunity to sneak into Miss Brenton's room and have a look through her things. You know, see if I could find any contacts' names written down or any information about her rendezvous with the rebels."

Nathaniel's mouth dropped open. "Good Lord, John! Had you taken leave of your senses? What if you'd been caught? Sweet Jesus, they would have turned that gathering into a bonfire, with *you* at the stake!"

His brother waved him off. "Oh, rubbish! I would never have allowed it to come to that! Besides, you said I could help with one of these assignments. And it all went very smoothly as a matter of fact, because the stupid footman didn't know which suite was Caroline's, and he took me straight to it and laid me out on one of her sitting-room sofas. So, once the fool left, it only took me a few moments to figure out whose room I was in and only a few minutes to find the damnable key to one of her trunks and have a good look through it."

Nathaniel leaned forward anxiously. "And what did you find?"

"The weapons," John said with a triumphant smile. "You can rest assured that the commander has the right woman."

"And?"

"And? That's all, I'm afraid. I'm sorry, Nathan. I did

160

my best. Perhaps, if I'd had more time, I would have gotten to look through her other trunk, but I heard the blasted footman returning at that point, and I had to rush back to the sitting room and pretend to be unconscious again. The dolt must have discovered that he'd put me in the wrong room, because he and some other servant came in and walked me to another suite. After getting a bit of sleep there, I decided to head home."

"But not before you had collected little Meara," Nathaniel interjected pointedly.

John's pallid face colored slightly at this. "As it happened, she was leaving at precisely the same time, and one thing simply led to another . . . fortunately for me."

Nathaniel was silent for several seconds, still fuming a bit as he mulled it all over. "Yes . . . well, if you don't mind my asking, little brother, how was she?"

John donned an indignant expression, but Nathaniel knew it was meant only in jest. "Really! I'm appalled that you would ask such a thing!"

"Oh, stop it, John, and just tell me. After the night I had with that bayou enchantress, I feel I've the right to a vicarious thrill!"

His brother looked genuinely surprised. "You mean you've never . . . *had* Meara?"

"No. I've come damned close on a couple of occasions, but I guess our timing has never been quite right."

John seemed pleased to hear this. A schoolboyish smirk tugged at the corners of his lips. "You mean she wasn't just another of your castoffs?"

"No," Nathaniel returned grudgingly. "Now, just

answer my question, or I shall flatly refuse to let you sit and nurse your aching head all day at the yards!"

John sobered slightly at this threat. "Well, she was . . . she was very nice," he replied, again groping for words. "Big and soft and white . . . like a pillow. Indeed, I would highly recommend her to you, were it not for the fact that I fully intend to go on seeing her myself," he concluded in as threatening a tone as he could muster in his debilitated state.

"Fine. I quite understand," Nathaniel said stoically. "There are plenty of others, I suppose."

"Pity, though, that you can't seem to count Miss Brenton among them. I mean, it would make your next meeting with Smythe so much easier if you could."

Nathaniel nodded.

"What exactly did she find unattractive about you? Did she say?"

Nathaniel laughed bitterly. "She said I'm too dark. She said she prefers blonds."

John scowled. "Most of the men in Boston go about in powdered wigs, for Christ's sake. What difference does it make what color your real hair is?"

Nathaniel shrugged and tried to smile. "It makes a difference to her, apparently."

"Well, couldn't you simply befriend her, then? You know, take her to some daytime events, yachting and such, and wheedle the information out of her that way? I mean, no one says you have to fall madly in love with one another."

"Yes, I was thinking the same thing last night. Until I danced with her. And . . . I don't know, John . . . something just overtook me and, like a bloody fool, I led her away from all the others and tried to kiss her. I

162

think that was when any hope of simply remaining platonic with her was dashed."

"Did she slap you?"

"No, blast it all! I only wish she had! I'd have preferred being struck to the humiliating speech she delivered instead. It was quite mortifying, really."

"I imagine. . . . It was the first time you received that sort of a response from a woman, wasn't it?"

"Of course. And, sweet Jesus, I certainly hope it will be the last!"

"When is Smythe due again?"

"This afternoon, I'm afraid."

"And you just plan to tell him to draft another man?"

Nathaniel dropped his gaze to the rumpled bed linens. He hadn't fully realized how humbling and distasteful a task this was going to be until his brother mentioned it. "Yes. I suppose so."

"That's a shame, Nathan, really. I know how much you want to help the commander. But perhaps another assignment would be best," he added, reaching out and giving his brother a consoling, albeit weak, slap on the shoulder.

"Yes . . . perhaps," Nathaniel conceded, rising from the bed once more. "But I had better get down to the yards now. What with my having to come back here and meet with Smythe later and you in the state you're in, I should put in some time at the office today."

"I'll feel better, once I've eaten," John called after him hearteningly as he headed for the door. "That is, when I feel well enough to eat."

Nathaniel laughed and smiled back at him. "Suit yourself. You've earned a holiday, I suppose." His smile faded as he stepped out into the corridor seconds later and began heading back to his suite to get dressed. He had put on a brave front for his brother, but the truth was, he just didn't know how he was going to face Smythe and admit defeat so soon—especially after having given his word that he'd meet the commander's request. It was going to be one of the most difficult things he would ever have to do. He'd just never been one to give up, and he hoped to God he'd find the words he needed to do so gracefully.

Smythe arrived fifteen minutes late that afternoon, and when he was finally shown into Nathaniel's study by the estate's steward, he was nursing a bleeding hand.

Nathaniel rose from his desk at seeing it. "Sir, what on earth happened to you?"

Smythe looked rather embarrassed, as he continued to hold his kerchief about the wound. "Ah, it's nothing, sir. I was just bitten by my horse, is all."

Nathaniel scowled. "Bitten by your horse? Well, good God, whatever did you do to provoke him to bite you?"

Smythe managed a pained laugh. "Oh, nothing, sir. It was simply that, after I hitched him up outside, I happened to feed him some dried apples I had with me, and I fear I failed to get the ball of my thumb out of his way in time."

"You seem to be bleeding through your kerchief there," Nathaniel noted, coming out from behind his desk and crossing to Smythe to have a closer look. "Let me call the steward and have him bring you a proper dressing for it."

Symthe shook his head and laughed again uneasily.

"I don't want to trouble you, Mr. Hamlin, and I must confess that I am in a bit of a hurry this afternoon. I'm expected back, in full dress, at my garrison in less than half an hour. So, I really shouldn't tarry."

Nathaniel had forgotten for a moment that this man was a soldier. With Smythe always showing up in civilian dress, that was easy to do, but it seemed Nathaniel had also forgotten the stoicism of military men. The bite must have been terribly painful, enough to make any other man grimace. Not a British soldier, of course, Nathaniel reminded himself. "But, Smythe, it does look as though you're about to begin dripping on my Oriental rug," he said gingerly, "so let's have you back up a foot or two, if you will, while my steward gets you a towel or something." Without another word, Nathaniel went to the study door and called for the servant.

Smythe still looked ill at ease when Nathaniel turned back seconds later to face him once more. "How did it go with the lady, sir?" he asked.

Nathaniel dropped his gaze and slowly walked back to his desk. "Well . . . I'll tell you, Smythe," he began tentatively, wishing he'd had the forethought to have consumed a glass or two of brandy before their meeting. "Do you want a drink by any chance?" he asked, turning back to his contact with a hopeful expression.

Smythe seemed surprised by this unprecedented offer. Nevertheless, Nathaniel was fairly certain that he wouldn't refuse it—liquor rations being scant in the army.

"I mean you look as though you could use one, what with that bite and all."

"Oh . . . very well, sir. I suppose one would do no harm. But just a little bit, please. As I said, I should be on my way soon."

Nathaniel smiled and quickly crossed to the cut-glass decanter standing on a nearby console table. He felt certain the liquor would help him get through the minutes to come.

"You were saying, sir?" Smythe prompted again.

"Um . . . yes. What was I saying?"

"Well, I don't know, sir. You hadn't really started saying it, you see. But I assume it was about the young lady."

"Oh, yes . . . Well, she was much, much tougher to finesse than I had thought she'd be," Nathaniel explained, turning back to face him a moment later with two brimming glasses of brandy.

"Oh?" Smythe replied coolly, and, as Nathaniel crossed to him and handed him his drink, it was quite clear that this wasn't at all what he wished to hear, much less to have to pass on to his commander.

"Sit down. Sit down," Nathaniel directed, a discomfited flush warming his cheeks. He had never, in all the time he'd known Smythe, offered him either a drink or a seat, but he knew he could do no less now. Fortunately, Smythe chose to rest his bleeding hand in his lap as he sank into one of the upholstered chairs Nathaniel had indicated, so Nathaniel was relatively sure the chair would not be indelibly stained. Nevertheless, he kept an anxious eye out for the servant and the towel he had requested.

"Well, you see," he continued, taking a seat in the chair opposite Smythe's. "She's a most unusual young lady. Very willful and unpredictable—" His words broke off as he again looked up at the study doorway and saw that the figure darkening it was not that of the servant he'd called for. To his utter amazement, the very woman whose nature he was attempting to describe to Smythe—Mademoiselle Brenton—stood there instead.

"Miss Brenton," he exclaimed, springing to his feet. Then he flashed Smythe a warning, sideward glance.

Smythe, looking equally amazed, also rose in deference to the young lady.

"Good afternoon, Nathaniel." Caroline's greeting was accompanied by a nervous smile.

"Good afternoon, Caroline."

"I hope I'm not interrupting."

Nathaniel began walking toward her, his smile welcoming. "No. We were just chatting . . . Mr. Smythe," he continued, turning back to his contact, "may I introduce Mademoiselle Caroline Brenton? She's Meldon Thorwell's niece, from New Orleans. Surely you know of Mr. Thorwell."

Smythe, still looking stunned, nodded stiffly and tried to produce a smile. "How do you do, miss?"

"Mr. Smythe is from a . . . a neighboring farm," Nathaniel blurted out, being hard pressed to find a plausible explanation for the man's rather shabby dress. He would never have stooped to introducing him simply as a friend. Nor did he care to go so far as to introduce him as a servant. He, therefore, felt he'd chosen a reasonably happy medium, and he made it a point to keep his eyes focused upon Caroline so he didn't have to receive any biting looks from Smythe.

"May I ask what brings you here?" he inquired of her in as cordial a voice as he could muster.

"Nothing pressing," she responded. Then she lowered her voice considerably, as though not wanting Smythe to hear. "Acutally, I had hoped to speak to you or John alone, if possible."

"I see. Well, John's not here. He's down at the yards, so you'll have to settle for me, I'm afraid."

She smiled demurely and let her gaze drop a bit. "That will do nicely."

"In that case would you mind terribly if Mr. Smythe and I concluded our little talk first? You may wait for me on one of the settles in the entrance hall, if that's agreeable."

"Of course," Caroline said, backing up a bit. When she did so, however, she bumped into the steward as he rushed into the study with the requested towel. *"Mon Dieu!* I'm sorry," she exclaimed, turning to the servant apologetically. "I'm so sorry. I didn't hear you coming."

Nathaniel played the diplomat. "It's quite all right, I'm sure, Caroline. The steward was just bringing a towel for Mr. Smythe's hand. It seems his horse bit him a few minutes ago, and he can't seem to get the bleeding to stop."

"I can."

Nathaniel furrowed his brow. "What?"

"I said, I can. I can get the bleeding to stop. It's one of my specialties."

"Specialties?"

"Oui. I told you that my *maman* and I are healers, didn't I?"

Nathaniel offered her a clumsy smile. "Well, you said something about midwifery, but I didn't realize it went beyond that."

168

"Oh, but it does," she replied, reflexively taking the towel from the servant and pushing past Nathaniel in the doorway. Her stride was so brisk in those seconds that Nathaniel didn't have time to stop her as she marched over to the redcoat and pulled his hand toward her so she could examine the wound.

"Oh, no. No, thank you, miss," Smythe said, shaking his head politely and obviously trying to free his hand from hers. "I'm sure it will stop bleeding by and by."

"Not if you keep it pointed downward like that, it won't," Caroline scolded, managing to free the blood-soaked kerchief from his palm. "That's a terrible bite! What could you possibly be thinking of, not tending to it at once, Mr. Smythe? Why, this could be very serious!"

"Oh, no. It's fine, miss," Smythe maintained, rolling his eyes at Nathaniel as she continued to keep a firm hold upon his hand.

"Now, keep it up . . . *up,* like this," Caroline snapped, elevating Smythe's palm, and Nathaniel found himself having to stifle a laugh, as he saw the British commander's messenger recoil slightly at the sharpness of her tone. "So the blood goes to your heart and not down to Mr. Hamlin's floor! . . . Sit down," she ordered. "You shouldn't be standing. *Sit!*"

Again her tone was so emphatic that Smythe seemed to have no other choice but to obey.

"Really, miss. It's all right."

"Shhh," she snarled. "I assure you, sir, that it's anything but all right! I've seen men die from such bites. Hard as rocks, they're found in their beds the day after, and you know it as well as I! Now, you must be quiet and shut your eyes and concentrate with me on

169

slowing your heartbeat," she explained, kneeling down before him and pressing the towel to his wound.

Nathaniel bit his lip, fighting the urge to smile as he saw Smythe blanch with pain. She obviously had a very tight grip upon him, a hold so excruciating that it kept him from even attempting to rise again, because he looked as though he were riveted to the chair. And all Nathaniel could seem to do for him in those seconds was offer him an apologetic shrug. He'd tried to tell Smythe that Caroline was both willful and unpredictable, and now the messenger was learning this firsthand. Unable to think of anything more he could do, and not at all anxious to have Caroline's snappishness turn upon him, Nathaniel continued to stand by the steward, looking on as the girl held Smythe's hand up and repeatedly counted to four in French. At least, Nathaniel *thought* she was counting to four. He couldn't be sure of it, however, because she was speaking so softly, so mesmerizingly that it sounded more like some sort of incantation than anything as banal as numbers. And, far from being amused by it all now, Nathaniel was beginning to find himself awestruck.

It was unlike anything he'd ever seen. Caroline seemed to be slipping into some sort of trance, a state that had her undulating from head to toe. It was obviously no longer just a count to her but a pulsation that had taken possession of her form, and it was most odd to Nathaniel to see such a civilly clad young lady in so eerie and primitive a state. To Nathaniel's further amazement, Smythe was no longer fighting her. He was, in fact, sitting there quite obediently with his eyes shut, and his body was exhibiting some of the same, odd motion as Caroline's. It was as if their two minds had somehow been linked, and though Nathaniel was tempted to tell himself that the whole scene was just an illusion, that his imagination was simply getting the best of him, he knew perfectly well that was not the case.

"What's happening, sir?" the steward asked him in a whisper, clutching Nathaniel's arm with obvious consternation. "It's as though they are possessed. Shouldn't we try to stop it?"

"No," Nathaniel ordered, holding the servant back. It was the most spellbinding display Nathaniel had ever seen, and he didn't intend to let anyone cut it short. He hated to admit it to himself, but there was something very erotic about seeing Miss Brenton move in such a way, and though it made him somewhat uneasy, he wanted to take in every instant of it.

After several minutes, when the trance began to wane, Nathaniel saw Caroline's hand fall away from Smythe's. Then she pushed away from him slightly, her body hunched over as though she were completely drained.

Smythe, in turn, slowly opened his eyes and sat back in his chair as if he, too, were fatigued by what had passed between them. Then, like a child peering down into a bird's nest, he lifted the towel from his wound and said something in a whisper.

"What was that, Mr. Smythe?" Nathaniel inquired, finally taking a few steps toward him.

"I said it's stopped. It's stopped bleeding," he declared, looking up at Nathaniel with the drowsy expression of one who has just been roused from a very deep sleep.

"It may start again," Caroline said softly, her voice still sounding a bit monotonous.

Smythe looked down at her. "What?"

She didn't respond, but fixed her eyes upon the blackened bricks of the nearby fireplace. "You may need some stitches."

"I . . . I really haven't time for that," Smythe stammered. "As I told Mr. Hamlin, I'm expected elsewhere in just a few minutes."

"Suit yourself," she said evenly. "But if that's liquor I saw in your glass, I suggest you forgo drinking the rest of it. It will only thin your blood and start you bleeding again."

Nathaniel knew this to be true. It was fairly common knowledge in the Colonies that most painkillers produced the nasty side effect of making one bleed faster. Being a soldier, Smythe was undoubtedly aware of this as well. "She's right about that," Nathaniel confirmed.

"You'd do better to put it *on* you, rather than in you. At least that's what my mother and I have found," Caroline continued.

Smythe raised a puzzled brow. *"On* me?"

"On your hand," Caroline clarified.

"Are you mad? That would burn like the very fires of hell!"

Caroline simply shrugged at this retort. "Suit yourself, *monsieur*. I can only tell you what I know to be true."

"Yes . . . well, I do thank you, miss. Truly I do. But I'm afraid I really must go." With that, Smythe rose and began walking toward the middle of the room, where Nathaniel stood.

172

To Nathaniel's surprise, Caroline made no effort to stop Smythe. She simply continued to sit on the floor, her legs tucked up under her billowy skirt and her gaze still locked upon the fireplace, as though she hadn't yet fully drawn herself out of her trance.

"What on earth?" Smythe snarled, once he reached Nathaniel. With his good hand, he took hold of Nathaniel's right arm. "A word more with you, sir. Outside, please," he whispered, moving toward the study door.

Nathaniel motioned for the steward to follow them out of the room, and, once they'd made their exit, he quietly shut the door, leaving Miss Brenton inside.

"Will that be all, sir?" the servant asked in a low voice.

Nathaniel nodded. "And not a word of what you just saw to anyone, Albert. Do you hear me?" he asked under his breath.

"Certainly, sir. Not a word," the steward promised before hurrying away.

"In the name of God, what went on in there?" Smythe demanded, still keeping his voice to a whisper as well.

Nathaniel shook his head. "I don't know. I was hoping you could tell me."

"She cast some sort of spell on me! That much was clear. You saw it for yourself."

"Yes, it did appear so, Mr. Smythe. But no harm done, I suppose. She did get your hand to stop bleeding, after all, or so you said in there."

At this Smythe unveiled the wound once more and held it up for Nathaniel's inspection. "Did you think I was lying simply to get away from her?" he asked indignantly. "Why just look at it. It's as though it's been cauterized, and that must be precisely how she did it, for her hand seemed hot as an oven toward the end of that madness. I tell you, sir, I've never seen or felt the like of it! She's a witch, is what!"

"That may well be. But neither of us is in the business of witch-hunting, now are we, Mr. Smythe. Therefore, I do think it best that we keep quiet about what happened and simply focus upon the task at hand."

"All right. What were you going to tell me, just as she came in?"

Nathaniel found himself unprepared for this question, and he realized now just how shaken he was by Caroline's display. "Well . . . only that she's not what one might call a malleable woman. I'm sure, after what just happened, you'd have to agree with that much."

"So . . . are you saying you can't manage the commander's request?" Smythe pressed irritably.

"Well, no. I'm only saying that, so far, I haven't had much luck with it. But I certainly hope to. I can tell you that she is indeed the smuggler you suspect her of being."

"How would you know that?"

"My brother did a bit of nosing around last night at the party Thorwell gave for her, and he found weapons in one of her trunks. Lots of them."

"Good. I'll be sure to tell the commander that. Anything else?"

"Yes," Nathaniel replied, beginning to gather his wits about him once more. "I've reason to believe that Earl McCrae might be one of her rebel contacts. They seemed to hit it off so quickly last night. Suspiciously so. You might, therefore, want to have him followed for a while."

"Very well."

"And perhaps it would be best if you don't stop by here for another report until we've let a fortnight pass. I've a feeling I'm going to need at least that much more time with her. Do tell the commander it's simply the best I can do, I'm afraid."

Smythe looked rather hesitant about this, but, after a pause, he nodded. "Very well, sir. But do try to move it along, will you? I really hate being the bearer of bad tidings where the commander is concerned. He's been very ill tempered lately."

"I shall work as quickly as possible," Nathaniel assured him, as he saw him to the front door. "And do give the commander my regards."

Smythe turned back to him before opening the door and taking his leave. "I shall. And good luck with her, sir," he said, rolling his eyes once more. "Looks to me as though you'll be needing it."

"Yes. Thank you, Smythe."

Nathaniel shut the front door. Then, drawing in a deep, bolstering breath, he turned and walked back to his study, to once again face the disquietingly unpredictable young lady who waited within.

Chapter 12

Nathaniel opened the study door and saw that Miss Brenton remained as they'd left her, slumped near the foot of the chair Smythe had occupied.

"Caroline?" he called out, concerned now that some bodily harm might have come to her as a result of what she had accomplished with Smythe. He'd expected that she would, at least, have gotten up off the floor by this time, but it appeared that she hadn't moved an inch.

To his further dismay, she showed absolutely no response when he walked over and bent down to look her in the face. Her dark eyes were vacant, almost lifeless, like those of the large bead-eyed, rag doll his sisters had played with in childhood. That doll had had the same eerie deadness to its eyes, the same limpness to its body.

"Caroline," he said again in a worried whisper, finding the he wasn't even able to tell whether or not she was breathing. "Let me help you up," he ordered. Trying to hide his trepidation now with a forthright and dutiful air, he bent down and wrapped his arms about her waist. Though he was lifting what felt like dead weight, he did manage to raise her almost to a standing position. Then he set her down in the adjacent chair. As he did so, he felt a chill run through him at the odd scent that filled his nostrils. He knew instantly that it wasn't her perfume. It wasn't at all like the heavenly scent she'd been wearing the night before as they'd danced beneath the Chinese lanterns. Rather, it was a much heavier, sweeter fragrance, like that of incense, and it was so overpowering that Nathaniel found himself drawing back a step or two as he continued to stare down at her.

"Caroline," he said again in a wavering voice, kneeling down before the chair to look into her face once more. "Are you all right? Answer me."

His emphatic tone seemed to jar her out of her stuporous state, and, an instant later, he saw a glimmer of recognition in her eyes. *"Qui'est-ce que—"* she asked in a barely audible voice.

"It's me. Nathaniel Hamlin. Are you all right?"

"Oui."

"What happened? Is there anything I can get for you?"

She shook her head and continued to gaze at him just as Smythe had, as though roused from a deep sleep. "No. I shall be fine. Just give me a minute or two more to recover."

"Does this happen to you every time you treat someone?"

Her voice was still ethereally soft as she answered. "No. Not every time. It depends on whom I'm treating."

"Well, obviously, Mr. Smythe was a real dandy!"

He expected her to smile at this bit of levity, but, to his surprise, her expression became more solemn. "Of course. Because he is evil, *mon ami.* You should have warned me about him," she added with a scolding edge to her voice.

Nathaniel felt his heart sink. He couldn't imagine how she could so quickly have deduced that the commander's go-between was an adversary. "Warned you?" he asked in as innocent a tone as he could muster. "Warned you about what?"

"About him," Caroline replied with obvious impatience. "A healer can sense these things, Nathaniel. The very essence of a person comes forth when there is a laying on of hands. And, if it's true that he's a friend of yours, I don't know how it is possible that you aren't aware of what kind of man he really is. He'd been cruel to his horse, you see. Did he tell you how he's beaten it? That is why it bit him. I could see it all very clearly in his mind."

"And that's why you say he's evil?"

"That's partly why, certainly. Anyone who is cruel to animals is either ignorant or evil, my friend, and, I assure you, Mr. Smythe is the latter. You would do well to steer clear of him in the future."

"Well, I'll . . . I'll try to be mindful of that," Nathaniel replied haltingly. "And that is what left you in such a state? This evilness you claim is in Mr. Smythe?"

"Yes. It is very draining to help one with such a dark side. But I'm sure I will recover."

"Ah, good. After seeing you slumped over as you were just now, that's very good to hear. I dare say your uncle would never forgive me, if he thought you had come to some harm in my home."

"I'm fine, Nathaniel," she affirmed. "Just a drink of water is all I'll require."

Nathaniel, accordingly, rose and crossed to ring for the steward once more. "I wonder . . ." he said hesitantly, as he walked back to where she sat and seated himself in the chair opposite hers. "Please don't think me indelicate for asking this, but what is that scent you are wearing? I don't believe I've ever smelled perfume like it."

"But I'm not wearing any perfume."

Nathaniel could feel his cheeks flush a bit in response, and he instantly realized that it wasn't just chagrin he felt but uneasiness. He sensed that she was telling him the truth, and that seemed to leave only an unearthly explanation for what he'd smelled.

"But you must be," he countered gingerly. "Can't you smell it? It's like incense."

A smile tugged at the corner of her lips, and she nodded. *"Ah, oui.* Now I know what you speak of. It sometimes comes when I treat people. But it won't harm you. Rest assured of that."

"I wasn't afraid that it might harm me," Nathaniel retorted defensively. "It was simply that it seemed so heavy. I just couldn't imagine what it was."

"I'm not sure I know either," Caroline confessed. "The spirits cause it, I'm told. But they are good spirits, my friend. You can be certain of that, because it is widely known that only good spirits can leave a good scent behind."

"Spirits?" he repeated, furrowing his brow. "Such as ghosts, you mean?"

She laughed. "Well, yes. I suppose so. Such as the

179

Holy Ghost, *mon ami*. Surely you've heard of Him."

Nathaniel scowled. "I hardly think you need be flippant! It seemed to me a reasonable enough question, given what just transpired."

She sobered a bit. "Oh, but I assure you that it was said only partly in jest, Nathaniel. You see, the healing power of my people has always come from God, the same God that you Puritans worship. I'm sorry, but I can tell you little more than that. It is a gift one seems to be born with or not, and, oddly enough, one can exercise it for an entire lifetime and not really understand how it works. I wish I could tell you more, but I simply cannot," she concluded apologetically.

Nathaniel's steward appeared at the study door once more. "You rang, sir?"

"Yes. Miss Brenton here would like some water, Albert. Please see to it at once."

The steward nodded and hurried off. Nathaniel, in turn, directed his gaze at his guest once more. "Smythe said that your hand felt hot as you stopped his bleeding. Is that so?"

"*Oui*. My hands always feel hot to me when I am treating people. So it stands to reason they would feel hot to him."

"Hot enough to cauterize such a bite? For that is what it appeared you did, Caroline."

"If that is how it appeared, then that must be what happened. I really don't know," she said, again in an apologetic tone. "My people have never considered it wise to question such things, you see."

Nathaniel sat back in his chair, his expression equally apologetic. "Ah, then you must think me unwise to do so. I am sorry."

180

"It's all right," Caroline replied. She was almost back to normal now. "I quite understand. Many outlanders are curious about our *traiteurs*. It is only natural, I suppose. I just wish I could tell you more, but I cannot. You must simply witness it for yourself and draw your own conclusions."

"And so I shall," Nathaniel declared, leaning forward a bit and raising a roguish, almost warning brow. "But I would beware of plying such skills here in the Colonies, my dear," he added. "Surely your father must have told you that, in the not-so-distant past, we burned women with such abilities at the stake."

"Would you have preferred it if I had simply let your friend continue to bleed?" she asked pointedly.

"No. Of course not. But my warning still stands, Caroline. Were I you, I would be more careful about whom I revealed such abilities to in the future. Why, Smythe was a total stranger to you. And you know little more about me."

Caroline flashed him a coy smile. "You? Why, you wouldn't turn me in for being a witch, now would you?" she asked, lowering her lashes and meeting his eyes in that instant with such daring that Nathaniel felt a provocative tingle run through him. Even the most experienced of the women he'd known had never displayed such an incisive regard, and he was seriously beginning to think this little, maiden niece of Meldon Thorwell's was anything but a maiden. Then, too, there had seemed to be an odd suggestion of a threat in her voice as she'd made the inquiry, something of a warning that a woman with her healing abilities could prove equally injurious to one's well-being, if given ample provocation. But perhaps he'd simply imagined this, he told himself.

"Of course not," he choked out. "I only thought it right to remind you that you're not in New Orleans now. This is a very different city."

To Nathaniel's surprise, Caroline suddenly dropped her gaze to the floor, as though saddened by what he'd said. "Indeed. Though Boston was the home of my paternal grandparents, and I have visited here a few times before, I must confess to hardly recognizing the city upon my arrival earlier this week. Forgive me for saying so, but it is like a town held captive. Don't you think?" she asked, gazing up at him again, her eyes betraying her great sadness about the situation.

"Well, I suppose it must seem that way to a visitor."

"Must seem?" she echoed incredulously. "But it is absolutely so! What else can be said of a city surrounded day and night by enemy soldiers? But then, I've said enough," she suddenly added, donning an obviously forced smile, and Nathaniel noted that her voice sounded stiff and diplomatic as she spoke again. "It is, in truth, your city far more than mine. And, after all, we Cajuns are under foreign rule as well these days. Spanish rule. So who am I to criticize," she asked rhetorically. "Who am I to assume that you don't favor the British presence here?"

Nathaniel cleared his throat and paused thoughtfully before responding. "Caroline, it was you who pointed out last night, that I refused an offer to build ships for His Majesty's forces. I do think that refusal is fairly indicative of where I stand."

She flashed him a warm smile. "I suppose it is. Do you worry, then, that some of your patrons, those who are Tories, I mean, will hear of what you did and take their business elsewhere?"

"I can tell, my dear, that you haven't been in Boston long," Nathaniel replied, an incipient smile tugging at the corners of his lips. "If you had, you'd know that few Tories would risk revealing their loyalties in such a way. Indeed, it is we rebels alone who dare to be vocal these days. But I am, nevertheless, cautious about discussing such things with my patrons. I've always thought it best for business to appear to be fairly neutral. Haven't you?"

"Yes, I guess you're right. I sometimes forget that I will one day be the owner of my family's company and will, therefore, be expected to play the part of the placater. It is rather an awesome position, isn't it? I mean, we are, you and I, in much the same boat in life, aren't we?"

Nathaniel nodded.

"I wonder, then," she laughed a little self-consciously. "do you hate it as much as I at times?"

Nathaniel laughed as well. "I'm sure I do."

She clapped a palm to her chest and expelled a sigh of relief. "Ah, good. Then it's not just because I'm a woman that I feel that way now and then."

"What way exactly?" Nathaniel prompted, certain he knew what she meant but wishing to learn more about her.

"You know. In over my head. Frightened, I suppose you could say, for want of a better word."

Nathaniel couldn't help flashing her a teasing smile as the steward finally arrived with the requested glass of water. "What's this, then? Admitting vulnerability to one of your most important suppliers? What would your father say?" he asked, motioning for the servant to come and hand the goblet of water to his guest.

Caroline bit her lip and fought a laugh as she received the water and the servant again took his leave. "I don't think he would approve. But you, of all people, should understand what I mean. Don't you?" she asked sheepishly.

Nathaniel nodded. "But what I don't understand, my dear, if you'll pardon my candor, is what you are doing here now in my study, discussing such things. I mean, after what you said to me last night, I truly thought I'd never see you again. So I hardly think it likely that you came over here today simply to chat." He was pleased to note that she looked sufficiently shaken by this comment. As a matter of fact, her hand was trembling as she raised the goblet to her lips and took a swallow of the water.

"No, I didn't," she responded, reaching out and setting the vessel down on the tea table that stood just behind where they sat. "I must say, Nathaniel, you're not a man who minces words, are you?"

"You were most direct with me last night, Caroline. Can you really be surprised to find that I am compelled to be the same with you now? I think I do have the right, after what happened, to know whether or not this call of yours concerns business or leisure. Or perhaps," he added with obvious displeasure, "it is my brother you came to see. I do recall your asking for him earlier." Nathaniel didn't care if she perceived his annoyance at the situation. It had been humiliating enough to have his little brother steal Meara Miller right out from under his nose the night before, and now it appeared that his quarry preferred his brother's charms as well!

184

Again, Caroline looked taken aback by his frankness. "No . . . either you or John will do, I imagine."

"'Do' for what?" he asked, trying not to sound suggestive.

"It has to do with some of the luggage I brought with me from New Orleans. It seems that someone went through it last night, during the party, and, quite frankly, your brother was the only one the staff saw go into my suite."

"Hmmm," Nathaniel looked directly at her. "It seems we're *both* resorting to bluntness now, doesn't it?"

"Perhaps it is the best way."

"Then exactly what are you inferring, my dear? Do you think John is to blame for this 'searching' that you say went on?"

"I suppose it is possible, though I can't imagine why he would do such a thing. I mean, it is no secret that your family is even wealthier than mine, Nathaniel, so I hardly think your brother would have been looking for any booty I might have brought along."

"Why? Was anything taken?"

"No. I don't think so."

"Then, I'm sorry, but I fail to see what your concern is."

"Well, it's just that I had some papers in there, you see. Business ledgers and such. The sort of records one doesn't care to have fall into the wrong hands, if you know what I mean. Surely, as a fellow businessman, you understand."

"Yes. I believe I do . . . Perhaps you should keep your luggage locked."

"That's just it. It *was* locked. What's more, the key

185

was hidden. Whoever opened it had to have done so quite intentionally."

"And you feel that, since John is a partner in our shipbuilding business, he would have reason to want to pry into the inner workings of your company?"

"Again, Nathaniel, I think your bluntness is a bit uncalled for. I've made no such accusation. I simply came here as a friend, to ask if you or John might know anything about this. If that is too presumptuous, I shall be quite happy to leave," she concluded, rising indignantly.

Nathaniel reflexively rose as well. "No. Don't, Caroline," he blurted out. "Stay, if you wish. You're most welcome here," he said softly.

Seeing his entreating expression, Caroline deigned to sit down once more. Nevertheless, her posture remained frostily rigid. "Very well. I suppose I can afford to stay a while longer. My aunt and uncle usually prefer to have supper served rather late."

"May I invite you to dine with me? John got down to the yards at such a late hour today, there is no telling when he'll be home, and I'd far prefer your company to dining alone," he said, a charming twinkle in his eye.

"That's most generous, Nathaniel, but my aunt and uncle will worry if I'm not back, I'm afraid."

"I'll send a footman to tell them you've chosen to dine here. Surely, they won't object to that, will they? It's not as though we'll be here all alone, you and I. The house is filled with servants, after all."

Caroline wasn't sure why, but she felt an odd tingle run through her at this obvious reference to the possibility of any impropriety occuring between them.

"Unless, of course, you feel that my being dark-haired will put you off your food," he added with a taunting smile.

She couldn't help laughing. "Of course not. As I told you last night, Nathaniel, you're a very handsome man. I don't find you unattractive."

He raised a skeptical brow. "You don't?"

"No, I don't. You're simply not . . . not my sort of man," she explained again. "I prefer—"

"Oh, please." He interrupted, raising a palm to her, a pained expression on his face. "Do spare me that patronizing speech of yours, my dear. If you promise not to repeat it and to have supper with me this evening, I promise I'll try to help you find out who might have gone through your belongings last night. Fair enough?"

"Fair enough. Was it really so hurtful, what I said last night?" Caroline asked, mild surprise in her voice.

Nathaniel nodded. "It certainly was. In fact, as I told John, I would by far have preferred to have been slapped."

Caroline knit her brows in amazement. "You would have?"

"Oh, yes. Take it from a man who has been slapped more than once by a woman, a slap only stings for a second or two. Wounding words, on the other hand, have a way of staying with one."

Caroline leaned toward him sympathetically. "Oh, I am sorry, *mon ami*. I wasn't trying to hurt your feelings. I just—"

Nathaniel interrupted her. "You see, there you go again, wanting to explain yourself. Let us just agree not to discuss it any further. All right?"

"Oh, very well. But I want you to know that I would

understand completely if you told me I simply wasn't the sort of young lady you found . . . well, you know, most desirable."

"You would?"

"*Mais oui.* Please do. Just tell me so. I promise not to take offense."

Several seconds of silence ensued.

"Well, go on," she prompted again. "Do your worst." To her surprise, in the pause that followed he took his eyes from hers and sat staring pensively downward. Seeing this, Caroline became serious. "I promise you, no matter what you say, I won't hold it against you, Nathaniel. You have my word that it will in no way affect the business our companies do."

Caroline recoiled a bit when he looked up at her an instant later, his big dark eyes conveying an emotion she couldn't seem to identify. At first, she thought it was sadness, but then she realized it was something else, something she really hadn't anticipated. *Longing.* Yes. It was a lovesick look, and she couldn't imagine what had provoked it. But, whatever it was, she suddenly realized that this wasn't simply repartee to him, as it was to her.

"I'm not worried about the business our companies do, Caroline," he answered finally, his tone strangely smoldering, and she instinctively knew she should not pursue the subject.

"May I give you a bit of advice?" he asked after a moment.

"You mean besides the tip that I shouldn't go about Boston giving people reason to accuse me of being a witch?" she asked with a chary laugh.

He laughed a bit as well. "Yes. Besides that."

"What is it?"

"Don't toy with men's hearts, Caroline," he answered in a tone that said he was dead serious. "You may not realize it, but you're far too lovely to go about taking the advances of men lightly. Fellows have fought duels and died over young ladies much less beautiful than yourself. And, after seeing you heal Mr. Smythe's hand, I can't believe you're the sort of girl who wishes to see blood spilt over you."

At this Caroline dropped her gaze to her lap, too surprised by his words to speak. "No, of course not," she said softly, almost repentantly. "And I do apologize for seeming to have toyed with you."

"Weren't you?" he asked pointedly.

She let her eyes slowly travel up to meet his once more. "Well, yes, I suppose so. A little. But I meant no harm by it. I mean, I hardly think Boston is the sort of city where anyone would fight a duel over me."

"Oh, you would be surprised, my dear, what acts of violence take place in the darkened corners of this town in times such as these! Why, even though your uncle's house is only a few minutes from here, you will need an escort home this evening."

"Why?"

"To protect you from the redcoats."

Caroline laughed. "To tell you the truth, my friend, I think they'd find me rather disappointing prey. I've very little money with me, and I didn't wear any jewelry."

He donned a knowing expression. "That is not all there is to steal from a young lady, Caroline. Surely you must know that."

Her cheeks flushed as she remembered what the

189

senior crewman on her father's schooner had told her, and Nathaniel's meaning finally dawned upon her. "Ah, yes. Well, I suppose it is wisest to be careful, then," she conceded. "But what I don't understand is how they bring off such things. With Boston's wives and sisters and daughters, no less. Don't you men try to stop them?"

"Of course . . . when we can. But there's a war being fought here, and whenever an enemy army's about, defenseless citizens are going to be hurt and killed. It isn't fair, of course, but it happens. Most of the British soldiers have been away from their homes and women for years. You can't really expect that they'd deny themselves the pleasures of the flesh all this time, can you?"

Again Caroline felt her face warming slightly with embarrassment. "No. I guess not."

"And, frankly, I doubt they earn enough to pay for such services, so they simply steal what they want. Such is war, I suppose."

"A dreadful business," Caroline replied, shaking her head sadly. "I'm so glad my people in Louisiana haven't had to experience it!"

"And do they ever expect to?" Nathaniel was fishing, knowing that anything he could extract from her regarding Louisiana's disposition toward redcoat attacks would be of value to the commander as well.

"Oh, I suppose they do, by and by. But the redcoats will have quite a fight on their hands if they march upon us, because the bayou is a great deal more treacherous than anything you'll find in New England. The British will not only be fighting Cajuns, they'll be fighting alligators, poisonous snakes, terrible heat, and insects of sorts you can't even imagine. I do think they would be well advised not to tread upon us. That area is really no place for Englishmen," she concluded, a defiant gleam in her eyes.

"You don't care much for the British, do you?" Nathaniel observed, striving to keep his tone incuriously even.

"Should I?"

He smiled and shrugged.

"In truth," Caroline continued, "I think it matters very little whether I care for them or not. This is not my war, Nathaniel; it's yours. You're the one who is being asked to build ships for His Majesty's fleet, so it is important that you and your fellow Bostonians know where you stand. But I will tell you that I don't care much for monarchs, be they English or Spanish. I think mankind has outgrown its need for kings and queens. Don't you?"

He smiled slightly at her, marveling a bit at the confident and sagacious way in which she'd spoken these words. "Outgrown?" he asked. "You mean, as a child outgrows its clothing?"

She nodded.

"How novel, my dear. I don't believe I've ever viewed the matter in quite that way. I shouldn't think King George would care much, though," he added laughingly, "for being cast off like an old pair of breeches!"

Caroline laughed as well. "No. I don't fancy he would. A pity," she declared, again with a clearly rebellious twinkle in her eyes. "In any case, we are all like one big child growing older with each generation, and, if His Majesty does not care to grow along with us, then he shall surely be left behind."

"You're a very interesting young lady, Caroline," Nathaniel noted, giving her a clearly admiring look. "How on earth do you think of such things?"

"Oh, thank you for the praise, but the truth is, I don't. Philosophers do. I simply read what they have to say. Don't you? Surely you've read the works of the Enlightenment thinkers, haven't you?" she asked, directing her gaze at his many shelves of books.

She expected him to return her enthusiastic smile, but, to her surprise, he looked rather disapproving. "I don't get much time for reading, I'm afraid. I find that overseeing the shipyards consumes far too many hours."

"Ah. What a pity." She rose and crossed to have a look at some of the titles in his bookcase.

"I must warn you that you won't find much of interest over there. They're about commerce and shipbuilding, in the main."

She perused the shelves for a moment or two, taking out a few of the books and flipping through them. Then she turned back to him, her expression teasing. "Oh, such a boring chap, Nathaniel! Whatever do you do for fun?"

He could not hold back an uneasy laugh. "I think it better you don't ask, my dear. Seemliness will only prevent my answering."

"Ah, *oui*. That's right," she replied with a smile and a nod. "All your lady friends. How silly of me to have forgotten. But besides that, what?"

He couldn't help flashing her a provocative smile, as he continued to eye her petite, hourglass figure, draped that day in a coral-colored satin gown, which seemed the perfect complement to her light hair and dark eyes.

192

"I'm afraid, Caroline, that, as far as I'm concerned, there is little else."

"Oh, come now," she scolded kittenishly. "There must be. Don't you even ride?"

"Ride what?" he asked, pretending to be quite serious.

At this, she planted her hands on either side of her tiny, cinched-in waist and clucked at him. "Oh, Nathaniel, really. You're incorrigible, you know. Can't you name even one other thing?"

He sobered a bit. "I like to fox hunt," he said after a moment. "And I used to like sailing, but the redcoats have made it rather more trouble than it's worth these days, I'm afraid."

"How?"

He shrugged. "They're always stopping John and me and searching our yawls for smuggled weapons . . . of all things," he exclaimed with a sharp laugh. He noted in that instant that she paled slightly, and he wasn't sure why, but it did bring him a tinge of satisfaction.

"Ah, yes. Of all things," she echoed with a nervous smile.

"But, short of tipping off a pint or two with my friends at our club, the one your Uncle Meldon belongs to," he explained, "my life is rather boring, and I'm sure I will be domesticated with frightful ease, when the right young lady comes along." Then, seeing how uncomfortable this last subject seemed to make her, he decided to rise as well and suggest that they leave the study and take a tour of the place. "But enough of me," he declared brightly. "You are far more interesting, my dear. Why don't you come along with me, and I'll show you around the house and the grounds while we get

193

better acquainted?" He extended a hand to her, and, to his relief, she slowly crossed to him and took it.

"That's odd," he said with a smile, as he escorted her out into the entrance hall and down the corridor that led to the grounds behind the house. "Your hand isn't at all hot now. In fact, it's rather cool, my dear."

She smiled at him uneasily, and when she quickly withdrew her hand from his. It was clear to him that she hadn't liked being put in the position of letting him touch her. "Well, I wasn't trying to treat you, Nathaniel," she explained in a faltering voice. "Though perhaps I should."

He assumed a questioning expression as they finally reached the double door that opened on to the back garden. "Whatever for?"

"For not having the good sense to take a little time for yourself now and then. An hour or two to read about something other than your business. The stern die young, my friend, if you'll pardon my saying so. Perhaps that is why I first pictured you in a grave."

"No," he countered with a laugh, opening the door for her and letting her lead the way to the garden path. "You said you pictured me digging a grave. Isn't that a different matter?"

She shrugged, then stopped to scan the large beds of delicately colored flowers on either side of her. "Maybe not. This garden, for instance, with all its beds. It must be the envy of all of Boston, don't you think? Yet, I'm willing to wager that you don't come back here to enjoy it but once or twice each summer."

He cocked his head at her. "And how would you know that?"

"Because the same can be said for my father. He's as

dedicated to his business as any man you'll ever know. And, I assure you, his incessant devotion to his work has taken a toll upon him, as I'm sure yours will, Nathaniel." Then, realizing what she'd just divulged, Caroline fell silent and bit her lower lip.

His next words were upon her with what seemed merciless swiftness. "What? Is your father ill, my dear?"

She could feel herself beginning to blush. "I . . . I really shouldn't say, I'm afraid. It seems I've revealed too much already."

"But what does it matter if I know? Why would you want to keep such a thing a secret?"

"I have my reasons."

"But everyone knows he's not a young man anymore. And it must be common knowledge by now that you will take the reins of the company when he dies, so I can't imagine why you seem so troubled about having spoken as you have."

"It's a very long story, *mon ami*. I'm sure it would only bore you. Let's just let it suffice for me to ask that you don't repeat what I've said to anyone else."

Nathaniel shrugged and continued to stroll at her side along the winding path. "Very well. But I must confess to having my curiosity piqued. I mean, so many secrets, Caroline. First, your mysteriously opened trunk and now biting your tongue this way about your father's health. You must feel as though you haven't a confidant in all of Boston with whom to share these things. Do you really consider this such enemy territory?"

There was so much concern in his voice as he asked this, she felt he deserved an answer. "I guess I do. You, more than anyone else, must know how lonely it is to oversee a large company. No doubt, you, too, find yourself able to trust only a precious few."

Nathaniel nodded. "Yes, I must admit to that. But, then, there are so few who are in my position. You are one of those few, my dear," he added pointedly. It had suddenly dawned upon him that stressing common ground might be the ideal way to persuade her to open up more with him, and he decided to exploit this tactic.

He stopped walking and again reached out and took her hand. But Caroline noted that he held it very loosely now, with almost an opened palm, as if to tell her that she was quite free to withdraw at any time.

"It would, therefore, mean a great deal to me, Caroline, if you would consider confiding in me while you're here in Boston. If I can't know you as a lover, please, at least allow me to know you as a trusted friend," he concluded, his dark eyes quite entreating. "That is, unless, of course, you already have enough friends here in whom you can confide."

"No," she replied, caught off guard by his sudden show of emotion. "I really don't have any friends here, not to speak of."

"Then you must agree to let me be one to you," Nathaniel insisted. "Given our similar stations in life, I'm certain there is much we could teach one another. For, though I would never deign to admit it to another man, I will admit to you that I, too, seek the comfort of a confidant now and then. And you seem such a perfect choice, considering just how mutually beneficial our two companies are. What do you say?"

Again Caroline found herself feeling rather speechless. "Well . . . I . . . I would need some time to think it over," she responded, though surprised at how intense their conversation had become. Were a passerby to have seen Nathaniel's expression in those moments, she thought, that person would surely have concluded that her host had just proposed something as serious as marriage.

Then, as if realizing how taken aback she was by his gushing, Nathaniel smiled apologetically. "Oh, please don't think me off my hinges, my dear. It is just that I do love the company of women so. And, finally to have found one who truly understands the demands and stresses of business, one who is in much the same station in life, and who seems genuinely in need of the friendship I have to offer . . . Well, words are inadequate to tell what a joy it is for me."

"I think I understand," Caroline replied, easing her hand out of his once more and resuming their strolling gait.

Nathaniel, of course, continued moving along at her side. "Good. I hoped you would. I mean . . . I hoped you would understand that I have no intention of taking unfair advantage of any time you may agree to spend with me. That is to say, I quite understand now that you have no amorous feelings toward me, and I would certainly never presume to treat you as though you did. I fully accept the fact that we are simply to be friends and nothing more . . . but there is so *much* I feel I can teach you," he continued enthusiastically. "I have, after all, been in business for almost as long as you've been alive. And I do know what it is to lose one's father to illness, having seen my own die not so long ago and having had to step into his shoes, as you will have to do with your father's one day. So, you see, it would do my heart good to think that I could actually be of service to you. Call it a penance, if you will. I fear I have unwittingly wronged so many young ladies like yourself throughout the years that to help right those wrongs, I feel compelled to offer my counsel and comfort to you now, in any way possible. Indeed, I feel it so strongly that I have actually said all of this to you and chanced your thinking me a fool. And, believe me, my dear, the Hamlin clan have always prided themselves on being dignified, so this is not at all easy for me!"

At this last declaration Caroline stopped walking and turned to him, a gentle smile covering her lips. "Oh, but I don't think you a fool."

"You don't?"

"Heavens, no. Not at all. It's just the English blood in you that makes you think so."

He offered her a puzzled smile, and she continued speaking.

"I do battle with it all the time, the stiff, English half of me that seems to think it is somehow shameful to cry or show emotion. I know that blood very well. And I've certainly been in the company of enough Frenchmen and Spaniards to have learned that they display little of the reserve we of English blood do, so it is not as though we humans were meant to be stern and unfeeling. It is only that some of us are taught, from earliest childhood, to be so. Believe me, Nathaniel, I see it in my father almost every day, and I think it is most unhealthy."

He couldn't help marveling at her. She had such an uncanny way of remaining uncommitted and turning the tables on him. He thought he had just delivered one of the most disarming speeches of his life, yet here she stood, seeming essentially unfazed by it and explaining to him how innately unhealthy he was, how defective his rearing. What was more, she actually seemed to expect him to take some comfort in what she'd said!

"Yes . . . well," he choked out at last, "I shall try to be mindful of that. Thank you. But what say you, my dear? Can we work at being friends, do you think?"

She started walking once more, and he, in turn, did the same. "As I said before, Nathaniel, I'll have to give it some thought. But," she added with a coy smile, "I would say there's a very good chance of it."

He would have to get her drunk at supper, he concluded grimly. He hated having to resort to such things with women, but she was, after all, proving to be a particularly difficult case. He had noted that she'd become more receptive the night before, once she'd had a cup or two, so he would simply have to ply her with some of his finest French wines. Then he'd sit back and let sweet intoxication lend him the hand he so obviously needed.

Chapter 13

With Caroline's consent, Nathaniel did, finally, send a footman to her aunt and uncle's residence to inform them that their niece had chosen to dine with Nathaniel that evening and to assure them that she would be returned to their home no later than ten P.M.

After insisting that Caroline take a tasting tour of his extensive wine cellar, Nathaniel ushered her back upstairs to his dining room, where they were served a supper of roasted turkey, squash, and potatoes, topped off by cherry tarts. As Nathaniel had hoped, his guest willingly drank two or three large goblets of the French wine he had his servants pour during the meal, and that, coupled with all the wine she'd tasted during their tour, had her pretty well inebriated by seven o'clock.

After sending his serving staff out of the room, Nathaniel sat chatting with Caroline for almost an hour following the meal, and he actually managed to get her laughing quite heartily once or twice, before he sensed that it was almost time to come in for the kill.

Get them laughing. Get them crying. Get them

talking. That was Commander Rushton's dictum for informers, and Nathaniel had always had pretty fair success with it. So, still adhering to this advice, he had saved his funniest story for last, and he was shooting now for a fitting capstone to the humorous phase of this endeavor.

"When I was ten," he began again, basking in the warm glow of both the table's lit candles and his guest's appreciative smile, "I sat on the front steps of the house one morning, taunting John. He was lying on his stomach, digging about in our mother's front garden. And I really don't remember what our quarreling was about that particular day, but, as I opened my mouth to hurl another affront at him, he reached up and threw a mudball of astounding proportions at me, and, so help me God, it lodged so perfectly in my mouth that my father actually had to cut it to pieces with a paring knife in order to remove it!"

To Nathaniel's delight, Caroline threw back her head at this and began issuing short bursts of laughter that were so pleasing to his ears, they got him laughing as well. He noted in those seconds that she had a sensually low, rich, laugh, one he liked very much and one which was, beyond a doubt, heartfelt in those moments.

"John was caned for it, of course," he continued with a chuckle. "But father decided to spare the rod with me that once. I suppose he felt a mouthful of mud was punishment enough. And he was right," Nathaniel concluded with a groan. "There was grit in my molars for nearly a fortnight afterward."

"Oh, stop," Caroline suddenly exclaimed, reaching out to beseechingly clamp his forearm and laughing so hard that she could barely speak. "I shall be sick from laughing if you don't stop!"

He leaned back in his chair, a satisfied smile on his face, deciding to grant her a little respite as he watched her reach up and dab her tearing eyes with her serviette. "I shall have a headache soon from all the laughing and all the wine," she said finally, glaring teasingly at him, "and it shall be all your fault, Nathaniel Hamlin!"

"Well, you're welcome to try to even the score, if you wish. Tell me some amusing tales about your childhood . . . I'd quite like that, you know, Caroline," he added, lowering his voice and affecting a disarming tone. "Learning more about you. You've said so little, really."

A silence fell between them, and Caroline directed her gaze downward for several seconds. It wasn't that she felt inhibited with him exactly. He had proven himself to be both vulnerable and sympathetic, and she'd actually come to like him over the past few hours. It was just that part of her was still a little afraid of that lusty, predatory side of him she'd sensed so strongly the night before. She was also frightened by the unspeakable feelings he stirred in her, the sinful thoughts especially now, alone with him, in the ardent glow of candlelight. His eyes seemed more penetrating than ever.

"Well, I haven't much to tell, I'm afraid. I've spent most of my life on my grandfather's ribbon farm on the Acadian Coast, and a farm is a farm, after all, no matter where it's set," she concluded, finally finding the nerve to look up at him once more.

"And do you dress this way when you're there? In such beautiful gowns?" he asked with an admiring smile. "I can't imagine that you do."

A soft laugh escaped her. "No. Of course not. My skirts would be covered with mud *tout de suite.*"

"Then, how *do* you dress, my dear?" He prodded, leaning forward again and brushing some stray wisps of golden hair from her eyes.

She would have objected to this action, had he not done it with such a platonic, almost big brotherly air. What was more, his eyes were so engaging, his attention so obviously fixed upon her every gesture and utterance, she wouldn't have dreamed of saying anything that might spoil the genial mood. "Well . . . as an Acadian, I guess. Surely you've seen one. There were so many sent to Boston as slaves twenty years ago."

He gave this several seconds' thought. Then he nodded. "Yes. I believe I did meet one or two. They dressed rather like Pilgrims, didn't they? Like our great-grandparents. Is that right?"

She smiled a bit self-consciously and nodded.

"Oh, then you must be quite irresistible, no? In your little white bonnet and simple frock?"

She shrugged, still feeling rather embarrassed by the subject. "I suppose so."

"Did you bring those clothes with you to Boston, perchance? I should like to see you in them," he declared, and she could tell that this was said only partially in jest.

"No. Of course not. I would look totally out of place here in such dress. What would my friends say?"

"I thought you said you didn't have friends here in Boston," he retorted, hot on the trail now of the answers to at least two of his key questions: who her contacts were and just how she planned to spend her time while she was here.

"Well, no," she stammered. "Not of the sort you meant. Not confidants really. But I do, of course, know people here. My aunt's friends mostly."

"Oh, yes? And what do you do with them while you're here?"

"Oh, *lady* sorts of things, mainly," she answered with a blushful laugh. "The pastimes that bore you men so."

"Such as?"

"Such as attending teas and garden parties and playing whist. Leaving our calling cards about. It is good for business, after all," she concluded in a dutiful tone.

Nathaniel fought a smile. "Indeed. How well I know it."

"There, you see?" she countered. "You do think it all silly and boring, don't you?"

"Oh, no. Not at all. In fact, I assure you, my dear, it would be quite impossible for me to find anything about you boring. On the contrary, Caroline, you're one of the most fascinating women I've ever met."

She clucked at him and laughed. "Mon Dieu! You could charm the fangs out of a serpent, couldn't you?"

"But I wasn't simply trying to charm you. I meant what I just said. I really do find you fascinating."

It was she who leaned back in the chair now, and Nathaniel was sorry to note that her expression continued to be a skeptical one. "What do you want from me?" she asked evenly, crossing her arms over her chest.

He didn't answer. He simply sat looking blankly over

at her, so she decided to venture a couple of guesses. "It can't be my family's money, can it? Everyone knows, after all, that you are wealthier than we."

"Really, Caroline! I'm appalled," he retorted. "I pity you, is what! Being so suspicious of one who is simply offering you friendship! Must I be after anything more?"

Caroline bit her lip, regretting that all the wine she'd consumed had made her speak so bluntly. "Well, no. I suppose not," she conceded. "But you really can't blame me for being a bit suspicious—all this food and expensive wine spent on a woman you've no hope of getting into bed, Nathaniel? You have to admit that isn't consistent with what I've heard about you."

"Oh? And just what have you heard?" he asked with a knowing smile.

"That you're a ladies' man, of course. And that you're very efficient, not one to waste time with matters and people who aren't apt to help you accomplish your ends."

He was cornered now, and he knew it. She was not like the other women he'd known, not one to be duped or charmed. He didn't even think it likely that she'd believe him if he said he was wining and dining her simply for the sake of their business relations. He knew he had to think of some other explanation and damned fast!

"Yes. I suppose it is suspicious," he agreed after a moment. "And I guess you were right to question it. . . . You're a very clever woman, Caroline," he continued, hoping that stalling with some flattery would give him a bit more time in which to come up with a plausible reason. Then, in an instantaneous brainstorm that he could only attribute to divine intervention, he devised what he felt was the perfect cover story, and he began to speak again. "You see, my dear, the truth is, I do have a favor I'd like to ask of you. But I needed to talk to you at length, as I have, to get to know you better and learn where you stand, before I could dare to ask it. And, in truth, I'm still not sure that I'm ready to do so."

Caroline furrowed her brow. "What is it? Has it something to do with our companies?"

"No, I only wish it were that simple. But, alas, it is not."

"So . . . what is it?" she asked again, this time more anxiously.

"Well, first you must swear to me that, no matter what your response to this request, you will never tell another soul I made it. Will you do that? Will you swear?"

"All right," she agreed. "I swear."

"Very well." He lowered his voice considerably as he spoke again, as though concerned about being overheard. "You see, it has to do with the rebel forces. Though few know it, I do count myself among them, and, well, let me simply be direct," he continued cautiously. "It's no secret that the Colonies can use all of the outside help they can get these days in order to win this war for freedom, and, frankly, Caroline, a woman such as yourself could prove most helpful to us."

Caroline was so surprised by all of this, she simply sank farther back in her chair and continued to stare expressionlessly at him. Part of her was compelled to laugh at the irony of the situation. Her good sense told her, however, that it was wisest to say and do nothing at all.

"Believe me, I know what you must be feeling," he continued in an allaying tone, "and if you wish me to take you back to your uncle's at once, I'll quite understand."

She gazed pensively down at her lap. "No. I don't think that's what I wish to do."

"Oh, good," he replied, breathing a sigh of relief. "I didn't think you would. Not after what you said earlier in my study. I mean the way you spoke against monarchy. I saw the defiant look in your eyes when you talked of the possibility of the redcoats attacking your people, and I just knew that you were different from most other women, that you were someone who possessed more wisdom and courage than most men I've met. I also knew that, sooner or later, I would just have to speak plainly with you and make you see that, while I find you very attractive, I seek much more than just dalliance with you."

"And that's why you came to meet me last night? To recruit me for the rebel cause?" She noted that he looked rather embarrassed by this question, as well he should have.

"Well, no. I came because your aunt and uncle invited me. I came to bid you welcome to Boston, just as everyone else did."

Though she was trying to fight it, her voice did sound a bit accusing now. "And what about your attempt to kiss me? Could that have been on behalf of the rebel cause?"

He, in turn, was starting to look somewhat indignant. "Of course not. That was precisely what it seemed, Caroline, the impulsive act of a man holding a beautiful young woman. In truth, I have always had a weakness for fair-haired young ladies such as yourself, and I probably always will ... but I've told you it won't happen again," he continued, rising from the table and beginning to pace vexedly about the room's hearth rug. "I gave you my word on that out in the garden, so I hardly think you need continue making mention of it."

She wasn't sure why, but she found this pledge strangely dispiriting. "Well, Nathaniel," she replied in a demure voice, "it is not so much that I object to being kissed by you, as it is simply that I object to being kissed for the wrong reasons."

He stopped his pacing and turned back to meet her gaze. On the one hand, he felt happy to hear this. It obviously meant that having an affair with her wasn't out of the question. On the other hand, he had hoped to catch her a bit more off guard, to have her jump at his bait and immediately admit to already being in cahoots with the rebels. Clearly, things weren't shaping up that way, however, so he decided to capitalize on what she might be willing to offer. "Oh, I see," he said with a whisper of a smile. "More wine, my dear?" he asked, crossing back to the table to pour it for her.

"No. *Merci*. I fear I've had too much already. What will my aunt and uncle say if I return after dark in such a compromised state?" she asked, smiling a bit teasingly.

"Well, perhaps they know that you truly are the experienced young lady you seem to be."

She gave forth a sportive cluck. "I'm surprised at

you, Nathaniel. Don't you know it's improper for a man to fish about regarding a young lady's chastity? I should ask that you take me home now!"

"You should," he agreed, still smiling. "But you won't."

"Oh? And why is that?"

"Because you sense what I do between us . . . some sort of animal magnetism that must come from us both being aggressors at heart, true competitors in the realm of business. A woman as perceptive as you, has surely noticed that much by now," he added, circling around to the back of her chair and hovering very closely behind her. He was so near that she could hear him breathing and she could feel his breath upon the crown of her head.

Her hands began trembling quite noticeably in response, and she quickly slipped them down under the table, onto her lap.

A virgin, Nathaniel concluded. He'd had his doubts, but her nervousness pretty well convinced him of it. So, he seized that instant to bend down and whisper in her ear. "A girl can get into trouble, you know, pretending to be more experienced than she is."

A tremendous chill ran through Caroline, and she knew, as she turned back to face him, that her eyes betrayed both her timorousness and her inexperience. "When . . . when will your brother be home?"

Her host looked as though this was the last thing he'd expected to hear from her, with their faces in such close proximity.

"I don't know. Does it matter?"

"Well, yes. You said you were going to try to help me discover who went through my trunk last night.

Doesn't that mean asking John about it when he returns?"

At this, Nathaniel issued a soft laugh and turned her chair about so she faced him more fully. Then he knelt down on one knee and began to speak to her once more. "Please don't go on worrying about that," he said, taking her hands into his, enveloping them with his huge warm palms. "You see, the truth is, it was John who went through your trunk, Caroline."

She opened her mouth to offer some protest, probably because he hadn't told her this when she'd first asked about the incident, and he reached out to press a silencing finger to her lips.

"And I didn't tell you so from the start," he continued, "because I didn't want you to leave. I figured that, once you had your answer, the answer you so obviously sought in coming here, you would simply leave and I might not have the chance to see you again, let alone to talk to you so privately and at such length as I have today. So, you see," he added, his eyes shimmering apologetically in the candlelight, "I couldn't tell you before, Caroline. I needed—I wanted—so desperately to have this chance to get to know you."

Caroline was too stunned to make an immediate reply. Then she felt herself beginning to seethe. "But what was he doing in my trunk? What right did he have to search for my key and open it? He was a guest in my uncle's home, not some common burglar! What on earth would compel him to do such a thing?"

"Oh, do calm yourself," Nathaniel replied, still keeping his voice assuasively low. "I'm sure he meant no harm by it. It's just John's way. He's always been rather unmanageable, as you saw for yourself at supper last night. And he's forever trying to gain the advantage in our company, so I suppose he sought precisely what you say you had in the trunk—your business ledgers."

"And what did he tell you about them?"

"Well, nothing, I'm afraid. He wouldn't have the advantage for very long if he shared what he'd seen with *me*, now, would he?"

"So he told you he saw nothing?"

A soft smile tugged at the corner of his lips. "No. Not exactly."

"Well, then, what did he say?" she demanded.

"What should he have said?" Nathaniel asked teasingly.

She glared at him. "Don't parry with me," she snapped. "After what you've just said to me—inviting me to join the rebel cause—you're certainly in no position to trifle with me!"

"Very well, then. I'll simply come right out and say it. We're both on the same side in all of this, Caroline. That much seems evident, doesn't it?"

"Then why this further attempt to recruit me?"

"Because there are many rebel factions in this town, my dear. I don't know which one you are helping, but I can assure you that, no matter how much you're planning to give or do, more will always be needed . . . and I am just hoping you would be willing to back us even further."

Caroline's heart was pounding so loudly now that she was almost certain he could hear it. "My . . . my aunt and uncle have nothing to do with all of this," she explained in a whisper, "so, please, whatever happens, don't let them be implicated in any way!"

To Nathaniel's surprise, he noted in those seconds

211

that her eyes were glistening with what appeared to be frightened tears. He reflexively reached over, took her serviette from the table, and handed it to her. "There's no need to cry, Caroline. Of course, I won't let them be implicated. We're on the same side. Don't you understand that?"

"Yes. I understand," she replied, fighting back her emotion. "But you weren't supposed to know about this. *No one* was supposed to know. I was to manage it all on my own!"

Seeing how upset she was now, Nathaniel seized the opportunity to take her into his arms and comfort her. "Shhh," he whispered, hugging her to him and bending down to kiss the crown of her head. "You've just had too much wine, is all. Things will seem clearer to you in the morning, I assure you," he added, rocking her consolingly. "Now, let us just get you home, my dear . . . before I lose what little restraint I have left with you and you find yourself with even more to cry about," he added under his breath.

"But what about John?" she choked out, pulling away enough to look him in the eye. "He won't tell anyone either? You're sure of it?"

"I certainly am. He is my brother, after all. It's hardly possible that we'd have different loyalties in this war, is it?"

"No. I guess not."

"Of course not," he confirmed, easing her up to her feet and pressing a tender kiss to her forehead. "Now, let us get you a wrap for the ride home. It does get rather chilly here at night."

"But you haven't told me what you want me to do for you and your rebel associates," she said weakly, reaching up to dab her eyes with the serviette.

"Oh, that can wait, I'm sure. At least until the next time we meet." He hadn't expected her to react this way, to become so wrenchingly tearful and vulnerable. It was a state he found most disarming in women, and he knew from past experience that he really couldn't trust himself with her very much longer. He was sure to begin ravishing her if given even a couple minutes more, so, in the interests of winning her confidence and building an ongoing relationship with her, he thought it best to see her safely back to her uncle's home at once.

"And when will that be?"

"When would you like it to be? Shall we wait until after your evening with McCrae?" he added, a resentful edge to his voice.

She laughed softly. "You really seem rather jealous of him, you know," she said charily.

"Of course I am. Why shouldn't I be? He'll be dancing with you all evening at the Winthrops'. I, on the other hand, have only been granted one dance."

"Then come to the Winthrops', *mon ami,* and dance with me as well. I'm sure Mister McCrae will permit me to have a few dances with you."

To Caroline's surprise he suddenly sounded admonitory as he spoke again. "No. Don't you see? Given how involved I am with the rebels, I'll only endanger you if you're seen with me too often in public. No," he said again firmly. "You'll simply have to come here when you can, and as secretly as possible . . . We'll go riding, all right? Saturday next, when I've finished for the week at the yards, you can call upon me in early afternoon, and we'll go for a long ride on the grounds. What do you say?"

"All right," she agreed. "One week from today."

"'Twill seem like ages until then, won't it?" he said, then almost laughed bashfully.

She stared up unflinchingly into his eyes, suddenly taking comfort in the knowledge that she really wasn't alone in her secret mission here. In fact, she probably had far more comrades than she realized, she told herself. "Yes, Nathaniel. I really think it will. And you don't know what a relief it is for me to have finally learned it was only John who opened my trunk and not my Aunt Margaret."

"Your Aunt Margaret?"

"Yes. My father's fraternal twin and, sadly, his sworn enemy as well."

"Oh, that does sound like a sad state of affairs. How did that come to be?"

"Well, it's a very long unpleasant story, and I fear I would only be doing my family a disservice by telling it to you or anyone else. Let us just let it suffice for me to say, had it been Margaret who had seen what John did in my trunk, the redcoats would have come for me already!"

Nathaniel did his best to look aghast at this, but, in the back of his mind, he was already entertaining thoughts that made him feel rather pleased. Her Aunt Margaret might prove to be the perfect scapegoat, he thought, should any accusations be made against him, following Caroline's seizure by the redcoats. He would simply have Smythe pass the word around that it was Caroline's Aunt Margaret who had informed on her, and, given the Brenton family's history, his fellow Bostonians would surely believe it. "Oh, dear. Then you would do well to deliver your cargo to your

214

contacts as soon as possible. Don't you think?"

She nodded.

"I do hope you don't have to keep it hidden for too much longer," he finished, inwardly delighted at the way the conversation was shaping up. To his disappointment, however, her next utterance was again aggravatingly vague. "No. Not too much longer."

"Good. I really would hate to see you get into any trouble, you know," he whispered, tightening his hold upon her and assuming an enamored air.

Caroline could see that his eyes were asking the same question they had the night before: would she allow him to kiss her? Not wishing to run the risk of having to dissuade him a second time and never having him attempt it again, she simply chose to shut her eyes, and, experienced as he obviously was with women, he immediately read her message.

Time seemed to freeze for Caroline in these seconds, as she felt his lips pressing down upon hers. She hadn't realized until that moment how much she'd wanted him to do this, and, as she stood, weak-kneed in his grasp, doing her best to reciprocate his penetrating kiss, she also realized that she didn't want him to stop. She'd expected the intimate caress to feel strained to her, overpowering and distressingly unfamiliar. Yet, to her surprise, it felt like the most natural thing in the world. His warmth, his seductively masculine scent combined with that of his barber cologne, and she was aware of his hot breath and of the expert way in which his hands held her, so comfortably, so lovingly.

How could she possibly have thought of him as a predator? Why hadn't she recognized him for what he was? A person much like herself, much like her father.

A wealthy, independent sort with the same enlightened values.

She had come home, at last, to the other half of herself, she thought in those moments, to the Bostonian half. And she realized that, of all the men she'd allowed to hold her—French plantation owners and wealthy Spanish merchants—she had never felt more at home in anyone's arms than she did in Nathaniel's.

"There," he murmured, as he concluded their kiss. Then he stood gazing down at her. "That wasn't so bad, was it?"

Caroline was still too transported by the embrace to answer, and, to her chagrin, the only response she heard herself offer was an aroused groan. "Umm . . . no," she finally stammered.

He laughed to himself, and then, to Caroline's further chagrin, he gave her posterior a brisk pat. "Come along now, my dear, before we're both reduced to groaning heaps. Thinking is never very far from doing, after all, and I can assure you that your father and uncle would be quite furious at what I'm thinking right now."

"And what is that?" she asked in a kittenish tone.

"Well, it has to do with your . . . your lips," he said, his voice still provocatively low, as he reached up and gently traced her mouth with the tip of his right index finger. "Those soft, full, peach-colored lips of yours, Caroline." He drew a deep, savoring breath in through his teeth. "They make me wonder what your . . ." His words died off, and it was clear that he had chosen to censor himself. "Well, if a man, in all propriety, is permitted to speak of a woman only from her neck up, then I would speak of your lips, my dearest, and of how

216

much I'm hoping you'll let me kiss them again when we meet once more, on Saturday."

"I think that is entirely possible," Caroline replied, feeling shaken by his having patted her. No other man had ever dared to do such a thing to her, to touch her on so unmentionable a part of her anatomy, and, ordinarily, she would have slapped the face of any man who had. But it had been different with Nathaniel, somehow. He'd done it with such a fatherly air, with such obvious concern about endangering their business relations by letting them both take things too far too soon, that it seemed quite understandable and forgivable in this case. What seemed less forgivable was the undeniable feeling of arousal it had provoked in her, the awareness she had now that—perhaps because she had denied herself sexual pleasure all of her adult life—she possessed even less self-control than he did in this area.

"That's good," he replied, looking as though he already knew that seducing her would be shamefully easy when the time came. "That's *very* good, Caroline. Now, let's get you home," he declared again, his tone becoming businesslike once more.

They rode back to the Thorwell's estate in relative silence minutes later. Caroline was still too atingle to speak much, and Nathaniel now seemed too determined to treat her honorably to risk further indulging in enticing conversation. Instead, he simply held her hand and gazed longingly over at her from time to time as they sat in the cab of his coach.

"You're truly a gentleman, Nathaniel," Caroline acknowledged, when the coachman finally drew the vehicle up to her uncle's front walk.

"Don't speak too soon, my dear," he replied with a gentle yet warning smile. "I can't promise I will be Saturday next. Not with a woman as lovely as you. So, please know that you're coming at your own risk," he concluded, raising a cautioning brow at her in the dim glow from the lantern he'd brought along. Strangely, he meant her to understand that his warning applied to far more than just sex. This was his final opportunity to encourage her to get away while she still could, before the redcoats' noose was placed around her neck.

"I shall," she answered with a wavering smile, as he stepped out of the coach and reached up to help her out of it.

"I mean it, Caroline," he warned again under his breath. "Please don't come unless you really know what you're getting into . . . I mean, with my involvement in this war, with all of it."

"All right," she said, her voice more firm. Then she donned a slightly questioning smile, to which he didn't respond. "Nathaniel," she said with a befuddled laugh. "If it will ease your mind to hear it, I'll think of little else but that till next we meet."

Seeming satisfied with this claim, he drew her right hand up to his lips and kissed the back of it with a telling wetness, which caused another wave of virginal shock to run through her.

"Good night," he said, his dark eyes smoldering once more as they looked, one last time, into hers.

She swallowed dryly, again feeling speechless at his obvious experience with women. "Good night," she gasped, as he turned and reboarded the coach. Then she stood and watched as the vehicle sped away in the darkness.

Was he one of the charmers of whom her father had warned her? One of those Bostonian bachelors who specialized in breaking women's hearts? No, he couldn't, she concluded. A heartbreaker would have taken her off to bed while he'd had the chance. He would never have given her the fair warning Nathaniel had. Nor would a man who was strictly a charmer have attempted to enlist her for so noble a cause as that of the American rebels.

And, she told herself, this Nathaniel Hamlin was far too plain-spoken to be anything but what he appeared to be, the heir of a wealthy shipbuilder. He was both an entrepreneur and a patriot—with, by his own admission, a bit of a weakness for women, and, as Caroline could well attest, a definite way with them.

Chapter 14

"Out seeing Meara again?" Nathaniel called out softly, from where he sat on the corner settle near the front door in the entrance hall.

It was nearly midnight, and John, having just crept in the door in the darkness, had obviously not noticed his brother. He was on the staircase now, and, as Nathaniel spoke, he gave such a startled jump that he had to take hold of the banister in order to steady himself. John turned back to his brother, and in the light of the lantern he now carried, his glare was evident to Nathaniel.

"What are you doing there? You nearly scared me into an early grave, I hope you realize, lurking about in the darkness like that! I thought for a moment you were father's ghost come to haunt me! You sounded so much like him."

Nathaniel laughed again and rose to step into the light John's lantern provided. "Never fear. 'Tis only me."

"Well, what are you doing up at this hour? I thought

surely you would retire early so you could get down to the yards at dawn and begin finding fault with what I did today."

"Oh, no, John. Not at all! Faulting you is the last thing on my mind tonight, believe me. In fact, I stayed up expressly to sing your praises."

John still looked growly as he sat down on the steps. "What for? And, I warn you, Nathaniel, if this concerns Meara again and what you've decided I can and cannot do with her, I swear to you, I'll battle it out with you right here and now!"

"It has nothing to do with Meara. It has to do with Miss Brenton."

"I didn't touch her! So help me God!"

Nathaniel laughed again. "I know that, you fool, and, I assure you, I wasn't going to say anything of the kind."

"Well, what is it then? Bloody hell, it's the middle of the night! Just say what you have to say and please let me get to bed!"

"She came here to see you today."

"Meara?"

"No. Caroline Brenton."

"To see me?" John asked incredulously.

"Well, more or less."

"Why?"

"To ask if it was you who had gone through her trunk."

John gulped. "Dear God! Well, why would she do that? Why would she want to call attention to the situation? I mean, why didn't she simply hide the weapons elsewhere and pretend the incident never occurred? That's what I would have done in her place."

"Yes. I wondered about that myself at first," Nathaniel replied. "But then she explained it to me. It seems her father's twin, her Aunt Margaret, is also her father's archenemy. The sort who's vindictive enough to undo Caroline, if she gets wind of the cargo her niece brought along to Boston. So, it seems that our little Cajun heiress simply came here to confirm that it was you who had opened her trunk and thereby put her mind at ease that it wasn't her wicked aunt."

"And what did you tell her?"

"I told her it was you, of course."

"Jesus, Nathan! *Why?*"

"Because she was so upset, you see, over thinking it had been her aunt."

"Yes, but what about me? Are you trying to get me thrown in gaol?"

"How could I? You didn't take anything, did you?"

"Well, no."

"Then, what can she do? You were a guest in her uncle's home, after all. It's not as though you were some stranger who sneaked in through the window."

"But do you really think it best for business, Nathan, telling one of our principle patrons that I went rooting through her belongings?"

Again Nathaniel laughed. Try as he might to fight it, he couldn't help enjoying this rare opportunity to see his brother squirm.

"Probably not. But it sure as the devil was good for the Tories. I told her that we're backing the rebel cause and, after you chanced to see what was in her trunk, we knew it was safe to ask her for aid for the Whigs."

"'Chanced to see what was in her trunk?'" John

repeated in amazement. "Sweet Jesus, Nathan! She may be a bog dweller, but that doesn't mean she's an idiot! She must know perfectly well that I had to search high and low for that key before I could open the trunk . . . that it was opened quite intentionally."

"Relax. I simply told her you were drunk and were doubtless sniffing around for any business ledgers to peruse. You know, trying to gain the advantage over me by getting some inside information about one of our patrons."

"Do you think she believed you?"

"She seemed to."

"And what if she tells her uncle or aunt about it?"

"Oh, I don't think she's apt to . They don't know about her rebel pastimes, you see, and she seemed quite adamant about their not learning of them."

John rolled his eyes. "Christ! You're going to get me publicly flogged one of these days! I'll never be invited to another party in all of Boston if word of this gets out! Some fine thank-you this is!"

With a broad smile on his face, Nathaniel crossed to his brother and extended a hand to help him rise from the lower steps of the staircase.

"Oh, she won't tell a soul about it, believe me. I've got her right in the palm of my hand now. Rest assured."

John didn't look at all convinced of this as he turned and they began ascending the huge carved staircase. "And so you've told her we're rebels?"

"Yes. And I also swore her to secrecy on that. I hardly think she feels in any position to spread it about, anyway, considering what we have on her."

223

"I gather you told Smythe you would continue with the assignment."

"Happily, yes. I was just on the verge of admitting to him that I didn't think I would succeed with her, when, lo and behold—*God bless you, sweet brother*—Caroline suddenly stood in my study doorway, as luminous as a tiger lily in those orangey satins of hers! It was just as if I'd somehow sent for her. And do you know what she did?" he continued, pausing on the staircase for emphasis.

John stopped as well, a step or two later, and glared down at him. "What? It's late, for God's sake, Nathan, and I'm still hung over from last night."

"Well, Smythe's hand was bleeding. His horse had bitten him just before he'd come in, and, I swear to you, Caroline simply laid her hands upon his palm and cauterized the wound, or so it appeared."

"Humbug!"

"No. It's true! I swear it. You can ask Smythe for yourself when next he's here. She's a healer, you see. One of those Cajun witch doctors, I guess."

John scowled. "Did she know who she was healing?"

"No. Of course not. But the uncanny part of it was, without hearing a word about Smythe, she sensed that he was her enemy. She came right out and told me, after he'd left, that he was an evil man and that I'd do well to steer clear of him."

"'Sdeath!" John replied with a shudder. "Sounds as though you'd do well to steer clear of her, also! It's far too bewitching an hour to be speaking of such things, don't you think?" With that John turned and continued up the stairs.

"Oh, but I don't want to steer clear of her," Nathaniel replied with a lusty laugh, as he followed him.

"Good Lord! Don't tell me you got her into bed already!"

"No. But I surely will the next time we meet."

"You're beginning to sound enamored of her," John warned, turning back to Nathaniel again once he'd reached the top of the stairs. "I'd be very careful of that with this one."

"Oh, but if you had kissed her, you would know that it's quite impossible to avoid making love to her. She's far too enchanting, you see. I'm afraid it just can't be helped," Nathaniel concluded dreamily.

John clucked at him. "And what if seeing her hung by Smythe's men can't be helped either? What then?" he asked, shaking his head. "No, Nathan. I think you should have simply gone ahead and told Smythe you wanted out of this assignment. A woman with powers such as you describe will surely prove more trouble than she's worth in the end."

Nathaniel couldn't hold back a soft, amazed laugh. "You know, John, you're starting to sound more and more like me every day. Don't tell me *you're* becoming the cautious one now."

"No. I hardly think so. I just think that woman has done something to your mind. I don't recall ever seeing you so smitten."

Nathaniel laughed again, a laugh that faded into a wavering smile. "Rubbish."

"Very well. Suit yourself. Why pay heed to me now? You never have before! Why should your work for the commander be any exception?" With that, John huffed off down the upstairs hallway, taking the lantern and leaving Nathaniel to find his way along in the darkness.

As planned, Caroline paid a call upon Nathaniel the following Saturday afternoon. She arrived in a lush russet-colored riding habit, complete with a smallish, veiled bonnet. It was an outfit her aunt's couturier had made for her just a few days before, and she was glad for the face-concealing veil now, glad for the anonymity it afforded her as she stood on the front steps of the Hamlin estate, awaiting a response to her knock. Nathaniel had warned her, after all, to be discreet about her comings and goings, and she felt he'd be pleased with the masking the habit inadvertently provided.

Several seconds later, Nathaniel's steward, the servant she'd seen in Nathaniel's study the week before, answered the door.

"Miss Brenton?" he inquired with a questioning smile.

"Oui," she said rather blushingly, raising the veil a bit to peer out at him.

"Ah, good. Come in, please. Master Hamlin is waiting for you down at the stable." He closed the front door behind her as she entered. "I'll take you down there straightaway if you wish."

"Please, *merci.*"

The steward began to conduct her down the long corridor that traversed the length of the ground floor and led to the back grounds. "Splendid, *mademoiselle.* Then we shan't keep the master waiting. He's really not one to be kept standing about," he added under his breath.

Caroline drew up beside the steward seconds later, as he held the back door open for her. "What was that?"

The servant's face reddened a bit, as they both proceeded out into the garden. "Oh, I simply said that Master Hamlin doesn't care to be kept waiting. He'd think me terribly remiss, I'm afraid, if I didn't escort you down to him promptly."

"Really?" Caroline asked with a casual cock of her head. "I wouldn't have thought it, somehow. . . . Tell me, is he a difficult man to serve?"

The steward laughed nervously. "My answer depends entirely upon who wishes to know, *mademoiselle,*" he said gingerly.

"Oh, you needn't worry," Caroline assured him. "'Tis only I who wishes to know. I'll not repeat a word of this to anyone, including Mr. Hamlin."

"Well, that being so, miss, I will confess that he's very difficult at times. Quite exacting in almost every area. But he's a fair man, nonetheless, and it really must be added that he does try to be fair to one and all."

"I see. Yes. Thank you," Caroline replied simply. She hadn't stopped thinking about Nathaniel during the entire week they'd been apart, and she immediately began pondering this new information on him.

Stern with his staff? Yes. It fit him, she guessed. It was that strict English blood in him, she concluded. He, after all, was twice as English as she, as was true of her father. So, she reasoned, some allowances would simply have to be made for this. Perhaps she'd even succeed in softening him in time, if given half a chance, much as she had her father through the years. And the thought of this brought a whisper of a smile to her lips as she continued to walk with the steward.

"Here you go, miss. He should be just inside," the servant declared minutes later, when they finally reached the stable. Then, giving a slight bow, he turned and headed back to the estate, leaving Caroline to announce her own arrival.

She couldn't help thinking the man rather remiss for this, but, seconds later, she was glad of it because she knew she wouldn't have wanted to interrupt what she saw happening inside for the world. It was Nathaniel communing with one of the most regal-looking horses she had ever laid eyes upon, and, as he stood feeding the animal from his hand, his manner was so reverent, so gentle that Caroline felt as though she had just come upon a priest alone in prayer. She lifted her veil once more and laid it up over her bonnet. Then she let her arms drop to her sides, and she continued to stand watching Nathaniel as stealthily as possible.

His dark eyes were fixed upon the horse, and he was speaking to it in a tone so low that Caroline couldn't make out what he was saying. She could tell, however, that these were words of great affection, and, for some reason, his face struck her as being very different from the way she remembered it from the week before. It was brighter now, much more animated and childlike then she had imagined it could be, as though he were speaking to his best friend, and she instinctively knew that she was learning more about Nathaniel in these stolen seconds than she had in all the time she'd spent with him thus far.

After feeding the horse, he reached out and began

228

stroking the side of its long neck. The animal, in turn, moved up until it was as close as possible to the stall door, as though wanting to soak up every ounce of attention it could get from Nathaniel. They were dear friends, long-time companions. That much was clear to Caroline as she went on silently observing them.

"I thought you told me you didn't have any *confidants,* Nathaniel," she said finally, keeping her voice as low as possible in the hopes of not destroying the lovely mood of the scene.

He turned to her with a startled expression that then gave way to a welcoming smile. "Oh . . . did I say that? Pardon me. As you can see, I was mistaken."

Caroline smiled as well. Then she sauntered over to where he stood and reached out to pet the horse. She could see, at this close range, that it was a mare of a breed totally unfamiliar to her.

"She's quite a prize, isn't she? I don't think I've ever seen a horse like this."

Nathaniel again directed his gaze at the horse. "No. I don't suppose you would have. Not in the New World. She's an Arabian, you see, and one of the very finest, I assure you. Not just for her impeccable breeding, mind," he added, his voice wavering with emotion, "but because she was a gift to me from my late mother. Shipped here from her clan in Belfast when I was still a boy."

"Oh? Your mother was Irish? I didn't know that."

"Yes. Part of the landed gentry there. My father met her in London, on one of his business sojourns, and it was love at first sight, or so I was told."

"Ah, *c'est très romantique.* Really, Nathaniel, how lovely for them."

229

He turned to face her more fully, one hand still stroking his precious mare. "Yes," he agreed with a sad smile. "But my mother died rather awfully, I'm afraid, and at a tragically young age. I was just a boy when it happened. She caught smallpox during a trip back to Ireland to visit her family, and she never returned. They chose, for some reason, to bury her in her native land, and father decided not to protest. . . . Perhaps," he continued with a dry swallow, and Caroline could tell he was fighting his emotions now, "that is why I found the words to the French song, the one to which we danced the night we met, so poignant. I did a lot of that myself, you see," he added, gazing downward at the stable's dirt floor, "that staring out to sea, wondering in vain when my mother might return."

"Ah, *mon chéri,*" Caroline said in a soft, quavery voice, sensing his great pain. She reflexively reached out and took hold of one of his hands. *"Quel dommage."*

They were both silent for several seconds. Then Caroline felt compelled to speak again. "And that is why this mare is so special," she acknowledged in a whisper. "A bit of your mother's spirit back again. A bit of her clan."

He raised his head once more with a stoic air. "Yes. Precisely."

"Well then, you must breed her, if you haven't already. You must keep the line going and pass one of her children on to one of yours. Don't you think?" she asked, and, as she did so, Nathaniel was so moved by her heartening expression and the sympathetic tears glistening in her eyes, that his breath caught in his throat. He'd made her cry, he realized, bitterly recalling the commander's dictum: *Get them laughing. Get them crying. Get them talking.* It stood to reason, then, that he was well on his way to making her *talk.* He acknowledged now, however, that he hadn't told her of his mother's death with that intent. In fact, in retrospect, he wished he hadn't bared his soul to her quite so completely. But she simply had that effect upon him, he concluded. Something about her brought out the very essence of him, and studying Caroline's luminous, young face, he was convinced that her abilities to do such things couldn't possibly have come from an evil source. She was simply too tender, too compassionate a woman to be the sorceress John thought her.

"I'm making a fool of myself," he declared after a moment, his face coloring a bit.

"Heavens, no! On the contrary, Nathaniel. I've never respected you more than I do now, having been permitted to see this gentle, vulnerable side of you. You mustn't go about hiding it, you know," she added, giving his hand a squeeze. "It's every bit as much you as the stricter side. And the world deserves to see it now and then."

"You're quite an advocate of that, aren't you? Showing all of one's self?"

"But of course. What else can one do? Your horse here . . . what is her name?"

"Matilda."

"*Oui,* Matilda. She has both sides, *n'est-ce pas?* The side that knows to be gentle with children and to simply stand and look adoringly up at you as you pet her. Yet there is also the side that would run for you on a fox hunt until she dropped of exhaustion, the side that is the serious worker. Isn't that so?"

"Well, of course."

"So, you're not so very different from her. You would do well, my friend, to let your gentler side show, too—and not just when you're with her."

He donned a thoughtful smile and lifted her hand up to his lips to kiss it. "I spoke too soon with you, I'm afraid. It's not just your trunks you should keep locked, Caroline, but yourself as well. You're the finest treasure to sail into Boston Harbor in ages, and I would hate to find any other man has discovered this as I have. . . . Speaking of which," he added with a teasing snarl, "how was your evening with McCrae?"

After indulging in a cagey laugh, she slowly withdrew her hand from his. "Very nice. Thank you."

"He didn't manage to get you off alone, did he?"

She bit her lip and laughed again, under her breath. "Oh, Nathaniel, what does it matter? I'm here with *you* now."

He suddenly looked very sullen. "But it matters to me. It matters very much," he declared, and Caroline could tell that he was fighting the urge to mutter an expletive or two in her presence.

She put her hands on her hips, and her expression became challenging. "And who are you? My brother? My father? My uncle? Who are you to be asking me such a question?"

He was clearly taken aback by her outburst. "Well . . . I simply thought that . . . after last Saturday . . . we had a bit of an understanding between us."

"Huh! What sort of understanding? It's not as though you proposed marriage to me, you know. The only thing I heard you propose was my joining the rebel forces, and that hardly requires my taking a vow of celibacy!"

"Shhh! Do keep your voice down," he cautioned. "My stableboys are never far away."

She fell silent, but she continued to glare at him.

"I'm sorry," he said after a moment. "It's just that, with McCrae being our key competitor in business, I can't seem to help wanting to compete with him in this realm, too."

"Well, you must stop it when you're with me, because it's not at all warranted. I give you my word that nothing happened between us. In fact," she added with a bit of a blush, "not even one of my dances with him came close to comparing to the one I had with you at my uncle's."

Nathaniel looked quite pleased with this news. "And his kisses?" he prompted once more.

Caroline scowled at him. "You're fishing again, and I've told you how rude I find it. He—" Her words broke off, for in that instant, to her amazement, he took her in his arms and kissed her—this time with no restraint.

She had to reach out and steady herself against the door of the mare's stall when he finally released her. She had thought he was going to ravish her right then and there, and what was even more surprising to her was that she realized she probably would have allowed him to do so! *"Mon Dieu,"* she gasped, looking at him as though he had taken leave of his senses. "What was that about?"

"Just to refresh your memory, my dear. So you could more fairly compare my kisses to McCrae's."

"But he didn't kiss me."

"He didn't?" Nathaniel asked incredulously.

Caroline reached up and straightened her bonnet with trembling fingers, hoping she'd soon gather her wits. "No," she answered simply. "And I was just about to tell you so when you . . . you grabbed me just now."

Nathaniel was clearly relieved.

"Really," she continued scoldingly, reaching up and fanning herself with one of her riding gloves in the hope of cooling down the surge of unspeakable feelings his kiss had caused to erupt in her. "You're going to get yourself into trouble one day going about and doing that to women!"

He smirked. "Why? I find that most of them like it."

"I dare say they like it too well, and that's what I mean about trouble, *mon ami*. It's sure to catch up with you, sooner or later."

His smirk broadened into a knowing smile, and he again wrapped an arm about her tiny waist. "And what about you, Caroline? Do you like it 'too well'? . . . I told you last Saturday, if you came back here, it would be entirely at your own risk," he added in a provocative whisper.

She pivoted out of his grasp and began fanning herself once more. "I came here for an afternoon ride and to discuss the rebel cause with you. I promised nothing more."

"Very well," he replied with a resigned, almost chilly edge to his voice. "Let's ride, then. And, while we do, you can tell me the truth about McCrae."

She furrowed her brow. "But I *have* told you the truth. He simply danced with me. Nothing more."

"No. That's not what I mean," Nathaniel retorted, moving down to the next stall and stepping inside to

234

lead out the already-saddled stallion that stood within. "I mean, now that we've established that you and I are on the same side in this war, I see no harm in your telling me that McCrae is among us as well. It's fairly apparent to me, after all, that he is one of your rebel contacts here in Boston." With that, he handed her the stallion's reins and walked back to begin saddling his mare.

"Where on earth did you get that idea?"

"Am I wrong?"

"Yes. Of course you're wrong. In fact, I've never even mentioned the war to Mr. McCrae, nor he to me."

"Really?"

"Really. And, even if we had discussed it, I wouldn't tell you where he stands, no more than I'd tell him where you do."

An admirable policy, Nathaniel thought. At least it helped to confirm for him that she was trustworthy. "Then why spend time with him?"

"Well, if you must know, it is for the same reason I'm spending time with you, because it is best for my family's business."

Though Nathaniel donned a wounded expression, she could tell it was mainly for effect. "Oh? And that's all I am to you, a business associate? Please, Caroline. I really did think we made more progress than that last Saturday night."

"Of course we did," she conceded. "But it wasn't my intention, you see."

"Oh, I see," he said sarcastically.

"So what are your intentions?" she countered, with obvious annoyance. "We seem to keep speaking of mine, and I think it's time we discussed yours. And

235

don't answer me with more talk of the rebel cause. I want to know about your *personal* intentions toward me."

A smile tugged at the corners of his mouth. "Oh, that's simple, my dear. I intend to go riding with you, then take you directly up to my suite and make passionate, heartfelt love to you . . . until such time as you absolutely must be returned to your uncle's."

She felt her face flush at this, and she directed her gaze downward.

"You did want me to tell the truth, didn't you?"

After several seconds, she nodded.

"Well, then, I suggest you take your leave now, Caroline, if you didn't like my answer. This seems to be your last chance."

At this she dropped the stallion's reins and walked back to the stable doorway. Then, knowing perfectly well that she really didn't wish to leave, she froze on the threshold and again stared downward. She wasn't sure what came over her when she was with him, but, whatever it was, she was finally realizing that she had absolutely no desire to go on fighting it. For the past six days, she had thought of little else but letting him make love to her, and her evening with McCrae had, to her surprise, only served to make such thoughts more intense. McCrae had, of course, been everything she'd expected him to be: polite, pleasant, a total gentleman. But, strangely, she had found that wasn't enough for her anymore. She'd had her fill of prim and proper suitors, and she yearned now for an enticing, unpredictable sort, like Nathaniel. In fact, she craved his provocative touch so much there seemed no point in continuing to pretend that she didn't. He'd clearly sensed what she felt about him, even the week before, so it seemed ridiculous to go on denying it. After all, she reasoned, if she had to lose her virtue to someone someday, why not to him, now? Why not to one of the wealthiest shipbuilders in the Colonies, a man who knew all too well what it was to inherit responsibilities like those that awaited her? A man who excited her more than any other she'd met. And he, perhaps better than anyone she had ever known or ever would, understood her, sensed the frightened, inexperienced core of her. Furthermore, given his standing in Bostonian society, he would surely make an honorable woman of her, should their intimacy lead to any unseemly complications.

"May I assume that's a yes, my dear?" he asked after a moment, as she continued to stand in the doorway.

A tingle ran through her, and she found herself nodding again. "But let's go to your suite now, Nathaniel," she replied timorously, finally finding the nerve to turn back and face him. "Anticipating it will make me far too nervous to even attempt to stay upon your stallion."

Apparently seeing the apprehension in her eyes, he quickly left his mare's stall, hitched the stallion to a nearby rail, and crossed to her. "Nervous?" he asked, wrapping an arm about her waist and ushering her outside. "Why?"

"Oh, come now," she said in an embarrassed undertone, again directing her gaze downward as they walked. "The reason must be obvious to a man as experienced as you."

"Well, whatever the reason," he said in a consoling whisper, as they continued to walk, "you needn't give it another thought. In spite of what I may have said to you before, I do strive to be, above all else, a gentleman."

"Oui," she answered with a wavering smile. "I guess I've sensed all along that you're not a man who would let me come to any harm."

"Heavens, no," he replied with a nonchalant laugh. Even as he said it, he felt a pang of conscience, but he did his best not to let it show.

Chapter 15

Caroline entertained the idea of asking Nathaniel to carry her back to the great house, but she somehow managed the trip on her own two legs. He couldn't have known, he couldn't possibly have realized the effect he had upon her at such times, how her legs seemed to melt out from under her like pats of butter. Knowing, even just imagining what awaited her up in his suite, was almost enough to make her keel over. She wished desperately for the company of one of her New Orleanian friends, a young woman a bit more experienced with men, someone who could answer all of her silly, fearful questions. But, of course, Nathaniel was her only companion now, and it wasn't likely that he'd be much comfort to her. He was the cause of her trepidation, after all, and he seemed so relaxed at this point, so nonchalant about what they were about to do, that she just knew, even if she tried to express her feelings, he wouldn't understand.

They were greeted at the back door by the steward as they returned to the estate, and Nathaniel addressed him with a steadiness of voice that Caroline found amazing.

"Miss Brenton and I wish to talk privately upstairs, Albert. Please see to it that we are not disturbed."

It was as simple as that, Caroline thought. Of a man, no questions were asked in such situations. It would not be so simple were Caroline escorting a male up to her suite. Such were the inequities that came with being a woman. But, in truth, she couldn't think of anything she'd rather have been at this point, because, clearly, nothing but a female could command Nathaniel's attention in quite the way she hoped to in the coming hour.

"What about John?" she asked guardedly, as they proceeded down the corridor and up the main staircase minutes later.

"Let him find his own woman," Nathaniel whispered laughingly, his arm still wrapped about her waist as they climbed the steps.

In spite of her nervousness, Caroline couldn't help laughing as well. "No. I mean where is he? Won't he see us coming up?"

"He's down at the shipyards again, my dear. And I don't expect him home for hours, so you needn't worry about that. I've told you, you needn't worry about anything, love," he added with a reassuring smile.

Caroline wasn't sure why, but she did take a great deal of comfort in his smile. It told her that perhaps he really did understand. Though it had doubtless been ages since he'd been an innocent, there was no denying that he did seem somewhat aware now of what she was feeling.

Once they got to the top of the stairs, he led her,

wordlessly, to the left and down the second-floor corridor to the very last door on the right. When they reached it, he stepped inside and held the door open for her.

She entered hesitantly and watched as he crossed to the bedchamber's window and closed the Venetian blinds, darkening the room considerably.

"Do shut the door, please," he called across to her, as he turned back to face her an instant later. "I think you'll find you want it shut, when all is said and done," he added in a provocative tone.

She slowly obliged. Then she turned to him, but she knew her expression was nowhere near as relaxed as his. "I think I have a confession to make," she said sheepishly.

He smiled. "And what's that?"

"Well, only that I . . . I lied to you the night we met."

"About what?"

"Well, I told you I didn't like dark-haired men, but I'm afraid that simply isn't true."

"It's not?" he asked, cocking his head teasingly.

"Heavens, no. You see, I only said it because I . . . I was frightened of you, and I wanted you to take offense and go away and let me be."

"Oh, I see," he said, nodding and doing his best to look as though he were taking all of this as seriously as she seemed to be. "Well," he began giving forth a sigh of relief, "do you feel better now, my dear, having unburdened your mind of that?"

"No," she confessed with an awkward laugh.

He laughed as well.

"Perhaps . . . perhaps we should go back downstairs and have something to drink first," she suggested in a wavering voice.

"As in liquor, you mean?"

She nodded.

"No need for that," he declared, crossing to the decanter that rested on a nearby console. "If you'll consent to drinking brandy, we've everything we need right here."

"Ah . . . *bon*," Caroline stammered, reaching up to untie her bonnet with fingers that were, once again, trembling. *"Je regrette,* Nathaniel, that you'll have to put up with French for a while, I'm afraid. I always speak it when I'm nervous."

He laughed softly and then turned to pour her a brandy. "But you haven't a thing in the world to be nervous about. On the contrary, Caroline," he declared seconds later, walking over to hand her a now-filled snifter. "I would like to think that you're in for one of the most pleasurable experiences of your life."

She donned a quivering smile and reached out to receive the snifter. To her surprise, however, he didn't let go of it once it was in her hand. Rather, he seized the opportunity to wrap his large fingers about hers and to stroke her hand with amazing adroitness.

"I . . . I've never done this before," she admitted, easing her hand out of his and taking a long swallow of the liquor.

He raised one eyebrow. "Really?"

"Oh, *s'il vous plaît,* don't mock me right now," she beseeched, turning about to set her bonnet down on an adjacent wing chair. "I feel like enough of a child as it is."

"Oh, believe me, love, you're anything *but* a child. Little girls never have this effect upon me."

242

"What effect?"

There was an enticing twinkle in his eye. "Well, why don't you come to bed with me, and I'll show you."

"I think I'd better sit down first," she declared, reflexively backing up to a chair and reaching up to remove her bonnet before she sank down upon the cushioned seat. She noted in that instant that it was a very high-seated chair. So, fortunately, she didn't have far to sink.

He was clearly fighting a laugh, as he drew up to her once more and squatted down to look her in the eye. "Better now?"

"Oui. Oh, oui. I've been needing a chair for quite some time, you see."

"You know, Caroline," he began again, his eyes focusing disarmingly upon hers as he reached out and took her free hand in his, "if two of the wealthiest business people in Boston can't succeed at something as elementary as making love, I don't hold out much hope for our generation."

She exhaled a long, tense breath. "No. I suppose not."

"Don't you think we've tortured each other long enough with all of this?" he continued, easing his hand out of hers now and slipping his fingers under the hem of her riding skirt.

She took another swallow of brandy as she felt him removing her shoes, and nodded again. *"Oui.* But I must warn you that I'm not sure I'll be much good at it."

"So, I'll teach you," he said softly, smiling up at her.

Then he began taking off her hose. "I'm honored, in fact, to be the one you're allowing to teach you."

243

"Yes, well . . . so am I. I mean," she added with an anxious laugh, "I'm glad that it's you."

He took the glass from her hand and placed it on the floor beside the chair. "I know what you meant." Then, still keeping his eyes fixed upon hers, he glided up and began kissing her neck, eliciting the same telling groan from her that he had when he'd kissed her the week before.

"Do you trust my ships, Caroline?" he asked in a heated whisper, near her ear.

"What?" she asked dreamily.

"When you sail up here from New Orleans, do you trust the ship I've sold you? Do you trust that it will take you safely where you wish to go?"

"Well, yes . . . *bien sûr,*" she replied, not at all sure where this line of questioning was leading.

"Then try, if you will, to put that same trust in me now. All right?" he asked, taking her bonnet from her lap and setting it on the floor beside him.

"All right," she murmured, looking on silently, as he carelessly removed his riding coat and let it drop to the floor. Then he slowly undid the bottom buttons of his vest, and he raised his right foot and let it come to rest beside her, on the seat of her chair. He then leaned toward her, an astounding bulge apparent in the center of his breeches.

"Shut your eyes," he said softly, reaching down to her with remarkable gentleness and taking hold of one of her hands. "It's all right," he assured once more in a murmur, when she hesitated to respond.

She again found comfort in his smile, and she shut her eyes an instant later, as he'd requested. Then, to her dismay, she felt him draw her hand up toward him and press it to that frightening point in his breeches.

At first, she gasped and tried to pull her hand away, but he held tightly to her wrist and kept her palm where he had placed it.

"*Feel,* Caroline," she heard him urge in a fervent whisper. "If you really wish to know all sides of me, then I must ask that you be open as well, and admit that this is what you've wanted from the night we met, what you've been hungry for. I've known enough women to have recognized it when I saw it in your eyes. It's a *hunger,* isn't it?" he continued, and, to Caroline's surprise, he was no longer pressing her hand to him. In fact, she could feel him drawing even closer to her. His hot breath was upon her neck as he leaned over her.

She, in turn, continued to keep her palm where he'd placed it. Perhaps, she thought, in an effort to keep him a safe distance from her. In the seconds that followed, however, she realized that she wasn't accomplishing that end at all. Rather, he was closer to her than he'd ever been before. His hands were sliding up her legs now, elevating her a bit and pushing her riding skirt up to a shamefully high level. Then he started touching her in much the same location she was touching him.

"Nathaniel!" she exclaimed, letting her eyes fall open once more.

"Shhh. Just listen. Trust me," he said assuasively. "Shut your eyes and *feel* . . . feel, Caroline, how very hungry you are for it. There's no need to go on being shy. Why don't you just let it satisfy you?"

She bit her lip and closed her eyes again, as she felt him easing her thighs apart and pressing his large downturned fingers to the unspeakable place that lay just beyond. Instead of trying to stop him now, however, she found herself sinking back in the chair with an acquiescent moan, inadvertently exposing more of this intimate region to him as her back inched downward.

He was absolutely right, she acknowledged, groaning again. She was hungry there. She felt positively insatiable as his fingers began to fondle her. And, all the while, he was kissing her neck and whispering the most shocking things in her ear, telling her he wouldn't let his fingers enter her now, not when he knew what she *really* wanted inside her.

He was teasing her, she realized, as her chest began to heave with all of the desire she'd suppressed throughout the years. This was some kind of erotic game meant to stimulate her all the more.

"Because, when this is done, I want you to know, to remember, that it wasn't just me doing this to you, but that you wanted it as well, my love. Tell me you want it, too," he urged, rubbing his free hand over her breasts, as they continued to rise and fall with her excitement. *"Tell me,"* he ordered again, his voice even more imperative.

"Oui. Yes," she declared in a whisper, throwing her head back and continuing to keep her eyes squeezed shut. She couldn't look at him now, she realized. Seeing his dark, penetrating eyes at a time like this would only cause her to lose what little self-control she had left.

"Here?" he asked. "Do you want it here and now? Or shall we wait and go over to the bed?"

"Here," she heard herself answer in a hushed, impassioned tone. "Oh, *mon Dieu,* Nathaniel, stop tormenting me and do it!"

"All right, *mon amour,*" he agreed, and she felt him take hold of her hips in those seconds and, with surprising strength, pull her farther downward in the chair.

She wouldn't watch, she told herself. She couldn't imagine how he was going to slip something as large as what she'd felt inside of her, and she thought it wiser not to look on as he did so. All she knew was that she wanted it. Even though she'd been told by some of her more experienced women friends that it was rather painful at first, she definitely wanted it. And, seconds later, after he'd draped each of her legs over an arm of the wing chair and, apparently, taken down his breeches, she began to feel her wish coming true.

His fingers opened her first with an expertness that made her realize just how many women he'd had in this way, how familiar he was with the female anatomy. Then she actually felt him beginning to ease his way into her, and she was aware that this wet, welcoming part of her was closing around him as he did so. At this, she gave forth an involuntary moan that, she realized seconds later, was probably far too loud to have escaped the notice of anyone passing in the hallway.

He had his hands under her now, holding her skirts up and helping her to stay arched toward him, and all she could seem to do in response was to keep whispering his name, along with various French expletives.

"Just a little deeper, my love," she heard him whisper, "and you'll have all of me."

She drew in a timorous breath. She had thought that this was all there was to it, but she realized now how much farther he needed to take it, and she couldn't help

247

opening her eyes again and staring apprehensively up at him.

"It will be all right," he promised, bending down to kiss her once more. "It will only hurt for a minute or two, and then you'll feel pleasure again."

She got a better grip upon the arms of the chair and, shutting her eyes once more, gave him a nod of consent. Her fingers dug into the upholstery an instant later, as he finally pushed all the way into her with what seemed compassionate swiftness.

"There," he said in an ardent tone, as though he, too, were experiencing some kind of ache. "There now, my dearest Caroline. The worst is over, the rest sheer heaven."

He was glad to see that her grip upon the chair's arms was loosening as he watched her emit a sigh, obviously of relief. He stayed still within her for a little longer, fighting his own urges in his effort to let her relax a bit more before he went on with it. Then, slowly, tenderly, he began moving in and out of her, his hands continuing to cradle her and prop her upward.

"How's that?" he murmured, again bending over her and kissing her neck.

She let out a rapturous sound.

"Excellent," he replied in a hushed, smoldering voice. But, much as he prided himself on being in control at times like these, he knew he didn't really feel that way now. In truth, he'd never felt anything quite as exquisite as being inside this Cajun heiress, and he knew in his heart he probably never would again.

She was using the same irresistible perfume she had on the night they'd met, the night she hadn't even permitted him to kiss her, and now, he acknowledged with a shiver of pride, he was doing a great deal more than that. He was holding her soft warm body to his. He was surging in and out of her like ocean waves hitting the shore, and he couldn't remember ever experiencing anything quite as wonderful.

He was amazed at how quickly she was taking to it—the French minx in her—wrapping herself around him, serenading him with the soft melody of her fervid sighs and moans as he continued his thrusts. He could even feel her hips beginning to move, starting to undulate ever so slightly in his cradling grasp, as she tossed her head, mussing her tower of upswept hair into a heedless disarray.

Oh, yes! She was the sort of woman who could wrap herself about a man's heart and never let go, and he hated himself for not having fully realized this until now, when it was too late, when he was pushing the entire length and breadth of himself so deeply into her. It wasn't she who was losing her virginity to him, but he who was losing *himself* to her, losing himself to this Cajun treasure, this forbidden fruit that would surely cause him considerable economic harm if her father or her uncle ever learned of the liberties he was taking with her.

Then, to his surprise, these thoughts seemed to get the better of him, and he—a man who had always been able to bring his sexual partners to several climaxes before he reached his own—began to feel himself on the verge of culminating the act. In spite of his efforts to be gentle with her, he found the front legs of the chair starting to leave the floor with his continued rocking movement, and he saw Caroline's eyes open again in alarm. He realized, however, that he could no longer comfort her. All of his attention was hopelessly locked upon what he was feeling in his loins, upon the ecstatic sensation that was continuing to make him move in and out of her, so impetuously now.

He heard her cry out once or twice. Then, he threw his head back and let out a long enraptured groan of his own. Seconds later, he slumped down upon her, feverishly kissing her and hugging her to him, and, to his delight, he realized that she was kissing him back, that she seemed as overcome with passion as he.

"Let's . . . let's get these clothes off, love, and get into bed. What do you say?" he asked breathlessly.

"Yes . . . yes," she whispered back with a light laugh, her voice reflecting obvious enthusiasm.

Minutes later, they lay naked together beneath the linens on his bed.

"That was wonderful," she praised, as he held her close at his side. "Even better than I thought it would be."

"Yes," he agreed, gazing admiringly over at her lovely profile. "But, regretfully, my dear, you're all that made it so. I must confess to being shamefully short-lived. I usually don't let that happen."

Her face was filled with childlike questioning as she turned to look into his eyes. "Should it have lasted longer?"

He nodded sheepishly and reached out to brush some wisps of blond hair from her eyes. "Indeed it should. But I lost control with you, I'm afraid."

"Why?"

"Because . . . because you just have that effect upon me, Caroline. I'm quite helpless when it comes to you, you see. But, if you'll stay here beside me a while longer, I promise to do better next time."

She smiled. "All right."

"Well, in spite of my brevity, there was a little something for good measure in it," he declared, chuckling.

"And what was that?"

"If you're smart enough to get up and leave now, you can still quite honestly tell your father that you've never been bedded."

"But I have, haven't I?"

"No," he answered with a soft laugh, drawing her more tightly to his side. "You've been *chaired.*"

She started to laugh as well. "What's the difference?"

"A bed's more comfortable," he replied. Then he raised a provocative brow at her. "As you're soon to learn. That is, if you still wish to stay."

"Oh, yes. I wish to stay. In fact, I've never felt as satisfied as I do now."

At this, he reached up and pressed a silencing finger to her lips. "Well, I'm very flattered, my dear, but I must warn you against seeming too enthusiastic about this sort of thing with men. They're apt to think you promiscuous, you know, and I wouldn't want anyone thinking that of you."

She scowled. "Oh. So men are permitted to enjoy this, but women are not?"

"Now, I didn't say that. I simply meant that you should be careful about letting it show."

She suddenly donned a coquettish smile. "Even with you?"

He laughed easily. "Oh, no. With me, you may let it show to your heart's content. In fact, I must confess that I'd be quite hurt if you didn't."

"Oh . . . I see," she replied with a knowing expression, "so it is just with *other* men that I shouldn't let it show."

He looked rather embarrassed by this deduction. "Something of the sort. Yes."

She rolled over onto her stomach and began running an index finger about the tiny forest of hairs on his chest. "You know, for a man who is rumored to have had so many women, you certainly seem possessive of me."

"Do I? I'm sorry. I don't mean to."

She looked unflinchingly down into his eyes. "Oh, yes you do. It's written on your face. I'm special to you somehow. But I haven't figured out yet in what way that might be. . . . I can tell you, though, that it's not altogether respectable, is it, Nathaniel? I mean, you value me, but not as a lover, really. More as one would value a precious gem or some such thing. Isn't that true?"

Maybe John was right, Nathaniel thought, doing his best to avoid her gaze in those seconds. He felt she was staring right through him, straight into his thoughts. "No," he declared, sportively clenching his teeth, and, in one fell swoop, he reached out and turned her on to her back and rolled on top of her. An instant later, he was straddling her, and he had her hands pinned up over her head upon the pillow. "No. That's not it at all, Caroline. I certainly *do* value you as a lover. I most *certainly* do," he added, bending down and kissing her with reckless abandon.

He concluded his kiss, and, to Caroline's surprise, his lips traveled down to give the same, vehement attention to her breasts. She, in turn, found herself becoming aroused all over again, wanting him to enter her once more, as he seemed to feed upon her as an infant would. This was the most shocking part of all to her. She truly had no idea that men did this sort of thing to women, this amazingly titillating act would surely have her blushing, should she try to recount it to any of her women friends. Yet he was actually doing it, his lips and tongue making the most ineffable noises against her flesh as he continued to keep her pinned to the mattress. The most astonishing part of all, however, was how reflexive he was about it, how uninhibited, as though it were the most natural thing in the world for a grown man to be doing.

Then, as if reading her mind, as if knowing what all of this was doing to the lower half of her, he slid his right hand down, under the bed linens and again began stroking that aroused region between her legs—this time not hesitating to slip a finger or two into her. His fingertips instantly found the very point that was throbbing most within her, and they began rubbing it with compelling vigor, causing a sensation that teetered between pleasure and pain, one she simply could not ignore.

Her legs stiffened, and, again, she found herself arching up toward him and groaning. How did he know, she wondered, precisely where and how to touch her? He's like a wolf, she thought, in those fevered, irrational seconds, coming in for the kill, knowing exactly where to bite its prey and how to get it to drop in its tracks with a minimun of effort and struggle. And, once again, all she could seem to do was writhe and moan beneath him.

Then, just as her body seemed on the verge of a

climax, she felt him withdraw his fingers and replace them with that hard, swollen part of him that had pleased her so earlier.

As his naked body glided up and down over hers in the minutes that followed, something seemed to explode within her, and she felt the depths of her suddenly opening and closing about him in spasms of ecstasy.

"Sacrébleu," she gasped. "What on earth was that?"

He stopped moving and smiled down at her. "What I hoped for. A chance to show you what I felt earlier, when things ended in such a chair-rattling manner. I'm so glad I could return the favor, Caroline," he added, bending down to kiss her neck with a reverent air.

Her heartbeat was racing like a cornered rabbit's, and such a shiver ran through her she knew the only thing that would warm her sufficiently was the heat of his body as it continued to glide over hers.

She was finally beginning to understand what it was to make love, to feel joined with a man, possessed by him, one with him, and, to her surprise, her eyes began to tear up with emotion.

"Am I hurting you?" he whispered, as he again gazed down into her face.

"No. *Pas du tout* . . . It's just that it's very nice, isn't it? This 'making love,' as you call it in English."

He smiled. "Yes, Caroline. Especially with one as lovely as you." With that, he reached over to blot her eyes with the edge of the pillowcase, and it was then that he noticed a red smudge on the linen, the blood on his fingers.

He froze, and Caroline noticed that his expression became a concerned one as he continued to stare down at her.

"You're bleeding, love, probably from the first time I entered you. Are you uncomfortable? Do you want me to stop?"

She was silent for several seconds. "Why would I be bleeding? This isn't the time for it," she added in a worried whisper.

"It happens the first time with a man, I'm afraid. It's quite natural though, I assure you."

"Well, then, don't stop," she murmured, not wanting him to uncouple with her and thereby take away the wonderful sheltering warmth of his body. She hadn't realized, until they'd made love, just how lonely she had felt since she'd left Louisiana, how isolated and vulnerable in her mission for the rebels. Now, however, in the arms of a fellow patriot, that feeling was finally starting to melt away, and she knew she wouldn't have let go of him for the world. He wasn't just satisfying her carnal needs but the deeper ones—for companionship, for communion with a kindred spirit.

To her relief, he finally resumed their love act, but she could tell that he was still concerned about her and was slowing things down a bit in an effort to avoid hurting her any further.

"Je pense que je t'aime," she whispered, as he bent down to kiss her once more.

Again he froze and lay still within her, his face reflecting what almost appeared to be distress as he lifted his head and stared down at her. "What did you say?"

She donned a soft smile. "I said I think I love you, Nathaniel. Isn't that what men and women say when they're making love?"

"Well, yes . . . I guess so. But I really . . . wish you wouldn't."

"Why not? Doesn't it please you?"

"Yes . . . but I wish you wouldn't say it, in any case."

"Why not? Are you afraid that it will obligate you to say the same to me? Believe me, *mon amour,* it won't."

"No. That's not it," he answered, his eyes again focusing upon the blood-stained pillowcase. It's because I don't want to be responsible for shedding any more of your blood, my dear, sweet, Caroline, he thought in that instant, a nauseating chill running through him. He knew, however, even as he had the thought, that he had no hope of explaining it to her. The very most he could expect was that their relationship would simply end with her thinking him a heartless ladies' man. Perhaps, with some luck, he might be able to rescue her before the commander's men closed in on her and her rebel contacts. He would have all the necessary information to do it—the date, the time, the place, all of the details he intended to pass on to Smythe—so it stood to reason that he might be able to do both, inform on her for the sake of the British cause and, at the same time, succeed in seeing that Caroline was spared. Yes, he decided, that seemed an outcome his conscience would abide.

"What's the matter, then? Why does it bother you so?" he suddenly heard Caroline asking.

He shook his head and narrowed his eyes, searching his mind for something to tell her. "Because we hardly know one another," he answered after several seconds. "I . . . I just don't want you to speak too soon, is all. You really must stop being so sweet and innocent. You'll be the end of me, my dear." Then, as if to punctuate these words, he could feel himself beginning to climax again within her, and, in another impassioned frenzy, his body began washing over hers.

A couple minutes later, they both lay still once more, breathless and exhausted.

"You keep doing that to me for some reason," he observed with a laugh, "and, for the love of God, I can't figure out why."

"Doing what?"

"Making me lose all control at times when I'm accustomed to being very much in command."

"I'm sorry."

He laughed again and eased himself off her. Then he lay on his right side and rested his head in the palm of his propped-up right hand. "No. Don't be. It's I who should apologize, Caroline. All I can tell you is that I will try to do better next time. That is, if you wish there to be a next time."

"I've told you, I think I love you. Is that not answer enough?"

"Yes, I suppose it is," he conceded, having heard a hint of annoyance in her voice and deciding it was best to try to smooth things over and then quickly change the subject. "Do you always wear this?" he asked, reaching out and running his fingers over the tiny gold cross that hung from a delicate chain about her neck.

"*Oui.*"

"Are you a Puritan then, like your father?"

She shook her head. "No. Catholic, like my *maman.*"

"Then these healing powers of yours, they come from God?"

"*Oui.* Of course. I've already told you that, haven't I?"

"Have you?"

"Yes. Remember? In your study last week, I told you about the Holy Ghost."

"Ah, yes. But I must confess, my dear, I wasn't sure that you were serious."

"Of course I was," she said scoldingly. "That is hardly something I would say in jest."

"Oh, no. I'm certain of that now . . . now that I've come to know you better. But I just can't help wondering, can these powers be used to work evil as well as good?"

"Evil?" she asked, as though this idea had never even crossed her mind. "Heavens, no. Well, I mean, I suppose one *could* use them to harm others as well as to help them, but I would never dream of doing so," she added firmly.

"No. Of course not," he replied with a chary smile, desperately hoping that she wouldn't sense how relieved he was to hear this. "Of course not. It hadn't even occurred to me that you would." But, in truth, it *had* occurred to him. More than once in the past week, he had told himself that when she finally realized it was he who was behind her eventual undoing, she might become like the very winds of a hurricane unleashed against him. He, of course, had had the fury of a female or two directed at him in his day. He assumed that no self-respecting playboy escaped that sort of thing. But the women who had raged at him thus far had been mere mortals, he reminded himself, capable only of doing him a fairly limited amount of harm. Caroline, on the other hand, probably wouldn't know such limitations, and there was simply no telling what someone with her obvious powers could conjure up against him. He now felt that he needed all the assurances he could get from her, in order to continue finding the nerve to press on with his assignment for the commander.

Then, as if to shame him, his thoughts took him back to the few battles he'd seen the redcoats wage against the rebel forces, back to the images of the brave British troops he'd seen wounded and killed as the unprincipiled and cowardly rebels had fired upon them from their hiding places. And he again acknowledged just how safe and easy his work for the commander really was. He, therefore, forced himself to proceed with it.

"I've been wondering, my dear," he said, "if it's possible that we are, unwittingly, working for the same faction of rebels. What can you tell me about your contacts here?"

Caroline took several seconds to respond, and he silently prayed that she'd neither evade the question, nor get angry at him for asking it.

"I can't tell you much about them, I'm afraid, *mon amour,*" she said finally, in an apologetic tone, "for, you see, I was not given their names."

This took him aback, but he managed to formulate his next question with admirable speed. "Well, then, how will you deliver your cargo to them?"

She smiled. "They'll come to me. At the right time and place, they will make themselves known to me."

"And when and where is that?"

Caroline didn't answer. She remembered how adamant her father had been about her not disclosing this information, and she found that she couldn't bring herself to tell Nathaniel anything more. "Oh, what does it matter?" she asked. "Even if they are the people with whom you work, that shouldn't affect your request that

I contribute more to the cause."

She was right, of course, he realized. She was, after all, not a slow-witted woman. Far from it! In fact, he found himself feeling a little surprised now that he'd gotten even this much out of her.

"Well, I do hope they don't intend to come to you at your uncle's house," he declared in an admonishing tone. "After what you said the other night about not wishing to involve your aunt and uncle in all of this, I would think that that would be the worst possible plan."

"Oh, don't worry, Nathaniel. They won't come there. I'll go to them, when the time comes. But you are a dear to be so concerned about me," she added, bending over and giving him a soft, appreciative kiss on the forehead.

"Oh, it's more than just concern," he countered, pulling her even closer to him. "I've really come to care for you, Caroline, in the short time since we met. And I truly can't bear to think of anything happening to you."

"It's all right," she assured him. "I'll be meeting with them well away from town, so I'm fairly certain there won't be any witnesses. Please don't worry, *mon amour,*" she concluded, reaching up to stroke his dark hair.

"I'll go with you," he suddenly declared. "That's what I'll do, my dearest. I'll go with you when you rendezvous with them. That way I'll be certain you don't run into any trouble. Simply tell me when and where we are to meet them, and I'll accompany you there."

She wore a blank expression for several seconds. Then, to his relief, a slight smile tugged at the corner of her lips. "All right. If, when the time comes, I feel I need to have you accompany me, I will send for you. How is that?"

It wasn't really what he'd had in mind, but he realized it was probably the best he was going to achieve, so he nodded. "Very well. But don't forget, mind, or, I warn you, I shall be very annoyed." He said this last in a fatherly tone that he sensed she'd find comforting.

Her smile broadened. "I won't forget. You have my solemn vow," she replied, and her laugh struck Nathaniel as being strangely insouciant.

"And do give me a couple of days' notice, will you, my dear? It is sometimes difficult for me to get away from the yards."

When she laughed again, Nathaniel wasn't at all sure what she thought of these requests. "All right, *mon amour,* a couple of days' notice. But I must tell you, Nathaniel you're even worse than my mother with your fretting! I fancy it comes from being the oldest child in your family. Don't you?"

He laughed softly, relieved to hear that her amusement was only due to the fact that she thought he was being overly protective and not because she found his offer to accompany her too ridiculous to act upon. "Ah, yes. That must be the cause. You're about the same age as my sisters."

"And this is what will happen to me, when I, too, am made the head of my family? I will spend my days worrying about my brothers?"

"You might. You might at that. You know, Caroline, it occurs to me that this business of becoming head of one's family is not so very different from the freedom we are fighting for here in the Colonies. I honestly thought that, once my father died, I would feel as though a yoke had been taken from my shoulders, as though I were freer than I'd ever been before. But I soon learned that, along with that freedom, came awesome responsibility, which keeps one in a kind of yoke for the rest of one's days, I assure you."

She sobered at hearing this. "What are you saying? Are you afraid that the Colonies are not prepared for such freedom?"

That was, of course, precisely what he was saying. He hoped to plant some seeds of Tory thought in her mind so that, when the time came for him to cross her, she might be less enraged with him and might better understand why he was doing so. But he could tell from the dissenting expression she wore that it would be most unwise to answer her question affirmatively.

"No. Of course not. But you must admit that our ability to defend ourselves against foreign invaders, once Britain has withdrawn her support, will be dubious indeed."

"Why?" Caroline retorted with a shrug. "It seems to me the Colonies are doing so now, against the redcoat invasion. And quite commendably, too."

"Do you really think so?"

"Oh, yes. Perhaps *you* don't think so because of the crippling control England has exerted upon the Colonies up until now. From the time our great-grandparents came here, England has prohibited the Colonists' from producing weapons and even such things as plowshares. All of these goods must be shipped here from England, *n'est-ce pas?*"

Nathaniel nodded.

"Of course, because in that way the British have every advantage. If they control the number of guns you have, they can be more certain such weapons won't be turned against *them*. To say nothing of the fact that they also receive more of your money and goods in exchange than they would if they simply allowed you to produce your own guns. And as a result you poor Colonists sit about, thinking that you're fairly defenseless against invaders and you need England's protection when all you really need is freedom from her constraints."

He furrowed his brow as he continued to gaze at her.

"Well, don't you see?" she continued. "It is just as with masters and slaves and men and women. Believe me, my friend, I've seen enough slavery in Louisiana to know that the first thing the plantation owners do is disarm the blacks, take away any means they'd have of producing weapons and rising up en masse."

Nathaniel agreed, never having been a big proponent of slavery. "No one could argue that point with you, my dear. But what is that you said about men and women? Do you see men as masters as well?" he asked, an intrigued smirk on his face.

"Heavens, no! Not at all. But you men do, and that's what I meant. A woman, a slave, a Colonist is subjugated only as long as he or she chooses to be weak and *allows* it to happen. You Colonists have decided not to let it happen any longer, and your years of effort will surely be rewarded with victory in the end."

Nathaniel couldn't help sounding skeptical about this. "Why is that?"

"Because the British simply *cannot* win this war. For, in order to win, they must not only fight to take control of each of your towns, but they must also leave enough troops behind to occupy what they've won, and that is essentially hostile territory. Besides, everyone knows that Parliament will never vote to send enough troops here to accomplish that. Surely they'd have done so by now, if they intended to. So, you see, from that perspective, the war is already won by you Colonists." With that, she settled back on her pillow, with the complacent expression of a well-fed house cat, and Nathaniel found that he could do little more than stare blankly over at her.

"Dear God, your mind works like a steel trap," he said finally in an awestruck tone.

She laughed, as though flattered. "Do you think so?" she asked, crinkling her nose a bit and rolling back onto her side to study his expression.

"Absolutely, my dear," he confirmed.

"Oh, good! Because my father says I will need such quickness when I inherit the company. I consider this very high praise, Nathaniel, coming from a man such as yourself. *Merci.*"

"Oh, you're most welcome, Caroline," he replied, fighting the urge to direct an amazed laugh at her.

"Does it bother you? Having a mere woman speak to you at such length about politics?"

"Well . . . no," he stammered. "It was I who started speaking of it, my dear, so I can hardly complain if you found you wished to expound upon it. Besides," he added, a note of admiration in his voice, "I must again admit to finding your ideas quite novel."

Her laughter was dry, almost biting. "Oh, heavens. There's nothing novel in my telling you that the British are ruffians, is there?"

264

"Ruffians?"

"Yes. Of course. What is a ruffian, after all, if not one who imposes his will upon another with the threat of violence? Why, you Colonists are little more than England's slaves if you don't rebel. Taxed out of all ho by a ruffian ruler who won't even allow you to send men to represent you in Parliament! And what do that ruffian ruler's henchmen, redcoats, do but go about conducting themselves like packs of *little* ruffians. Raping your women and pillaging your homes. Well, if you ask me, it would be absolutely disgraceful if you *weren't* fighting this war!"

"Hmm," he said, striving to keep his face fairly unreadable as he nodded once more. "Well, you do seem to have matters all sorted out, don't you? An answer for everything. Right, Caroline?"

Her face colored a bit. "I'm boring you, I fear," she declared with an uneasy laugh. "I'm starting to preach again. My mother has warned me about it, but I do tend to slip into it now and then, nonetheless."

"No, no, my dear," he quickly assured her, regretting that he'd let his disapproval of her words show. "You're perfectly charming, as usual. I find your thoughts most enjoyable, in fact."

"But my body more so," she countered with a knowing smile.

"Yes. Well, such is a man's lot, I'm afraid."

"And you're a man who's not accustomed to taking a young lady to bed and ending up discussing the ethics of rebellion, *n'est-ce pas?*"

"I suppose that's true," he confessed.

"Then, perhaps, you should finally tell me, Nathaniel, what it is you want me to do for you and your rebel faction, so we can stop discussing the matter and begin acting upon it. You know I am most anxious to help in any way I can," she concluded, an enthusiastic twinkle in her eye.

Though he'd known all week that he would sooner or later again be faced with this question, he found himself with precious little to say. He'd simply planned on stalling her a bit longer on it, having her call upon him a time or two more before having to come up with some elaborate and risky ruse in which she could play a part. "Well, I—that is, my rebel contacts—would like to meet with you here one day soon to discuss it."

"Which day is that?" she asked evenly, leaning toward him and cradling her chin in her upraised palms.

"Um . . . Thursday afternoon . . . at two," he blurted out scouring his mind for something more to tell her. John would cooperate with the scheme, of course, but he again acknowledged that he'd have to scare up at least two very *trusted* friends to participate in the ruse as well.

"Thursday at two?" she repeated, her tone indicating she wanted more details.

"Yes. I'm planning a fox hunt. Will you come?"

She bit her lip and gave the request several seconds' thought. Then she reached out and playfully pressed a finger to the tip of his nose, punctuating each of her next words with a tap. "I'll come because I fancy you, *mon amour* . . . but not because I believe in hunting down poor, defenseless, little foxes," she added reproachfully. "You should be whipped for such cruelty, you men," she declared, shaking her head with obvious disgust.

"Ah, yes," he agreed, adopting some of her previous jocularity. "Whyever do you ladies put up with us?"

"Simple. You're a necessary evil."

He laughed, marveling at her cheekiness and poise. Less than an hour before, she'd been a frightened little virgin, and now she lay, completely at ease, in the buff with him, firing back the perfect retort to his every comment. Only her luminous, young face attested to the fact that she was just twenty-one. The wisdom and wit in her words would have made Nathaniel think she was at least ten years older, had he not known better. He had indeed met his match in her, and he was finally beginning to realize it.

"That's odd," he replied at last. "We men have been saying the same of you ladies for ages." Then, wishing to see her return to the ruffled maiden once more, he reached out and began tickling her, and they slipped into another round of love play.

At five o'clock, Nathaniel called for the steward and had him deliver a light supper for two to his suite. Then, at six, knowing that her aunt and uncle were sure to be expecting her, Caroline dressed and took her leave, with Nathaniel once again acting as her escort.

When Nathaniel returned to his estate a little while later, he felt strangely drained and slightly disconcerted. He knew it wasn't just their rounds of lovemaking that had left him this way, but also some of the things Caroline had said. Though he'd been resisting the notion, he was starting to think that it wasn't he who had succeeded in planting some seeds of his Tory thought in her, but she who had planted some rebel thought in him. He was, above all else, a pragmatist, and something within him was starting to

267

tell him that she might have had a point when she had said that there was a certain futility in the redcoats having to fight for the same ground over and over again. For that was precisely what they were destined to keep doing if Parliament didn't start sending them enough backups to fully occupy the towns they'd won in battle.

But then he caught himself, and a voice within him began scolding him, telling him that just because a cause looked futile at times, was no reason to give up on it. He still believed in King and country, after all, still held his oath of allegiance to them. And, even if Parliament was temporarily blinded to the debt it owed the Loyalists, the Loyalists had no call to become blinded to their obligations.

John had been right to chide him about getting too close to Caroline, he acknowledged, taking his riding coat off and tossing it onto the entrance hall settle as he passed through. Then he went down the corridor to the drawing room that led to the garden, and stood looking out over the rolling back grounds.

On their childhood hunts, his father had always warned him and John of getting too close to their prey. "Near enough to hit it, yes, but never near enough to start to care," the patriarch had admonished. It was just all too easy to begin caring . . . when one got close enough to see the cute little face of a fox, the frightened look in the eye of a deer. And that, unfortunately, was exactly what Nathaniel had done today. He had simply gotten too close to Caroline to continue doing his job well. He'd told John from the start that he was going to avoid doing so, that he was going to be "mercifully swift" with this assignment, and then, as always happened to him with beautiful women, he'd stopped thinking and begun *feeling*. He'd thought with his loins, rather than his brain. As a result, he'd gotten himself in a spot. Now he could only bring himself to inform on Caroline and her contacts if he was certain she would be spared, and he wasn't at all sure how that could be achieved.

The first thing to do, he concluded, recalling that Smythe had told him the commander intended to have Caroline's comings and goings watched while she was in Boston, was to send Rushton a message saying that he had obtained the requested information from Miss Brenton and would be sending on the specifics soon. This, at least, would help to assure that he and Caroline wouldn't be tailed when he accompanied her to her rendezvous with her contacts. Then, once the rendezvous was over, he would send word to Rushton that the weapons delivery had taken place earlier than planned and that Miss Brenton had escaped the scene before he could seize her, but that he had managed to apprehend her contacts.

Maybe Rushton would actually believe such a claim. And then again, maybe he wouldn't. Only time would tell. One thing was certain, however, Nathaniel would have to work with lightning speed at the rendezvous if he was going to succeed in getting Caroline safely out of Boston before the commander began an all-points search for her. Nathaniel had never known Rushton to be the sort of man who settled for any fewer than the number of heads he set out to bag, and there certainly wasn't any reason to believe he'd be more easygoing with his procedures this time.

Chapter 16

Sergeant Smythe sat on a log, putting his short leggings on for the Sunday morning roll call and again contemplating the problem that had been plaguing him for days, his mounting gambling debts. He knew it wasn't going to be long before his card-game cronies came to collect, and such a visit from them was sure to lead to his commander getting wind of his illicit activities. In which case, he would be expected to pay his debts, not only with his future wages but with his very hide. Rushton was never one to sentence a man to fewer than two-hundred lashes for this sort of offense, and such a sentence, delivered as it often was with a cat-o'-nine-tails, could prove fatal.

Naturally, Smythe didn't relish the idea of being whipped to death! In fact, he honestly believed that he would take his own life with his pistol, before he would submit to such punishment. But the fact of the matter was, at the relatively young age of twenty-five, he didn't relish the idea of having to kill himself either. Still, he knew that was what he would be forced to do if he didn't lay his hands on a great deal of money and damned quickly!

There was, of course, a slim chance that he and his grenadier company would be sent off to help defend a British fort in one of the southern Colonies. There had been some talk of that around the garrison of late. But no one was certain when such a command might be handed down and to whom, so Smythe knew he couldn't count on getting out of Boston before his creditors came after him.

He was, by no means, above stealing the required sum, if necessary. There were a number of wealthy Colonists to prey upon, after all, and, strange as it seemed, Smythe knew that the commander would probably be much more lenient with him were he caught stealing from some Whigs than over the matter of his gambling debts. This seemed odd on the surface, but it was commonly known among the redcoats that the British commanding officers usually ignored complaints that their men had stolen from or attacked American civilians. As frustrated by England's lack of support as their subordinates, officers like Rushton had simply decided to take advantage of the fact that such random acts of terrorism on the part of their men proved a fairly effective means of keeping the Colonists in line. Yes, Smythe decided, stealing was probably the course to follow, if he was to pay off his creditors before they came around to the garrison and made a fuss.

Having decided this, the sergeant rose and was bending down to go back inside his tent and get his grenadier's cap when he heard someone calling his name. He froze and looked out toward the east, to see a

271

man in civilian clothes running toward him, clutching what looked like a letter in his hand. Once the fellow was just a few yards away, Smythe could make out his features, and he saw that this was one of Nathaniel Hamlin's footmen. Having determined this, Smythe started walking toward the servant, a questioning expression on his face.

"Are you Sergeant Smythe?" the footman asked breathlessly, when they were finally face to face.

Smythe nodded.

"A message for you, sir. From Master Hamlin," the servant declared, handing him the sealed note he carried.

Smythe scowled. "Is he daft, sending you to a redcoat post? He's not supposed to do that! It's far too risky!"

The footman shrugged and continued trying to catch his breath. "I don't ask questions, sir," he answered with an uneasy smile. "I'm sure you understand."

"Yes," Smythe confirmed, taking the note from him. "But just be off with you now, man, before you're seen by the rebels! And tell your master not to do this again," he growled, as the servant turned and began heading away.

"Yes, sir. I shall, sir," the footman called back over his shoulder, as he dashed off.

Smythe was still scowling as he made his way back to his tent seconds later. The seal was definitely that of Nathaniel Hamlin, he noted. He had seen it many times before on the messages he'd conveyed from Hamlin to the commander, and he was now certain that this intrusion upon the post was a legitimate one and not some rebel trick. Nevertheless, there was simply no excuse for Hamlin having endangered himself and his footman in this way, and Smythe made a mental note to remember to tell the commander about this indiscretion when he delivered the message to him.

That having been decided, Smythe snapped the wax seal in half, opened the note, and skimmed its contents. As he read, he suddenly stopped walking. Hamlin had already done it! Though he'd asked that Smythe not return for any news for a fortnight and only a week had passed since they'd last met, the note clearly stated that he'd already succeeded in extracting the rendezvous information from Mademoiselle Brenton. It went on to say that this message would be followed by another containing the specifics about the rendezvous: its date, place, and time.

Smythe smiled. This was good news, indeed, and Rushton was sure to be pleased. It was strange, though, that Hamlin hadn't simply waited another week for Smythe to return to him for the news, as planned. Strange, too, that he had felt compelled to jeopardize his work for the commander by having the message brought to the post. And stranger still, it seemed, that, if he already had the specifics, he hadn't just included them in this note but again planned on running the risk of sending one of his servants to the post.

All of this would have to be brought to the commander's attention, Smythe concluded, continuing to walk now. But then he was struck with a brainstorm, and he stopped in his tracks once more. What was to become of the *mademoiselle* if the commander sent men to her rendezvous point to seize her? She would be hung most likely. That was what had happened to the last few Whig smugglers the redcoats had intercepted. They had been unlawfully hung, treated as though they were simply the victims of the terrorism the British troops had been routinely employing against the Colonists. Yes, Smythe concluded, Miss Brenton and her contacts would be "made an example of." They'd be executed, and their bodies would be left hanging in the trees for all Whig passersby to see.

Ordinarily, Smythe wouldn't have thought a thing more about that situation. He had, however, come to know quite a bit about this particular quarry of Nathaniel Hamlin's. He knew that Miss Brenton's family was worth a fortune, and he figured that, because Caroline was the heir apparent of the clan, her uncle would probably be willing to pay quite a pretty penny to get her back from the redcoats alive.

This being the case, things were starting to look brighter for Smythe regarding his gambling debts. Since Hamlin had already procured the necessary information from the Brenton woman, her contacts could be rounded up and hung, with or without her being present at the rendezvous. Why, Smythe reasoned, should he let such a valuable young lady simply end up hanging from a tree, when she could fill a useful role as a captive held for ransom? He knew a little bit about her comings and goings. He knew where her uncle lived. And, since this mademoiselle had already met him at Hamlin's, she wasn't likely to see any reason to refuse him if he paid her a call and asked to speak to her alone for a moment or two. Then, once he'd knocked her out and had her securely bound and gagged, he could haul her off to some secluded point outside of town—some place not too far from his garrison—and he could hide her there, until her family responded to his ransom note.

Yes! That was a capital plan, he decided, smiling again. With any luck, he might even be able to talk one or two of his fellow grenadiers into assisting him with it. Surely the Brenton clan was sufficiently wealthy to provide him with enough money to be split three ways.

The only problem with the scheme might be with the Brenton woman herself, Smythe suddenly thought. After what she'd done to his hand in Hamlin's study, it was clear that she was a witch, and God only knew what else she was capable of doing if provoked by the abduction. But Smythe knew that was simply a risk he'd have to run. Perhaps, if he took the time to explain to this *mademoiselle* that her rendezvous with the rebels was going to be thwarted by the redcoats and that he had, in effect, saved her life by kidnapping her, her wrath could be quelled. He would simply have to hope so, because given his circumstances, her wrath did seem the least dreadful of the adversities that could befall him.

All in all, though, abducting her seemed a pretty good way out of his predicament, he silently concluded, as he finally reached his tent. If he acted quickly enough, he might actually be able to extract the money from the Brenton family before his creditors came poking around the post. He might even go to them and offer them more than what he owed, just to keep them at bay for a few days longer.

In accordance with Nathaniel's request, Caroline arrived at the Hamlin estate at two o'clock the following Thursday afternoon. As she stood at the front door, waiting for a servant to respond to her knock, she couldn't help hoping that Nathaniel's other guests had not yet arrived and that he and she could have some time together for an embrace or two. It seemed their lovemaking a few days before hadn't so much curbed her yearning for him as it had increased it. Indeed she'd thought of little else in the past week but finally being allowed to lie with him again. However, as the steward of the estate opened the front door to her seconds later, she could tell from his distraught expression that this was not going to be the sort of day that would allow for such intimacy.

"Miss Brenton. Come in. Come in," the steward said hurriedly. "I'll take you to Master Hamlin. He is expecting you, of course . . . but we've some trouble here, I'm afraid."

"What sort of trouble?" Caroline inquired, following the servant down the corridor that led to the back grounds. As enamored as she now knew she was of Nathaniel, her mind was already racing with gut-wrenching possibilities. Perhaps the British authorities had learned of his work for the rebels and had decided to arrest him or his brother. Maybe he'd been hurt somehow, perhaps while out riding. She just couldn't imagine what it could be, but the servant's pale face had told her that, whatever it was, it was very serious. "Nathaniel is all right, isn't he?" she asked in a wavering voice.

"Yes, thank heavens," the steward replied, not turning back to face her as they continued their hurried walk through the house. "But his most prized horse, Matilda, is not. Perhaps he showed her to you when you were last here."

"Yes. What's happened to her?"

"Well, the stableboys say a pack of drunken redcoats stole her and ran her until she dropped, poor beast! The equerry found her just half an hour ago, in a clearing a few miles away. She was brought back to the stable in a wagon, and the veterinary is down there now with Master Hamlin, tending to her. But the word is, he doesn't hold much hope for her, poor old thing. It's just far too warm a day for her to survive such a running," he concluded, shaking his head.

Caroline grimaced at this and quickened her pace as they went out into the garden. *"Mon Dieu!* He'll be heartbroken if she doesn't pull through."

"Oh, you needn't tell me, miss. Everyone in the household knows the redcoats just couldn't have chosen anything more dear to take from him. And I do pity the stableboys on duty when that gang came through. Heads will roll before this day is over, *mademoiselle.* I can assure you of that!

"Well, I suppose the soldiers thought the horse a novelty," he continued after a moment, in a less harried voice. "It's not often one sees an Arabian in the Colonies. And I'm sure she must have simply caught their eyes, as they came marauding through. Filthy buggers," he exclaimed, and then, as though he suddenly remembered that he was addressing a lady, his face reddened and he fell silent.

They walked the rest of the way without exchanging another word, Caroline struggling to keep pace with his long-legged strides, her heavy, clinging riding skirt slowing her up.

Once they reached the stable, the steward took his

leave, and Caroline was again obliged to go inside alone. The only difference this time was that her throat was filled with an awful, almost breath-stopping lump. She knew she cared too much for Nathaniel to see him as beside himself as this situation was bound to make him, and she reflexively reached up before entering the stable and pressed her fingers to the cross that hung from her neck. Then she offered up a silent prayer that she would, somehow, find the words to console him.

There were five men gathered about the mare's stall as Caroline went inside seconds later. One of them was Nathaniel's brother, John, and the rest she hadn't met. She could tell from the way two of them were dressed that they were stable hands. The other two, being clad in obviously expensive riding costumes, had to be guests for the hunt.

With a dry swallow, Caroline lifted her skirts once more and made her way around to where they stood. John was the first to notice her. He offered her a hurried smile and again directed his gaze down at where the mare lay, with Nathaniel and an elderly man kneeling on either side of her. Nathaniel was stripped down to his breeches and shirt. His ruffled sleeves were rolled up to his elbows, and several strands of his dark hair had come free of his tie-back bow. He wore a most disconcerted expression.

After hearing just a few words of what the older gentleman was saying to Nathaniel, Caroline knew that he was the veterinarian to whom the steward had referred.

"I don't know," he said in a low disheartened voice, shaking his head all the while. "I doubt we'll bring her back to health. She's terribly dry, and I've never seen a horse brought out of such a grave state. Much as I know you don't wish to hear it, Nathaniel, I fear I must recommend that we simply shoot her and end her suffering."

At this Nathaniel drew away a bit, straightening his posture, but he continued to stare forlornly down at the animal.

Caroline stared down at her as well, at her lustrous black hide, torn and bloodied in several spots now by some sort of whip. Her eyes were open, but her face was so still that Caroline couldn't really tell whether or not she was breathing.

"Can't you get her to drink?" she heard herself ask. To her chagrin, all of the men turned in that instant and scowled at her, as though she were the last person they'd expected to hear from or had wanted to.

She felt her face color, but she forced herself to push forward, past the others and into the stall, where she immediately dropped to her knees beside Nathaniel.

"This is no place for you," he said with obvious annoyance. "You'll dirty your skirts in here."

She reached out and gave his hand a sharp squeeze. "But I'm not worried about my skirts, Nathaniel. What's the matter with you?" she whispered through clenched teeth. "I'm worried about you and Matilda. Now, do get out of the way so I can examine her!"

Nathaniel looked over at the veterinarian with a questioning expression. "She's a healer of sorts, from New Orleans," he explained.

The vet shrugged. "May as well let her have a look then. She can hardly do any harm at this point," he concluded, rising resignedly and reaching up to wipe his palms on his vest.

Nathaniel, in response, rose as well and cleared the way for Caroline to pass through to the horse's head. She wasted no time but bent down, opened the mare's mouth, and pressed a finger to her gums. They were white, not pink as they should have been, and, as Caroline drew her finger away, she saw that the indentation it had made remained for several seconds longer than it would have, were the horse not so terribly dry. White and spongy. Yes. The veterinarian was right; the horse was dehydrated. One final test: a pinch at the mare's neck, and again the skin remained dented where she'd pressed. Old Matilda was in a very bad way. That much was clear.

"Water," Caroline declared. "Get me buckets of *cool* water. Not cold. And hurry!"

"But she won't drink," the vet said scoldingly. "Don't you think I would have gotten her to drink by now if she were inclined to?"

"It's not for drinking. It's to pour over her. Now, *move,*" Caroline snapped. "You'll lose her for sure, Nathaniel, if you don't bring me some water and quickly! And get me some towels as well. At least a dozen of them," she ordered, turning back and glaring up at the circle of men.

Within seconds, the requested water arrived, and Caroline began pouring it over the animal's neck.

"What on earth are you doing?" the vet asked.

"Cooling her down. If you can't do it from the inside, you do it from the out," she answered evenly.

When, at last, the requested towels arrived, Caroline dipped them in the water and started wrapping them about the horse's legs and applying them to her neck. Then she took the last of them, got it drenched, and placed it in the mare's mouth. Raising the horse's head, she closed her muzzle, in the hope that some of the water would drip down her throat. She proceeded to do this two or three times, each time cradling the mare's head in her lap and tilting it upward. Finally, the animal emitted a groan of sorts, and Nathaniel stooped down in amazement.

"That's the first sound we've heard from her since she was found," he whispered in awe. "Maybe she'll live, after all. Maybe she honestly has a chance!"

"Of course she does," Caroline replied, smiling over at him. "'Ye of little faith,' Nathaniel. Have you no room in your life at all for miracles?" she asked, staring into his eyes with a look so poignant, it was difficult for him to keep from tearing up.

"Well, I'd better make some," he acknowledged. "Hadn't I? With *you* around." He was relieved to see that she could tell what he was thinking in those moments, what his words really meant. She knew, so he didn't have to say anything more. He didn't have to risk having the others detect the deep feelings welling up in him.

"But we're still not past danger with her," Caroline continued. "There is something else I would like to try. Do you think you can get me some piping?"

Nathaniel was still too awed to really understand her question. "What?"

"You're a shipbuilder, for heaven's sake. Surely you have some leather piping about somewhere. You know, the sort you use on boats."

"Well, yes. But what for?"

"I want to try to run some water down, past her throat and into her stomach. There may be some risk, but I think it's worth a try."

"Oh, that's preposterous," the vet exclaimed. "You'll choke the poor animal! Or, worse yet, drown her if you should happen to enter a lung!"

"But it could work, Nathaniel," Caroline declared, choosing to ignore the veterinarian. "I saw it done once by a treater on Bayou Manchac."

Nathaniel wavered for several seconds. Then he offered Caroline a soft smile and a nod. "All right, then. If you say so, my dear, we will try it." With that he turned back to his brother. "Go down to the yards and fetch what she's asked for—as quickly as your horse will carry you, John!"

"This is madness, Nathaniel," the veterinarian hissed. "You'd be daft to even try such a thing!"

Nathaniel gazed up at the vet apologetically. "But she's very good at healing, Doctor. I've seen her ply her craft before, and I can assure you of that."

"Well, do what you will," the vet replied with a huff. "But I, for one, do not intend to stand about here, being party to such lunacy!" With that, he took his coat off the side wall of the stall, where he'd tossed it earlier, and bent down to pick up his medical bag.

"Get some salve from him before he leaves. To soothe her lash wounds," Caroline whispered out of the side of her mouth.

Nathaniel rose and went after the veterinarian as he stormed out of the stall, and Caroline could hear their hushed conversation in the seconds that followed. She was still too busy tending to the horse to pay much attention to what was being said, but, whatever it was, Nathaniel had obviously managed to sweet-talk the man a bit, because he returned to Caroline a couple of minutes later with the requested jar of salve.

"Clean her wounds," Caroline directed, as Nathaniel knelt down at her side once more. "Then start applying the salve to them. And *gently,* mind!"

A teasing smile tugged at the corners of Nathaniel's mouth as he replied, and in such a soft tone that only Caroline could hear him, "You certainly are a dictatorial wench at times like these."

She glared at him. "And if it were you, lying here in her place, Mr. Hamlin, would you really want me taking the time to say please and thank you to one and all?"

"No. I suppose not," he conceded, picking up one of the wet towels and starting to carefully apply it to the mare's wounds. "It seems I've forgotten my manners in the midst of all of this, Caroline," he sheepishly admitted. "I've neglected to introduce you to my two friends up there, Mr. Barney Quin and, to his left, Yates Kenyon," he explained, tilting his head up toward the stall wall to their left.

Caroline turned about and flashed each man a quick smile.

"Mademoiselle Caroline Brenton, gentlemen."

"How do you do, miss?" they both asked, almost in unison, and one of them tipped his riding hat to her.

"They're my compeers in the rebel cause," Nathaniel added, clenching his teeth as he continued cleaning the mare's wounds. "And now that the redcoats have done this to my Matilda, we're more fiercely commited than ever," he growled. "Aren't we, chaps?"

The two men were silent for several seconds, as though not quite sure how to respond. Then one of them, Barney Quin, answered in a faltering voice,

"Ah . . . yes, Nathan. Yes, indeed."

"Well, actually, they could be of help with *this* cause at present," Caroline interjected, doing her best not to sound quite so "dictatorial."

"How is that?" Nathaniel asked.

"One of them could go and fetch some lard from the house."

"Lard?" Nathaniel echoed. "Whatever for?"

"To lubricate the piping, when John returns with it. We're going to need all the help we can get to slip it down into her."

"Yes," Nathaniel agreed. "Capital idea, my dear. Barney, would you go and get us some?"

"Oh, aye," his friend agreed, pushing away from the stall wall and hurrying out of the stable.

"And what should I do?" Kenyon inquired.

"Go and find the men who did this to my Matilda, and lash them until they die," Nathaniel snarled.

"I wish I could, Nathan," his friend replied in a sympathetic tone. "But it seems Matilda there is the only one who got a good enough look at them."

"Yes," Nathaniel said resignedly. "What can Yates do to help, Caroline?" he asked after several seconds.

She was still busy, again wetting the many towels and reapplying them to the horse. "I can't think of a thing right now, *mon cher.*"

"Well, I can," Nathaniel declared, looking up at his friend again. "You can go and fetch a bottle of brandy."

"For Matilda?" his friend asked in amazement.

"No. For *me!* And please be quick about it, will you? I've been needing a drink for over an hour now," he confessed with an uneasy laugh.

Although he seemed to be doing his best to sound

perfunctory as he made the request, Caroline knew that he really did have need of the liquor. Though his friend wasn't close enough to see Nathaniel's fingers trembling as he worked, Caroline was, and she wasn't sure whether it was due to worry over the horse or simply rage at the mare's assailants. But, whichever it was, she wished they were alone, so she could reach out and give him the consoling hug he so obviously needed.

"You'll find a bottle in my study," she heard Nathaniel go on to say. "Near the door. The steward will show you."

"Yes, yes, Nathan," his friend droned, waving him off as he headed out of the stable. "Don't you think I've had enough brandy in your study to know where it can be found?"

"There's a good chap," Nathaniel called after him.

Caroline glanced back then, to make certain the two stable hands she'd seen standing beside the stall earlier had gone off as well.

"Yes. We're alone at last," Nathaniel confirmed. "And damn glad I am of it, too! Thank you, Caroline," he murmured, again looking near tears. "Thank you for all you're doing to save her."

Caroline turned to him more fully and wrapped her arms about him, and, though he looked a bit surprised by this at first, he wasted no time in putting his arms about her as well. "I've been thinking of you—all week," he admitted in a whisper. "Until this happened, I was thinking of nothing but you."

"And I of you," she replied, keeping her voice equally low. She would have been content just to hold him again, but she could feel him drawing away a bit and sliding her bonnet back so he could kiss her. She didn't resist when his lips pressed down upon hers, but she knew they couldn't afford to indulge themselves for long.

"Oh, now . . . let's not start that again," she said with a chary laugh, easing away from him a few moments later. "Matilda needs our full attention, I'm afraid. For the next couple of hours at least. So, please don't distract me, love."

"All right. All right," he agreed, drawing away from her once more and continuing to tend to Matilda's wounds. "But do say you'll stay for a while, once the others have gone. I need you here with me tonight, Caroline. I'm not myself . . . not after what's happened."

"Yes. Very well. I'll stay . . . I *want* to stay, in fact," she added in an enamored whisper, and again, as their eyes met, it was clear to them just how strong their bond was becoming.

When John returned with the piping half an hour later, Caroline did succeed in channeling some water into the mare's stomach. Before doing so, however, she placed several spoonfuls of sugar into the water to help nourish the horse and some ground willow bark to ease her pain and help her sleep.

By eight o'clock that evening, Matilda, though still unwilling to stand, was taking a bit of food from Nathaniel's hand and was starting to drink a little on her own. Nathaniel's friends had long since departed, agreeing to come back at some other time for the canceled fox hunt. John had gone off as well, claiming that he wanted to go over some ledgers at the yards.

Nathaniel knew, however, that his real plan was to spend the evening with Meara Miller. John had been seeing her more and more in the past few days, albeit surreptitiously, and Nathaniel considered it a pretty good measure of his growing affection for Caroline that he no longer felt even a smidgen of resentment over his brother's liaison with the redhead.

With everyone else gone, Caroline and Nathaniel again found themselves alone in the stable. They were standing now, leaning back against the left wall of Matilda's stall, a cooling, evening breeze from the adjacent window wafting past them. While they were both weary from the ordeal, there was a comfortableness in their silence, a peace that came from knowing they had done all they could for Matilda and she was pretty well out of danger.

"I can't believe the redcoats did this to me," Nathaniel suddenly muttered, shaking his head. "I mean to her, to Matilda," he quickly amended. He'd been in a stunned state since Matilda had been found, and he couldn't seem to shake that dazed feeling, so he was finally allowing himself to give voice to it, in the hope that would make the terrible sense of betrayal he felt wane a bit. "To a poor, defenseless animal like this," he added, hoping that Caroline hadn't detected his underlying feelings.

"Defenseless as the fox you were going to hunt down today?" she asked pointedly.

He responded only with a pained look.

"Oh, I shouldn't mock you at a time like this, I know," she said apologetically. "I'm sorry. I guess I'm just tired."

"It's all right. It's just that I . . . I simply don't

287

understand how this could have happened to me," he noted once more in bewilderment, and, again, a voice within him began scolding him for daring to express such feelings.

"But it didn't happen to you, Nathaniel; it happened to Matilda, as you said. And you, of all people, should know how the redcoats are. They don't care who they bully. They take what they wish from *anyone* they wish, Whig or Tory. They're ruffians, as I told you. Nothing more, nothing less!"

"Yes," he agreed rather numbly. "I guess you're right about that . . . I shall sleep down here," he suddenly declared, taking his riding coat down from where he'd hung it, over the stall door, and putting it back on in the evening's chill. "I won't let her be taken from me again!"

"Oh, don't be silly. You're just tired and hungry, that's all. Neither of us has eaten since midday, so why don't you simply let your stableboys look after her for an hour or two while we go up to the house and have supper?"

"The stableboys?" he repeated huffily. "But that's what they were supposed to be doing when she was stolen! The bloody fools!"

"Then post your steward down here for the night, why don't you? You can trust him, *n'est-ce pas?* Because believe me, love, you'll be of no earthly good to Matilda or anyone else if you're half-dead yourself," Caroline admonished, slipping a hand behind him and rubbing his back with her opened palm.

"You've such wonderful hands," he said, shutting his eyes for several seconds and issuing an appreciative sigh. "Such wonderful *healing* hands." With that he reached back and brought her palm around and up to his lips, so he could kiss it. "It was amazing what you did here today, bringing poor Matilda back from the brink of death like that," he added in a venerative whisper.

He saw, in that instant, an evening star twinkling through the opened window, and the cobalt blue sky framed Caroline's face as she stood with her back to it.

"Do you realize, I wonder, just how amazing it was?" he continued. "It frightened the others a little, I must confess. I could see it in their eyes," he added with a laugh. "But, Caroline, I want you to know that it didn't frighten me. On the contrary, I've never cared more for a woman than I do for you now. And, far from fearing your healing powers, I almost wish I possessed them myself. I wish that the very holding of your hand could somehow pass some of that ability over to me. I've always known great power in Boston, you see. Always been among the wealthiest men here. Never wanting for anything. Never being crossed by anyone . . . until today by the redcoats. And it was as if they *knew* precisely what to take from me, exactly what it would hurt me most to lose. You saw for yourself that all my money and power could do naught to help me or my horse. You heard the veterinarian. He'd have shot Matilda if you hadn't gotten here when you did. Such was the help my money could buy today . . . No. Only *your* power, my dear, made any difference. And I think it is because yours seems to come from the very heavens themselves."

Caroline was caught so off guard by his worshipful manner, she hardly knew how to respond. "Oh, dear," she said finally with a tremulous smile. "There was really nothing divine about it. I was simply doing what I saw another treater do a few years back."

"No," he countered. "I was a witness, and, as soon as you began touching Matilda, she started to rally. It was your *touch* that did it," he maintained, continuing to hold her hand in his and intermittently pressing his lips to her fingers. "Your wonderful, wonderful touch. And every inch of me longs for it now," he confessed.

Caroline felt an impassioned shiver run through her in response.

"Stay the night with me, love," he said in an urgent whisper. "Please say that you will. I won't sleep a wink without you at my side. I really do need to have you with me tonight . . . I know it was silly to have gotten so upset over a horse Matilda's age. All this troubling to keep her alive, when everyone knows she only has a couple more years left to her, in any case. But *you* understood. Even now you understand—I know you do—that she's really all I have left of my mother. . . ." He broke off, and Caroline reflexively reached out and hugged him to her.

"Yes. I do understand, and I want to stay. Really I do. But I can't. What about my aunt and uncle? They'll be worried sick about me if I don't get back to them soon."

"Oh, yes," he muttered, as though that had completely slipped his mind. "Well . . . I could have one of my footmen take word to them of what happened to my horse, and my man could explain that you've chosen to stay here overnight so you might look after Matilda until you're sure she's out of danger," he suggested, a hopeful rise to his voice.

"I suppose so," she answered tentatively. "But I

really hate lying to them, Nathaniel. I'm sure you understand."

"But you wouldn't be lying to them in that case, *I* would."

Caroline smiled. "But I'd be a party to it. Besides, what lie do we tell them the next time I want to spend the night with you, and the time after that? Sooner or later, we'll have to start telling the truth, won't we?" she asked rhetorically.

"But you did tell the truth, love . . . the other day," he added, bending down to kiss her neck. "When you told me you loved me. And it was again I, sadly, who didn't want the truth to be told. But I do now, Caroline," he added, in a heated whisper. "Dear God, how I do now!"

"I . . . I didn't say I loved you," she stammered, starting to feel rather frightened by his intensity and easing away from him a bit.

"You did," he declared, pursuing her and pinning her to the far corner of the stall. "I heard you say it."

"No, I said, *'Je pense que je t'aime.'* I think I love you. And that's not really the same thing."

Nathaniel laughed softly. "Well, I don't know how it is where you come from, but here in Boston, the two are very close, indeed." With that, he bent down once more and again started kissing her neck, and she could feel her legs beginning to melt beneath her.

"Really Nathaniel. Must we have this discussion out here in a horse stall? Can't you at least give a poor girl some supper before you seduce her?"

He lifted his head and smiled because she knew he intended to try to get her into bed once more and was offering so little resistance. "I'll give you anything you

291

want, love. You have but to name it! And, please, do take me up on this offer," he added gingerly, "because it's not one I've made to anyone else."

"I . . . I don't know what I want," she replied, finding herself a bit dumbfounded by this.

"Well, how about me?" he suggested. "I could give you me . . . to have and to hold, for ever and ever. You know, that sort of thing. What say you?" he asked with a sportive smile.

"I say . . . I think you've had a very trying day, and all that brandy you drank is finally catching up with you."

He opened his mouth to speak, and knowing that he was sure to object to what she'd said, she pressed a finger to his lips. "I also say that I want some supper and a nice big soft chair to sit back in for a while."

His smile became roguish. "A *chair?*" he asked pointedly.

"Oh, Nathaniel, really! Is that all that's ever on your mind?"

"With you, my dear, yes. I'm afraid so. In case it hasn't come to your notice, I absolutely adore you—and you were right about everything. Everything you said the other day. Right about all of it, including telling me how you feel about me. In fact, if you hadn't had the courage to come out and say it, I surely never would have. And now I think we should go right up to the house, get you some supper, and then start trying to beget a little heir apparent like ourselves, an offspring who can assume both of our burdensome lots, once we're dead and gone."

She furrowed her brow. "Just one moment, Nathaniel. I know I'm a relative stranger to Boston, but, in

Louisiana, a man proposes marriage to a lady *before* he 'proposes' motherhood! And, I do believe that is how it should be!"

"Oh, indeed," he agreed, looking amply contrite. "I quite agree. And, though I do seem to have the two out of order, you have my solemn vow that I shall propose *both* to you." In time, he thought. In just the time it would take to send the commander another message, telling him of the atrocious act some faction of his redcoat battalion had committed that day and, accordingly, refusing to offer him any further assistance.

For the moment, however, Nathaniel's mind was on Caroline, on seeing that she was well fed and well loved and making certain that his only words to her from this point on were meant to praise and win her and no longer to entrap.

Chapter 17

Nathaniel decided to take Caroline's advice and send his steward down to the stable to watch over Matilda for the night. With that matter finally settled, he had an intimate supper with Caroline, then took her up to his suite. Though she still wouldn't agree to stay all night, she did consent to having one of Nathaniel's footmen take word to her aunt and uncle that she was helping with the care of Nathaniel's wounded horse and wouldn't be home for a few more hours. Happy to be allowed even that much more time with her, Nathaniel resolved to make the very most of it.

Though Caroline still looked a bit blushful as they reached his bedchamber, she didn't seem nearly as apprehensive as she had the first time they'd made love. Nevertheless, Nathaniel sensed that she'd feel less inhibited if he didn't light the room's candles, so he simply crossed to the window and raised the blinds, allowing more of the evening's twilight into the room. He'd learned through the years that there were some things best left to nature, and at that moment he knew that lighting was one of them.

He then walked back to the bedchamber door and shut it behind Caroline, and, in the moments that followed, they stood in the gloaming, happily tipsy on the dinner wine and slowly undressing one another.

Once Nathaniel had Caroline disrobed, he reached up and slipped the large comb out of the tower of curls at the top of her head. Her golden waist-length hair cascaded down her back, and, for the first time since he'd met her, Nathaniel saw her as nature had intended her to look, as she was each day when she awoke— before she and her handmaids had labored to create the elaborate hive of curls that usually perched upon her crown.

Caroline gasped. In part this was because she knew she would never be able to restore her hairdo before returning to her aunt and uncle. That would provoke some embarrassing questions. What was more, no one had ever done such a thing to her, and it struck her as being almost a barbaric action.

Even now, as Nathaniel stood running his fingers down the length of her curly mane, she felt strangely afraid of him, frightened by the low, smoldering sounds he was making deep in his throat. There was such an energy about him, such heat emanating from beneath his ruffled shirt with each button she undid, such seduction in every whiff of the manly, almost gingery-scented barber cologne he wore, that she could almost feel herself aching inside, aching with the stabbing pain of the first time he'd entered her. And, though she knew it was probably irrational, she began to freeze up at the thought of what was about to happen between them. He was, after all, miles beyond her as a lover, worlds wiser and more experienced, and, once again, she felt like an unversed child as he stepped out of the last of his clothing and took her into his arms.

"Na . . . Nathaniel," she choked out.

He simply responded by shushing her, as he continued to hold her tightly to him. Then, to her amazement, his body began to sway, to rub against hers in a kind of dance that allowed her to feel for herself just how aroused he was. Again the memory of being deflowered seemed to shoot through her, real as it had been just five nights before, and she wondered if it would hurt that way again tonight, if her body would have to adjust to it each time with a man.

She couldn't help freezing up once more as she wondered about this, but, to her surprise, her body kept swaying with his, in his guiding grasp, slowly, rhythmically, as the breeze from the window caressed them both. She seemed to have no choice but to cooperate, her long hair warming the back of her as his undulating torso continued to warm the front.

"Have you been to the tropics?" he asked in an enticing whisper.

She shook her head, still feeling too taken aback by his actions to speak.

"Oh, I must take you to them one day, so you can see for yourself how the native women go about, with their hair down, like yours is now . . . and, I must forewarn you, wearing very little more!" His hands, which had, only seconds before, been brushing across the curled ends of her long hair, traveled downward now, and her breath caught in her throat as she felt him not only touching her well-rounded posterior but clutching it to him. To make matters worse, she remembered in that instant how he had slapped her there on the second night they'd been together, and she felt her legs go weak.

"Oh, Nathaniel, please," she entreated. "Can't we please go and lie down?"

"Yes, of course. Is something wrong?"

"No," she lied, embarrassed to admit that he already had her feeling too weak-kneed to continue standing. "I'm just a little dizzy from the wine, I think."

"Very well," he replied, taking hold of one of her hands and leading her to the bed. As they reached it, however, he surprised her once more by pulling the quilt from it and wrapping it about her. "Come on," he urged, taking her hand again and drawing her toward the door to the adjoining room. "You can lie down in here, if you wish."

She furrowed her brow. "In where?"

"In here. Just past the sitting room. Come on." He continued to coax, stepping behind her and directing a tickling whisper down the nape of her neck. "I'll show you." With that, he led her to the next room.

"Where?" she asked again, peering about in the dim light as they stood on its threshold. There were only camel-back sofas and chairs within, and she knew she really wasn't up to being "chaired" again, as he had put it.

"Out here," he said softly, crossing to the French doors and resting his fingers on their handles. She heard a smile in his voice now, but she definitely didn't feel as lighthearted as he. His huge arousal was clearly visible to her, in the moonlight which shone in through the glass doors, and all she really felt was an odd sense

297

of misgiving.

"Out on the balcony?" she asked, making no effort to hide the fact that she thought the suggestion daft.

"Yes. Come on. It's so lovely and cool out here on summer nights, and there's a wonderful view of the creek that runs across the grounds."

"But we're . . . we're not dressed, for heaven's sake! What if someone should see us?"

"You've got the quilt," he said, shrugging. "And there's plenty of room for you to lie down out there, if you wish. Oh, come on, Caroline. There's no one out there at this hour. Come on, love," he concluded, crossing to her and firmly taking her hand in his. "Come and share your quilt with me."

She did go along with him, albeit hesitantly, and, a few seconds later, found herself outside, far above the rolling moonlit land beyond. Though she still had the quilt wrapped about her, she felt the evening breeze slipping upward, past her ankles, and sweeping gently over her body. And she had to admit to herself that it was quite sensual and exhilarating, this being outdoors in the nude. There was something sinful, almost wicked about it, and she couldn't help letting an uneasy giggle escape her as she continued to stand just outside the French doors.

"You see," he said, turning back to her with a smile. "It's nice, isn't it. Just as in the Bible, before Adam and Eve came to know shame. Pity it's been with us ever since," he added, shaking his head.

"Do you do this often with your lady friends?" Caroline inquired, slowly, cautiously, drawing up next to him and leaning, as he was, against the balcony's balustrade.

He again took his gaze from the bluish scenery below and offered her a subtle smile. "Only with the very special ones, Caroline," he said, reaching out and pulling her up to his side. "We wouldn't want the local vicar to get wind of it, after all."

Caroline laughed easily now. "Heavens, no! And who would even think it of a prim and proper Puritan such as yourself? I'm shocked. Truly I am."

"No, you're not," he said knowingly. "You and your French and Spanish suitors. I'll wager there's no end to what those hot-blooded sorts do!"

"I wouldn't know," she answered coolly. "I came to you a virgin. Remember?"

He nodded and continued to smile. "So you did, but if you'll share your quilt with me, I'll gladly teach you a thing or two to take home with you . . . when you go . . . *if* you go. If I *let* you go," he added, drawing a savoring breath in through his teeth as he turned her toward him and slipped in next to her under the voluminous bedspread.

"Will they hurt? These things you want to teach me?" Caroline asked in a wavering voice.

He emitted a surprised laugh and reached up to brush some wisps of hair from her eyes in the soft blowing wind. "No. That is to say, they shouldn't, love . . . not if they're done right. And I'm pleased to report that, so far, on my rather infamous course as a lover, I haven't heard any complaints." With that, he bent down and began kissing her neck.

"What . . . what do we have to do?" she whispered bashfully.

"Well, that's the really lovely part, my dear. *You* don't have to do anything but go back inside and lie

299

down on the bed. It is I who must do most of it."

This sounded both inviting and a trifle scary to Caroline, and she really didn't know how to respond.

"Come back inside," he directed, "and you can see what you think."

She moved along with him under the quilt, but she still had some qualms. "And if I don't like it?"

"You can simply tell me to stop. You're not my prisoner, after all, love . . . though, God knows, I really wish you were," he confessed with a soft laugh.

"But I thought you taught me everything the other night."

"Hardly."

"I think I need more to drink," she suddenly announced, when they had returned to the bedchamber, and her eyes lit upon the liquor decanter that rested on his console.

He looked on adoringly, as she slipped the quilt off him and crossed to the console to pour herself some brandy, managing all the while to keep the covering securely wrapped about her. Once she'd poured the liquor, she tipped her glass back with a trembling hand and took a long swallow of it.

"Oooh," she exclaimed, setting the glass down with a shudder. "How dreadful! I hate the taste of strong drink!"

He smiled. "Then why are you drinking some?"

"Because I think I'll be needing it."

"Oh, nonsense, love," he declared, laughing as he walked over to where she stood. "Besides, I want you awake for this, not numbed by brandy. So, come on, Caroline," he urged, pulling her to him once more. "Come to bed with me."

His voice reminded her of thick dark honey, low, seductive, confident. And, as he bent down and kissed her lips, she again felt her legs going weak. She was grateful, therefore, to finally be reclining a moment or two later, for, upon concluding the kiss, he'd taken her up in his arms and carried her over to the bed.

He was right, she realized, as he set her down upon the mattress; this was precisely what she needed, simply to be allowed to lie back and enjoy his touch. To her surprise, however, just as she was nestling in beneath the quilt, he climbed in next to her and reached out and rolled her onto her stomach.

"What are you doing?"

"You'll see soon enough, my angel," he answered, pressing a trail of kisses to the side of her face and neck.

His hands were upon her, as well now, his fingertips gliding up and down the length of her back with a whisper-lightness that felt just wonderful. They tickled a bit, too, but, not wishing to spoil the amorous mood, Caroline bit her lip and did her best not to laugh. Then, seconds later, her urge to laugh was replaced with a feeling of both abashment and trepidation. His hands were moving so far downward that they were actually brushing past her derrière and down between her thighs, to that unmentionable part of her that he had repeatedly entered a few nights before.

She gasped and tried to get up, but he pressed her to the mattress and bent down near her left ear to again address her in a voice that seemed capable of melting steel. "Come on now, Caroline. Do give it a chance, will you? I know you'll enjoy it. And you needn't feel embarrassed, you know, my dear, sweet love. You don't possess a thing that I haven't seen or touched

301

before. I assure you."

This was probably true, she acknowledged, as she did her best to relax once more. It had been abundantly apparent, the last time she'd been with him, that he knew his way around the female anatomy better than most naval captains knew their ways around their ships! Besides, she told herself, he'd touched her there before, quite thoroughly and adeptly, just a few nights ago, and, far from being painful, the second and third times around had brought her indescribable pleasure. It was the sort of pleasure that made one want to cry out, in fact . . . as she was starting to do now at his probing touch. He was simply taking a more round-about route this time. A route that was, to her surprise, even more titillating. And all she could seem to do in response was to give forth some appreciative sighs and hope that he couldn't feel or *hear* how he was making her heart race.

It was rather odd, really. Half of her was so self-conscious and apprehensive that it wanted to get up and go lock itself away forever, and the other half wouldn't have stirred now for the world. But it was she who had sought him out this time, she silently reminded herself. This time *and* the last. In truth, it was precisely this sort of excitement, the kind of provocative uncertainty she was feeling now, that kept drawing her to him like a moth to flame.

Then, just as she was actually beginning to relax a bit and really feel and enjoy what his fingers were doing to her, he stopped the foreplay. His hands slipped upward, under her stomach, and he lifted her up so that she was resting upon her hands and knees. And, before she could utter a word of objection, she felt him move back behind her and slip that aroused part of himself into her lower lips with one smooth thrust.

"Mon Dieu," she gasped.

His hands reached up and cupped her breasts, and again he softly shushed her. "Does it hurt?"

She gave the question a few seconds' thought. "No," she answered finally, realizing it had only been shock that had made her gasp and, in truth, felt quite nice.

It was the most incredible thing she'd ever felt, far surpassing the way they had made love before, and there were goose bumps traveling over her, as he continued to surge deeply into her and then withdraw—again and again. Then, as his movements quickened, she was forced to bend down and bite the pillow before her in order to stifle the ecstatic cries that were welling up and starting to pour out of her.

"Oh, *mon Dieu! Mon Dieu,* Nathaniel," she heard herself exclaim into the muffling pillow, and suddenly, her outcries were accompanied by clutching and clawing, as her fingers closed around the pillow as well. It was the most exquisite experience she'd ever had— his every move seeming to push her farther and farther upward, toward heaven itself. And, just when she thought it couldn't get any better, he apparently started to climax within her, and she was swept up into such a torrent of motion and orgasmic sensation, she couldn't help lifting her face and letting a moan or two escape into the air.

A moment later, Nathaniel, windless, fell over onto his side. Being still joined with him, Caroline naturally fell too, and she instantly settled into his curled-up form with a gratified sigh.

"My God, *mon amour,"* she said after several

303

seconds. "Where on earth did you learn such a thing?"

She heard him laugh to himself. "Oh, it comes rather naturally. Don't you think?"

She shrugged. "I . . . I don't think I'll be in any shape to think again for at least a week!"

"As good as that?" he asked, in a tone that reflected mild surprise. "Why, thank you, my lady. It's comforting to know I haven't lost my knack."

"I think, though, that your staff may have heard me," Caroline said blushfully.

"Oh, I shouldn't worry about it. They're terribly discreet. They know it's the one thing that's really required of them. Besides, the only one of them who sleeps on this side of the house is the steward, and, as you know, he's down with Matilda tonight. Thank God!"

Caroline laughed. "It's only right, I suppose. We did Matilda a good turn today, and she simply returned the favor."

"Yes," he agreed, smiling. "So, what do you think, love? Have I persuaded you to stay the night? We could do this again, you know . . . and probably go a lot longer the second time around."

She released another satisfied sigh. "Ah, Nathaniel. You'll be the end of me. I've spent enough summers on my grandfather's farm to know that you'll have me 'with calf' *tout de suite,* if I let you keep doing that . . . and that would put poor Uncle Meldon in a most uncomfortable position, wouldn't it? Having to explain that to my father?"

"I should think *I'd* fare even worse," Nathaniel retorted uneasily. "But, of course, I'd marry you, my dear, with even just an hour's notice, so perhaps he'd have mercy on me."

"*Oui.* I think so," she said thoughtfully. "That quickly?" she asked after a moment with a surprised rise to her voice.

"What?"

"You'd marry me that quickly, if I found myself in such a state?"

He hugged her to him, as his hands continued to fondle her ample breasts. "You could have me *tonight,* Caroline, and you know it. I've been smitten with you since the night we met, and you've been aware of it all along, you little temptress," he concluded with a teasing laugh.

"No I haven't," she declared. "This is news, indeed. Believe me!"

"Well, it's the absolute truth. I would marry you tonight, if not for . . ." Fortunately, he stopped himself in time. If not for the fact that I still work for your enemies, Caroline, he thought. If not for the fact that I haven't yet broken ties with the British, and I can't do so until tomorrow, when I'm again able to send a messenger to the commander.

He wanted to tell her that. After what had been done to Matilda that day, he wanted desperately to break down and confess his misguided loyalties, as if she were a clergyman. He knew, if their relationship was to prove a lasting one, he would have to make a totally clean breast of things with her, tell her all of it, so that the lies and deception could be put behind them forever. Clearly, however, he wasn't in a position to make such a confession yet, and, luckily, he was just sober and awake enough to have stopped himself in time.

"If not for what?" she asked.

"Oh. I'll . . . I'll try to explain it to you, the next time we're together. For now I can only tell you that it involves some rather divided loyalties."

"In business, you mean?"

"Well . . . sort of. But let's not talk about that now. There has been enough unhappiness here today with what happened to Matilda. I just want you to let me spend my last few minutes with you tonight, holding you like this. All right?"

"All right."

"And what about you, my dear?" he asked gingerly. "Would you marry me with only an hour's notice?"

"No," she answered, without, to Nathaniel's dismay, even a second of hesitation. Oddly, though, there had seemed to be a smile in her voice as she'd said it.

"This really isn't a laughing matter, you know," he said sternly, doing his damnedest not to sound as wounded as he felt. "If you're old enough to sleep with men, you're certainly old enough to know when you're breaking their hearts."

"I know it's serious, Nathaniel," she replied, sounding soberer now. "I just wouldn't agree to marry you with so little notice, because it would take at least twenty-four hours for me to have a suitable wedding gown made. And, then, of course, I would need father's consent. And we've so many friends and relatives in Louisiana who would be shattered if I didn't marry in New Orleans, so they could attend the ceremony."

His mouth dropped open. "Dear God, girl! What on earth have I gotten myself into?"

"A very big Cajun family, *mon amour,* if you marry me. So, do consider yourself forewarned," she said with a soft laugh. "And then, of course, my dearest," she added with a teasing tsk, "there is your rather marginal French. I mean, I've only heard you speak a word of it here and there, so I'm sure you've a lot to learn . . . if you're to have any hope of conversing with anyone besides my father in the southern half of the Brenton clan."

Nathaniel groaned. "Sweet Jesus! All I did was fall in love with two beautiful brown eyes, the face of an angel, and a sensational pair of hips, and, next thing you know, I'm having to speak a second language and take vows before a *priest!* . . . Caroline, please tell me—will you—that at least *some* of this is negotiable," he concluded with a pleading laugh.

She laughed as well. "But of course." Just as she was about to say more, however, she heard a nearby clock sounding the hour of ten, and she drew away from him and slowly sat up. "I should go now, my love. We did promise my aunt and uncle that I would only be a few hours more, and they've shown me such kindness since I arrived, I really hate to worry them. I guess we'll simply have to discuss our plans when we're together next. We can talk then about what you and your friends want me to do for the rebel cause. All right?"

"All right," he answered, offering her a resigned smile.

Caroline bent down and pressed a kiss to his cheek before she rose from the bed and walked around to where they had left their clothing, near the door.

Nathaniel rolled over and got up as well. "I'll see you home," he declared, reaching out to the adjacent night table and feeling about for a flint and striking steel. Once he found them, he lit the hurricane lamp. "That is, if you're really sure you must go now."

"I am," she replied, having already managed to climb into some of her undergarments in the darkness.

"And when will you come to me again?" he asked in a fervent tone.

"I don't know. When I can get away, I suppose."

"Tomorrow night?" he asked eagerly, crossing to her and reaching out to hug her once more.

"Now, now, Nathaniel," she countered, slipping out of his embrace. "As much as I love having you hold me, you really mustn't start that again. I'll have enough on my hands, after all, just trying to explain to my aunt and uncle why my hair is in such a state."

He laughed and hurriedly began slipping into his breeches and shirt. "Just tell them you got so much straw and such caught in it, after spending the day in the stable, you decided to take it down and comb it out."

"*Oui.* I suppose they would believe that . . . Button me, will you?" she asked after a moment, turning her back to him once she'd stepped into her riding skirt. "Can you see well enough here?"

"No. Come over by the light," he replied, taking hold of the waist of the garment and drawing her over toward the night table. "This is ridiculous, you know," he grumbled, as he began struggling to get the row of tiny buttons fastened and she stood feverishly retying the drawstring ribbons on her blouse. "We're like two adolescents, having to scramble back into our clothes at this hour. I shall be quite happy when you can finally just stay the night."

"Well, you'll have to march me down a church aisle first, love, because I'm afraid my family would never allow it."

"Ah, yes. We're back to that, aren't we?"

"Oui," she said with a kittenish kind of firmness.

"Oh, very well, then, my dearest. You have my word that I'll propose to you when I see you next, and then you can go forth and make all the arrangements. Will that keep your family happy?"

She smiled. "I think so . . . yes. In fact, I must confess that Uncle Meldon has been doing more than his share of fishing of late about my trips to see you. And I dare say, nothing would please him more."

"And what about your father?"

"Oh, *Papa* is sure to approve as well. Indeed, I think he half hoped I'd choose a Bostonian like himself. It's *Maman* who will be a trifle disappointed. She seemed to favor a Frenchman for me. *Naturellement.* But she'll come around to my way of thinking in time."

"I certainly hope so. Because, if she's anything like her daughter, I would really hate to have her cross with me."

"Oh, she won't be," Caroline assured him, as he finished buttoning her skirt and she turned about to face him once more. "When all is said and done, I know she'll want what pleases me most, and that's you, Nathaniel. . . . Now, let's find my shoes and riding jacket," she declared, going up on tiptoes to kiss his cheek again. "And let's get into a coach. The more punctual I am, the more likely my aunt and uncle are to receive our news well, when the time comes to tell it."

Nathaniel simply stood watching her as she dashed back to the door and began searching around for her remaining garments. He wondered what his own family would say. In truth, John was really the only one who had to be told about his plans to marry, and, even if his brother didn't approve, he certainly was in no position to keep such a union from taking place. Nevertheless, it would be nice if John could find it in his heart to confer his blessings upon the union. But, of course, his reaction was sure to hinge rather heavily upon how Nathaniel broke the news to him. Deciding to change both one's political loyalties and one's marital status, all in one day, did seem a bit drastic—even considering what had happened to poor Matilda. So, Nathaniel concluded, it would be best if he didn't attempt to tell John about both matters in one blow. He'd just have to try to get both across to his brother a little at a time.

With that decided, he walked over to where Caroline was standing and slipped back into his shoes. He would simply have to make John understand that he'd given all the years he could to both bachelorhood and the redcoats, and it was finally time to follow his heart. He was sure he was right in this—as sure as he'd ever been about anything—and, with that kind of certainty behind him, it didn't seem likely that John could oppose him forever.

Nathaniel did not get out of the coach when he saw Caroline back to her uncle's estate some fifteen minutes later. Not wishing to make her any more late in getting home than she already was, he had simply decided not to bother putting his riding coat back on and combing his hair. No one was going to see him, after all, he reasoned, not if he didn't walk her to her uncle's door. So, after giving her a lingering kiss and asking that she dine with him at his place on the coming Saturday evening, he bade her good night.

He looked out of the coach's window at Meldon Thorwell's front walk an instant later, and saw Caroline heading for the estate's door. As she disappeared from view, into the shadows cast by the adjacent hedges, he felt satisfied that she would be safely inside in just seconds. He, therefore, tapped on the front panel of the coach, signaling his driver to pull away.

Chapter 18

Nathaniel was roused in the middle of the night by a thunderous knocking at his bedchamber door. It was so loud, he found himself sitting bolt upright in bed before he even realized he was awake.

"Who is it?" he called out.

"It's me," he heard his brother declare. "Are you alone?"

"Yes."

"I can come in?"

"Yes! Yes, for Christ's sake, come in!"

The door swung open an instant later, and John stood on its threshold in his nightshift, holding a lit candle.

"What the bloody hell is the matter with you?" Nathaniel hissed. "Knocking like that in the middle of the night? Why, it's still pitch-black outside!"

His brother was squinting as he began heading in Nathaniel's direction with the candle extended far out before him. "Caroline isn't with you?"

"No. I just told you I was alone! What is the meaning

of this, John? Are you walking in your sleep again?"

"No. I'm quite awake. I assure you! It was Meldon Thorwell's knocking that roused *me.*"

"Meldon Thorwell?"

"Yes. He's downstairs waiting for you, and he's demanding that you send Caroline down to him at once."

"Caroline? But I took her home hours ago."

John shrugged. "Well, Meldon doesn't seem to agree. He says she came over here for the hunt this afternoon and that was the last he and his wife have seen of her."

"Dear God," Nathaniel exclaimed, springing out of bed and snatching his robe from where it lay, on the seat of a nearby chair. His initial response was to dread the wrath that Meldon doubtless had in store for him. His dread was instantly overridden, however, by his concern for Caroline.

"He's very angry, Nathan. I should be careful if I were you," John warned, as his brother threw on a robe and swept past him, taking the candle from his hand. "I had everything I could do to keep him from storming up here and searching your bed for her," he continued, rushing after Nathaniel and following him down the corridor.

"I'll be careful."

"And what will you tell him?" John asked, keeping his voice guardedly low now.

"The truth, of course. What I've just told you. He'll simply have to believe me."

Nathaniel heard his brother emit a skeptical "Huh" in response to this. Then he heard his footsteps behind him on the stairs.

313

"Good evening to you Meldon," Nathaniel called out, as Thorwell became visible where he stood, just to the side of the staircase. "Or I should say good *night,*" he added with an uneasy laugh.

Thorwell simply glared up at him in the eerie glow from the lantern he carried. "Where is she, damn it, Hamlin?"

"If you're referring to your niece, I escorted her back to your house at about ten o'clock, just as my footman promised I would," Nathaniel answered, as he reached the bottom of the stairs.

"Well, then, *where,* I pray thee, is she? Amelia and I waited up for her, and she never came in! So, move aside, Nathaniel, and let me go up and have a look for myself," he ordered, pushing past his host and stomping up the stairs.

"As I've told you, she's not up there," Nathaniel thundered, going after him. "And I must warn you, sir, that I really don't take kindly to being called a liar!" He managed to catch up with Thorwell on the same stair on which John had been standing, frozen for the past several seconds, and it was there that Nathaniel grabbed Meldon by the back of his coat collar and addressed him through clenched teeth. "Did you hear me?"

Thorwell broke away from him and, looking equally enraged, turned about to snarl, "Yes. Of course I heard you, my boy. Everyone in the house must have! And, if what you're saying *is* true, you should have no objection to my having a look for myself!" With that, he hurried up the remaining stairs, Nathaniel still on his heels and John bringing up the rear.

"I may not be the cleverest of men, mind, but I'm not

314

fool enough to let you go on stalling me while my niece is wriggling down some trellis in her smock! Now, where is she?" he demanded, stopping at the top of the stairs and turning back to them. "You were once responsible for two younger sisters, Nathaniel. Surely you understand my position," Thorwell appealed. "Tell me where I might find your bed!"

"To the left," Nathaniel answered grudgingly, moved by Thorwell's mention of his own responsibilities. "The last door on the right."

At this, Meldon hurried off down the corridor with the Hamlin brothers still close behind.

"You're a nice enough lad, Nathan," Meldon continued amenably, as he rushed along, "and we've certainly no objection to you courting our Caroline. But keeping her the night is simply out of the question! Her father will have my hide if he gets wind of such a thing!" He finally reached the designated suite and wasted no time in entering it.

Nathaniel and John entered it as well an instant later, and they watched as Thorwell made a beeline for the bed and stood perusing it for several seconds by the light of his upraised lantern. He then circled around to inspect the floor on the other side of it. Then he concluded that portion of his search by dropping to his knees and peering under the bed.

Nathaniel let out a weary sigh. "Have a look in the wardrobe and the sitting room, Meldon, while you're about it. And, by all means, go at once and see if she is, indeed, lowering herself down my trellis or balcony. But, no matter where you look, you won't find her, because, as I've said, she was returned to your home hours ago."

Thorwell, though looking a bit surprised by Nathaniel's encouragement of his search, went ahead and checked all the places suggested, and, minutes later, he returned to the bedchamber with a discouraged expression. "I guess she *isn't* here," he conceded.

"Quite right," Nathaniel retorted. "And, believe me, I only wish she were, because then you and I wouldn't have to face the fact that she seems to be missing. . . . You don't suppose she could have headed back to New Orleans, do you?" he asked worriedly.

Meldon furrowed his brow. "In the middle of the night? Why would she?"

"I . . . I don't know," Nathaniel stammered.

"Well, her clothes and such are still in her suite, so it doesn't appear that that is what happened." Thorwell's tone was clearly a suspicious one, as he spoke once more. "But why would you ask such a thing?"

"I don't know," Nathaniel said again. "It was just the first thing that came to mind."

Meldon's expression became even more quizzical, and he took a couple of steps toward Nathaniel, his stance plainly threatening, "What did you say to her, Hamlin? Did you say or do something that might make her want to go home to her parents?"

"No. Of course not."

"Well, you must have said *something* to her today. God knows you were with her for eight hours or more!"

"Well, I . . . I think I proposed to her. But that was all."

Nathaniel heard his brother, who stood just beside him now, issue a horrified gasp at this.

"You *think* you proposed to her?" Thorwell echoed in amazement.

"Well, yes, yes. I guess I did . . . after a fashion. But it was all very tentative, you see. And I hardly think that sort of thing would make a young lady flee in the middle of the night. Do you, Meldon?"

"I suppose not," he said after a moment. "Well, not a girl like Caroline, in any case. I think she'd simply have railed at you, if she considered it too bold."

"Yes," Nathaniel agreed, having long since discovered that Caroline wasn't one to sit still for anything she found objectionable.

"You didn't, perchance bag a child with her, did you?" Thorwell inquired charily.

Nathaniel did his best to look indignant. This was not so much for his sake, he realized, as for Caroline's. "What manner of question is that to ask? Really! I'd have you thrown out for that, Meldon, if not for the fact that you're Caroline's uncle, and I, therefore, feel obliged to show you some courtesy!"

"Yes . . . well," Thorwell muttered, looking a little less angry now. "I suppose it was a bit premature, given that she's only been in town for a couple of weeks. Not even *you* could have gotten her with child that quickly, I guess . . . But, damn it all, Nathaniel, I *must* find her at once! I'm telling you, this has my Amelia in such a state that I shall have to call for a doctor soon!"

"Well, you're not alone in it, I assure you, Meldon," Nathaniel declared, daring now to draw up close to him and place a consoling hand on his shoulder. "I'm as worried about her as you are, my dear fellow. Probably even more so, if that be possible. And you have my word that I'll spare no time or expense to help you find her! I'll even be happy to double any sum you care to put up as a bounty for her return."

317

This offer, as Nathaniel could have predicted, brought another protestant gasp from his brother, and he chose to respond to it this time by simply turning and glaring at John. Then, as Nathaniel returned his gaze to Meldon an instant later, he saw a panicky expression on the man's face.

"You don't suppose the redcoats could have gotten hold of her, do you?" Thorwell asked.

Nathaniel froze. He simply hadn't been aware of the situation long enough yet for such a dreadful possibility to have crossed his mind. Now that Meldon had mentioned it, however, an even worse possibility came rushing to the fore. What if Caroline had, without informing him, gone off to rendezvous with her rebel contacts that very night? And what if she'd been tailed by one of Rushton's men in the process and had thereby, ended up in redcoat hands? She could be dead by now! Hung, without a trial, in the woods outside of town, as Nathaniel's previous quarry had been . . . But this was all too horrible to continue contemplating, so Nathaniel stopped himself and did his best to make his expression unreadable. Even if this was how events had unfolded for Caroline that night, he'd promised her that he wouldn't involve her aunt and uncle in her dealings with the rebels, and he saw no gain now in even intimating to Meldon that his niece was taking part in the war.

He would simply have to go to Rushton on his own in the morning, Nathaniel concluded. God knew, after what had happened to Matilda, he was simply blinded with rage to run such a risk. And now, with Caroline missing as well, there was no doubt in his mind that going to the redcoat garrison in person was what he'd have to do. "I . . . I doubt it," he said to Thorwell at last. "As I told you, I rode right up to your front walk with her, and I saw her head for your door."

"But did you see her go inside?"

Nathaniel pondered this question for several seconds. "Well, no. But I'm fairly certain she did. She was just a few steps from the door, after all."

"But you didn't actually *see* her go in?"

"No," Nathaniel confessed, shaking his head. "I suppose I should have stayed and done so, but it just didn't seem necessary at the time. I'm sure you understand."

"Of course," Meldon replied in a tone that Nathaniel found irksomely patronizing. "But understanding won't bring her back to us, will it? We're simply going to have to start a search for her at once."

"I quite agree. And I'll gladly get dressed and come with you now . . . as will John."

John greeted this declaration with a clearly dissenting groan. He seemed to acquiesce an instant later, however, as Nathaniel elbowed him sharply.

"What about any note she may have left around for you or Amelia?" Nathaniel asked. "Have you searched for a letter of explanation from her?"

Thorwell shrugged. "As well as we could after dark. But it will be morning, I'm afraid, before we can really know the answer."

"Yes. I suppose so," Nathaniel agreed, resolving now to keep a calm and level head about himself and not to start panicking until they knew for certain that some harm had befallen Caroline. She was a fiery sort, after all, he reminded himself, the emotional, unpredictable kind of girl who might simply have wandered off in search of a clergyman to whom she could confess even in the middle of the night. He'd heard that Catholics were rather keen on that sort of thing. Or perhaps she'd hidden her cargo for the rebels outside the Thorwells' estate and, once he'd taken her home, had slipped away to bury it somewhere for safekeeping. There were probably dozens of reasons why she'd gone off on her own for a while. So Nathaniel knew it was best not to get too wrought up, until the situation seemed to warrant it.

"Hell of a day, ay, Nathaniel," his brother grumbled. "First Matilda's missing and then Miss Brenton!"

"Yes," Nathaniel replied, shaking his head and silently praying that his dear Caroline would come out of all of this in better shape than his horse had. "Yes. Most disturbing, indeed. Now, please, do go and get dressed, John, so we can begin helping Meldon look for her. And go rouse what staff you can, as well. I want to have as many people searching for her as possible."

Caroline wasn't sure whether she was awake or simply dreaming as she felt the night's chill start to make her shiver. Her head ached, and she was aware of a spinning sensation, but only the surrounding cold really told her that she was probably conscious.

She couldn't see, though she was certain now that her eyes were open. The explanation for this came soon enough, however, as she began to realize that there was a band of cloth running across her eyes and tied at the back of her head.

Even without the aid of vision, though, she knew she was lying on the ground. She was resting on her left side, and she could feel the dampness of the soil beneath her, against her cheek. She could also smell its earthy scent. And, as her senses of touch and smell began to return, her hearing seemed to pick up as well. She heard voices very nearby—low, male voices that seemed to sport British accents.

Finally, as she started to stir, she discovered that her hands were bound at the wrists and positioned behind her, and that was what triggered her to feel her first emotion since . . . Since *when?* she wondered, straining to remember. It was panic she was starting to feel now, an emotion she had rarely experienced nor permitted herself. She had learned, through the years of assisting her mother as a healer, that panic rarely served a useful purpose and usually made matters worse. It was, after all, the ultimate denial of the power one possessed. Yet, to her dismay, panic was definitely what she was feeling as she continued to stir and found that her ankles were bound as well.

Where am I? a frightened voice within her demanded to know. She realized, however, that she simply had no answer. She had been walking toward a door. She remembered that much. Yes. She had been approaching the front door of her aunt and uncle's estate. Nathaniel had just kissed her good night, and she was hurrying up the front walk. Then, suddenly, there'd been a terrible, crushing pain at the back of her head, and she'd felt herself sinking to the ground.

Someone had abducted her. That much was clear to her now, and she felt a lump forming in her throat at this awful realization. She tried to speak in the seconds that followed, but, to her further dismay, all she heard come out of her was a pained groan.

321

"She's come to," a male voice declared, and, a moment later, Caroline was aware of someone, perhaps two people, standing next to her. She then heard a couple of soft thumps upon the ground beside her, and she could tell, from the subsequent warmth she felt and the sudden shelter from the evening wind, that they were kneeling down before her.

"Where . . . where am I?" she managed to say. Unfortunately, she realized an instant later that she'd voiced the question in French.

"Bloody hell, Smythe," she heard one of them growl in response. "You didn't tell us she doesn't speak English. How are we supposed to understand her?"

"She speaks English well enough," the second man countered. "As well as any Colonist, she does. Don't you, *mademoiselle?*"

Caroline suddenly felt a heavy hand on her shoulder, shaking her a bit, as if trying to wake her. "So, what is it you said, lass?"

She struggled to voice the question again in English. "Where . . . where am I?" she asked, and the words sounded so slurred to her that she wasn't at all sure that her captors would be able to make them out.

"She wants to know where she is, I think," the first voice declared after several seconds.

"Ah . . . you're in good hands, Miss Brenton," the second voice offered. "And that's all we can tell you for now, I'm afraid. But we saved you from the redcoats, just remember that," he added gingerly, as though rather fearful of her for some reason.

"The redcoats?" she echoed.

"Yes. They'd have hung you if we hadn't taken you when we did."

Caroline furrowed her brow. "You saved me?"

"Yes."

"Then . . . why am I tied up and blindfolded?"

"Just a precaution we must take for a time, *mademoiselle*. But, don't worry yourself; we'll see to your every need while you're with us. And, if you'll kindly keep from crying out for help, we won't have to make you all the more uncomfortable by gagging you. What say you to that?"

"Very well," Caroline replied in a tremulous voice, having not even considered the fact that she could have found herself gagged as well.

"No point in crying out, anyway, miss," he stated in a resigned tone. "We're too far out of town for anyone to hear you. But I must caution you again that my companions and I will gag you, nonetheless, if you holler. None of us want to listen to your complaints, I'm afraid."

"I'll be quiet," Caroline agreed again. "Who are you, anyway?" she asked cautiously after several seconds.

There was a long pause before he answered. "I'm sorry, but we can't tell you that, not at present. You can rest assured, though, that our plan is to return you safely to your aunt and uncle, and as soon as possible."

"Why can't you take me back to them now?"

Another pause ensued. "Again, I fear you've asked a question we're not at liberty to answer. But you have our promise that you will be returned to your family soon . . . In the meantime, is there anything you've need of? Can we get you anything?"

"*Oui!* A blanket," Caroline answered without hesitation. "I'm cold. It's cold here on the ground."

"Ah, yes, miss. How stupid of us not to realize

that. . . . Go and fetch her some blankets," he ordered. He was apparently speaking to the man next to him now, because Caroline heard his companion object almost instantly.

"Not *ours,* Smythe," he replied, as though appalled at the thought of it.

Caroline heard an odd snarl from one of them, and then they both suddenly rose and walked away. This was followed by a barely audible dispute between them. Then she heard their voices rising once more. "Yes, ours, you fool," one of them snapped. "Who else's can we give her at this hour?" It was the second voice, Caroline realized, the same voice that had been doing most of the talking with her. "Now, go and fetch them," he continued, "before she grows cross with us."

"She?" Caroline echoed in her mind. She who? Was it possible that he meant *her?* And, if so, why would they care if they made her cross? Wasn't having been abducted by them reason enough for her to become angry? Why would they fear angering her further? It simply didn't make sense to her, and she again began to wonder if she really was awake or if this was all just a nightmare as she had at first suspected. But, if it *was* only a bad dream, it was certainly the most lifelike she'd ever had. Everything, from the pain at the back of her head to the frightened racing of her heart, seemed as real as it could be.

And what about the name she'd heard the first voice call the second? Smythe, was it? It sounded familiar to Caroline. Yet, for the life of her, she couldn't seem to place it. She only knew that, wherever she'd heard it, she'd attached some very negative feelings to it.

Her thoughts were interrupted an instant later, as the

men finally returned to her and declared that they had the blankets she'd requested. She was delighted to hear this, but, before she could express her gratitude, she felt one of them gather her up in his arms, and all she could seem to do in response was let out an apprehensive gasp and stiffen like a board. Her fearfulness was allayed, however, as she felt herself being lowered back to the ground an instant later and set down upon the requested blanket. Then, to her further relief, they spread a second cover over her and hurriedly tucked it in all about her. The blankets were coarse and thin, but they did seem to be sealing out the night's chill, so she saw no point in complaining.

"Merci . . . thank you," she heard herself say at last.

"Oh, it was nothing, miss," the second voice answered. This was the one called Smythe, she told herself, the man the other one had called by that name.

"We should have known you'd be cold, even in that hide dress of yours," she heard him go on to say.

"It's a riding habit," she explained.

"Ah . . . yes," he said awkwardly. "I guess I knew that."

"What is it your companion called you?" Caroline asked gingerly, sensing that this had been the topic that had gotten the two of them arguing earlier.

"Just a nickname, miss. I don't go by it much," he answered, the finality in his voice telling her it would be in her best interest to simply drop the subject.

"What time is it?" she asked after a moment.

"Just about midnight, I guess," the other man quickly volunteered. "Time for all of us to get some sleep before dawn breaks," he concluded pointedly.

"And what happens at dawn?" she fished.

"You'll be alone for a little while," the one called Smythe replied. "But no need to worry. One of us will be back to see to it you get some breakfast and such."

"And will you untie me then?" she asked hopefully.

"Ah, yes, so you can have a bit of privacy if you need it to relieve yourself. Yes, miss, I'm sure we can grant you at least that much . . . that is, if you'll just be so kind as to keep quiet now so that we can sleep a bit," he added guardedly.

"Yes . . . of course," Caroline hesitantly agreed, again sensing an odd sort of fear in him, in the wary way in which he put things to her. They weren't acting much like kidnappers. They seemed a little too polite somehow, yet she instinctively knew that they would deny her requests if she failed to comply with theirs. And theirs, at present, was that she stop asking questions and simply let them shuffle back, to wherever they'd been when she'd awakened, and get some sleep. So, still feeling woozy and tongue-tied from the blow on her head, Caroline concluded that it *was* probably best to save her questions until morning, and she obligingly bade them good night.

They both wished her the same, and then she heard them walk away. She knew without being told, however, that they wouldn't be far from her.

Chapter 19

As she approached the Thorwells' front door, Margaret Brenton Prentiss wasn't entirely sure what she would say to her relatives. She supposed that they'd believe her if she simply told them she had come to visit with Caroline. She was, after all, Caroline's aunt. She was certainly as much her aunt as Amelia had ever been, she told herself, as she neared the estate's entrance now. Yet, as always happened when she came to this place, she felt her mouth growing dry and a lump forming in her throat. She knew she wasn't really welcome here, and she hated always winding up having to make all the conversation whenever she paid her sister and brother-in-law a call. To make matters worse, Margaret already knew that this visit would prove particularly tricky, because today was the day she'd chosen to come in for the kill. Caroline had been in town for over two weeks now, and God only knew how long she intended to stay. So, finally deciding that their time was probably more limited than they realized, Margaret and her husband had come up with a plan for doing away with this barrier to their economic betterment.

They were going to host a gathering in her honor, much as Amelia and Meldon had, so Caroline would feel sufficiently obligated to attend. To make doubly certain that she'd be there, Margaret had already begun inviting several of Boston's most prominent citizens to the function. It was to be a fox hunt. After tailing Caroline off and on since her arrival, Margaret had learned that her niece was seeing a great deal of Nathaniel Hamlin, and everyone in Boston knew how fond he was of fox hunts. He hosted them frequently, and it was common knowledge that he'd never declined an invitation to one. So, once Margaret procured his agreement to attend, Caroline was sure to follow. Then, just to cinch the plan, Margaret would rather offhandedly inform her niece that she was inviting several of Boston's most eligible maidens to the function, as well. Surely that would be all it would take to insure that the heir apparent would agree to come. Caroline had, after all, already shown herself to be wise enough not to let a catch like Hamlin fall into another young lady's hands.

Then, once everyone had arrived, some beverages would be served and the hunt would begin. It would be followed by an outdoor banquet, which would also be held on the grounds of Margaret's home.

Unfortunately, however, the day would end in tragedy when it was discovered that Caroline Brenton had fallen from her horse during the hunt, after having struck her head on a low-hung tree branch. This seeming accident was, of course, to be carefully engineered by Margaret and her husband.

It would begin as they first saw to it that a trace of hemlock was slipped into their niece's beverage, prior to the hunt. This wouldn't be a lethal amount of the poison, of course, because the cause of such a death was too easily deduced. It would simply be enough to induce the initial sympton of hemlock poisoning, slight motor paralysis.

Once the hunt began, Margaret's husband would be careful to stay closely behind Caroline, so that he'd be present when the poison took effect and Caroline started to lag. Then, when she eventually lost control of her horse and fell from it, Mr. Prentiss would be there to finish the job.

With all of the other riders well ahead of them by that time, he'd simply get off his horse and go and deliver a death-dealing blow to the front of his niece's head with a branchlike object.

It was admittedly a precarious scheme, one that would hinge very heavily upon Caroline being assigned to just the right, rather volatile horse. And, of course, if Hamlin, or any of the other guests, happened to notice that Caroline was lagging and decided to drop behind to be with her, the plan could be foiled as well. But, desperate as Margaret and her husband were to regain a hold on the Brenton family wealth, it did seem as sound a scheme as any they were apt to devise in what time remained.

Margaret took a deep bolstering breath as she finally reached the front door of her sister's home. Again assuring herself that, as the first-born of her generation of Brentons, her mission here today was justified, she reached up to take hold of the knocker. As she did so, however, she heard a flat, papery kind of slap at her feet, and she looked down to see that a note of some sort had fallen onto the estate's front step. Noticing that it was addressed to Meldon and Amelia Thorwell in an urgent-looking kind of scrawl she bent down to pick it up, her curiosity getting the best of her.

Fortunately, it wasn't sealed, so Margaret wasted no time in ducking into the adjacent hedge and reading through it. Her mouth dropped open an instant later, and her heart began to pound with excitement.

We are holding your niece, Caroline, for ransom. If you wish to have her returned to you alive, leave six hundred pounds in Massachusetts bills of credit in a purse in the bushes in the northeastern corner of the green that lies before the governor's palace—by five o'clock tomorrow evening.

The note was, of course, unsigned, and it bore the previous day's date.

Margaret was frozen with shock for several seconds. Then she clapped the missive to her chest, offering up a silent prayer of thanks. Incredibly, as if by divine intervention, some dear souls had already come along and done her dirty work for her. All she had to do now was stash the ransom note in her drawstring purse, walk back to her livery carriage, and see to it that the message was safely burned, once she got it home. Then, with any luck, Caroline's kidnappers, whoever they might be, would grow annoyed with waiting for a response to their note and simply follow through with what they'd implicitly threatened to do if the money wasn't awaiting them by five—kill their captive.

Suddenly realizing, however, that she would be the prime suspect in her niece's disappearance if it were attributed to kidnapping, Margaret decided it was best to go ahead and knock on her sister's door and proceed with her previous plan of action, rather than making a quick getaway. Surely Amelia and Meldon would be less likely to point an accusing finger at her if she continued as she'd planned, pretending not to know a thing about Caroline's abduction.

With that decided, she stuffed the note into her purse and stepped up once more to knock on the door. The most important thing was to appear the same as always, she told herself in those frenzied seconds. Above all else, she knew she mustn't let her jubilation show. This was going to be difficult, she knew, as she heard someone rushing to answer the door. It was probably going to be one of the toughest things she'd ever had to do.

As the front door opened to her an instant later, Margaret was surprised to see that it was Meldon himself who had come to it. Always, when she'd called before, he and Amelia had been careful to let the servants answer the knock. The reason for this deviation was clear to Margaret as soon as she saw her brother-in-law's face. Even in this soft, early-morning light, he looked as though he had just risen from the dead. The bags under his eyes were much more pronounced than usual, and his clothes were terribly wrinkled, as though he'd slept in them. He was worried sick about Caroline, and he'd obviously been hoping that it was she who had knocked or someone bringing word of her whereabouts.

"Dear Heavens! What's happened to you?" Margaret asked with a gasp.

Meldon, looking even less enthused than usual to see her, simply responded with a groan and called off in the direction of the parlor. "It's only your sister. Should I send her away?"

"No. Show her in," Margaret heard Amelia call weakly.

Margaret donned an amenable expression. "I could come back some other time, Meldon, if this is not convenient."

"No. Come in," he said with a grunt, as he stepped aside for her to enter. "I can't imagine that even *you* could put Amelia into a worse humor than she's in already."

"Well, whatever is the matter?" Margaret asked blankly, slowly making her way into the entrance hall.

"Oh, don't tell me you haven't heard. I thought that was why you came."

She offered him a mystified scowl. *"What* was why I came?"

"Because of Caroline, of course."

"Well, in truth, my visit does regard Caroline," Margaret explained, spotting Amelia who lay, rather forlornly, on a camel-back settee in the adjacent parlor.

"What about her? Do you know where she is?" Meldon asked anxiously.

"Well, she's *here,* isn't she? I came to invite her to a hunt."

"No. She's not here, you dolt. Half of Boston's been out looking for her since midnight, for Christ's sake! She's missing!"

Margaret pressed a palm to her bosom and tried to look sufficiently taken aback. "Well, dear Lord,

Meldon, how was I to know? We live so far out, after all. It sometimes takes a couple days for news to reach us. How was I to know?" she asked again almost tearfully. He looked so frosty at her show of emotion, however, that she thought it best to go and throw herself upon her sister. "Oh, my dear Amelia," she exclaimed, rushing into the parlor. "You must be worried half to death about her, you poor, dear thing!"

Amelia, looking even more pallid than her husband, struggled up to a sitting position as she saw her older sister making a beeline for her. She'd managed to dress, but her blondish hair was still hanging down about her shoulders. It looked as though she hadn't even taken the time to run a comb through it. She made a feeble effort to hug back as Margaret bent down and threw her arms about her. Nevertheless, Margaret could tell from her expression, as they ended the embrace, that she was absolutely the last person Amelia had wanted to see that morning.

"What happened to her?" Margaret asked, reaching down to slide Amelia's legs back a bit on the settee, before attempting to perch upon it herself. "When did you see her last?"

"Yesterday afternoon," Amelia answered, her voice still sounding weak as though she'd made herself hoarse with crying. "She went to Nathaniel Hamlin's for a hunt, and she just never . . . never . . . returned," she explained, faltering due to her emotional state.

"Well, have you spoken to Mr. Hamlin?"

"Of course we have," Meldon answered scoldingly from where he now stood in the parlor doorway.

"I was speaking to my sister," Margaret snapped back, forgetting herself for a moment.

"But, if you had half a brain, Margaret, you'd see that your sister is in no mood to speak to you."

Margaret couldn't help gritting her teeth at his rudeness. He and Amelia had admittedly always been on the curt side with her through the years, but this was the first time either of them had been so biting. "Let me remind you, Meldon Thorwell, that Caroline is *my* niece, too. More mine, than she is yours! And, on that basis alone, I think I have the right to know what you two can tell me about her disappearance."

Meldon, looking a bit shaken by this irrefutable retort, responded at last with a weary groan. "Oh, take pity on us just this once, will you please? We've obviously been up all night, and were worried senseless about the girl. So, won't you please take my word for the fact that there's nothing else to tell?"

"And what will you tell her father?" Margaret inquired gingerly after several seconds.

"Well, we're hoping she'll return to us soon so there'll be no need to worry him."

"I think you're deluding yourself, Meldon," Margaret replied, raising a critical brow at him. "You're a stupid dreamer, and you always have been."

"And you're a *snake*," he spat. "In fact, it wouldn't surprise me in the least, if you and that scheming husband of yours are the ones behind all of this!"

"Oh, Meldon, *please*," Amelia pleaded, slumping forward on the settee.

Margaret narrowed her eyes spitefully at her brother-in-law, and she felt compelled to rush over and slap his face in those seconds. Given her sister's pathetic plea, however, she forced herself to stay where she was. "Though I shouldn't have to, Meldon," she declared, looking him squarely in the eye, "I am prepared to swear on a stack of Bibles that neither I nor my husband had anything to do with Caroline's disappearance. In fact, I came here this morning expressly to extend an invitation to her, as I told you. But, if that is truly how you feel about me, I think it is best that I go now . . . and to you, dear Amelia," she added, reaching over and giving her sister's right hand a condolent squeeze, "I offer whatever asistance my family and I can render in finding our niece." With that, Margaret reached up and made a show of dabbing her eyes with the handkerchief that protruded from the right sleeve of her gown. Then, she cleared her throat with a stoic air, rose, and made her way back to the front door, completely ignoring her brother-in-law en route. "Send for me if you need me, and good day to you both," she concluded, exiting and shutting the estate's front door behind her.

Excellent, a voice within her praised, as she strode back to where her coach was waiting, and she felt a triumphant chill run through her. She had given what she considered to be a damned convincing performance, and there was no denying that things were finally looking up for her!

Though Nathaniel was definitely seeing red by the time he reached Rushton's garrison the following morning, he still had the presence of mind to go through conventional channels in order to meet with the commander. Crazed with rage and worry as he now was, he did realize that attempting to storm through the British camp and barge into Rushton's barracks

335

would only end in his being shot, and there seemed no point in allowing the redcoats to claim yet another victim. He, therefore, followed a more levelheaded procedure. He handed a note, asking to meet with Smythe, to one of the sentries posted on the periphery of the camp, and waited as patiently as possible for Smythe to come to him. When at last Smythe did appear, he looked amazed to see that Nathaniel really had dared to come there in person.

"Good morning to you, sir," Smythe said by way of greeting, obviously wishing to avoid speaking Nathaniel's name in front of the other soldiers. "What can I do for you?" he asked uneasily.

"You can take me to see the commander," Nathaniel replied through clenched teeth.

"Ah, yes. Certainly . . . But a word with you first, sir, I pray thee," Smythe added, taking Nathaniel aside so the others couldn't overhear.

Nathaniel was tempted to take a swing at him at this point. But, knowing how much more difficult it would be to obtain an audience with Rushton if he acted on such an urge, he refrained from doing so.

"Have you taken leave of your senses, Mr. Hamlin?" Smythe asked an instant later. "First sending your poor footman here the other day and now coming here yourself! Could it be that you actually *want* to find your house burnt to the ground by the Whigs, sir?"

Nathaniel continued to speak in a growl. "Mr. Smythe, in the past twenty-four hours, I have been forced to conclude that I would indeed fare better at Whig hands than at those of you redcoats! Now, take me to the commander at once!"

Smythe, fearing now that Hamlin might somehow

have found out it was he who was behind Miss Brenton's disappearance, thought it best to question him further on the nature of his visit before granting this request. "Well, obviously, sir, you are most upset, and you have my word that we'll do all we can to put matters right with you. But it would help greatly if you could tell me a bit more about what is troubling you."

"Gladly! It concerns my horse, stolen by redcoat soldiers yesterday and beaten and run nearly to death! It concerns Crosley Fergusson, found hung without trial in the woods, after *I* informed on him to you. And, most importantly, it concerns my latest quarry, Mademoiselle Caroline Brenton, who mysteriously disappeared last night and has not been seen or heard from since! I know you took her, Smythe, so don't bother to deny it!"

"*I,* sir?" the sergeant asked with a horrified gasp.

Nathaniel waved him off in annoyance. "Well, not *you* specifically, you fool! But you redcoats in general. I know, without having to be told, that you are behind it!"

"Sir, that is quite a grave accusation to be making, don't you think? And I really must warn you that the commander is not apt to receive it well. Might I manage to persuade you to come back later when you're not quite so wrought up?"

Feeling unable to restrain himself any longer, Nathaniel grabbed Smythe by his gorget. As he drew his arm back to punch the man, however, he felt someone take hold of him from behind, and he knew that the sentries had decided to intervene.

"It's all right," he heard Smythe declare, as he was being pulled backward by one of the guards seconds

337

later. "He's here to see Commander Rushton. Just frisk him and let him go, so he can come with me. He won't try that again," Smythe added with a chary laugh. "Now will you, sir?"

"No," Nathaniel conceded in a snarl, seizing the chance to jerk free as the sentry's grip upon him loosened. As raving mad as he still felt, he realized now, while the other guard was obediently frisking him, that the redcoats would simply pick him up and toss him out if he didn't get a grip on himself immediately. He, therefore, took the time to draw in a long calming breath and straighten his coat and vest before following Smythe into the post a moment later.

"I am sorry about all of that," Smythe began again, gingerly, as he stopped walking for a second or two and allowed Nathaniel to catch up with him. "But we really can't afford to run the risk of having the commander shot by a crazed civilian, you understand. And, frankly, Mr. Hamlin, I don't believe I've ever seen you in such a state."

"Yes. I understand," Nathaniel choked out, continuing to fight to keep himself under control.

Smythe entertained the idea of asking for more details regarding what had happened to Hamlin's horse, but, considering this man's outburst before the sentries, it seemed wisest not to mention anything that might get him worked up again. Consequently, they walked in silence the rest of the way to the commander's barracks.

Once they reached it, Smythe asked that Nathaniel wait outside while he went in to announce him to Rushton. Then, having done so, he returned to Nathaniel and showed him inside, advising that he keep his visit brief because the commander had an inspection to conduct straightaway.

"Thank you, Sergeant," Rushton said to Smythe, dismissing him with a salute.

Smythe, in turn, saluted and took his leave. Once he was outside the barracks, however, he ducked around to its right side and stood next to a window, straining to hear the conversation that ensued.

"Well, Mr. Hamlin." The commander hailed him from where he sat, behind a French writing table, partaking of breakfast scones and tea. He was a large, piglike man with ears that bowed out from under the pannier curls of his white wig like two huge apricots. "We meet again, it seems. And what a surprise! Smythe told me you had gone so far as to send a footman here the other day, but I certainly had no idea you'd take matters quite this far. You're aware, surely, of the risk you're taking by coming here, aren't you?"

"Quite, sir. But it didn't matter to me, you see."

"Do sit down and have some tea," Rushton continued evenly, as though he hadn't even heard Nathaniel's response.

"I prefer to stand," Nathaniel said coldly.

Rushton raised a brow at him. "Well, suit yourself," he replied with a shrug. "Smythe tells me you've all the details we requested on your latest assignment."

"Are we free, Commander, to discuss such matters in present company?" Nathaniel asked, directing his gaze at the two soldiers who were busily sorting through some papers on the table, behind which Rushton sat.

The commander greeted this question with a caustic laugh. "Good heavens, Mr. Hamlin. I can hardly believe you'd be concerned about such a thing, after having ridden out here, in broad daylight for half of Boston to see!"

"The question still stands, sir, nevertheless," Nathaniel growled.

Rushton laughed again. "Yes. It's quite all right. They're simply my assistants. Nothing you say will go any farther than this room, sir. You have my word on that."

"Your word," Nathaniel mocked. "Believe me, Rushton, it's worth less and less to me these days!"

The commander looked angered by this, his cheeks reddening a bit. Nathaniel was fairly certain that the officer would choose to remain civil, however. He had been an asset to Rushton for quite some time now, and, given how difficult Tory spies were to come by these days, Nathaniel knew he had a way to go before it was decided that he had overstepped his bounds. "I'm very sorry to hear that," Rushton responded, amenably enough. "Might I ask why that is?"

"Oh, I'm here to tell you, Commander. Rest assured!"

Again Rushton looked like he was fighting the urge to lash out at Nathaniel. "Well, then, please do."

"Firstly, there's the matter of Mademoiselle Brenton. I demand, sir, that you take me to her at once!"

Rushton drew his head back, looking baffled by this request. *"What?"*

"She disappeared last night. At some time after ten, and I demand to know what you've done with her!"

To Nathaniel's surprise, the commander continued to stare at him blankly, as though honestly believing he'd taken leave of his senses.

"Well, *we* don't have her, Mr. Hamlin," he said

finally. "I thought we agreed that it was you who would keep an eye on her."

"Oh, rubbish!" Nathaniel thundered. "You've taken her off somewhere and hung her, haven't you? Just as you did Fergusson!"

"We've done nothing of the kind," Rushton declared, and his tone was so convincing that Nathaniel was tempted to believe him.

"Then, where is she?"

The commander shrugged. "I have no idea. In fact, I was hoping that you had come to tell me what you could about her and her rebel contacts . . . when she plans to meet with them."

"Well . . . not for a while yet," Nathaniel stammered, too chagrined to admit that he'd been premature in sending word to Smythe that he had acquired the details about the rendezvous.

"In that case, let us hope she comes to hand before that time, or all of your work will probably be for naught. Aye, Mr. Hamlin?"

"Yes. I'm afraid so," Nathaniel admitted. "But you can't deny that your men hung Fergusson," he began again angrily. "It was all over town that they were the ones responsible!"

At this, Rushton dropped his gaze remorsefully to his tea cup. "Yes . . . quite regrettable, that. I did mean to arrange to speak with you personally about it. You know, try to explain to you how matters purportedly got out of line on that particular evening and how I didn't intend to allow the incident to set a precedent in such cases. Sorrily, however, I failed to do so, and for that, sir," he continued, looking Nathaniel squarely in the eye now, "I do apologize to you most profusely. But you have my word that no such fate will befall Mademoiselle Brenton or any of the other suspects we may assign you to in the future. So, please, don't worry yourself about it."

Though he wasn't sure why, Nathaniel was certain that Rushton was telling him the truth. "You *don't* have her," he said, his confoundedness evident in his voice.

"No, sir."

"But I thought you had planned to have her comings and goings watched while she was in Boston."

"Yes. Smythe was tending to that, you see. But, once you sent word that you'd already obtained the requested information from her, I had him discontinue those efforts."

"So, you really don't know where she is." Nathaniel was unable to hide his worry now. If they didn't have her, who did?

"That's right, Mr. Hamlin," the commander answered wearily. "However, I promise to send word to you straightaway, if she should be found. And I trust you'll do the same for us."

"I'm sorry, but I'm making no more promises to you, Rushton," Nathaniel replied in an ominously low voice. "In fact, I refuse to tell you what I've learned about Miss Brenton's rendezvous—until you've given some answers to what I've asked!"

"And so I shall, my dear fellow, when I *have* them," the commander declared through gritted teeth. "I've already promised you that! And, as for your service to His Majesty in this war, might I remind you that it has been completely voluntary all along? Therefore, I fail to see why it would be any different now," he concluded resignedly.

"Well, it most certainly isn't," Nathaniel spat out.

Rushton offered him a patronizing glare. "So I just said, sir. Is there anything else on your mind before I take my leave? I'm late for an inspection of my troops, I'm afraid."

"Yes. There is something else," Nathaniel blurted out. "What about my horse? What have you got to say about that?"

Rushton furrowed his brow and gave forth a light bewildered laugh. "Your horse, sir?"

"My Arabian. The horse my stableboys saw some of your redcoats run off with yesterday afternoon!"

The commander looked concerned once again. *"My* redcoats, Mr. Hamlin? Are you certain of that?"

"Well . . . no," Nathaniel confessed. "But they were, sure as hell, *someone's* redcoats, Commander, and you could, at least, offer to look into the matter for me, considering the services I've rendered to you!"

"Very well," Rushton agreed after a moment. "Now that I've been informed of it, I shall look into it." With that, he rose and reached out to shake Nathaniel's hand, as though anxious to get rid of him and proceed with his duties.

Nathaniel grudgingly stepped up to the table and accepted the handshake.

"I'll send word to you the moment I hear anything about either Mademoiselle Brenton or the men who took your horse," Rushton pledged, looking unflinchingly into Nathaniel's eyes. "How is that?"

"Fine," Nathaniel said, still seething.

"And is that all you wished to discuss?" the commander asked again.

"Yes. I suppose so," Nathaniel muttered, mad at himself for not having been more forceful with the

343

man. But he simply hadn't had enough sleep, he told himself, as Rushton gathered up his frock coat and left the barracks. He'd been up most of the night with Meldon and John and the rest, searching for Caroline. Then, when the breakfast hour had finally rolled around and there was still no sign of her, he'd found himself too distraught to eat so much as a slice of toast. He was exhausted and hungry, a voice within him noted consolingly, and he just hadn't been thinking clearly enough to handle a confrontation with one as formidable as Rushton—especially at this early hour.

Perhaps another time, he thought. Maybe, if Caroline didn't turn up in a day or two, he'd ride back out to the garrison and stand up to the commander again, when he was more rested. For now, it was probably best just to go home and try to steal a few hours of sleep before rejoining the others in the search for Caroline.

He acknowledged, however, that this visit hadn't been in vain. He'd obviously caught Rushton by surprise and had gotten some seemingly candid answers out of him, along with the pledge to look into what had happened to both Caroline and Matilda. Things could certainly have gone much worse, Nathaniel concluded, heading out of the barracks as well now.

Chapter 20

It was the second day after Caroline had been abducted, and she'd finally recalled where she'd heard the name Smythe. It was the surname of the man she had met in Nathaniel's study a couple of weeks before, the man whose hand she had treated and whom she had sensed was evil. And, even though her captors still had her blindfolded and she hadn't seen any of their faces, she knew that the one who'd been called Smythe that first night was indeed the man to whom Nathaniel had introduced her.

It wasn't his voice that told her this, because in truth, she didn't remember anything about it. She hadn't been with him long enough on the day they'd met to recall its qualities, and it hadn't struck her at the time as being in any way distinctive. He had, however, had an English accent—as did each of her three captors. Still, what had finally confirmed for her that he was the same man was the evilness she'd sensed in him the day they'd met. It was undeniably present in this fellow as well. What was more, she'd made it a point to ask for his hand whenever he'd taken his turn at leading her about in her blindfolded state, and she had, thereby, had the chance to run her fingertips across his right palm. There she had felt, as she'd suspected she would, the large crescent-shaped sort of scar that only a horse bite could cause.

She didn't think it wise, however, to let on that she knew who he was. Assuming he and his companions really were going to set her free, as they'd continued claiming they would, it just didn't seem prudent to disclose this to him. They had, after all, been very vigilant so far about keeping her blindfolded, so it only stood to reason that they didn't care to let her be able to identify them, once she was released. She had chosen, therefore, to keep her mouth shut about what she'd deduced and to simply try to be as cooperative as possible, in the hope that it wouldn't be long before they set her free.

Nevertheless, this secret deduction had stirred up a number of disturbing questions for her. If this *was* the man to whom Nathaniel had introduced her, did that then mean that Nathaniel had had something to do with her abduction? Was it possible he was behind it all?

No. Absolutely not, a voice within her declared, and she hated herself now for even having entertained such an appalling thought. She'd all but promised to marry him, for heaven's sake, when they'd last been together, and it was he himself who had insisted upon seeing her safely back to her aunt and uncle's estate the night she'd been kidnapped. No, it didn't seem likely that he was in any way connected with what had happened to her. Furthermore, Caroline distinctly remembered that his manner with Smythe had not been a terribly friendly one. He had, in fact, seemed rather brusque and dutiful with the man, as though their relationship had been strictly one of business.

Because Nathaniel had said that Smythe was a farmer, Caroline had gotten the impression that the man was somehow involved in supplying food to the Hamlin estate, and she really hadn't thought to ask Nathaniel anything more about his association with him. One thing had been evident to her, though; Nathaniel hadn't seemed to know very much about Smythe. Even when she'd scolded him for not telling her that Smythe was evil, he'd simply looked at her blankly, as though he knew too little about the fellow either to admit to or refute the claim. Again, Caroline told herself, perhaps only for the preservation of her sanity now, that Nathaniel was not involved in what had happened to her. The only thing he might have been guilty of was simply having, unwittingly, introduced her to an opportunist of some sort. And that, Caroline resolved, was all she would conclude about the matter, until she was reunited with Nathaniel and he was able to explain and defend himself.

It wasn't that being kidnapped had proven so terrible, really. The truth was she hadn't come to any harm in her captors' keeping. They were feeding her three times a day with nutritious, if somewhat tasteless, food, and they'd certainly seen to her other needs with compassionate regularity. It was just that she'd grown frightfully bored and restless after so many hours of being blindfolded and bound, and, of course, she was most concerned about how her disappearance was affecting her aunt and uncle. She could almost feel their worry and torment as she sat thinking about them, hour after hour, day and night, but all she could seem to do in response was try to silently convey to them the message that she was still alive and well, and that her kidnappers had promised she'd be safely released.

Nevertheless, she'd gotten the impression that something had gone wrong with her captors' plan in the past day or so. They didn't seem nearly as heartening with her now as they had the night they'd abducted her. There was a note of discouragement and sometimes even of annoyance in their voices when they talked to her of late, and, though it was never loud enough for her to hear much, they seemed to be quarreling quite a bit now as well. She'd overheard only enough to know that their bickering had to do with the fact that they hadn't been paid some money as they'd expected. She could, therefore, only conclude—though they refused to confirm this for her—that they'd asked her family to ransom her.

Naturally, she found all of this disturbing. She was certain that her aunt and uncle would be happy to pay just about any sum in order to have her returned to them. Yet it appeared that they were hesitating for some reason, and she couldn't imagine what it might be. But, just as with her suspicion of Nathaniel, she had decided to push any unsavory conjecture to the back of her mind for a while longer, because now, more than ever before, she needed to believe in the loyalty and support of her loved ones. In fact, helpless as she felt in this situation, she found that she was positively clinging to such a belief for emotional sustenance.

Perhaps it wasn't her aunt and uncle her kidnappers asked for a ransom, a voice within her suddenly suggested. They could be attempting to extract money from *Nathaniel* for her return. Maybe Smythe had been observing Nathaniel closely enough to deduce how close the shipbuilder had become to her, and he had decided that Nathaniel was as good a rich man as any to try to wrest such a sum from. Perhaps that explained why her kidnappers hadn't received their money yet. Maybe Nathaniel, feeling it would be unseemly for him to pay ransom for a woman to whom he wasn't yet even formally engaged, had passed the demand on to Caroline's aunt and uncle, and they needed some time to respond.

Yes. That sounded plausible, Caroline told herself. That might be the reason for the delay in all of this. She'd simply have to ask her captors who it was they were endeavoring to exact a ransom from and see if any of them were willing to answer. That question would have to wait for a while, however, a voice within her cautioned. The two men guarding her at present had been quarreling off and on for almost an hour, and she instinctively knew it was best not to make such an inquiry until they'd all had supper and seemed to be in better moods.

As Smythe rode back to where they were holding Caroline that evening, he decided that he would be taking her with him when he and his company moved out of Boston the following morning. Even if her aunt and uncle didn't care enough about her to respond to his ransom note, it was a pretty sure bet that her parents would, and, as chance would have it, her home territory of Louisiana was precisely where Smythe and his fellow soldiers were being transferred.

Admittedly, taking her along would entail some risks. While the *mademoiselle* had been fairly cooperative so far—having been told that she was being held just outside Boston—she might become quite unmanageable, once she realized she was being taken out of Massachusetts. And there was no telling what a woman with her ominous powers was capable of doing in retaliation. On the other hand, she also possessed the power to heal, Smythe reminded himself, a skill that was apt to come in very handy if he and his company found themselves fighting rebels or Indians along the way. So, perhaps the good she could do would outweigh the bad. And, in truth, Smythe thought, just how uncooperative could an unarmed girl in the middle of a savage-ridden wilderness be?

What was more, she had been born and raised in Louisiana—not far from Fort Bute, if Smythe's memory served—so she might also prove helpful as a guide, once they reached that area. He'd be sure to tell his company captain that, if any questions were asked. He doubted they would be, however, because women were almost always found in redcoat camps. They served as both nurses and laundresses, and they even marched into battle with the men they worked for, from time to time. So, Smythe doubted that his fellow soldiers would even raise an eyebrow, as Caroline accompanied them.

Yes, all in all, he told himself, taking her along did seem a better plan than simply succumbing to the Thorwells' stubbornness and setting her free. He had intended to knuckle under a bit to their unresponsiveness and send them another ransom note. Once his company received its transfer orders, however, he'd realized he had to think of another way to benefit from the kidnapping, and, given how little time there'd been in which to make a decision, he felt he'd reached the best one.

Nathaniel was leaning back against the left wall of Matilda's stall now, stroking the mare's back. Her lash wounds were healing remarkably quickly for a horse of her age, and it was clear to Nathaniel that there was every chance he'd get several more years of riding out of her—thanks to Caroline. Ordinarily, this realization would have brought him great joy. With Caroline still missing, however, he was finding that the only emotions he seemed to be feeling of late were sadness and, of course, rage at whoever had taken her. This, in fact, was the first time in nearly three days that he'd allowed himself to just stand about and feel nothing at all for a few minutes. Unfortunately, though, this respite had come about for the worst of all possible reasons: they had simply run out of places to look for Caroline.

Nathaniel and Meldon, along with at least one hundred friends and family members, had spent the last sixty-four hours searching for her, and not a single clue had been found. Still thinking that Caroline might have gone off to rendezvous with her contacts, Nathaniel had even gone so far as to talk Meldon into letting him have a look through her luggage for any clues. This hadn't been easy, of course, considering that Nathaniel was still unwilling to reveal to the Thorwells that their niece was involved with the rebels. And, even though he'd been allowed to go ahead and search her suite, the effort had revealed nothing conclusive. Naturally, he'd hoped to find that the weapons John had seen were still hidden in one of Caroline's trunks. As he'd feared, however, he'd found that none of her luggage contained the contraband. Nevertheless, this wasn't absolute proof that Caroline had gone, without forewarning him, to her rendezvous. After the episode with John, a girl as bright as she would probably have taken the weapons out of the house and hidden them elsewhere—especially in light of her concern about not letting her aunt and uncle become implicated in all of it. So, the fact that the contraband was missing still didn't offer any solid clues as to her whereabouts. And, even though Nathaniel and Meldon had offered a veritable fortune as a reward for Caroline's return, no one in Boston could seem to offer any solid clues either.

Though the Thorwells and their household staff had searched their estate upstairs and down for some written explanation from their niece, none had been found. Nor had they received any kind of ransom note telling them she'd been kidnapped. Nathaniel, too, was finding himself left equally in the dark. He still hadn't heard a word from the commander in response to the questions he'd asked, and he was certain he would have, had Rushton had anything to report. The situation was beginning to look more and more desperate with each day that passed.

To make matters worse, Nathaniel had become so run-down since Caroline had disappeared, he'd caught a cold and was running a slight fever, which he couldn't seem to shake. Perhaps because of this feverish state, the ballad kept rolling around in his head, the one to which he and Caroline had danced the night they'd met. It seemed to haunt him day and night now, the sweet, high tones of the dulcimer and violins that had produced it sounding to him more and more like the cries of a young woman than notes from the strings of instruments. And a part of him knew they were the telepathic cries of a girl who was lost and alone somewhere in a strange war-torn land.

Though he hated himself for it, the music made him feel like that sad young lad again, the one who had, against all reason, tearfully awaited his mother's return from Ireland, at the harbor, night after night. He couldn't recall precisely how long it had taken for his father to finally convince him that his mother was dead and that no ship, not even the finest the Hamlin ship-yards could build, would be able to bring her back to Boston alive. Nor was he sure which words his father had used to finally make him understand and accept this tragic truth. Whichever ones they were, however, Nathaniel prayed now that he wouldn't have to hear them again, in connection with his dear Caroline. As strong-minded and resilient as he'd prided himself in being since his father's death, he just didn't think he could bear that.

His thoughts were suddenly interrupted by the sound of someone entering the stable, and he looked up to see his brother's shadowed form darkening the doorway. "What news, John?" he asked, swallowing uneasily.

As his brother proceeded to Matilda's stall, his features became clearer in the light from the adjacent window, and Nathaniel could see John looked far too relaxed to have come down to the stable about anything of great importance.

"Not much," he answered with a shrug, leaning up against the stall door with his hands and forearms resting across the top of it. "It's just that it seems your friend, Smythe, has been running up quite a few gambling debts of late, and his creditors are most annoyed with him."

Nathaniel furrowed his brow. "What? Where did you hear that?"

"At the Blue Boar Tavern. After what you said the other day about Smythe being the one Rushton assigned to keep an eye on Caroline, I didn't think it would do any harm if one of us did a bit of eavesdropping where he and his bloody-back friends lollop. You and Meldon seemed so busy with investigating the other possibilities, I just decided to take care of this on my own. And guess what else I learned."

Nathaniel continued to scowl. "What?"

"Smythe's been sent off to Louisiana, of all places. To some British fort called Bute, on some bayou down there. . . . *Quelle coïncidence*, right, Nathan?" he added with a dry laugh.

Nathaniel didn't reply. He simply stood staring expressionlessly at his brother, racking his brain for any connection that might be made in all of it.

"Well, what do you think?" John prompted after a moment. "Do you think he may have had something to do with Caroline's disappearance?"

"Holding her, perhaps, to raise money to pay off his debts, you mean?"

John nodded. "Something of the sort."

354

"But there's been no ransom note. And, as you said, he's been sent out of Boston. It just doesn't make sense."

John shrugged. "Well, he only just received his transfer orders, and maybe it wasn't a ransom he sought for her. Maybe he simply sold her to someone."

Nathaniel knew that his face was paling now, at the very suggestion of this. "You mean, as a slave?"

"Well, yes. Why not? She'd probably bring a good sum, after all. And who better to snatch her than a man who'd been assigned to watch her comings and goings for the past few weeks?"

"And he received a note from me, stating that I had already gotten the requested information from her, so he knew her disappearance probably wouldn't interfere too much with Rushton's objective," Nathaniel interjected.

"Precisely."

Nathaniel's eyes narrowed knowingly. "And that might explain why he was so hesitant to let me see the commander the other day."

"It just might," John replied.

Nathaniel could feel his heart beginning to race. "When did Smythe leave, do you know?"

"This morning sometime, I think I heard someone say. And his company's traveling by land and riverway, I was told, because the higher-ups apparently want a reconnaissance done en route and, with Parliament flagging so, they claim they can't spare any ships at present."

At this, Nathaniel pushed past his brother and rushed out of the stable. He heard John running to catch up with him, as he headed up to the great house in the seconds that followed.

"You're going back out to the garrison, I take it," John acknowledged breathlessly.

"Yes. I should have thought to question Smythe myself, after Rushton told me that it was he who had been assigned to keep an eye on Caroline. But, fool that I was, I simply concluded that if Smythe knew anything about what had happened to her, he would have told me so. Now, I can only pray that I'm able to overtake the bastard, before he's too far out of Boston!"

Chapter 21

"Smythe took Caroline with him, and I'm going after her," Nathaniel announced breathlessly, when he returned home from the British garrison later that day.

John, obviously trying to catch up on some paperwork at home rather than go down to the noisy office at the shipyards to do it, sat at the desk in Nathaniel's study, gaping up at his brother. *"What?"* he asked, setting down his quill.

"You heard me, John. I've found out that Smythe has Caroline, and he's taking her down to Louisiana with him. And I'm going after them. I simply came back to inform you of it and to ask you to tell Meldon what I've learned and where I'm going."

"But how do you know Smythe has her?"

"Some of the soldiers at the garrison told me. They said he and his company left for Fort Bute with a blond nurse in tow."

"But that doesn't prove anything. There must be a number of blond nurses in Boston. How can you be certain it was Caroline?"

"Because they described her riding habit to me, the color of it, the cloth, the cross about her neck—all of it. It all fit, John, and I can't afford to stand here quibbling with you over it! I've got to gather what staff I can and go after them! They already have a twelve-hour lead on me."

"But *think,* Nathan, will you?" John exclaimed. "Smythe's not alone out there. He's with his company, scores of men. Even if you do overtake him, you'll be far too outnumbered to stand a chance of getting Caroline away from them."

"So, we'll sneak into their camp by night, while they're sleeping, and free her. Please, John! Just say you'll talk to Meldon for me, so I can be on my way!"

"And I suppose *I'm* to manage everything at the yards while you're gone," his brother snarled. "No matter that it could be weeks, perhaps even months before you return!"

"Yes. You'll have to do so. I'd do the same for you, were your fiancée kidnapped," Nathaniel assured John, looking his brother in the eye with an entreating air.

"Oh, don't draw the longbow with me! She isn't your fiancée. It's not as though you've given her a ring. It's not even as if the dear girl had accepted your proposal."

"She would have . . . in time. We even discussed where the wedding would be held."

"Well, go after her, then. If you must," John snapped. "I suppose there's nothing I can say to prevent it. But I do think you're carrying all of this too far. I mean, when I told you the news about Smythe earlier, I had no idea it would lead to this! . . . Why, for heaven's sake, must it be *you* who goes after her? Why can't you simply send some of the staff or, better yet, Meldon? I mean, you must admit, he has more call to go after her, than you do."

"No," Nathaniel said firmly, lowering his head and glaring at his brother with hooded eyes. "It is I who must go. Sooner or later she's going to piece things together and remember that she met Smythe here, in this very room, and that I introduced her to him. She's going to realize I was loyal to the redcoats and played a part in what's happened to her. And, if I'm not the one who goes forth and troubles to rescue her now, she'll never forgive me for it!"

At this, John rose from the desk chair, obviously intending to make a last-ditch appeal to his brother. "But, Nathan, look at yourself. You're sick. You're tired. You haven't slept and eaten as you should in days! You've been like a caged beast since she disappeared. And I wouldn't be at all surprised to learn that that fever you've been running still hasn't subsided. . . . Just, please, take it from me, it would really be for the best if you let someone else go in your stead."

"No. It must be me, for without her, I'd stay sick in any case, dear brother," Nathaniel choked.

John dropped his gaze at this, as though embarrassed by his sibling's show of emotion. "Can't we simply send word to her parents that she's been kidnapped and is being hauled down to their neck of the woods?" he suggested finally. "Perhaps have them arrange to have a rescue party waiting for her halfway up the Mississippi?"

"And what if the redcoats should decide to do away with her en route? Or what if they're forced to fight rebels or Indians along the way, and she's accidentally wounded or killed?" Nathaniel shook his head once more. "No. This is simply a task I cannot shirk. I am the one, after all, who acquainted her with that vermin, and I owe it to her to be the one who comes to her rescue now. I know you're only concerned for my welfare, but I'm afraid this simply can't be avoided."

"But why try to overtake them by land? Why don't you simply sail down to Louisiana and make your way up the Mississippi from there? You'd reach them much more quickly, you know."

"Yes. But we'll need weapons in order to defend ourselves, once we meet up with them, and you know, as well as I, that the British fleet won't let any of our ships out of the harbor with guns and such aboard."

"They let Caroline in with them," John countered. "She managed to smuggle them through."

"Of course. Because they *meant* her to, John. Use your head, please! I haven't any more time to stand here debating with you, don't you see? I must go now!"

"And what if something happens to you en route? What then?" John asked in a tellingly quavery voice. "How will I manage?"

At this, Nathaniel crossed to the desk and reached out to place a hand on his shoulder. "As you have all along," he said with a soft smile, "I know I've been tough on you since father died. I've criticized and berated. And we're both aware that sometimes it's been uncalled-for. But such is an older brother's lot in life, I'm afraid. I never meant to have you take it too seriously. I never meant you to start believing that you couldn't handle the company on your own, if you had to. In truth, little brother, you've done quite well,"

Nathaniel added, patting his shoulder. "And that, John, is all you need remember, should I fail to return."

John dropped his gaze to the desk, and he bit his lip, as though fighting back tears. "Well, in that case, go," he said finally, in a growl that was obviously meant to mask his softer feelings. "For God's sake, go, Nathan, while you still have some hope of overtaking them!"

It was nearly sundown, and Caroline had been marching with the redcoats for over twelve hours by the time they stopped to set up camp for the night. She'd been shocked that morning, when her captors had finally removed her blindfold and she'd seen that she was in the midst of a British company. She had thought all along that she was simply being held by a trio of civilians with some personal motives for kidnapping her. Instead, she'd found, to her great dismay, that she was some sort of prisoner of war.

But why? she wondered. What had she done to deserve such a fate? They hadn't mentioned the weapons she'd smuggled to Boston, so surely that wasn't the reason, and her efforts to question Smythe that morning, in what little time there had been before they'd gotten under way, had yielded no real answers either. He had simply told her, with a curiously raised brow, that they still intended to return her to her family. She realized now, though, that this response had been nothing more than a subterfuge, because they'd been traveling due west all day, and it was obvious they were heading out of Massachusetts.

So, as they finally stopped the march, and Smythe dropped out of formation and came forward to collect

Caroline, she again attempted to question him about his actions. He had warned her that she'd be shot, if she tried to break away from the company as they marched. He'd also told her that she should not attempt to speak to anyone during the journey. Now, however, with their march so obviously over for the day, she knew he'd have no further reason to refuse to let her speak.

Her eyes narrowed spitefully at him as he reached her and took her by the arm, apparently to lead her to their campsite for the night. She would tell him now what she hadn't dared to tell him when they'd still been in Boston, when she'd still believed that he intended to return her to her aunt and uncle.

"I know who you are," she hissed. "I've known all along that you're the man I met in Nathaniel Hamlin's study. I felt the scar on your hand, so there's no denying it!"

He laughed at her. "So?"

She continued to glower at him, unfazed by his obvious amusement with her plight. "So, did Nathaniel know you were a redcoat? Did he know who you really were?"

"Of course."

Caroline was taken aback by this, but she tried not to let it show. "I don't believe you," she declared, jerking free of his grasp.

"Suit yourself, *mademoiselle,*" he replied with a huff, turning away from her and slipping out of his knapsack's straps. He set the pack on the ground and immediately knelt down and began detaching his bedroll from it.

"*Why* did you kidnap me?" Caroline demanded, reaching down and tearing at his arm, in the hope of

362

receiving his full attention once more.

He turned back to face her. "I warn you, miss, I shall go back to keeping you bound nights if you don't behave!"

Caroline recoiled at his gruff expression. "Just tell me why," she said again, tearfully. "I deserve to know that much after all this time!"

"For ransom, of course. But your stingy uncle never came through, I'm afraid," he said bitterly, "so we'll try your father now."

"My father?"

"Yes. I guess there's no harm in telling you . . . we're headed for Louisiana."

"Louisiana?" she echoed in amazement. "But that will take weeks to reach, even going downriver."

Again he laughed. "Ah, you'll survive, *mademoiselle*. There are other women marching with us, as I'm sure you've seen today. And, what's more, if you want to get home alive, you'll do as you're told!"

"But you said, that first night, you were *saving* me from the redcoats, and now I see that you're one of them! Why would you tell me such a thing?"

"Because, if I hadn't snatched you before your rendezvous with your rebel contacts, some other redcoats would have, and they'd most likely have hung you, miss. That's what they did with Hamlin's last quarry."

Caroline furrowed her brow. "What?"

"Don't tell me you still haven't figured it out," he said with an amused scowl. "I thought you brighter than that."

"Figured *what* out?"

"Well, I suppose, since we're so far out of Boston, it

363

won't matter, if I tell you . . . your Mr. Hamlin was a Tory spy. I mean, we knew about you smuggling weapons to Boston well enough, but the commander wanted to find out who your rebel contacts were. You know, catch the lot of you in the act. And that was Hamlin's job, you see . . . to get the date, time, and place of your meeting with the rebels. And, once he sent word to me, saying that he'd done so, I just figured I was doing you a good turn, snatching you as I did. No harm done, after all, right? And, if you're nice and cooperative along the way, you just might find yourself safe and sound and back home with your parents, in due time." With that, he picked up his gear and began heading toward a nearby gathering of his fellow soldiers. They were already setting up tents for the night, and he obviously intended to help them.

Caroline wanted to go after him once more and question him further, but she found that she couldn't seem to move. It was clear that he really hadn't intended to be cruel to her. He'd just said it all too offhandedly for that to be the case. Nevertheless, his words had sliced through her, like the blade of a sword, and she simply stood, frozen now, where he'd left her, gaping into the orangey glow of the western sky as the last of the sun's rays faded from view. She knew she should walk over to him again and continue her line of questioning, but her feet felt as though they were on fire due to the day's march, and sheer exhaustion, combined with her shock at what he'd said, were enough to make her want to sink to the ground in a heap.

"But Nathaniel can't be one of you," she muttered

364

after a moment, finally finding the strength of mind to pursue him once more. "Not after what you did to his horse."

Smythe, in response, turned back and glared at her, as though he didn't care to continue discussing the matter with his fellow soldiers all about him. He, therefore, took her aside and spoke to her in a growl. "I had nothing to do with what happened to his horse, miss."

"But he was furious about it," Caroline countered, doing her best to humor him by keeping her voice low now as well. "He forswore you redcoats! He said he wanted to see you beaten and run nearly to death, as his horse was at your hands! So, I *know* he'll come after me. I know he'll piece it all together and come and rescue me!"

Again Smythe laughed at her, a dry, cynical laugh that made her heart sink all the more. "Oh, yes . . . that's right, *mademoiselle,* isn't it? You knew him so *well,* didn't you?"

"But I did! I *do,*" Caroline quickly amended. "He all but proposed to me when last we were together!"

Smythe offered her a surprised smirk, and his eyes twinkled with amusement. "Did he? . . . Yes, I fancy he probably did. That is to say, I wouldn't put it past him. We came to realize through the years that he'd say or do almost anything to learn what he needed to in order to assist us. And that is precisely why we engaged his services so often," he explained. "Now, if you'll just pitch in and help us get some supper cooking, *mademoiselle,* it would be much appreciated. The captain has a rule for civilians who accompany us, you

365

see: 'If you don't work, you don't eat.' And you have my word that that's going to apply to *you*, Miss Brenton. As I'm sure you learned today, there'll be no privileged class on this journey . . . and I shouldn't attempt to break away from us, if I were you," he added. "Not unless you relish the idea of traveling alone and unarmed in Indian country."

Chapter 22

By the end of the third week, the journey with the redcoats had become a death march for Caroline. They rose every morning before dawn, and never walked for fewer than twelve hours a day. At nightfall, Caroline would drop down upon her bedroll, in a tent she shared with some of the other women on the trip, and she would sleep dreamlessly, like a rock, until morning came around once more and it was time to begin marching again.

What sleep she got seemed to make little difference. She was constantly exhausted, and the redcoat diet, which consisted mainly of boiled meats and stale bread, was only serving to make matters worse. She was starting to show the signs of scurvy—weakness and bleeding sores in her mouth—and she was certain that others with the company were experiencing these symptoms, too. She didn't dare mention them to anyone, however, because she knew the redcoats would simply leave her behind if they thought she was growing too ill to keep going. And God only knew what fate would befall her, should she be passed into the hands of strangers in one of the few settlements they traveled through. At least, in redcoat custody, she'd come to know what she could expect and what was expected of her, so staying with the British troops did seem the wisest choice.

She had long since stopped thinking about Nathaniel and all that she'd left behind in Boston. It was just too painful and draining to go on contemplating such things when every ounce of her energy was required merely for survival. The only thing she was focusing on now, therefore, was continuing to find the strength and will to keep putting one foot in front of the other, hour after hour, day after day, until they finally reached the Allegheny River and their journey could, quite literally, become more downhill.

She was well aware that the only thing keeping her alive these days was the hope that she would be reunited with her family in Louisiana, as Smythe had proposed. Consequently, she did her best to concentrate on that hope and not let her thoughts stray to anything wounding or demoralizing. There was one other matter, though, that she permitted herself to ponder from time to time, and that was one of the things Smythe had told her on the day they had left Boston. He'd said that Nathaniel had sent him a message, stating that he had already obtained the details from Caroline regarding her rendezvous with her rebel contacts. Yet, even in her more-dead-than-alive state, Caroline knew this just wasn't true. She hadn't given that information to Nathaniel, so he simply couldn't have passed it on to Smythe. Why, then, she wondered, had he told Smythe he already had it?

It didn't add up, yet, as Caroline continued on the tedious trip, trudging, day in day out, in the midsummer sun, she *had* seemed to make some sense of it. Nathaniel had obviously undergone a change of heart of some kind while he'd been with her. That much seemed clear to her now. Rather than continuing to deceive her, he had apparently begun trying to deceive Smythe toward the end. And the only conclusion she could seem to draw from all of it was that some part of him had started to sympathize with her, to devise a plan for saving her from being hung, as Smythe claimed she would have been, had she been able to follow through with meeting her contacts. And that, for what it was worth, was about all she could surmise about Nathaniel and his motives.

Caroline realized now that, in spite of her father's warning to her about both Tory spies and Boston's beguiling bachelors, she had unwittingly fallen into the clutches of both. And, on those very rare occasions when her thoughts drifted for a few seconds to the memory of Nathaniel's dark princely features, his almost ominous intelligence and charm, she acknowledged that she was still falling into his clutches. Some three hundred miles from him now, she still nearly swooned at recalling his amorous touch, the way he'd made love to her, and she realized that, no matter what he'd done, how he'd deceived her, some part of her would always be his.

*   *   *

Nathaniel and his party had followed the redcoat company all the way through Massachusetts and halfway across New York before Nathaniel really began to regret not having taken his brother's advice that he travel down to Louisiana by ship. They'd encountered a small group of unfriendly Indians, and though the ensuing skirmish hadn't left any in his party dead, seeing properly to the wounded men did further delay them.

He was definitely on the redcoats' trail. He was certain of that, because Rushton had, albeit grudgingly, given him a map that showed the route the grenadiers were to follow to Fort Bute. What was more, the Colonists and settlers Nathaniel had questioned along the way, had all confirmed that the troops had traveled the same ground several hours earlier. But, in spite of the fact that Nathaniel seemed to be shortening the distance between his party and the redcoats, he just couldn't seem to catch up with them, and he was beginning to realize that he and his servants probably weren't going to do so by land. Rather, they would be forced to build a raft and put forth upon the Allegheny River, when they finally reached it, continuing to pursue the redcoats by water. One thing was abundantly clear to Nathaniel, however, he was just too far along now to even consider turning back to Boston and starting the journey over again by ship.

By the time the British company reached the southern flow of the Allegheny, Caroline's dearly bought riding habit was beginning to fall apart, and she had to borrow a cotton frock from one of the laundresses the redcoats had brought along. Part of her was glad of this, because cotton would be preferable to her heavy, hide outfit in the heat, once they began traveling southward. She chose, nevertheless, to keep the habit's jacket, in order to shield herself from the nights' chill as she slept. And, in the long run, she was glad she had.

The redcoat diet seemed to be getting more and more paltry with each day that passed. Smythe offered no objection, therefore, when, after a day's travel, the British paddled their canoes to shore, and Caroline went off to put to use some of the herbalism her mother had taught her by gathering those weeds and berries that she knew were used to treat scurvy. She would then return to the camp with her pickings and stir them into whatever stew or soup the soldiers were preparing for supper.

There seemed to be no question in Smythe's mind, at such times, that Caroline could be trusted to return to the encampment. The redcoats were, after all, managing to feed her—something she wasn't sure she could do on her own, especially without weapons. In addition, with the nightly posting of sentries, they were keeping her guarded from both Indians and wild animals as she slept, and it went without saying that she couldn't do that for herself, were she to try to flee from them. What was more, Smythe's repeated warnings to his fellow soldiers that Caroline possessed some rather fearsome supernatural powers seemed to be preventing them from attempting to harm or molest her. As a result, she felt fairly certain that, if she continued to

371

follow their rules, she would have nothing to fear from them.

In the week that followed, they canoed through Pennsylvania to Pittsburgh, where the Allegheny met the Monongahela River and went on to form the Ohio. A few weeks later, the Ohio River finally led them to the Mississippi, and their course to Louisiana became the same as that followed by many of the Acadians, when the British had expelled them from Maritime Canada some twenty years earlier. Caroline could, therefore, more fully appreciate now what her maternal grandfather had gone through, when he and his neighbors had fled a generation before, and she began to derive a sort of spiritual strength from this, from knowing that she came from that same, resilient stock.

By early September, the redcoat company reached Fort Bute at last, and, for the first time in over two months, Caroline was able to take a hot bath and look forward to sleeping up off the ground that night, in a bunk. She couldn't believe how luxurious this seemed to her, being allowed to spend her nights indoors once more, fully sheltered from wind and rain, and she knew, in her heart, that the grueling journey had served at least one useful purpose. It had taught her that, if returned to her family, she should never again make the mistake of taking her privileged way of life for granted. Nor would she have any further excuse for being ignorant of the needs of those less fortunate than she.

Caroline was pleased to note that, upon their arrival at Bute, Smythe had immediately sent a message-bearer off with a ransom letter for her clan. He was obviously as anxious to get his hands on the money, as Caroline was to be returned to her family. However, given that Caroline's nearest domicile was her grandfather's ribbon farm, and that was at least a week's journey away, she knew they both had a bit of a wait ahead of them. She would, therefore, simply remain with the redcoats until the matter was settled. She had, after all, just gone through the most hellish experience of her life, simply trying to stay alive until she could reach her home ground, so she knew she'd be a fool now to run the risk of being shot while attempting to escape from the fort.

Nevertheless, she couldn't help feeling terribly homesick, surrounded as Bute was with such familiar landscape. And, after she'd had her bath and dinner had been served, she asked Smythe for permission to climb to the top of the fort's guard tower, so she could quell her homesickness by taking in the marshy terrain that lay all about. Smythe gave his consent with a shrug, and Caroline went up to the top of the tower and introduced herself to the sentry posted there. Then she proceeded to survey the scenery below with great yearning.

The Iberville River lay just beyond, and right across the way from them was the Cajun town of St. Gabriel. She'd only been to St. Gabriel once, but today, after having traveled for so long over such strange ground, it almost looked to her like home, almost like the tiny village near which her grandfather's farm was located. And, to her surprise, her eyes began to fill with tears.

"Are you all right, miss?" the sentry asked.

Caroline felt herself blush a bit, as she turned to look at him, and she instantly reached up and dabbed her eyes with the sleeve of her dress. "Oh . . . yes," she stammered, hoping he'd simply take her word for it and not continue to question her. She didn't think it wise to tell the fort's staff that she was a Cajun, so she hoped the sentry wouldn't press the issue and force her to lie to him.

Fortunately, he did not, and she quickly returned her gaze to the Cajun horizon. As she did so, however, she bit her lip at what she saw. A regiment of soldiers was approaching St. Gabriel from the Cajun side of the river, and, even from this distance of nearly a mile, Caroline could tell that they were Louisianan troops. She'd just never seen them in such numbers, however. There were six hundred of them by her estimation, headed directly for Fort Bute, and, again, she turned to look at the British sentry.

He didn't see them, a voice within her acknowledged. The sentry spyglass was trained in an entirely different direction, and Caroline decided she would be damned if she would stay there an instant longer and risk calling his attention to them.

"I'm going back down," she suddenly declared, her heart racing with excitement. "But thank you for the look."

"You're most welcome, miss," he called after her, as she hurried to the stairs and began descending them.

Six hundred men, she thought, as she rushed downward. More than enough to overrun the meager number of redcoats who occupied Bute. Even with Smythe's company present now, the British probably didn't stand a chance. Apparently, the tower sentry agreed with this assessment of the situation, because she heard him cursing seconds later, and then he began

374

shouting warnings down to the guards posted below.

But where should I go when the fighting starts? Caroline asked herself, as she reached the bottom of the stairs and then began heading for her barracks. She'd simply have to hide, she concluded. The redcoat officers were already starting to shout combat orders to everyone afoot, including the women, and Caroline knew that, unless she wanted to find herself fighting her own people, she'd simply have to dart off somewhere and hide. She, therefore, changed her course now, skittering across the fort's parade ground and slipping into some barracks she knew to be unoccupied. Once inside, she got down on the floor and slid under one of the bunks on the far side of the room.

Governor Galvez was finally doing it, she acknowledged, her heart soaring. And on the very day of her return to Louisiana! She reached up and snatched a pillow from the bunk overhead, in order to make herself comfortable in the minutes that followed, and then went on basking in the triumph of this turn of events. Her people's leader had at last caught on to the fact that the British intended to attack Louisiana, and, as a result, he'd amassed what would surely prove one of the nastiest, most formidable regiments on earth. Caroline could be certain of this, because she knew her people very well. They were slow to anger, generally easygoing and loving. But, just as with her Acadian ancestors who'd had all but their farm tools taken from them when they'd finally been forced to fight their British persecutors a generation before, these men wouldn't hesitate to tear the occupants of this fort limb from limb, if necessary. She also realized that all she could hope for now was that her command of Louisianan French and her knowledge of the surrounding territory, would keep them from killing her as well.

The first sounds she heard, several minutes later, as the battle began, were the blasts of Bute's cannons. The redcoats were apparently trying to ward off the attack by mowing down the Cajun troops as they approached. This was, however, as Caroline could have predicted, to no avail. She knew perfectly well—as the British must have known it, too—there were just too many Cajuns coming for a few cannon bursts to make much difference.

Minutes later, this was confirmed for one and all, as Caroline heard her people beginning to pound upon the fort's gate with what must have been a battering ram. Unable to contain her curiosity any longer, Caroline crawled out from her hiding place and crept over to the front window of the barracks to peek out at what was happening. In the seconds that followed, she saw the enormous latch of the fort's doors crack in half. Then the gate flew open, and the Cajun soldiers came pouring into Bute like a spring tide.

Even though she knew she should have gone back and hidden under the bunk again, Caroline felt spellbound by the scene, and she continued to stand off to one side of the window, peering out at it. She'd never had occasion to see men at war before, and she had a sneaking suspicion that this wasn't a battle she should miss. It was definitely one she'd be asked to recount dozens of times to her family and friends, once she was returned to them.

To her dismay, however, all of the musket smoke and chaos produced in the minutes that followed pretty much obscured what was happening, and she began to realize that her wisest course at this point was probably to seize the opportunity this turmoil offered to make her way out of the fort. The Cajuns, after all, didn't look as though they were stopping to ask questions before shooting, and, Louisianan French or not, Caroline sensed that she might not even be given the chance to speak, once they finally reached the barracks and began rifling through them for any survivors.

Having decided this, she hurried to the back window. She stuck her head out first, to make certain that no one was approaching from either direction. Then she slipped outside and began creeping along the back side of the row of barracks. When she reached the last of them, she dashed to the palisade, and, dropping to her hands and knees, began creeping along that, as well.

It was slow going, to be sure. En route, she had to stop several times, in order to avoid being caught in the line of the fire or being stepped on by the participants in the hand-to-hand fighting. By and by, however, she did succeed in making her way to the fort's entrance, and she honestly believed that she could leave Bute without being stopped.

She put a hand out to brace herself against the stockade fencing, and she lifted her skirts an instant later and got back up on her feet. Once up, however, she stopped dead at what she saw in front of her— *Nathaniel* and several of his estate's staff, standing at the mouth of the fort. And, even though staying inside Bute seemed certain death for her now, Caroline found herself taking a step or two back into the fortress in response.

"*Mon Dieu,*" she exclaimed. "What are *you* doing here?"

He looked almost equally surprised, as though he hardly recognized her in her tattered, cotton frock. "Caroline?" he said, and, though she could barely hear him over the din of the battle, she could tell from his expression that he had uttered it in a tone of almost reverent disbelief.

Her eyes narrowed vengefully as she shouted her next words to him. "You'd better get out of here, before they realize you're on the British side!" With that, she pushed past him and his men and hurried out of the fort.

As she did so, however, he grabbed her arm and pulled her back toward him, his strength amazing. "But where are you going? I came all the way down here to rescue you!"

"Well, you're too late, aren't you? It looks like my people have already taken care of that."

"But I can explain about Smythe . . . about all of it," he stammered, paling, and, as incredible as it seemed, it was apparent to Caroline that he feared her wrath more than the fury of the entire Cajun regiment. "You must, at least, come with me for a moment . . . out of here and let me explain!"

"No! *You* must release me, you traitorous dog, and let me go home to my grand-père's farm!" With that, Caroline jerked free of him, causing him to tear her dress's sleeve. "They're your King's troops, Mr. Hamlin, so why don't you go and help them fight?" she spat out, but before she could turn away from him, something dreadful happened.

He was just standing there, his brow furrowed and his expression an anguished one, as though her words were ripping his heart out. Then, suddenly, someone behind him caught Caroline's eye. It was a redcoat soldier, and he had his musket trained on Nathaniel. Before Caroline could cry out a warning, however, the soldier fired, and Nathaniel lurched forward, his eyes wide with shock.

Without another second's thought, Caroline rushed to him and threw her body up against his, as two of his men slipped under his arms and began propping him up as well. They instantly moved him out of the gateway and over to a grassy spot, just to the right of the fort's entrance.

"Oh, *mon Dieu*." Caroline gasped, still clutching him. She was too afraid to pull away from him and assess the damage done. "Is he dead? Did it kill him?"

To her amazement, it was Nathaniel who replied. "No, my dear," he answered weakly. "But it's kind of you to care," he added, with a dry laugh that, to Caroline's dismay, instantly turned to what sounded like a death rattle.

"Oh, dear God! Dear God," she continued, finally letting go of him. "Turn him over! Let me see what's happened."

Nathaniel let out a pained groan as his men rolled him onto his stomach, and Caroline began examining his wound.

"Is it deep?" he asked in a voice so faint she could hardly hear him.

"No, thank God," she replied. "But don't talk. You

shouldn't be talking! You'll only make the bleeding worse."

"Can we move him again, miss?" one of his men asked.

"*Oui.* I suppose so. If you're careful."

At this, the two men who had whisked Nathaniel aside only moments before slipped his arms over their shoulders and hurriedly conveyed him to a sheltering thicket, several yards away. Caroline, of course, rushed after them, as did the rest of Nathaniel's servants.

Once they reached the thicket, Nathaniel was again laid down on his stomach, and Caroline dropped to her knees beside him and immediately began tearing some strips of cloth from the hem of her dress. She knew she would need them in order to clean and bandage his wound. Meanwhile, another of Nathaniel's men removed his jacket, rolled it up, and slipped it under his employer's cheek, obviously to serve as a pillow.

"Water," Caroline commanded, wadding a strip of fabric.

One of the men quickly obliged her, reaching out from amidst the huddle of servants and handing her his flask.

"They thought I was Cajun, didn't they?" Nathaniel acknowledged a moment later, as Caroline lifted his shirt and began trying to clean his wound.

"Quiet now," she admonished.

"But I'm right, am I not?" he prodded, lowering his voice. "It *was* a redcoat who shot me."

"Yes," Caroline confirmed.

"It's ironic, you must admit," he continued. "I once served them so faithfully, and they seem to do nothing in return but try to destroy me and everything I hold dear."

"There's nothing ironic about it," she retorted. "They're ruffians, as I told you, and they're finally getting what they deserve!"

"And what do I deserve now, dear Caroline? That grave you told me you saw me digging for myself?"

"Don't say that," she said through clenched teeth. "I've told you this wound isn't deep enough to kill you, and you . . . you *must* believe me," she added trying to fight back her emotion.

"Would you care if it did?" he asked.

"Of course. Of course, I would, *mon amour,"* she replied tearfully. "But, please, don't keep speaking," she entreated. "You're only making it worse."

"I must speak, though. Don't you see?" he countered faintly. "I've so much to explain to you, and I don't know how much longer you'll be willing to stay here with me."

Without an instant of hesitation, she bent down and spoke softly into his right ear. "I'll stay for as long as you need me, Nathaniel. Surely you must know that."

Again she heard a dry laugh from him. "Oh, be careful what you promise, my love, for that could be a very long time, indeed. Say . . . a lifetime?"

"I'll stay and take care of you. Just rest assured of that," she said firmly. "Such . . . such loyalty you displayed, after all, in coming all the way down here to rescue me." She choked up, and tears began to trickle down her cheeks.

"Ah, but that's the English way of seeing it, isn't it?" he replied, and, for some reason, these words sounded stirringly familiar to Caroline. "You French would say instead that what I displayed was love. *N'est-ce pas?*"

Caroline wiped her tears away with her sleeve and sniffled a bit, recalling in that instant that these were the very lines she'd spoken when relating the story of that French ballad to him, the night they'd met. *"Oui,"* she answered in a quavery voice.

"Mais, oui," Nathaniel agreed, reaching back and giving one of her hands a squeeze. There was such fervor evident in his grasp, that Caroline was finally certain he wouldn't die. He'd simply come too far for her to succumb to death now. He'd simply come too far for her ever to turn away from him again.

Epilogue

From Baton Rouge to Pensacola, Bernardo de Galvez's Cajun regiment went on to win every battle it undertook against the redcoats, ultimately freeing West Florida from British rule. Had the Cajuns decided not to enter the Revolutionary War exactly when they did, many historians believed the redcoats would have begun a third front in the conflict, thereby enabling British forces to invade the new republic from the west, by way of the Mississippi River.

As for Nathaniel Hamlin, he did, indeed, live and recover fully from his musket wound. And, as Caroline and her family nursed him back to health at her grandfather's farm, Nathaniel was given plenty of time in which to explain all that had happened in Boston; how he'd decided, early on in his relationship with Caroline, to abandon his services to the British and to save Caroline's life when he accompanied her to her rendezvous with the rebels. He also made it clear that no ransom note was ever received from Smythe, either by himself or Caroline's aunt and uncle, and that

Meldon and Amelia had, naturally, been beside themselves with worry when Caroline had disappeared. The Thorwells, of course, confirmed all of this for their niece, when they sailed down to New Orleans a month later for Caroline and Nathaniel's wedding.

Though not invited to the wedding, Caroline's aunt Margaret did send a letter of regret, explaining that she and her family would be unable to afford to travel down for the ceremony. Margaret went on to congratulate the couple and to express her great relief at having heard that Caroline had finally escaped from her redcoat captors. Caroline's father, knowing his twin as he did, responded to this with nothing more than a skeptical grunt.

On October the fifth, 1779, Caroline Élise Brenton and Nathaniel Jerome Hamlin were finally wed, or, in the earthy, Cajun vernacular, they began "boiling the pot together."